Charma ✓

║█║▌║█║▌║█║█║▌║█║

D0816277

The strains of the waltz were lilting, mesmerizing—but no more so than the man who held her, sweeping her out onto the floor . . .

Lithe, lean, with a sensual grace that tempted, taunted, Ransom drew her into his arms, and, Cecily thought, into something far deeper.

"It—it seems I owe you an apology," Cecily said, attempting to break the intense spell he seemed to hold over her.

"Shall I tell you what you owe me, Gloriana?" Ransom's muscles were hard, taut, the planes of his face carved with an intensity that terrified her. "A night's sleep, and dreams . . . that you stole from me last night. I lay abed, thinking of a kiss. . . ." His eyes, green, blazed with devastating longing.

"Captain Tremayne, I hardly think it proper to—"

"After what we shared a day past, 'tis past time to concern ourselves with what is proper . . ."

_____

. . . from the author of *Crown of Mist,* hailed by *Publishers Weekly* as "exciting, satisfying, and most unusual."

Books by Kimberly Cates

Crown of Mist
Restless Is the Wind

Published by POCKET BOOKS

Restless is the Wind

Kimberly Cates

POCKET BOOKS

New York   London   Toronto   Sydney   Tokyo

This book is a work of historical fiction. Names, characters, places and incidents relating to non-historical figures are either the product of the author's imagination or are used fictitiously. Any resemblance of such non-historical incidents, places or figures to actual events or locales or persons, living or dead, is entirely coincidental.

An *Original* Publication of POCKET BOOKS

POCKET BOOKS, a division of Simon & Schuster Inc.
1230 Avenue of the Americas, New York, NY 10020

ISBN: 0-671-63395-3

First Pocket Books printing August 1989

10 9 8 7 6 5 4 3 2 1

POCKET and colophon are trademarks of
Simon & Schuster Inc.

Printed in the U.S.A.

To Susan Carroll Coppula,
who threw open the doors
to a Regency ballroom
and made me fall in love
with an era.

London, 1813

Chapter One

THE CLOAK FLOWED OUT in nightmarish waves, ebony edges melting into the maze of gold-tissue gowns and gleaming Hessian uniforms gracing the boxes of the Theater Royal in Drury Lane. Lady Cecily Arabella Anastasia Lansdowne swept a wayward tendril of night-dark hair from her delicate features, her shaking fingers all but crushing the gilded quizzing glass clasped in her hand. Eyes the hue of Lancashire violets strained across the dimly lit theater to the ominous presence.

The antics of the players drew raucous laughter from the lowlings in the pits, and well-bred chortles of amusement from the haughty lords and ladies ensconced within their private boxes. But Cecily heard them not. The farce she had once anticipated with such pleasure now seemed a sinister mockery set against the scene being played out in the shadow-veiled theater box across the way.

Whoever lay beneath the veiling of ebony cloak was destroying the one person Cecily loved above all others in her once-sheltered world. Her father.

For nigh a quarter of an hour she had fought desperately to pierce the shroudings of dusky light, struggled to glean some hint of what secrets lay within the heated words the two figures were exchanging so far away. But she had gained

1

naught except the sharp tang of danger, heretofore as foreign to her as the frenzied gaiety of London's elite.

Even from a distance, she could see Charleton Lansdowne's silvery head silhouetted in stark contrast against the mysterious cloak, could see his waxen, scholarly features pinched with some inner agony that had turned a serene, ever-loving man into a haunted specter. And as the width of the Theater Royal yawned between Cecily and her beloved father, it seemed as endless, as hopeless, as a chasm in some dark night terror, banishing the shield of security and love that had been Cecily's bastion for all her nineteen years.

"Cousin, in case you failed to notice, the stage is *that* way." The acid-sweet voice made Cecily start, as a fan jabbed sharply into her knee. Her gaze leapt up to abundant moon-pale tresses and wide blue eyes drowning in feigned innocence. Lady Lavinia Lansdowne drew pouting lips into a smirk. "After all of Mama's trouble in dragging you to this performance, the least you and your *father* could do is to pay some attention to Miss Siddons and the rest. But then, as Mama says, one can scarce expect good manners from rustic poor relations."

"You'll have to excuse us poor rustics." Cecily gritted her teeth so hard her jaw ached, her gaze still straining toward the distant box. "We've not had the benefit of your *impeccable example* overlong."

Lavinia waved one white-gloved hand in breezy dismissal. "Faith, but the best way to demonstrate your gratitude is to secure yourself a husband with all haste. After all, your father thrust you upon us during *my* first season. And with my *elder sister* yet clinging to spinster's row . . ." Lavinia accented the words as though the absent twenty-year-old Mirabelle were a crabbed crone. The cruel chit's mouth curled in an aura of such infinite satisfaction, Cecily pitied the cousin she had never met. 'Twas little wonder Mirabelle was supposedly languishing at Duke Harry's country estate in the wake of some illness—an hour in Lavinia's company had proved far more draining to Cecily than the bout of scarlet fever she had suffered as a child.

At the fleeting memory of those long, weary days, Cecily's

eyes stung afresh. She could yet see her father's haggard face, could hear his voice, hoarse from reading aloud her favorite stories over and over while she fretted upon her mound of pillows. Never once had he left her side, even after the doctor had sworn she was past danger. Always her father had been there to aid her, no matter what mischief she had wrought, what tiny sorrow saddened her heart. And now, for the first time Cecily could remember, *he* was the one bearing some burden. . . .

Lavinia's goadings droned on, but the veiled barbs that had turned Cecily's first days of London society into the purest of miseries were lost on her as the roar of final applause filled the theater, the raising lights washing gold over the building's elegant appointments.

Cecily's hands knotted, the quizzing glass cutting into her soft palm as the shadows receded from where her father sat, bathing his face in a hellish orange-gold light. It was as if some lurking evil had banished all but those two figures from Cecily's vision, the rest of the company blurring into a whirl of garish color.

She caught her lip between her teeth, raw panic jolting through her as she saw the cloaked stranger's fist flash out, grasping her father's cravat. She surged to her feet, unable to stay herself, expecting at any moment for the menacing figure's fist to crash into her gentle father. Instead, Charleton Lansdowne lunged from his seat, his own arm dashing the cloaked figure away, as though the person's touch had somehow soiled him.

Cecily stumbled back a step, the rage contorting her father's face piercing her to the very core of her being. Never in her life had she known her gentle father to lay a hand on anyone in anger—from his lowliest hound, to the laziest kitchen lad. And the sight of Charleton Lansdowne in agonized fury terrified her as nothing in her life ever had.

"Merciful heavens!" Cecily heard Lavinia's high-pitched squeal. *"Tell* me that *cannot* be Uncle Charleton. . . ."

Cecily caught a glimpse of Honoria Lansdowne's turbaned head whisking around, the duchess's hawklike eyes turning the blasting force of their disapproval upon the distant box. But Cecily heard naught of the duchess's umbrage, saw naught except the swirl of midnight velvet as the cloaked figure spun and stalked into the crowd exiting their seats.

The quizzing glass clattered to the floor, her violet feathered fan spilling to her feet as Cecily scooped her heathershaded skirts into her hands. Cries of outrage and indignation from the duchess and the hateful Lavinia welled behind Cecily as she bolted down the aisle, fierce protectiveness and desperation roiling inside her. The domed foyer was a blur, the elegance of the entrance hall below a whirl of Doric columns, immaculate waistcoats, exquisite gowns.

Cecily fought to break through the masses of people descending the stairways, her single purpose to gain her father's side. But her ribboned slippers had scarce touched the bottom step when she saw it—tiered layers of black velvet rippling out from shoulders stiff with anger.

Her eyes locked upon that whirl of darkness, mysterious, taunting, filling her mind with images of the inner agony her father had refused to share. Would even still refuse to share, Cecily knew with sudden certainty—his red-rimmed eyes would bar her from his torment as surely as he had barred her from hying off to India upon the "ship" she had built in the stables when she was eight.

No. This time she would not allow her father to wrap her in some gossamer-soft web of dreams, protect her. If he would tell her naught, there were other ways of discovering what was amiss. And who was responsible. Her eyes tracked the black cape flowing toward the wide-flung doors. If she could but catch a glimpse of the menacing stranger's face, gain some clue as to his identity . . .

The delicate curve of her chin thrust out in the defiant resolve that had struck terror into the hearts of countless governesses and housemaids. Her feet trampling heedlessly upon toes, her elbows digging thoughtlessly into soft paunches, she plunged through the disgruntled crowd. She burst through the stream of London's elite as they spilled out the doorway, the night embracing her in chill arms.

If that blackguard gains a carriage, I'll never find him, Cecily railed inwardly, frustration crushing her chest as her violet eyes locked upon the cloaked form fast sweeping into the night. *And if I fail to find him . . .* The thought died within her, trailing into stark hopelessness as the sinister form was swallowed by myriad people two coach lengths away from her.

A sob balled hot in Cecily's throat as she ran, the gas-lit street a-blur with unshed tears as her gaze focused upon the scene in front of her. A maze of cloaks blotted out the dirty cobbles, at least a score of the rich garments the shade of a raven's wing. Desperately she tried to identify the figure she had been pursuing, her gaze raking through the mob, her throat tight with despair.

She stumbled, numb, the glossy toe of an officer's boot suddenly snagging her slipper, catapulting her between a dandified buck and the angel-faced Cyprian he was escorting. The notorious lady of pleasure gave a squeal of alarm, all but spilling her blush-tinted bosom into her protector's hands as Cecily hurtled past them.

Cecily felt the smack of a palm between her shoulder blades, heard a coarse, high-pitched giggle. With a choked cry, she fought to keep herself from crashing to the cobbles, but the momentum hurled her through the wall of cloaks and gowns that had barred her but moments before. She felt the sting of chill air against her cheeks as she broke from the crowd, felt herself falling in the midst of what seemed a ragged ring.

A flash of white silk shirt streaked before her eyes as an arm, hard as burnished steel, dug deep under her ribs. The breath left her lungs in a choked gasp as she felt herself being jerked back to her feet, something hot, wet, from that steely sinewed arm soaking through the thin fabric of her gown to wet the soft skin below.

Blood. She knew it in a stomach-churning instant—that sickly sweetness she had smelled a hundred times while tending her father's injured tenants in the cottages of Briarton. For a heartbeat her gaze locked with eyes of molten emerald, straight black brows slashing in fury above their fiery light as the man catapulted her back toward the crowd. Yet in that second his striking countenance seared into Cecily's very soul.

Hair the color of burnished gold tumbled about his sharp-carved features, an angry scar slashing bronze-dark skin from the crest of one arrogant cheekbone to the square jut of a granite-hewn jaw.

Cecily staggered back, struck suddenly with a primitive sense of danger, but the mass of people had closed behind her, waving fistfuls of pound notes, levying wagers on the battle before them. For it was a battle—a battle to the death. Cecily had seen it in the gold-tressed stranger's eyes as he spun back to face his beleaguered opponent.

"Get 'im, Tremayne!" a masculine voice roared from somewhere behind her. "Show him what a gentleman learns at Jackson's!"

There could be no doubt as to which of the fighters the person addressed. Cecily's gaze shifted from the sleekly muscled Tremayne to the other man—a hulk staggering up from the cobbled street, his broad face bloodied, torn. Sparse orange hair clung to his bull-like neck, dull bestial eyes and coarse features crumpled in a mask of dumb terror. Heedless, Tremayne faced him, menace carved in every line in his whip-cord taut body. Richly tailored pantaloons clung to the hard curves of tight buttocks, the white silk shirt screaming of elegance in spite of its smearings of dirt and blood.

Yet it was the unholy glee seething from those piercing eyes that chilled Cecily's blood. For even from where she stood, she could see that the man was taking infinite pleasure in every crack of his fist into the dullard's slack face, was reveling in his opponent's terror as if it fed some fearsome hunger burning within his own lean frame.

Of their own volition her fingers drifted up to her slender throat. This was a man who could snap someone's neck in but a heartbeat, then set those strongly sculpted hands to gaming at Whites.

"He's done for, Ransom!" a snipe-necked sergeant exulted. "You taught him what it means to bloody a cursed Tremayne!"

"Go back to your barracks!" a red-faced buck bellowed, clutching a handful of pound notes in one meticulously groomed hand. "Five pounds says the big one still takes him!"

The voices blended into a cacophony of cheers and jeerings aimed at the man, Ransom Tremayne, the sound drowning Cecily as he raised his fist again. She shut her eyes, unable to watch as his knuckles slammed into flesh. But the force of the blow seemed to reverberate through the circle of spectators, their roars of approval making her want to scream.

"He's down!" "Ransom's trounced the lowling bastard!" The cries of triumph and groans of defeat filled the street. Flooded with naught save the need to flee the blood-thirsting crowd, Cecily opened her eyes, then froze as that devastating green gaze slashed to but a sword's length from where she stood.

'Twas as though even the man lying battered in a groaning heap upon the street were not enough to satisfy the hunger in the whip-taut grappler, and she could feel the fury yet coiled within those daunting shoulders. She took a step back, her own gaze following his just in time to see what looked to be a bundle of filth-laden rags shrink back, a pinched, terrified child peering out with eyes that seemed to swallow its whole face. A whimper parted pale babyish lips, the boy's side grating against the harsh stone as he tried to escape that searing glare.

Tremayne's black snarl made Cecily jump, stunned, as he paced toward the child with the grace of a stalking jungle cat, eyes blazing with some emotion too terrifying to put a name to. Outrage seared through Cecily lightning fast, obliterating her own sense of fear as she lunged to put herself between Ransom Tremayne and the trembling urchin. But in that instant a glimmer of light striking steel caught her eye and she turned, stunned to see a long-bladed knife clutched tight in the red-haired brawler's beefy hand.

"Beware!" she cried out, hating herself for warning the

ruffian who had terrorized the child, yet knowing that she could not have stood by and allowed even the most despicable of men to be stabbed from behind.

With stunning agility Tremayne dove out of the weapon's path. Cecily heard one broad shoulder thud into the cobbles, saw him roll and lunge to his feet.

Cries hissed from the eager mouths of the crowd as they scented blood, their voices high, thin, renewing wagers that turned Cecily's stomach. Yet even through the noise of the crowd, through her own fear, the sound of childish sobbing nearby touched her more deeply than any danger the battling men might hold. Ever aware of the blade flashing blue against the night, Cecily dashed across the space that separated her from the lad, felt the quavering urchin fling himself into the meager shelter of her skirts. She caught scarce a glimpse of wizened little features, eyes devastatingly old in a child's pale face, before the boy buried his damp cheeks in the folds of her gown.

"'Tis *me* boy, 'e is!" Cecily heard the huge man shrill, lips pulling back from blackened teeth as he turned the hilt of the knife in one giant paw. "Ye'll ne'er live t' take 'im!"

Cecily's face went cold, her heart icy as she half expected either the hulk or the blaze-eyed Tremayne to attack her. But the drink-glazed eyes of the red-haired man were fastened upon Tremayne's face with the eagerness of a boar closing for the kill.

She saw Ransom brace lean legs to meet the giant's charge as the man drove his massive body forward. Jaundiced eyes glowed in an instant of triumph, then crumpled in agony as Tremayne's arm shot out, crashing into a brawny elbow. The clatter of the knife striking the ground mingled with the sickening sound of bone shattering.

She felt the child jump against her, Cecily's own stomach wrenching in horror as the huge man's arm jackknifed at an impossible angle, his great bulk crashing to the ground. Writhing, wailing, he clutched his beefy arm with one grimy fist. "Broke it! He cursed broke—"

But even with the man's screams of agony echoing through the street, Tremayne's face was impassive as marble. He planted the polished heel of one boot on the man's belly, forcing him back against the cobbles until the pain-hazed eyes met his own. "Next time it will be your worthless neck."

"But 'e's *mine*," the drunkard blubbered. "Legal-like, I swear—"

"Swear to me you'll never come near him again, or I'll snap your neck now and save myself the trouble of—"

"I swear it! I swear it!" the man sobbed, eyes wild. "Ye be daft! Daft! 'E's naught but a boy!"

Cecily saw Tremayne's granite jaw knot, his heel biting deeper into the drunk's chest. For an instant she feared the man would make good his threat. But after a moment the lethal fists uncurled, one hand swiping across the exquisitely wrought trousers, as if the drunk had tainted him.

She felt the child quaver against her, and was aware again of the danger exuding from Ransom Tremayne's lean form —danger to the boy, danger to herself glossed in that hard gaze. Deprived of their spectacle, the crowd was already melting away. If she could but take the child, hasten to a constable . . .

Cecily clasped the waif's stick-thin wrists in her hand, trying to pry his fingers from her skirts, free them both to escape the seething Tremayne's wrath. But the child clung as though he were drowning, and she was the single thread that kept him from being sucked down.

"Hasten!" she pleaded, battling the child's grip. "Let go of me and—"

"Spare the angel's gown?"

Fire hot, ice cold, the voice sent jolts of panic bolting through Cecily's veins. She stiffened her spine, her chin jutting stubbornly at the arrogant bronzed visage so close to her own. Her hands dug tight into the waif's narrow shoulders as she met Tremayne's glare.

"I vow I'll call the constable!" Her own voice sounded strange to her ears, haughty, with no trace of the fear even now thrumming in her senses. "This child—"

"Is no concern of yours." Cold green eyes slashed to where the boy's matted hair was crushed against her gown, the fragile fabric soiled beyond repair as the boy scrubbed at his dripping nose with a fistful of lace.

"I beg to disagree. This boy will not leave my hands until the authorities—" Cecily flinched, her breath catching in her throat at the hate blazing in Tremayne's lean face.

"Plague take your authorities!" His lips curled in dismissal as his gaze raked a humiliating path from the gold-satin ribbons woven through her curls to the slippers peeking out from beneath her hem.

One bruised hand dug into his pocket, withdrew gripping a wad of pound notes. "This will pay for your *damages* a dozen times over," he bit out, jamming the currency into her hand. "Bow Street has far more dangerous criminals than this lad to run down this night."

"Curse you—" Cecily sputtered, rage firing her cheeks. She hurled the bills to the cobbles, more furious at Tremayne's callous dismissal of the child, and of her, than she had ever been in her life. Instinctively, her hand swept up, her open palm smacking into Ransom Tremayne's scarred cheek.

In that instant she saw something flare in Tremayne's face, something wild, terrifying, mesmerizing. His hand closed upon her wrist, the long fingers dark against her skin, his grip so strong, she knew in that instant he could crush her if he chose.

"Don't leap into the fire, little girl, unless you plan on getting burned." The words were a silken warning, but within the arrogant curve of Tremayne's mouth was a new wariness, a watching. It pulled Cecily in like a whirling tide, sweeping her deep into those eyes with the hue of shattered emeralds. She was lost in them, prisoner.

The silken chains snapped with a sudden jerking tug, and Cecily gave a tiny cry as the child's grasp tore free of her skirts. She turned wrathful eyes upon Tremayne, her jaw set, hard.

"Stop!" she commanded, clutching the tattered hem of the boy's jerkin as Tremayne swept the child into his corded arms. "Do not you dare . . ." Her protest trailed off, lost in a swirl of midnight cloak, as a tall figure burst from the dispersing crowd. Outrage surged through her afresh as strange beringed hands loosened her fingers from the child's rags. She spun, furious, upon the person who now held her. But at the sight of the blandly handsome features bending so near her, she gave a cry of relief. "Uncle Bayard!" She caught the immaculate sleeve of the rising politician who had been her father's closest friend during her girlhood at her father's estate of Briarton.

Bayard Sutton, Baron of Wythe, sketched her a most graceful bow. "My Lady Cecily, it seems I am destined to extricate you from scrapes," he drawled with an urbane smile. "Let me see, the last time, you were seven years old, I believe, and you were having an altercation with a most querulous goat."

"Yes . . . no . . . I mean, thank heaven you happened along!" Cecily cried. "This ruffian had seized this child, and I—"

Cecily started to fling a glare at Ransom Tremayne, but she stopped, frozen. The planes of his face seethed a hatred so virulent, it drove her back a step toward the safety of Sutton's narrow chest. Corded tendons stood out on Tremayne's throat, muscles knotted in a jaw thrust out in fury, while his eyes glittered, shards so menacing, Cecily could feel the danger crawl cold upon her flesh.

She scarce felt Sutton's grip tighten about her, his arm catching her about her waist. "Tremayne." Bayard's nostrils flared in distaste as his cool gaze swept from the other man's rigid features to those of the child. "What is amiss? Did one of your street rats gnaw through its leash?"

Cecily saw Ransom take a furious step toward them, heard the child whimper as the man's fingers clenched tight around its small frame. "Sutton, I should—"

"Before you attempt to bludgeon me the way you did that other poor wretch, you'd best count the cost."

Cecily started at the venom in Bayard Sutton's voice.

"If you release that urchin, he'll bolt," the baron observed, brushing a fleck of dust from one kid glove. "And you will lose yet another specimen from your little . . . *'collection.'*"

"No, Uncle Bayard," Cecily stammered in confusion at Sutton's cavalier dismissal of the beggar lad's plight. "The child doesn't belong to—"

"I can assure you, Captain Tremayne takes most especial care of little boys, do you not, sir?" Sutton's voice held the sneering, velvety tone that had oft daunted the House of Lords.

"You bastard." Tremayne's oath cut raw through the night. "You cursed—"

"Spare me your observations upon my character," Sutton said, his grip about Cecily stunningly strong as he urged her away. "'Tis time I removed this lady from your churlish company."

"The child . . . the constable . . ." Cecily pleaded desperately, trying to break Bayard's grasp. "We have to—"

"These are not the lanes of Briarton, Cecily, my dear," Bayard said, his fingers bruising tight upon her waist. "And you . . . you have grown far too lovely to risk amongst London rabble."

A strange discomfort swept over Cecily at Sutton's frank appraisal as he all but dragged her toward the duchess's awaiting coach. She strained her gaze toward the figures yet silhouetted in the middle of Drury Lane, the daunting man, his face a mask of fury, his iron-honed body dwarfing the pitiful one of the child imprisoned in his arms.

Cecily shivered, her skin prickling with a chill of foreboding as she felt those emerald eyes searing into her flesh, a hatred so violent, it struck her through with the sensation of being trapped—a butterfly snared within a silken web.

Chapter Two

THE CHILD WHIMPERED against Ransom's chest, thin limbs twitching, face crumpled with pain even in sleep. Ransom shifted the exhausted boy in aching arms, his battered hand holding the stallion to a walk upon the night-black London streets. So many bruises, Ransom thought, his jaw clenching as his eyes traced the boy's shrunken face. Yet at least, now, that beast of a man the lad had called father had tasted of a fist himself.

Grim satisfaction warmed Ransom's belly as he drew the ebony folds of his cloak more tightly about the child's huddled form. Despite the purplings splotching Ransom's own flesh from the huge man's body-shattering blows, Ransom had not gleaned so much pleasure from a brawl in longer than he could remember.

His lips curled in a savage grin, the tender skin about his eye throbbing as it pulled tight. He'd bear a shiner to rival any boxer at Gentleman Jackson's on the morrow, but the drunken oaf who had abused this lad would fare fortunate if he ever used his cursed arm again. Ransom's gaze drifted down to where the child clung to his shirtfront, one small hand curled against the bloodstained white silk.

It was so fragile, that tiny hand, and could have been so full of wonder, but its fingers would never grip the reins of a horse, wield a cricket bat, or skip stones upon a crystal pond. Ransom winced inwardly, his stomach lurching at the sight of those tiny fingers—crippled not by some sanctimonious God's will, nor by the cruel fate that crushed so many of the poor, but rather, crippled by choice, the delicate tendons severed by the child's own father.

The better to beg with, Ransom knew, fury surging through him afresh. But the boy had not gleaned enough from the decadent rich streaming into the Theater Royal this night to satisfy his father's thirst for gin, and the oaf had been well on his way to mutilating the lad's remaining hand when Ransom had stalked from the theater during the last act.

And if the violet-eyed shrew had held her own way, the child would most likely not only be suffering under his father's cruelties this night, but the wrath of the constabulary as well.

God knew Ransom had witnessed a hundred horrors since the day he put ashore from his own ship, intending to find some beauty, some grace in one of the most "civilized" cities in the world. Yet, in spite of the scores of children he had snatched from Tothill Fields and Covent Garden's stews, waifs such as the one he had discovered this night never failed to fill him with a soul-searing despair.

Whenever he witnessed the callousness of London's elite as they trampled over the starving in their wake, the rage that had built in him since the days of his own childhood ate away at him like poison. He shut his eyes, the relentless African sun burning again beneath his eyelids, hunger clawing like rats in his belly as he scrabbled through trash piles for food in the filth-laden slave port of Baytown upon the Gold Coast.

Always, through years of a slavery as horrible as any the captive blackamoors were forced to endure, Ransom had clung to the certainty that far away from Baytown, from the greedy, cunning power of his cruel master, Tuxford Wolden, there lived people the like of those few families that resided at the outskirts of the slave port's walls. People with little girls garbed in ruffles, their hair tumbling in masses of perfectly combed curls, and small boys with fresh-scrubbed faces, their cheeks not hollow with hunger.

Ransom swallowed the bitterness, remembering the hard, cold feel of the coin one of the children's pretty mothers had pressed into his filthy child palm on a steamy hot day so long ago at the jungle's edge. There had been such sorrow in the woman's dark eyes as she had looked down at him, such gentleness in her slender gloved fingers as she had smoothed back a tendril of his filthy hair.

Despite the certainty that Tuxford Wolden would beat him for disobedience and deprive him of even what meager edible scraps the brothel master allowed the spawn of his trade, Ransom had been unable to bring himself to slit the ribbons of the beautiful lady's reticule as planned. The woman's single, tender touch had been well worth the flogging Wolden had served him. And as the days passed, Ransom had taken time from playing cutpurse to question anyone who might know something about the gentle lady.

From London town the family was, a bandy-legged sailor had told Ransom at last. And he had clung to that distant city as the dark-eyed woman's son had clung to a rag-stuffed rabbit, taking out the memory to finger lovingly when alone.

But the fairy city he had conjured in his mind had proved more elusive even than the sea creatures the sailors wove tales of late at night. And when he had stepped, a man grown, upon the London quays six years past, he had not found a haven brimming with compassionate angels, but rather, beneath the glitter of wealth and position, hard-faced women with brittle smiles that battered down those beneath them.

Ransom's lips twisted in disgust, the shadowy street seeming to hold eyes the hue of violets, a face molded to steal men's souls. A fallen angel . . . the incongruous thought flitted through Ransom's mind. A pampered darling of the London elite who would no doubt have demanded the crippled child's head for daring to have wept upon her gown. The loathsome Sutton had called the girl

Lady Cecily, groveling at her feet as if she were some crowned princess.

Ransom's teeth clenched at the memory of that face, the aristocratic nose tipped up, the delicate chin thrust out in spoiled defiance. He himself would have lief seen that cursed "princess" humbled—those haughty lips crushed red beneath his own, those soft hands that had proved so ready to condemn a child, eager instead upon Ransom's own shoulders.

'Twould give him as great pleasure as breaking the drunkard's arm to drive that air of superiority from *Lady Cecily's* beautiful face with his kiss—then hurl into her perfumed hands the knowledge that the man who had humbled her held the same lowling blood as the child she had been willing to cast to the devil.

Ransom swallowed, his throat strangely dry at the image his mind had conjured. From the first time he had seen her, tumbling into the midst of the brawl, a whirl of silk ribbons, heathery satin, and defiance, he had felt some strange tug deep in his vitals, something that had jolted through his callused palms when they had curved around her bare arms.

He had been half mad with blood lust in the midst of the fight, but in that instant he had touched her, the feel of her—soft, warm, scented of violets—had pierced like a saber thrust through his very core.

The child cradled against him whimpered, and Ransom eased him more fully into the lee of his shoulder. "Aye, little Pip, 'twas naught but the clamorings of lust," Ransom sighed to the still-dozing boy, bitterness brassy on his tongue. "And a night with that dark-haired witch would most like turn a man's heart to ice. Mayhap I should not have taken such pains to avoid Lysandra and Suzanne during the play. God knows they were both hungry enough at Aurora's last musicale." Ransom grimaced suddenly, unutterably weary at the prospect of sharing either of the beauteous women's silk-draped beds.

Gripping the reins in his other hand, he reached up to the pale little face cradled against him, tenderness and fierce protectiveness constricting his throat. "No, 'tis well I slipped from my box before those two she-cats were able to descend upon me. For if I had not . . ."

His hand clenched upon the reins, images seeming to dart through the shadows—the giant of a man battering the cowering child, the tiny scarred hand, useless, limp, the loathing blazing from Lady Cecily's violet eyes.

Ransom drove the images ruthlessly from his mind, dragging gritty eyes to where a rambling rose-brick house glimmered in the moonlight. Its spacious gardens brimmed with shadowy swings, ropes for climbing, platforms anchored high in spreading tree boughs.

"Let the whole of London burn in hell," Ransom grated as he reined the stallion to a halt at the garden's gate. "You're home now, Pip." Ransom's voice caught in his throat as he smoothed a dusty brown curl from the child's pale brow. "And I vow to you that no one will ever harm you again."

The fire was dying. Cecily fastened her bleary gaze upon the glowing embers in the marble hearth, despair knotting in her throat. 'Twas as if the silent bedchamber mocked her, the cast-off quills, inkpots, and well-worn books scattered about the apartments allotted to her father at Duke Harry's Moorston Hall bringing to the town-house rooms the aura of security that had always seemed to cling to her father's beloved possessions.

From the time she had been able to toddle, she had been welcomed amidst her father's books, her lopsided child's letters often crowding beside her father's precise script. Nothing within her father's life had been kept from her—from the simplest act of tying a troublesome cravat, to the meetings Charleton Lansdowne had reveled in holding within Briarton's huge library, during which a dozen of his brilliant friends would gather to discuss Plato and Machiavelli.

Yet now even the shadows seemed to whisper of secrets, jeer at her from the place where her father's nightshirt lay, folded upon the vacant bed. "Where in God's name could he be?" Cecily whispered to the first threadings of mauve softening the darkness beyond the mullioned glass windows. "He never stays abroad till dawning—*never*. Even the night of his accident he—"

Cecily swiped her fingers over her burning eyes as she fought to banish the memory of four weeks past—a wild shot supposedly from a poacher's gun, a riderless gelding, her father's head swathed in white-linen bandages as the doctor hovered over Briarton's huge mahogany bed.

An accident, Charleton had assured his distraught daughter later, a moment's carelessness. Yet that carelessness had come close to snapping his very neck. And though half the menservants at Briarton had combed every corner of the Lansdowne property the next day, there had been no evidence of any game having been taken. Cecily crossed her arms tight beneath her breasts, a chill prickling the nape of her neck as she remembered the patrols her father had set to roving over Briarton thereafter—burly men, with pistols secreted beneath their frock coats. True, she now much doubted her father's tale of careless riding and a skittish horse. But who . . . what enemy would wish to harm gentle, kind Charleton Lansdowne?

She shook herself, trying to banish the threadings of panic snaking about her, as exhaustion spawned within her a nigh supernatural dread of the ebony velvet creature who had eluded her. 'Twas as if the cloaked figure were woven of every nightmare that had beset her as a child—a faceless image, claws dipped in her father's blood.

Cecily's jaw clamped tight, nails cutting deep into her palms as she fought to crush the budding hysteria roiling in her breast. "You'll stop this foolery at once, Cecily Lansdowne!" she railed at herself between clenched teeth. "Whoever was skulking about beneath that cloak was naught but a man, and you've never yet encountered any rogue you couldn't best in a contest of wits. For all you know, Papa might have whisked back to the town house before Aunt Honoria's coach arrived, and then darted out again. Mayhap he found someone just perishing to dissect Shakespeare or Pericles."

Even as she spoke the words, she knew her hopes to be groundless. A meeting with the Bard himself could not have spurred the methodical Charleton Lansdowne to forego his sleep. And not so much as a shirt stud was disturbed upon the glistening mahogany table, the chamber appearing exactly as it had when Cecily had bounced in to thank her father for the new slippers he had placed upon her pillow before the fateful trip to Drury Lane.

The moment the house had lain quiet, she had slipped her wrapper about her shoulders, stealing into her father's room armed with her vow to force him to confide in her. She had paced his apartments an eternity, listening for the tiniest creak of the stairs.

But still he did not come.

Cecily picked up her guttering candle, its meager light painting eerie shadows upon the room. Reaching out one trembling finger, she trailed it across the broken nub of a cast-off quill, her palm skimming the embossed leather spine of her father's most treasured possession, next to the miniature of his long-dead wife.

"Papa . . ." Cecily said, unable to stem the waves of misery washing over her as she touched the gilded pages of Charleton Lansdowne's beloved journal. "Papa, if you would only *talk* to me. You ever bore the time to discuss any joy, any sorrow. And now your silence . . ." The whisper caught, jagged-edged in her throat. "Your silence hurts more deeply than anything I've ever known."

She shivered beneath the thin lawn of her night robe, her gaze straying to the tiny gold frame tucked lovingly amid the clutter upon her father's desk. The mother Cecily had never known peered out at the world with tranquil eyes, her soft pink lips curved in a smile of such loving, the painted image seemed aglow with its light.

Seldom had Cecily felt the loss of the woman who had borne her, then succumbed to dread child-bed fever three days later. Charleton Lansdowne had showered his little daughter with love, delighting in acceding to the childish demands she set forth with such a regal air. And only the interference of one of the grande dames of the surrounding nobility, or the chance of danger to Cecily herself, had been able to drive him to deny her what she had desired.

No, Cecily thought, swallowing hard. She had counted herself fortunate to have escaped a childhood chained by the harsh rules of propriety that other regency misses endured at the hands of their mothers. 'Twas only rare moments like these that she felt an emptiness inside her, a numbing need to bury her face in rose-scented skirts, feel soft, tender hands soothe over her curls.

"Mother . . ." Cecily's voice cracked over the word. The tears she had fought to hold at bay stung her weary eyes. "I vow I'd bargain with Satan's own if I could but know Father was safe."

Cecily brushed trembling fingers across the soft skin of a wrist that hours ago had been banded by Ransom Tremayne's hard-rough palm. Now the golden-maned rakehell's mocking sneer seeming to fill the dimly lit room.

Satan's own . . . Had she not nigh been ensnared by him hours ago? Fierce, dangerous, sinfully handsome, the scar that slashed one cheek but added to that bronzed visage's dark fascination.

Don't leap into the fire, little girl, lest you want to get burned. . . . Tremayne had warned her, his muscled arms holding the boy captive. And she had let Bayard Sutton drag her away from the night-veiled street, away from the frightened child and the man who had held him.

Yet in truth she had escaped nothing—not the menace concealed behind a black cloak, not her father's inner pain, nor Ransom Tremayne's dark fury.

Cecily dashed the hateful tears from her lashes with her knuckles. "You'll not waste your time wailing like some witless babe, cowering from the shadows," she said between gritted teeth. *"Think, Cecily. Think!* There must be something—"

She started as the candle suddenly guttered and went out,

spilling darkness across the bedchamber. Steeling herself against the unreasonable sense of panic washing over her, Cecily hastened to the small table beside the empty bed, her fingers closing about the silver doves gracing the unlit branch of candles.

Voices drifted through the pitch-dark corridor, the words indiscernible, but the tone . . .

"Papa?" The plea was but a choked breath as Cecily padded silently through the darkness to the chamber door, her fingers groping for the doorknob, loosing the latch. "Papa, is that you?"

She stilled, straining desperately to gauge the direction from which the sound had come. But the old section of Moorston Hall allotted to Cecily and her father gave no clue. The drafty corridor was riddled with little-used passageways, doors to rooms whose bolts had but rarely been unlatched in thirty years. With unsteady fingers Cecily snatched a single taper from the branch of silver doves and hurried to the hearth to plunge the wick into the glowing embers. The wick flared to life, and Cecily, heart hammering against her ribs, eased through the door, into the darkened hallway.

Ancient armor—the previous duke's passion—lined the narrow passage, morning-star maces, massive broadswords, Saracen daggers dripping from the dark-paneled walls. Cecily shuddered, her slippered feet deathly silent as they stole across the floor, the light from her candle oozing over terrors from another century. She paused, listened, detecting the origin of the faint voices that had drawn her into the night.

The gardens . . . Her gaze swept down a narrow flight of stairs to where a sliver of rose-gray sky crept through the crack of a half-opened door. Her fingers clenched tight about the candle, hot wax spilling down to burn her skin. But she scarce felt it, as a ragged, tortured voice came from beyond the partially closed portal.

". . . Ninon . . . sweet Christ, if they discover . . ."

'Twas her father, Cecily thought, her heart lurching, his

voice nigh unrecognizable, shattered. Cecily scooped up her trailing ivory wrapper in her other hand as she hastened down the steps, but another sound stayed her just as her fingertips touched the door's latch—a purring, raspy voice, drifting velvet across the night.

"They'll discover nothing about that cursed ship," the voice said firmly. "Even if they should suspect the truth, there would be no way to prove their charges. There is naught to do now except wait till whoever wrote the missives makes the next move."

"Nay, we cannot lay back and do nothing! God knows—"

"We cannot do anything else!"

Cecily shrank back into the shadows as the other voice bit out the words.

"Think you I do not realize how much you stand to lose? My life's ambition is within my grasp, but if, by some chance, you are exposed, I will be ruined as well." A harsh laugh grated out, and Cecily could feel the sneer in that raspy purr. "Surely you did not think that *I* was responsible for this. . . ."

"You were the only other person who could know." Charleton's voice was strained, beaten. "I thought—"

Cecily heard her father drag in a shuddering breath.

"Dear God, I do not know *what* I thought. I was grasping at anything . . . so terrified that Cecily would be snared in this morass. 'Twould destroy her . . . and she . . . she is innocent of all except being the daughter of a fool."

"She will never suspect the truth, Charleton. Do you think I would ever let anything harm her?"

"No. I know you would not. I . . . Bayard, forgive me for accusing you. 'Twas my greatest folly of all."

Cecily caught her lip between her teeth, stunned that the sinister voice she had first discerned was that of a friend.

Bayard Sutton . . . She felt a prickling where his arm had curved about her waist, felt his grip, shockingly strong as he had maneuvered her away from Ransom Tremayne and the child. Yet instead of filling her with relief, the pervasive sense of unease she had felt in the shadow of the theater whispered over her again, blended with a sharp tang of anger.

"'Tis forgotten," Sutton said, and Cecily could hear the muted thud of his palm striking her father's shoulder.

"Nay. 'Tis not forgotten . . . never forgotten," Charleton choked out. "It will haunt us both till the day we die."

Cecily heard the soft crunch of Sutton's boot soles retreating down the back garden's path. She stole to peek through the crack in the door, grief and fear twisting deep inside her as she saw her father bury his face in gnarled hands.

"Mad . . ." he muttered brokenly, his narrow shoulders shaking. "Dear God, 'tis driving me mad. . . ."

Cecily's throat knotted, her hand shaking where it held the candle. She wanted to twine her arms about that bent gray head, but she knew that if he suspected she had seen him so broken, it would shatter the last of his pride.

She drew back into the shadows as she saw her father turn slowly toward the door. Panic jolting through her at the certainty that she would never reach her own room at the end of the hall, she hastened up the stairway, darting partway down the darkened corridor. As she heard her father start up the stone steps, she turned, struggling to appear as if she had just slipped from her own chamber, praying that her father would believe her little ruse.

"Papa?" she called softly as Charleton Lansdowne's stooped figure came into sight. "Papa, is that you?"

She saw his head jerk upright, his shoulders squaring. "Yes, child."

Cecily pretended to rub her eyes, and feigned a yawn. "I heard . . . a noise . . . thought it was . . . housebreakers. . . ."

"And if you had surprised some rogue making off with your aunt's silver, what would you have done?" She could hear her father battle to infuse his accustomed teasing tone into his words. He failed.

"I would have requested that they ply their trade more quietly."

"Requested? Commanded, more like." Her father's lips

twisted in a mockery of a smile. "But I fear there is no one about but me. I had some difficulty in sleeping. Took a stroll in the gardens."

"Is everything . . . are you well?" Cecily couldn't stay the tremulous inquiry.

"Go to bed, child." Charleton dragged a weary hand through his disheveled hair, evading her question. "With your cousin Mirabelle arriving on the morrow, the duchess will no doubt be hauling you off to every fete in London. You'll be in sad need of your rest."

Cecily took a step toward him, wanting to brush his pale cheek with a kiss, but at that moment she saw something flutter from his waistcoat pocket.

She bent down, retrieving a small rectangular card, her eyes scanning the word scrawled across it.

"Ninon . . ." she read aloud, praying her father would betray some hint of what was tearing at his soul. "Papa, who . . . what is—" Cecily flinched at the stricken look that flashed across her father's face as he snatched the bit of paper from her fingers, his Adam's apple bobbing convulsively in his throat.

"Nothing," he said in a strained voice. "No one."

"'Tis a lovely name, I—"

"Go to bed!"

She winced at the sharp words, fear surging through her anew as the candle's light illuminated the pain in Charleton Lansdowne's thin face. Crushing the card in his fist, he stalked toward his own chamber. She saw him fling the door wide, the empty echo as he slammed it shut behind him reverberating through the hallway.

Cecily stood silent in thought as the shadows painted black upon the walls. Ninon could be the name of the boat he and Sutton had been discussing, the ship causing her father such agony.

"My lady?"

The touch of fingertips upon her arm made Cecily jump and wheel toward the quavering voice thick with the accents of Cornwall.

Framed in a ruffle of mob cap, Bess Kinsey peered up at her mistress. The maid's eyes appeared as round as they had been the day Cecily had plucked her from the midst of a bevy of tormenting farm lads who had snatched the girl's rosary.

"My lady, when I found you gone from your bed, I feared—"

"I was just waiting up for Papa." Cecily sighed. "He—He had some affairs to be about late, and I wanted to hear his news."

"More papers to bury his nose among?" Bess asked with a lopsided smile. "I vow, 'tis a wonder Lord Charleton is not cross-eyed, the way he is always—" Bess broke off her chatter, stooping down to pull something from beneath the toe of a suit of Elizabethan armor. "Look," she said, bobbing up again with something clasped in one chapped hand. "The master must have dropped—"

"Let me see that!" Cecily's hand flashed out, whisking the stiff paper card from the surprised maid's fingers. Cecily's own hand trembled with foreboding as her gaze locked upon the rectangular card. It was identical to the one her father had crushed in his hand, except for the single word it held.

Baytown.

Baytown? Cecily's brow knit in confusion. First, the name of some mysterious ship, scrawled upon a card, then this. 'Twas a settlement, most likely, situated somewhere upon a coast. Perhaps that harbor bore some connection to the Ninon . . .

Her lips set in a determined line.

Once, as a child, she had scaled every tree in Briarton's orchard in an attempt to discover which nest a baby wren had fallen from. She had succeeded. Surely she could find out about a ship, and perhaps its harbor. . . .

Cecily closed her fingers over the scrawled word, stuffing the card hastily into her wrapper's pocket under Bess's confused stare.

"Lady Cecily, what—"

Cecily grasped the girl's plump arm, pulling her into the

chamber, closing the door behind them. "Bess, something is amiss. I cannot tell you what it is. I don't even know myself. But I need you to bring out my rose-checked muslin, my braided straw bonnet, and—"

"My lady, what—"

"I have to slip away before anyone else awakes," Cecily rushed on.

"Away?" Bess paled. "I don't understand."

"I have an errand to serve without anyone else knowing. Especially Papa. I will be back before anyone else awakes."

"But 'twould not be proper," the timid girl quavered. "If the duchess discovered, she would die of apoplexies."

"Please help me!" Cecily hated the desperation in her voice, her agonized gaze locking upon the maid's face.

Loyalty brightened the girl's eyes, her lips parting in adoration. "After all you've done for me—sweepin' me up from the village, making me a right respectable lady's maid? Of course I'll help you, miss," the girl said stoutly, giving Cecily's hand a bracing squeeze.

Cecily swallowed hard, hating herself for revealing her anxiety even to this girl she had known since childhood. "You owe me naught, Bess. And I should not even ask you to go with me."

"I've ne'er seen you turn your back on any as needs help, trouble or no," Bess broke in. "I'll not turn away from you now." She bustled to gather the checked gown in her arms, and Cecily was glad that the maid could not see the tears stinging her eyes.

"So," Bess said briskly, "where is it we are to be off to?"

"The docks."

"The *docks?*" Bess spun around, her mouth forming a stunned O. "But—But 'tis the worst part of town, miss. So full of thieves and cutthroats, the shipmasters had to make 'em nigh a fortress, and—"

"I've already faced the worst cutthroat London could muster," Cecily snapped, surprised at the grating edge of nervousness that suddenly beset her.

Her eyes strayed to the window, where the dawn was just

touching the city's streets—her imagination betraying her with sword-sharp images of the violence in Ransom Tremayne's lean visage, the scar ice white against his skin.

"There is nothing to be afraid of," she said fiercely, and wished that she believed it.

CHAPTER II THE WIND

within the water's surface, the shape rolling and seeking the old man's presence within the streaming pattern, a dim outwash leaning. The sun on either current lay within... *** *** *** ***

Through a transparent forms of the darkening and inside water's eye, beheld

Chapter Three

Spices from Cathay, sugar from the Caribbean, and diamonds from Africa filled to bursting the holds of the ships looming across the Thames's dark waters. Like the most formidable of sentries, the towering masts stood at attention within the maze of London's vast docks, as though the ships themselves could see past the quayside defenses into what lay beyond—a dark, twisted world of murderers and brigands, their vermin-infested haunts clustering greedily about the seaborne fortresses.

Yet no knight-valiant stood guard amongst the dazzling treasures. Rather, a ragtag army mounted watch, salt-weathered and surly, their eyes as hard as the butts of the pistols thrust into their baggy canvas breeches.

Cecily straightened her shoulders within her daffodil satin coat, trying to keep from showing the unease gnawing at her confidence. But the weight of a hundred stares pressed in upon her from all sides, months at sea and barrels full of gin blending in a daunting mixture of temper and lust.

For nigh on an hour she had borne it, the once-crisp ribbons of the reticule clasped in her gloved hand now wilted with the perspiration gathering on her palm, the baitings of the sailors she had stopped to question yet jangling her frayed nerves. Stones and bits of splintered wood cut into the soles of her slippers, and it seemed already as though she were searching for a wisp of thread in a hay rick. All of the sailors she had dared to stop had regarded her with unbridled suspicion, none of them owning to knowing of a port called Baytown or the elusive Ninon.

"'Ay, there, me partridge, what would ye be chargin' me t' pluck ye?" a swarthy boatswain with tattoos ringing his thick neck volunteered from the midst of a crowd of savage-looking mates, his teeth flashing white in a game grin. "I vow I'd be willin' t' part wi' my last voyage's wages in full if ye'd come gauge the qual'ty o' me sheetings wi' me."

Cecily heard Bess gasp, the maid scurrying in the shadows of the rose-checked skirts like a timid mouse. But Cecily gripped the reticule containing the stiff paper card all the harder, forcing herself to meet the sailor's hot-eyed leer with an icy glare of her own.

"My lady!" Bess squeaked, grabbing a handful of Cecily's coat and digging her heels into the ground. "You cannot mean to question that—that lout! He'd slit you from nose to knees with his saber, or hurl you over his shoulder an' carry you off . . . 'prison you in his ship as his—"

"He shall do no such thing," Cecily bit out, crushing her own bounding fears as she dragged the girl toward the bevy of grizzled blackguards. "'Tis daylight, and we're fair drowning in witnesses. No one would dare." Cecily steeled her spine as her eyes swept the hostile faces all around her, not at all uncertain the men beneath the bright bandanas and scraggly beards would fail to dare any danger—even that of hying off one nameless young lady in a daffodil-yellow coat.

Cecily ground her teeth as Bess told off more beads of her rosary upon shaking fingers, prayers the girl had been repeating since the moment the hackney cab had let them down nigh the dock's gates.

"Ah, so she 'tends t' take ye up on yer offer, Gibbon!" one of the sailors guffawed. "I vow, missy, drive a hard bargin wi' the man, 'cause I can promise 'e'll drive a right hard one at yer tup!"

Cecily battled the heat of humiliation threatening to flush

her cheeks, the lust in the faces of the sailors turning her stomach. "I do not intend to strike a bargain with anyone," Cecily said, drawing the regal tones about her like a mantle. "I've but come to seek—"

"Some thrice-cursed officer, no doubt t'spread yer pretty legs fer," the tattooed leader sneered, his grin turning ugly.

"Oh, aye, Gibbon, she be away too fancy fer the likes o' ye!" a balding man chortled. "Most like she be shipped in special fer Captain Donnelson. 'E has a fresh 'un brought 'round whenever 'e strikes the shore."

"I know nothing of *any* captain, let alone one named Donnelson," Cecily protested evenly. "I but need some information. I have this card—"

"A callin' card, is it?" a chirruping cricket of a man chimed in, scratching his half-bared belly. "'Scuse us fer not providin' a silver platter t' leave it on. But we be short in the amenities 'ere."

"She'd be the only amenity I'd need!"

Cecily heard the voice from somewhere behind her, and was suddenly aware of stinking, sweat-laden bodies closing about her and Bess from behind. Daring a glance backward, she was terrified to find the surly mob of seamen surrounding her while their tattooed leader took a measured step toward her, his full lips wet with spittle.

"Leave 'er be, ye sotted fools!" Bess's shrill voice shocked Cecily, the maid's eyes popping from her face in fear. "Me mistress is a lady, she is!"

"An' I be Princess Charlotte!" the balding man guffawed. "A *lady* would scarce be a-pawin' about the London docks with naught but a skinny witling the cut o' ye to guard 'er, would she, me little doveling? Nay, methinks yer *lady* is but the pet o' one o' the swells 'at leave us starve on weevily biscuit an' soured water whilst they cram their bellies wi' salt pork an' Madeira."

"Or drink our cursed blood," Gibbon spat, his black eyes glowing in malevolent slits. "That bastard Donnelson flogged me six weeks past till scarce a strip o' me hide was whole, he did. But with Donnelson's sweeting, here, mayhap I can gain back a bit o' me own, eh?"

One grimy finger reached out to trace the yellow silk that hugged the curve of Cecily's breast. Instinctively, Cecily's hand flashed out, her palm connecting hard with Gibbon's thick arm. The burly sailor yelped in surprise, his eyes dulling with a fury that struck terror into even Cecily's stout heart.

"I told you I know nothing of your brute Donnelson," Cecily declared, fighting to keep the building fear from her voice, sensing that to betray it to these men would be like scattering bloody carcasses to a school of savage sharks. "All I wish is to—"

"Your wishes mean less than nothing to me, my *lady*." Gibbon's hand swept out, his hard palm crushing the tender flesh of her arm. "'Twas a long voyage we set out on, the boys, here, an' me. An' we be ashore now fer a bit o' diversion. *You*, my pretty doxy, be the most tantalizin' one we've come across as yet."

Indignation mingled with fear, then welled over it, as Cecily caught a glimpse of Bess's face, tear-streaked now, terrified.

Cecily tried to take a step back, rip her arm from Gibbon's grasp, but the fingers holding her clenched tighter, his other hand reaching up to shove the braided straw bonnet from her head.

"Release me this instant." Cecily's voice was low, even, yet full of silken threat.

"Oh, aye, I'll let ye go, doveling," Gibbon snarled. *"After* ye settle the score ye've tallied with me. Nobody makes a fool o' Cavan Gibbon an' gets away wi' it."

"I can assure you, Mr. Gibbon, 'twould be a waste of time for me or anyone else to 'make' a fool of you." The words poured out before she could stop them. "You play the part so admirably on your own."

'Twas as if some unseen blade had severed the throats of every man clustered about her. Silence fell, seeming to last an eternity—an eternity in which Cavan Gibbon's eyes transformed to those of an enraged animal.

Cecily swallowed the lump of panic in her throat. Fixing a dazzling smile upon her lips, she started to sway toward his bull-like chest, the memory of the only brawl she had ever witnessed flashing through her mind.

The elbow . . . Ransom Tremayne had struck at the elbow . . .

Clenching her jaw, she drew her fist back, ramming it with all her strength into Cavan Gibbon's arm.

Spikes seemed to shoot into her shoulder, her knuckles bruising against the sailor's hard flesh.

She waited for his shrieks of pain, but instead a bellow of rage blasted her ears and her courage. Bess screamed as Cecily felt brawny hands close over her throat. She knew in that heartbeat that Cavan Gibbon full intended to crush that slender column between his palms. Fingers curling into claws, she raked at the reeking sailor's cheeks, gouged at his glittering eyes.

Then, suddenly, the whole dock seemed to explode in a roar of gunfire. Cecily heard the sailors surrounding her cry out, felt Gibbon's fingers loosen to but a whisper about her throat as she battled to focus upon what looked to be a pistol jutting toward the sky. A tendril of smoke wisped up from the still-hot barrel.

Cecily dragged her gaze from the battered, gnarled hand gripping the weapon's butt, down a wiry arm to the wizened face of a man who peered at her with unconcealed disgust. "What be the matter, boyos? Hoardin' too many pennies t' buy a doxy willin'-like?" the man asked in a voice sour as aged vinegar. Cecily shot her unlikely savior a look of gratitude, and was stunned to see the old sea dog's mouth twist in dislike.

"Now, Gibbon." The sailor shifted on a carved peg leg and raked Cecily with a scathing glare. "I'm certain-sure the wench has vexed you, and most times 'twould be fine with me if you wrung any o' the clinging little witlings' necks, but I can na' have ye makin' a mess on the steps o' Defiance Enterprises. Makes the captain inside there passing surly, it does."

"I did nothing!" Cecily attempted to protest, her throat burning like fire, but all that came out was a raspy croak.

"Then I'll take 'er away from your precious captain,

Jagger," Gibbon said, his fingers knotting in Cecily's hair. "This harlot an' me, we got business t' settle—"

Cecily tried to jerk away from her captor, wheel to face him, but Gibbon's hand yanked her back upon her hair, her backside smacking hard against his filthy breeches. The wiry little sailor merely thrust his pistol into his scarlet sash, then drew the weapon's twin from his other side.

"Gibbon," the man sighed, "ye know I've endured a flood o' women in me time, but I've ne'er met a-one worth dyin' for." The gnarled hand closed on a leather pouch tied at the old sailor's waist. He yanked hard on it, snapping the string. "Here," he said, tossing it at the swarthy Gibbon's feet. "There be enough coin in that t' get ye all drunk as lords an' fancyin' the favors o' any lady ye please at One-Eyed Jack's."

"Jagger, the bitch—"

The sound of Gibbon's protest was interrupted by the metallic click of the pistol hammer being pulled back.

Cecily felt Gibbon's hands tighten upon her, heard his foul curse. "Aw, what the hell, Jagger's right," he snarled at last. "Ye're not worth dyin' for." His fingers closed about Cecily's chin, bruising hard as he wrenched her face up to his. "But stay the hell out o' my way, pretty," he said, with a sea shark's smile.

Cecily stiffened her own spine, quelling her fear as she gave him a haughty stare. "Should be . . . no problem to . . . outwit . . . a—"

The world seemed to reel as she felt herself jerked from Gibbon's grasp, the livid face of the man called Jagger inches from her own. "I'll murder ye myself, if ye don't shut yer yap," he hissed low. Then, with a forced laugh, he uncocked his pistol and shoved it beside its mate in his sash. "Save a pot o' Molly's finest for me at the Jack," Jagger said. "I'll be over as soon as I wash my hands o' this rubbish."

"Rubbish!" Cecily bristled.

Her blusterings were lost in the guffaws of the sailors as they hurled coarse jests amongst themselves at her expense. She clenched her fists, more furious with her rescuer than the man who had assaulted her, but Jagger's gnarled fingers were as strong as tempered steel as he propelled her away from the crowd of men.

"Move yer hindquarters, ye whinin' wench, lest I leave ye," Jagger flung out to the terrified Bess. Bess stumbled along after them, clinging to Cecily's skirts.

"Leave her alone, you great oaf!" Cecily blazed, the sound of her maid's muffled sobbings filling her with guilt. "Can you not see she is terrified?"

"Alone?" Jagger spat. "If I'd left ye both *alone,* ye'd be ridin' Cavan Gibbon's pike staff by now, my fine lady, an' this chit would really have somethin' t' be caterwaulin' about."

Cecily cringed inwardly at the vivid image Jagger's words conveyed, but if the old sailor were *trying* to rouse her to fury, he could not have chosen his words for more effect. "She has every right to be wailing to the heavens if she has a mind to!" Cecily said. "I hauled her out here against her better judgment, those ill-mannered blackguards assaulted us— And *you!* Then you barged in, yelling loud enough to deafen—"

"Gratitude," Jagger interrupted, rolling eyes permanently squinted from years at sea. "The greatest o' female virtues."

"We—" Cecily nearly choked on the words. *"I* thank you for coming to our aid. Of course, in another moment I would have had the situation well under control."

Cecily squirmed inwardly at the blatant lie, and the look Jagger shot her made her cheeks flame.

"Well, I be glad t' hear it, missy, 'cause once ye get out o' these gates, even the captain can't fault me when ye get yer fool neck slit."

Cecily looked up, suddenly aware that the crotchety sailor had been steering her and Bess toward the dock's gates. With a tiny cry she planted her slippers upon the ground, slamming to a halt. "No, Mister . . ."

"Jagger. Jest Jagger."

"We cannot . . . cannot leave before . . ." Cecily dug into the reticule still caught over her wrist, ignoring the old sailor's ripe swearing. "Though I know you'll not believe it,

34

I did not come down on the docks here just to ruin your day. I need to—have to gain some information. . . ."

"Ahhh." Jagger drew out the syllable in such a guise of male arrogance, Cecily ground her teeth. "So ye be spyin' on yer man, eh?"

"No! 'Tis not like that. I must discover what this means." She held out the card, and with a half-snort of contempt, the old man ran a glance over it. Suddenly his breath hissed, sharp, between graying teeth, and his expression veiled so quickly, Cecily wondered if she had seen it at all.

"'Tis naught but a port in Africa." He shrugged. "Ye'll not take my advice, I know, but ye'd best yank yer nose outa whoever's business ye be meddlin' in afore ye get it snapped off."

"I have no other choice. I have to . . ." Cecily swallowed, trying to keep the pleading from her eyes. "There was another card," she said, her hands knotting into fists. "It was exactly like this card. Even the script was identical, except that it read 'Ninon.'"

"Mother o' God!"

Her gaze leapt up to his face, saw him pale beneath his teak-hued tan.

"Ninon." Jagger's eyes pierced her. "Why in the name o' Satan are ye stirrin' up that cursed hellhole?"

Cecily felt dread prickle like slivers of ice over her skin, and she had fleeting memories of the Greek myth she had once read about a woman named Pandora and a box. . . .

"Someone is trying to use whatever is written on those cards to harm a person I love. I have to discover . . ." Cecily paused, knowing she was making little sense, knowing also that she dare not slip and somehow betray her father.

Jagger's eyes narrowed to slits, the black orbs seeming to bore into her very soul. Cecily held her breath, hoping, praying . . . fearing . . . 'Twas as if a war raged inside the crabbed sailor, and she knew if Jagger cast his lot against her at this moment, a cannon could not dislodge whatever information he might hold.

"Should boot ye both out o' these gates by the tails o' yer

petticoats," Jagger said, raking his hand through snow-white hair. "I should. But he . . . he'd want t' see ye, damn 'im . . . Cannot leave it alone.

"Stop yer snivelin', then, an' give a man some peace!" Jagger groused at the sniffling Bess with a ripe oath. "I'll take yer cursed mistress t' someone who might aid 'er."

Hope raced in Cecily's breast, then slammed dead as she caught the muttered words: *"Aye, or someone who might cast 'er in the Thames."*

With that cryptic comment, Jagger wheeled, stalking off through the maze of crates, barrels, and coils of rope. Grabbing Bess by the arm, Cecily hastened after the wizened old man, scarce able to keep pace with him despite his wooden leg. She was gasping for breath when at last Jagger neared the weathered steps of a long, low building, pristine in a coat of fresh whitewash. The brass-plated sign in the shape of a compass rose fairly quivered above the door, the name DEFIANCE ENTERPRISES seeming to fit perfectly whatever scene was being played out behind the open door.

"Perfect," she heard Jagger mutter, flinging the portal a jaundiced glare. "Jest perfect."

Cecily caught her lower lip between her teeth as a deep, furious voice from within the building thundered in her ears.

"Donnelson . . . burn in hell where . . . belongs!" the voice railed. "Any man with . . . good sense to jump ship under his command deserves . . . berth on . . . Defiance—deserves . . . goddamned medal for bravery!"

A muffled reply cut in, indecipherable, yet bearing a calm the other voice did not.

"Like Hades! . . . saw Tom Waring's back—"

Cecily jumped as the muffled voice's interruption was drowned out by a deafening roar. "Donnelson *was* three points off on his compass! If Waring hadn't been cowardly and insubordinate, Donnelson's hull would have been making love to a blasted coral reef, though, by God, if he was the only man to go to the bottom, 'twould have been cause for a national holiday. Now, *out!* Get off of my cursed property, and tell your master if he tries to pull Tom Waring from one of my ships, 'twill be the high and mighty Donnelson who feels the bite of a lash."

Jagger stepped away from the foot of the wooden stairs, his eyes fixed expectantly upon the doorway. "One," the old sea dog counted. "Two—"

Suddenly the doorway erupted in a flurry of dark-blue coat and gold braid, an oily little man clutching a huge leatherbound ledger in his arms bolting pell-mell down the risers.

"Three," Jagger said, with such infinite satisfaction that Cecily managed to smile in spite of herself.

But whatever odd amusement she had gained from Jagger's actions was banished in the next second as something from the inside of the building struck the wall beside her with such force that the sign above the door swayed drunkenly.

"Ever bearin' a saintly mood," Jagger grumbled to himself. Cecily's gaze followed his to the door, unease knotting in her stomach as she regarded the lair of what seemed to be a most cantankerous dragon. But before she could draw another breath, the doorway filled with broad shoulders, clenched fists, and well over six feet of scarcely leashed fury.

"Jagger, blast it, you're late!"

She almost dove behind the scowling Jagger's back as the morning light flashed white over a wicked scar, a green eye blazing from the midst of swollen, purpling flesh. The grime and blood from the brawling the night before had been scrubbed from the taut bronzed skin; a fresh white-linen shirt and biscuit whipcord breeches clung elegantly over muscles still rippling with latent power.

"You!" Ransom Tremayne's hot gaze seared Cecily's face, and she felt a dull panic wrench at her resolve as she stared at her nemesis of the eve before. "If you've come seeking that boy, I'll—"

"Mind yer temper, ye ravin' maniac!" Jagger broke in. "The chit has come t'—"

"I give not a damn why she crawled out from under her velvet-lined rock. Get her the hell out of—"

"Ye *will* care, lad." The old sailor's voice was gruff with emotion, edged with what, even to Cecily's battered eardrums, seemed tenderness.

Tremayne's dark brows swept low. "Jagger, what—"

The sailor's gnarled hand reached out, curving over the rigid muscles of Ransom's forearm. "The *Ninon,* boy. She be pokin' about the docks seekin' word o' the *Ninon.*"

Cecily felt something twist in the pit of her stomach—fear, dread, and something she dared not identify—as she saw Ransom Tremayne's lips whiten, the eyes that swept to her face piercing, yet hinting at a vulnerability she would never have believed possible in that hardened rogue. Her breath caught in her throat as she lost herself in those emerald eyes, saw for a fleeting instant the gateway to some private hell.

"Sweet Christ."

'Twas but a breath, half profanity, half prayer, but those two words struck Cecily as nothing else that day had. 'Twas as if she were standing on a precipice, with Ransom Tremayne's bronzed hand reaching out to draw her into some abyss.

"Get ye inside." The sound of Jagger's voice shattered the web that had seemed to entrap both her and Ransom, and the daunting Tremayne stepped aside, gesturing for her to enter.

But when the drooping Bess made to follow her, he shook his head. "Nay. Only your mistress."

"Bess was almost accosted once," Cecily objected. "I'll not abandon her to—"

"Jagger will see to her." Tremayne's voice was hard again.

Cecily glanced at the white-haired sailor and was surprised to find his lined face studying her in amazement and, mayhap, a touch of respect. "An' I thought 'twas the maid who was s'posed t' shield th' frail society miss," Jagger muttered. He gave Cecily a gentle shove. "Go on, girl. No man on these docks'd touch the hair of so much as a ratling on the captain's holdings. Yer woman here'll be safer than in her mammy's cradle."

Cecily felt a sudden fierce urge to beg Jagger to stay with her as she confronted Tremayne, the bad-tempered sea dog suddenly seeming a shield against the green-eyed black-guard. But even before the thought had fully formed, she quelled it. Appearing a coward in either man's eyes seemed more unbearable than any havoc Ransom Tremayne might wreak.

"I shall return in a little," Cecily said to Bess. "Draw a long drink of water for yourself and rest a bit."

"A-Aye, my lady," Bess sniffled.

"'Twill all be well, Bessie," Cecily added, as she saw the girl's wide eyes swim with tears. "I promise."

Forcing her hands not to tremble, Cecily laid gloved fingertips on the rail, her arm brushing against the hard wall of Tremayne's broad chest as she swept past Ransom into the shadowed shipping office.

Light streamed across the wooden floor through a huge bow window that opened out across the harbor, the sunlight picking out the rich, dark texture of two huge leather wing chairs flanking either side of the curved panes. The soft gold walls were papered with scores of charts and maps, awkward charcoal sketchings of fantastical monsters tacked up beside countless rows of schedules and shipping lists.

A huge desk in the center of the room overflowed with ledgers, a crumpled cravat—obviously torn from Ransom Tremayne's muscled throat in a fit of impatience—and, incongruously, a bedraggled doll, a makeshift eyepatch banding its delicate head. Cecily stared at the unique plaything long seconds. Was it some holdover from Tremayne's own childhood, or had he snatched it from the arms of some hapless waif?

Her fingers twisted the gold ribbons of her reticule as she crossed the width of the room to examine a colorful rendition of Africa—*not,* she reassured herself inwardly, *to place distance between her and the green-eyed warrior.*

The whimsical sea creatures drawn by the mapmaker's pen wavered before her eyes, seeming almost to have a life of their own, their gaping mouths appearing to jeer at the fears trickling through her. Drawing in a deep breath, she turned to face her own menace.

The door latch clicking shut bore the sound of a pistol

hammer being levered back, and Cecily turned half expecting Ransom to bring to bear a weapon. But in that instant she would have preferred to face the barrel of one of Napoleon's cannons rather than the unreadable expression upon Ransom's arrogant features. As if she were in Wellington's army, she steeled herself for the charge.

"'Tis most pleasant to see you again, *Captain* Tremayne." Cecily gave him her most haughty smile. "Especially with your eye so deservingly adorned."

"'Twould be wiser not to discuss what I or anyone else deserves, my lady." His voice was silky soft, dangerous. "Unless, of course, you want to spur me to deliver payment in full for your actions of last eve." Cecily saw those insolent eyes trek to her lips, something firing in Tremayne's face—dangerous, tempting.

"I did naught last night but—" Cecily hated the defensiveness that beset her voice, steadied it, lifting her chin with studied hauteur. "I demand to know what you did with that boy."

"So you can cry off with his head? I think not, 'Gloriana.'"

"Captain Tremayne, I—"

"He is far out of your reach, I assure you. However, you, Lady Cecily, are not out of mine. I suggest you leave off trying my patience."

"Your patience!" Cecily blustered, indignation firing her cheeks. "Of all the conceited, swell-headed—"

"The subject is closed. Now, either state your business or stop wasting my time."

Cecily's nails gouged deep in her palms as she struggled to maintain what little rein she yet held on her temper. She wanted to slap Ransom Tremayne's mocking face and sweep out of the room with the air of the queen he had tauntingly named her. But in all the time she had spent scouring the docks, this man, with his insolence and his acid tongue, was the only person she had encountered who had even heard of the *Ninon,* which she had by now gathered was a ship. No fit of pride was worth risking Charleton Lansdowne's peace of mind.

With every ounce of fortitude she possessed, she drew in a deep, calming breath. "Captain Tremayne," she began again, leveling a gaze at him. "I need information. Anything you can tell me about—"

"The *Ninon.*" He spoke the name as though it said everything, said nothing. And she sensed a tensile eagerness about him, the coiled power of a predator waiting to pounce upon its victim.

"Yes, the *Ninon.* I need you to tell me whatever you know concerning—"

"I give less than a damn what you need, 'Gloriana.'" Tremayne sneered, his mouth hard. "What *I* need is to know why the hell one of Bayard Sutton's princesses is wandering about in the filth of these docks."

"Has the battering you endured the night past affected your hearing as well as your eye, Captain Tremayne? I want information."

"You're naught but another of Sutton's spies, then? Trying to wheedle secrets free with your body? Well, I vow I'm a bit tired today, and I've little interest in sampling your charms."

"How dare you!" Cecily's cheeks flooded with heat, her fingertips fluttering to where Ransom's gaze had fixed upon the swell of her breasts.

"I'd dare much with you, milady. After all, 'tis why Sutton sent you trotting down here, is it not?" He paced toward her with lazy, dangerous grace.

Indignation surged through her, and she clung to it against the tempest raging in Tremayne's black-fringed eyes. "For all the concern it is of yours, Lord Sutton is a man of honor! Far too noble to stoop to crawling about, spying in corners, unlike you who brawl in the streets—"

"Nay, Sutton would not dirty his gloves fighting his own battles." Ransom stalked closer. "He lets other men 'brawl' for him. Aye, and die. Die like the poor devils on that cursed hell ship."

"The *Ninon?*" Cecily felt a shiver scuttle between her shoulder blades.

"Aye. The *Ninon.* But what happened upon that ship

41

holds not half so much fascination for me as the fact that a woman the like of you is so eager to know what befell it. Fifteen years the *Ninon* has been buried so deep within the ocean's floor that God himself cannot find it. And now . . . of a sudden, you sashay in here with your haughty demands, seeking . . . seeking what, princess?"

Cecily felt the probing of his gaze upon her, a gaze far too adept at stripping free any ruse the world could offer. She looked away, fearing that he might discern something that could inadvertently betray her father.

"You appear to be a woman far more taken with the tedium of *haute façon* than naval history," Ransom said. "Tell me, Lady Cecily, are you one of those twisted young chits with a penchant for gruesome tales? Or are you merely trying to find a way to ruin some enemy by resurrecting old ghosts?"

"I am not the one who bashed his way across Drury Lane last night!" Cecily wheeled to face him, infuriated at the blatant aura of male arrogance in his tone. "I want to harm no one. 'Tis just that if I could discover anything about the *Ninon* and Baytown, I might be able to aid someone I love."

There was a flashing of some emotion she dared not name in those implacable green eyes, a hardening of the line of his mouth as his gaze flashed to her lips. It was as though her words had angered him in some mystical way, or issued some primal challenge even she dared not face. "I stumbled upon two cards with those words scribed upon them," she said, rushing on in an attempt to secret away the effect Tremayne's flaming gaze bore upon her. "Words mysterious to me, yet holding some secret that is destroying my—" She stopped, appalled at what she had almost revealed, feeling those eyes that saw all, knew all, boring into her face.

"What secret, Gloriana?" The tiger's paw was toying with her. "You already know that the *Ninon* was a ship, and Baytown—'tis naught but a patch of misery carved out of the jungle. What could a haughty miss the like of you have to do with such a place? Such a ship? And who, my lady Cecily, are you battling to protect?"

"That I will never reveal to you," Cecily said, meeting the probing force of his gaze.

"Then how the hell am I to gain the information you seek? Without a name? Without somewhere to start searching?"

"That is your affair, Captain Tremayne. All I can promise you is that whatever you can do to aid me will be richly rewarded. I will pay—pay most handsomely for any information you gain."

He was close, so close her hip brushed the taut muscles of his thigh, the warmth of his hard flesh washing over her despite the bare inches that separated them. Her breath caught at the savage beauty sculpted into the harsh planes of his face, primitive despite the trappings of elegance—bewitching, Ransom Tremayne was, Cecily thought numbly. Bewitching, yet more dangerous than a roiling tempest.

"So," he said in a deceptively bland voice. "I am not worthy enough for you to *trust*, but I am hungry enough for you to *buy*, eh, your highness? You can but cast your coin at your feet and expect a lowling the likes of me to scramble to lap it up like a trained hound?"

"I have a great plenty to offer you, Captain Tremayne—a purse full of guineas. My father said—"

"Guineas?" Deep laughter came from his hard lips, and Cecily was shocked at the richness of the tones.

"Take them all—every one—if you will just—"

"Every one? I can take every one? A trough full would scarce be enough to buy the ribbons on your coat, yet you expect me to spill out my soul for a handful of them."

Cecily felt a blush mount in her cheeks, but she kept her shoulders straight. True, at Briarton she had never had need of money, and she had been in London such a short time, she had had small experience in handling the currency, but her father had said . . .

"Ah, so you honestly believed your little reticule held a treasure Croesus would envy." There was a softness around the edges of Ransom's voice she had never heard before, a brushing of amusement. "Poor Gloriana."

His mouth curled in a disarming half smile, one strong

finger reaching up to stroke the pulse point at the hollow of her throat. Cecily flinched at the slight contact, stunned at the power in the merest brush of that work-roughened flesh against her. The blood flowing beneath its fragile layering of skin heated, raced, the lazy circles he drew there with the tip of his finger sending strange sensations tingling to her breasts, and lower, to her loins.

She tried to evade his touch, but her legs were leaden, the soles of her slippers seemingly fused to the ground. "C-Captain Tremayne—"

"Fear not, milady." His voice was husky deep, tinged with a humor she had never thought to find there. "I bear no need of your crowned jewels, but mayhap if you would offer some other recompense . . . say, a generous portion of that cursed aristocratic pride?"

Cecily saw his eyes darken, those mocking lips part with obvious intent. He was going to kiss her. She saw it in his eyes, felt it in the tensing of his muscles where they brushed against her. Yet there was in his face an incongruous shading of bored arrogance, as though the meeting of their lips would prove a task to be endured, not pleasure to be savored.

She started to protest, sensing the danger in him, her palms pressing hard against the wall of his chest. But before she could speak, his mouth lowered to hers.

Never, in her most fantastical dreamings, had she suspected that the merest brushing of a man's lips could hold such incredible heat. Yet Ransom Tremayne showed her. Whisper soft, taunting, tantalizing, his mouth promised dark pleasures, yet held them just out of her reach, making her ache for them all the more. Cecily struggled to capture the magic he offered, hold it, but the wondrous sensations Ransom was loosing inside her danced like star fire, elusive, mesmerizing.

She whimpered, melted closer against his hard frame as she felt his fingertips trail up from where they had rested at the base of her throat, thread through the silken skeins of her hair to unravel some mystery he alone understood. He had delved to the very soul of more worldly women than she, aye, and had found them lacking, Cecily sensed through the drugged haze his lips were weaving about her. Yet she could no more have stopped him from taking in the very essence of her being than she could have stayed the tides.

"Open for me . . ." The command was husky, hot, and blue flame seemed to spear down into her very womb as Ransom's tongue skimmed the curve of her trembling lips, then delved past them to seek out the mysteries of her mouth.

She gasped, shocked at the bold, exquisite mating, her fingers curling into the rough satin of his hair, her whole body liquid, aching.

His mouth drew from hers, shaped hers, made love to hers in a way that was so stunningly intimate, shockingly sensual, 'twas as if he had breached far more than her lips with the touch of his own. Every inch of her body throbbed with primal, hypnotizing passion. Yet untutored as she was, she sensed that he was gifting her with far more pleasure than he would ever be able to draw. Gifting her? Or mocking her?

Half afraid, Cecily willed her eyes to open, the lids seeming weighted as she fixed her confused gaze upon the bronzed visage bending so near her. With obvious reluctance, Ransom's lips left hers, his breath warm, scented of spice, yet feathering across her face, his thumb soothing mesmerizing patterns upon the inside of her elbow.

She was quivering. Ransom could feel it beneath the daffodil satin, could see the blaze he had meant to stir raging within her luminous eyes. Wide with wonder, they stared at him from beneath lush black lashes, the rose-hued petals of her lips swollen, trembling from the expert assault of his mouth.

He had seen women ensnared in the web of his lovemaking a hundred times—women far more experienced and nigh as desirable as this pampered angel. Yet never had the sight of lips damp from his kisses affected him so strongly. For beneath Cecily Lansdowne's beauty, pride, lay an openness, an innocence a man the like of him bore no right to taint.

Ransom's lips curled with a depth of bitterness he had not

felt since the day he had first landed upon London's shores, and regret seared him as he saw the unsullied amazement within Cecily's gaze falter. He felt a fierce urge to draw her back into his arms. And crushed it.

"That, my lady, was a most intriguing deposit upon your account." The words brimmed with a studied insolence, intended to wound, to spark off the temper ever ready to blaze in the sheltered beauty's eyes. "If you are prepared to continue like payment—"

"Payment?"

The lightning-fast flash of pain that pierced the glow of her face twisted in Ransom's belly—something tearing in his chest as he saw her veil her hurt in anger.

"How dare you, you . . ."

"Bastard?" He supplied the word, one corner of his mouth tilting in a half smile. "Aye, I am. In birth as well as in temperament. 'Tis one thing, Gloriana, you shall have to learn to endure if we are to seal this . . . business arrangement."

"If you think you can force your foul kisses upon me as some sort of twisted payment, Captain Tremayne, you are sadly mistaken. I'm not some—some harlot who revels in being mauled by any man in breeches!"

Ransom's smile turned brittle, a dull pain clenching in his own heart. "Contrary to popular belief, your highness," he said softly, "few 'harlots' revel in aught but misery. However, you . . ." He let his gaze sweep a lazy path to her lips. "You seemed to take no exception to enduring my 'foul kisses' but a moment ago."

"'Twas naught but shock," she flung back defiantly. "I am hardly accustomed to being grabbed and forced—"

"You've never been 'forced' to do anything in your life, princess." The words were harsh even to Ransom's own ears, filled with a bitter pain ever lurking within his soul. He wheeled away from her, angry, hurting, fearful that she might detect something in his face that would betray him—betray that little boy who had lost his very soul in the stench of the African jungle.

He could feel her icy pride goading him from where he stood, and despite the fact that he kept his eyes averted from her siren's face, his mind held an achingly clear picture of those porcelain features, violet eyes.

"Mayhap you are right, Captain Tremayne." Her voice held a thread of steel. "I have rarely been 'forced' into anything in my life. And I have never failed. If you know about this so-called hell ship, *Ninon,* others must as well. Men not so low as to barter information for the use of someone's body."

Ransom's jaw clenched at the self-righteousness in her voice, and he spun toward her, his face scarce a breath from the rose-tinted perfection of hers. "Gloriana, if you knew just how *low* this man is, you'd run away, screaming in horror."

He took savage pleasure in the slight tremble of her lips, the flicker of uncertainty in those huge violet eyes. He had made men back down from the fury in his face—burly sailors hardened by battle. But the graceful girl before him shifted not so much as an eyelash; rather, she met the turmoil in his eyes with fire and ice of her own.

"I seldom scream, Captain Tremayne," she said in frigid accents. "And I never run away."

"Mayhap you should start." It was a warning he wished she'd take, knew she never would.

The curve of her delicate chin jutted out in the stubborn line that was already too wrenchingly familiar, and he wanted to catch it in his fingers, drag her lips again to his. But the strange, beguiling innocence beneath her veiling of elegance stayed his hand.

"Well, Captain, what is it to be? Do you aid me? Or do I begin to search out someone else?"

"There is no one else. No one who truly knows about the hell ship. They're dead. All dead except . . ." Ransom let his voice trail off, his mind churning with memories he had tried to banish for fifteen years. . . .

A cargo hold crammed with human bodies, ebony-hued skin layered with filth, scarred by whips, chains—a crotchety old sailmaker pulling tight the stitches he was setting in a half-crazed boy's cheek—and flames, writhing up from the bowels of the ship, devouring all entrapped upon it like some ravening monster.

He felt bile rise in his throat, the stench of burning flesh again searing his nostrils, the feel of the sea's cold arms folding around him, washing his skin with a blessed chill.

Aye, they were all dead now, except for that elusive man who had turned the *Ninon* into hell, and the golden-haired urchin who had stowed away below its decks. The child who had witnessed disaster and vowed to destroy the man responsible . . .

Ransom raised his eyes again to those of the child-woman before him, her face drawing into agonizingly clear focus. She was desperate, despite the bold facade she had struggled to maintain. God knew, he had been in the throes of desperation oft enough to recognize the signs. But 'twas no mission of mercy this time that drew him to give her help, 'twas not compassion that drove him, nor even lust. Never had he suspected that such a hideous dark side lurked within him, a beast of a man who would prey upon the fears of a woman to gain his own ends.

Nay, a voice railed inside him, *'tis not vengeance for yourself you seek, but rather for all the others who were murdered. 'Twould be a greater betrayal still if you let this woman walk away, let whoever she hides behind her petticoats escape, merely because Lady Cecily bears an enchantress's face.*

He bit out a curse under his breath, hating himself as he leveled his gaze upon her. "Aye, damn it, I'll aid you," he said. "But only upon the condition that you give me something . . . someplace to start. If you truly fear for this person you're trying to protect, Gloriana, you have to at least give me a name, else you've risked this trip to the dock, aye, and suffered rousing my temper for naught."

"I cannot—"

"You cannot *fail* to reveal the truth to me. You may think me as dense as the dolt I trounced outside the theater, but I bear enough wit to know that you must have been terrified out of your mind to come plunging down to the riverside. *Let me help you,* Gloriana. Tell me!"

She stared at him endless seconds through eyes tortured with indecision and a pain that sickened him with guilt. But Ransom forced himself to meet her gaze, gritting his teeth against the certainty that the expression upon those delicate, beautiful features would haunt him for eternity.

Trust. There was a reluctant trust in the creamy curve of her brow and in the ripe sweetness of the lips he had just melded with his own. Trust laced with the starkest of fear. He saw her shoulders go rigid with a surrender that only served to heighten the aura of pride that clung to her angel face. "Very well, then," she said, her voice but a whisper. "'Tis . . ." Her gaze flickered away from his face, her voice catching in her throat. "'Tis my father Charleton Lansdowne."

The words struck Ransom like an axe blow to his chest, the honesty, the vulnerability in her face filling him with self-loathing. Her father . . . Ransom's fingers gripped the edge of his desk, the wood cutting deep into his hardened palms as his mind filled with images of his own little Lacey, the dark-curled imp who fair worshiped her papa with the blind faith the devout reserved for God himself.

He closed his eyes, picturing the woman before him as she would have been the year the *Ninon* set out upon its disastrous voyage—an innocent, trailing hair ribbons for kittens to pounce upon and weaving crowns of lavender and gillyflowers. 'Twas evident in every line of her face, the tiny crease of worry betwixt her finely drawn brows, that she adored this father she was attempting to shield. And if it was as Ransom suspected—if her father actually proved to be the man he had sought since the day the *Ninon* surrendered to flame—then Cecily Lansdowne had just unknowingly betrayed the father she loved to the very man sworn to see him hanged.

"Will you aid me?"

He started as Cecily repeated the words, and he raised his

eyes to where she stood—proud, so proud and graceful, her face so cursed beautiful that to touch it seemed a sin.

"Aye. I'll aid you." He turned away, trying to blot out the image of Cecily Lansdowne's face, drive from his ears the tauntings of demons he thought long dead.

Aid her, they mocked him.

Aye, and then destroy her. . . .

Chapter Four

Cᴇᴄɪʟʏ ʙʀᴀᴄᴇᴅ ᴏɴᴇ ʜᴀɴᴅ against the threadbare squabs of the hackney's seat, gritting her teeth in frustration as the vehicle ground once again to a rumbling halt. Two dozen times since they had pulled away from the dock's gates the coachman had hauled back on the reins of his plodding horses to avoid trampling anything, from a saucy milkmaid to the scrawniest of hounds. The cabman saw it as his bound duty to pass judgment upon whomever or whatever blocked his path, and the vocabulary of one of London's less-cultured inhabitants had considerably enriched Cecily's meager collection of cursings.

But she had exhausted even those gleanings of oaths but a little ways back, during the time the cabman had taken a full five minutes to rail at some creature Cecily had not been able to see.

Straining to see out the window, Cecily bit back a curse as her gaze focused upon the object responsible for this latest delay—a rough-hewn cart a-brim with fat green cabbages, the farm lad perched upon its crest beaming at the throng of people as proudly as if his cargo were faceted emeralds.

"Thunder in heaven!" Cecily grated, stomping her slipper against the coach's filthy floor. "At this rate Papa will have nigh called out half of Bow Street by the time we gain Moorston." Her eyes swept up to where the sun was struggling to pierce the ubiquitous pall of dun smoke lying over London's rooftops.

"By now Lettice has most like flown belowstairs with the tale that I was not abed to receive the infernal cup of chocolate she is always pressing on me of a morning. Aunt Honoria is shattering the crystal with her railings about my ingratitude, Lavinia is half foxed with gloating over my disgrace, and Father . . ." Cecily's hand knotted into a fist and she thunked it hard into the cushion beside her, trying futilely to blot out the image of Charleton Lansdowne distraught with worry.

Huddled into the corner beside Cecily, Bess buried her peaked face into a ragged apron, muffling a sob. "The master . . . he'll put me out for certain-sure," the maid mourned. "If her grace herself doesn't hurl me into the cookfires first for allowing you to roam so. 'Twill be off to the crofter's they'll be exiling me again, and you—they'll be lockin' you in your rooms till you're eighty."

"Don't be dramatic, Bessie." Cecily ground her teeth at the maid's sniveling. "Papa would never lock me up a day past my fiftieth birthday."

"If—If his lordship 'spected the half of what we were about this morn, he'd most like ne'er let you out of his sight again—" Bess gave a wounded hiccough. "What with bandying with dock ruffians, 'tis a wonder we're both not 'neath the undertaker's care. And that scar-faced rogue—a devil he was, certain-sure."

Unbidden, Cecily's fingertips drifted up to her lips, the feel of Ransom Tremayne's mouth yet imprinted upon her own. A devil? Yes, she had deemed him dangerous from the first moment she had seen him upon Drury Lane, glorying in battling with his fists, his face rife with savage beauty. Yet the far greater hazard for her lay within his carnal lips, his lean, jungle-cat body.

He had kissed her—a snarling ruffian buried chin deep in pitch and tar and salt-sea tempests. She had knocked the heir to a dukedom into a rosebush for daring less, but Ransom Tremayne had left her no time for indignant protests, nor, in truth, had Cecily wanted anything from the moment his lips touched hers, except to feel the sensual promise in those exquisitely molded lips. He had wrung from her mouth, in every nuance, the essence of her being. Yet despite the bone-melting magic of his mouth, 'twas as though Ransom himself were searching for something in each kiss—ever searching for something that eluded him. Even when his mouth had been pleasuring hers, there had been, for the first time, a vulnerability about the gold-maned rakehell, something that made Cecily want to trail her lips across the scar that marred his cheek, delve deeper still to other scars she sensed lay buried deep within Ransom's broad chest.

She fought to shove away the welling of empathy that rose in her toward the roguish seaman, forcing herself to see him as he had appeared outside the Royal Theater—ruthless, violent, reveling in the joy of battle.

"Captain Tremayne may have Lucifer's own temper. Still, he's naught but a man." Cecily kept her voice firm, yet even as she spoke, she could feel the wine-dark sweetness of Ransom Tremayne's mouth taking hers, the hard-muscled length of his body against the yielding softness of her own. A man . . . aye, Ransom Tremayne was very much a man.

". . . And now . . . now this . . . this contraption." Bess's incessant wail swept the remembered sensations from Cecily's mind. "Sweet Mary, my lady, we'll ne'er reach Moorst—"

"Perdition!" Cecily hissed, the maid's blatherings fading as Cecily caught a glimpse of a most impressive purple turban, bedecked with scarlet ostrich feathers. In a heart-beat Cecily dove to the hackney's floor, ducking her head in an effort to shield her face from the all-seeing eyes of her aunt's esteemed friend, the eccentric Mrs. Ambercrombie. The ever-present turban that was the balding old woman's most fiercely held concession to vanity was too unique to be mistaken, even had Cecily not glimpsed the long hawk nose and daunting jut of bosom that constantly threatened to burst the grande dame's bodice.

"'*Twould* be my cursed luck to find that vulture out shopping at this absurd hour!" Cecily groaned. "And the way that blasted coachman is bellowing— Get down, Bess! Hasten, before she swoops down upon us!"

"She already is, my lady!" Bess squeaked, crossing herself as though to ward off a dreaded banshee. Cecily strained to peek over the coach's window ledge, her heart hammering in her throat as she glimpsed the purple-turbaned form sweeping inexorably in the direction of the coach.

"Bess—" One glance at the maid's pinched face told Cecily that the girl understood all too well the implications of an encounter with the approaching dowager. Bess gaped at the bobbing scarlet plumes with the terror of a rabbit beneath a goshawk's eyes, but Cecily had no intention of being devoured by the gossip of Mrs. Ambercrombie or any of the other interfering biddies that took such joy in destroying young girls' reputations.

Before the older woman could break free of the crowds thronging the shops, Cecily flung a handful of coins at the driver, and, grabbing her snuffling maid by one ice-cold hand, leapt from the coach and darted betwixt the front of the cab and the cabbage-laden cart.

Snatching the yellow-satin coat ankle high, Cecily dashed down a narrow alleyway on the hackney's opposite side, praying that the vehicle would conceal their escape. Yet they had barely rounded the corner when Cecily crashed head-long into a set of elegantly clad shoulders, the heel of her slipper stomping onto the instep of an impatiently tapping black-leather pump. She choked out an apology, trying to shield her face with the fall of hair that had tumbled loose from its pins. But before she could dodge around the figure, a hand caught her, tight, about the elbow.

She spun around, certain that the redoubtable Mrs. Ambercrombie had commanded one of her cheery but penniless nephews to snare her. But the flash of relief she felt at discovering that was not the case disappeared as her eyes took in the face shielded beneath the brim of a tall-crowned beaver hat.

"U-Uncle Bayard," she stammered, a hot flush rising to her cheeks. "What—What a surprise."

"Undoubtably." Lord Bayard Sutton's lips parted in the

elegant smile that had aided him in securing great heights in the Whig party, the tiniest tautness about the corners of his mouth hinting at both shock and some carefully veiled annoyance. Eyes the hue of molasses searched the mob of people for an instant. Then Sutton's gaze swept back to Cecily, skimming over her tousled hair and muddied hem, the politician's patent disapproval giving Cecily the uncomfortable feeling of being ten years old again, caught plundering the sugar sack.

She waited endless seconds for the baron to demand to know what she was about, dashing through the streets of London at an hour when all proper young ladies lay at home, scarce up from their beds. But Sutton said nothing, merely dissecting her with his gaze, until 'twas as if that infuriating stare dragged words from her reluctant throat.

"I . . . Bess and I were searching for some ribbon to refurbish a gown for . . ." Cecily battled to fabricate some reasonable alibi, groping desperately for some approaching fete to name.

Sutton arched one finely drawn brow over eyes that seemed far too canny. "For Lady Lyton-Snow's ball?"

"Yes!" Cecily seized upon his words a bit too eagerly. "I—I tipped an urn of ratafia over my rose gown and—"

"Your father expects you to waltz about Lady Lyton-Snow's ballroom in stained furbelows?" The doubt in his voice was scarce perceptible—a razor whispering through a sea breeze—yet Cecily could feel the bite of the steel slicing away her subterfuge.

Her first impulse was to unburden herself, confessing as she had when caught stirring up tempests as a child. But then she felt the quick, sharp simmering of her temper rising. 'Twas not the fact that the baron had seen through her Banbury tale that sent the blood boiling in her veins. Rather, 'twas something so subtle in his expression that Cecily could scarce put a name to it—as though he were concealing beneath that bland face a kind of twisted enjoyment in watching her squirm about, pinned by her own falsehood.

"Of course, Papa would buy me another gown if I wished

it." Cecily's chin swept up in her most queenly aura. "But the rose muslin—it was my favorite, and I hadn't time to have the seamstress stitch me up something as lovely."

"You would be exquisite if the rest of your gowns were naught but flour sacking, my dear," Sutton said in acidly amiable tones. "But sweeping about in charwomen's rags is no way to glean yourself a husband. And, from the way you seem to always be charging into trouble, I affirm that you need a man's firm hand to your reins."

Cecily stiffened, the patronizing tones of male arrogance exacerbating her already deteriorating mood. "I fear that the man who attempts to put spurs to me shall find himself dumped most soundly into the nearest streambed, Lord Sutton. Now, if you will excuse me."

A dull red flush washed up above the starched cravat at Sutton's collar, his nostrils pinching in with what Cecily knew was irritation. His hand tightened about her arm. "So it is to be 'Lord Sutton,' is it, now that I have dared to attempt to curb your reckless ways?" His white teeth bared in a smile as one immaculately gloved finger swept up to trace her cheek. "Well, perhaps 'tis best for us to abandon the cry of 'Uncle' between us. After all, as you are attempting to demonstrate to me most clearly, you are quite grown up now." The dark eyes swept to hers, something in their depths souring Cecily's stomach.

She reached up, forcing his fingertip away from her skin. Clean . . . the gloved hand was so clean, she thought incongruously, spurred by Ransom Tremayne's bitter words. And she suddenly wondered if in truth the gloves shielded bleedings, physical and emotional, shed by those Sutton had overtaken upon his rise to political power.

"You play the untouchable beauty to perfection," Bayard said, his fingers yet poised in the air inches from her cheek. "Yet you allow just enough spark to darken those eyes of yours to challenge a man. I predict that you will be the toast of London before a fortnight has passed. And after . . . if you are wise . . ." His lips curved in a smile rife with secrets. "Who knows what heights you might attain."

Something clammy seemed to crawl into Cecily's stomach

as she met the baron's chilly gaze. "Lord Sutton, since being thrust in the 'marriage mart' by Aunt Honoria, the single thing I am certain of is that I bear little thirst to reach any 'heights' at all with the wealth of fortune-hungry fops swarming about the ton." She broke the baron's hold upon her arm, feeling the skin tingle with bruising where his fingers had bound her. "And as for being wise, I have always found that state excessively tedious."

Sutton's gloved hand dropped to his side, and Cecily took intense satisfaction in the single scowl line marring the perfection of his high brow. But even still, his gestures betrayed nothing of his annoyance with her, no hint of the true feelings Cecily guessed lay beneath that infinitely urbane countenance. And, despite herself, Cecily found she preferred Ransom Tremayne's open ragings to emotions concealed beneath down-wrapped velvet.

"Well then, my lady," Bayard said at last, "perhaps in this one instance you will prove wiser than is your custom. Since I am also invited to Lady Lyton-Snow's ball, I could relieve you of the attentions of these—how did you say it?—fortune-hungry fops . . . by claiming you for the first set."

"I do not think—"

"'Tis not so great a boon to ask, my dear. Most men would demand a far higher forfeit to keep silent about such a beautiful young lady's escapades."

Cecily met his gaze, sensing something hidden within the mild brown depths. 'Twas not a threat . . . could not be. And yet . . . For a moment she wavered between her natural tendency to meet any challenge with a stiffer one of her own and the need to shield her father from any further worries. For if Bayard Sutton chose to reveal her "sins" of the past two days, she bore little doubt that 'twould be her father whom the baron would enlighten about her conduct. And Charleton Lansdowne was already a pale copy of himself, gaunt with worry.

Hating the feel of being somehow silkily cornered, Cecily forced her lips into an engaging smile. "Very well, Lord Sutton," she said. "But the dance at Lady Lyton-Snow's ball shall be deemed"—how had Ransom Tremayne phrased it?—"payment in full for your silence."

"As you wish, of course."

Cecily ground her teeth at the condescension in his perfectly modulated voice. *No,* she wanted to say, *'tis not as I wish at all.* But she merely lifted her chin, brushing back one of the tendrils that clung to her brow. "I had best be hastening back to Moorston," she said, "else your vow of silence will gain me naught. Half the house is most like about by now, what with my cousin the Lady Mirabelle arriving."

"Mirabelle Lansdowne?" Sutton's lips pulled into a slightly unpleasant smile. "They are dragging her back from the country once again? With your aunt bringing out the Lady Lavinia, I had assumed the duke and duchess had given over hope that the chit would find some beau, ahem, 'worthy' of her hand."

"If she is at all like Lavinia, I vow I'll send a mourning ring to the poor dolt who weds her," Cecily muttered, not really caring if Sutton heard. But Cecily felt somehow defiled as his brows arched in a kind of sly taunting.

"Seeing as I have now witnessed *two* of *your* indiscretions, my pet, let me commit one of my own to warn you that the Lady Mirabelle is far worse than the Lady Lavinia has ever dreamed of being."

"Worse?" Dread at the thought of being chained to another cruel, smirking witch congealed in a cold lump in Cecily's stomach. "In what way—"

"Your pardon, miss, your pardon," Bess's high-pitched voice interrupted, her hand tugging insistently upon Cecily's sleeve. "'Tis Mrs. Ambercrombie boiling along this way."

Cecily hazarded a glance over her shoulder, seeing, indeed, the plumes of the magnificent turban poking out above the crowd.

"Perdition!" Cecily said between gritted teeth. "Hasten, Bessie!"

"Until the ball, my Lady Cecily."

Bayard Sutton's voice lingered over her name as though

he were greatly savoring her discomfiture. But Cecily took no time to consider the grating of Sutton's velvet-soft tone upon her nerves. She dove into the crush of people, struggling to lose both herself and the skittery Bess amongst the cooks buying baskets of vegetables and the farmers' wives running rough-hewn, covetous hands over figured muslins and silks.

The sweet-laden window of a corner confectionery bowed out to tempt the passersby, its glistening curve promising Cecily shelter from Mrs. Ambercrombie's piercing eyes. Cecily hauled Bess around the corner, then cast a final glance over her shoulder. The redoubtable dowager had vanished into one of the numerous shops that lined the street, her purple turban no longer bustling through the crowd like a tempest about to break.

Cecily started to heave a sigh of relief, then stopped as her gaze snagged upon the other familiar figure yet visible in the crowded lane.

Lord Bayard Sutton stood not where she had encountered him, but rather, withdrawn to a shadowed corner, the pale-gray hazings revealing in the planes and curves of his features something dark . . . expertly hidden. Or was it, Cecily thought suddenly, that Sutton was trying to secret himself away amongst the shadows?

His elegant lips were curled in a smile pulled so tight over his teeth it resembled a snarl, as he glared into the throng of people around him, his head giving an imperceptible shake as though to ward off something . . . or someone. Cecily followed the direction of his gaze, stunned to find it locked upon a splash of scarlet satin sweeping toward him.

A woman, it was, statuesque, mysterious, so oddly compelling, Cecily paused a moment longer, mesmerized as the scarlet-garbed figure glided ever nearer Sutton. A fragile veiling of gold net hid the woman's features from view; only her hair was revealed to those about her, the strands draping in a silken waterfall past her knees, tresses dark as sin. Yet Cecily sensed that the hidden face held the exotic beauty of a jungle lily dipped in subtle poison.

She saw Sutton's eyes dart about the crowd, but 'twas as if

the woman defied the fury Cecily sensed in the stiff lines of Sutton's shoulders—or took some sort of hidden pleasure in inciting the baron to anger.

Sutton's mistress? The notion flitted through Cecily's mind for but an instant before she dismissed it. The scarlet-clad beauty seemed more like a jewel-hued spider than a woman imprisoned by a man's carnal whims. There was something aloof, untouchable about her.

Cecily swallowed hard, a chill creeping beneath the yellow satin of her coat as she watched the exotic woman lay a sugar-cake brown hand upon Sutton's chest, her face tipped up toward the baron's taut features. As Cecily watched, she felt herself drowning in some encroaching blackness.

She was being foolish, she thought, shaking off her fears, as fanciful as flighty Bess, with her wild imaginings of intrigue in the simplest of things. A mistress, that's all the woman was. And Sutton . . . Despite the veiled manipulations, the acid in his smile, Bayard Sutton was naught but the same man who had posed as her "Uncle Bayard" for nineteen years—the bland, obsequious friend of her father.

She would be wiser, far, to turn her concerns to her father's desperation when he discovered she was gone, and to the cousin arriving this day at Moorston Hall—the cousin who, if what Sutton claimed were true, would make the coming weeks a subtle form of hell.

Mayfair glittered, a queen's tiara set amidst the tarnish of old London. Criers of every persuasion plied the hallowed streets with their wares, whilst gentlemen in high-perch phaetons or astride blooded stallions roved about at their leisure, generations of aristocratic pride carved into their lazily arrogant features.

Cecily caught her lip between her teeth, wincing as a sharp-edged stone sliced the much-abused sole of her slipper. She should be rejoicing that the lot of them found beneath their notice the two bedraggled women struggling along on foot. She had no wish to be fodder for the gossip hounds. But it chafed at her that the very men who had rushed about providing her with punch and plying her fan in the crush of a ballroom took no interest in the two obviously exhausted women dragging themselves beneath those selfsame "gentlemen's" very noses.

Cecily jammed an unruly lock of hair back from her cheek, frustration spawning burning tears at the back of her eyes. 'Twas futile, now, to hope that she and the terrified Bess might creep into Moorston undetected. The time was long since past when any excuse Cecily might conjure would be found acceptable. Guilt pricked her conscience with a dozen relentless needles. Her father was no doubt beside himself with worry, his ears ringing with the duchess's rantings about Cecily's shortcomings.

With his confidence so horribly shaken by whatever inner agony was tormenting him, he would no doubt heap blame for Cecily's wayward behavior upon his own stooped shoulders. *After all,* Cecily could almost hear her aunt's sneerings, *what else could Brother Charleton expect—stuffing the child's head full of that Socrates' philosophical nonsense.*

Cecily's chin jutted stubbornly, glaring at the elegant town houses lining Mayfair. Her lips set in a grim line as she pushed her aching muscles ever onward toward the Lansdowne residence just visible at the end of the street. It had proved naught but a cruel jest, this London season that had promised to hold so much gaiety. For it had not only stolen her naive admiration of those of elegant society, but had robbed her of her unshakable trust in Charleton Lansdowne as well.

A sigh eased the burning in Cecily's lungs. "Mayhap this whole day will turn out for the best after all, Bessie," she said to the wilting maid trudging in her wake. "This grand faux pas might well disgust Aunt Honoria so greatly that she will fling Papa and me from her house. And if we could hie back to Briarton, things might . . . we might gain peace."

Cecily had to clamp her teeth together to quell the sob threatening to betray her. Briarton. What would she not give to be curled in Papa's library chair this very instant, her feet tucked beneath her as she devoured one of Cook's raspberry trifles and one of her father's volumes of Byron at the same time.

Mayfair seemed to fade around her, replaced by tangles of briar roses, an old Elizabethan knot garden, and rolling, well-tended fields spilling out from beneath the delightfully whimsical Carolinian manor house that had been her home for nineteen years. She fought back the wave of homesickness that threatened to engulf her, refusing to cry before all the elegant, icy people who were her aunt's peers.

So fierce was her longing for home that she was oblivious to the rumble and the clattering of a coach bearing down from the rear.

"Sweet Jesus! You, girl! Watch out!"

The warning came almost too late. She lunged to the side, stumbling, cracking down hard on one knee as the vehicle ground to a stop. Cecily blinked back tears of pain, struggling to her feet as she felt warm blood run from her scraped flesh. Her stomach churned as she looked toward the coach that had almost run her down, an exquisitely painted box looming up before her—its lavender, green, and gilt-appointed sides emblazoned with some heraldic seal blurred before her stinging eyes.

"God's feet," Cecily muttered to herself, praying for the coach to rumble off on its way. But before the driver could touch his whip to the magnificent team of six snow-white horses, Cecily heard a timid thumping from within the coach, and the driver again reined in his beasts.

Cecily saw the coach door open, a face peeking out through the aperture. 'Twas a young woman's face, bearing little beauty except in its infinite gentleness. A dove-shaded bonnet hid all but a few tendrils of soft-gold hair, the brim framing gray eyes that seemed to swallow the whole face. She wet soft lips nervously with her tongue, and Cecily could see the dainty hand upon the coach door clench, white-knuckled, about the wood's gilt trim. "G-Good morrow," the young woman stammered. "I mean, I am sorry . . . sorry you fell. Are you all right?"

"Naught but my pride is bruised up a bit." Cecily brushed the dirt from her palms.

"But your dress . . . 'tis quite ruined, is it not?" 'Twas

impossible to mistake the genuine concern on her pale features.

Cecily sucked in a deep breath, her mouth twisting in a wry expression as she pulled aside the soiled yellow satin of her coat, revealing the torn checked muslin beneath. "I fear 'tis most certainly beyond help," Cecily allowed. "But 'twas my own fault, stumbling about the streets in a daze—stumbling about the streets at *all*, my aunt Honoria would say." Cecily pursed up her lips in perfect mime of the duchess's expression of severe displeasure. "No lady of any quality would—" The words lodged in Cecily's throat as her eyes caught the glinting of sun off of the coach's gilt seal. Moorston—'twas the crest of the dukedom of Moorston.

Cecily groaned audibly, half expecting the young woman in the coach to transform before her very eyes into a simpering shrew like Lavinia. But the girl's pink lips only curved in a most engaging smile, a faint dimple playing about one cheek. "She would say that, would she not? And, I fear, a great deal more."

Cecily's stomach sank to the toes of her slippers as she recognized the girl's slight resemblance to Lavinia. Her face was possessed of such a quiet dignity, Cecily did not notice at first that, though Lavinia's lips were ever simpering, slightly cruel, the girl before her bore a mouth of the same shape, yet softer, with a smile that touched her heart.

"You—" Cecily swallowed hard. "You are Lady Mirabelle Lans—"

"Naught but simple Mira," the girl interrupted, her dimple deepening. "And you must be the cousin Cecily I've been hearing such a great deal about."

Cecily flushed. "Most of it ill, no doubt. And unfortunately most of it true."

"Of a certainty. From the single letter Lavinia dashed off to me, I gauged that you must be absolutely delightful and the most beautiful belle to come out this season."

"Lavinia said that?" Cecily gaped, stunned.

"No. Lavinia claimed that you were a rollicksome hoyden with the manners of a buttery maid. And, she said that you hurled yourself at the gentlemen in a most unseemly fashion."

Cecily bristled, her eyes blazing. "I do not hurl—"

"Nay, don't upset yourself." Mira reached out one hand to clasp Cecily's stiff fingers. "'Twas from that very letter that I knew I would take such pleasure in your company. You see, Lavinia deems any girl with the least bit of sparkle to her bearing a hoyden. And as for the gentlemen . . . Lavvy cannot tolerate anyone outshining her. She ne'er takes the time to insult any but the most beautiful, witty, and . . ." Mira looked down shyly. "I just never expected to stumble over you quite so literally before reaching Moorston."

Cecily felt a smile tug at the corner of her own mouth. "You may wish to have the coachman drive you about London awhile before pulling through the town house gates," Cecily said. "Else you'll lay in peril of losing your hearing. My homecoming this morn will most like prove quite an ordeal. I—" She looked up into Mira's clear gray eyes, instinctively trusting her quiet cousin. "I had to creep out this morn with my maid, Bess, full intending to return before anyone discovered I was gone. But things went awry and—" Cecily gnawed upon her lower lip, her father's stooped shoulders rising in her mind. "Papa . . . he'll be so worried. . . ."

"There is naught we can do about that." Mira gave her hand a sympathetic squeeze. "But I can at least aid you in avoiding at least one of Maman's apoplexies. If you and your Bess can but climb into the coach, we'll bundle you up in my cloak to hide the damage to your gown, and—"

Gratitude and a sense of some inner kinship filled Cecily as she managed to haul herself up into the plush vehicle, Bess but a step behind her.

It seemed they had scarcely sunk into the equipage's soft seats before the coach drew to a halt at the grand entrance of Moorston. The lion-carved door burst open with an immediacy that boded ill for the scene awaiting them within, a babble-eyed footman bolting down the stairs three at a time to fling wide the coach's door.

"Lady . . . Lady Mira . . ." the beet-faced young man blustered, "thank heaven you're here! Her grace—she's in a most precarious temper, and your cousin—"

"'Tis all right, Alistair." Mira gave the man a solemn smile. "Thank you for the warning, and for the welcome." Mira extended her hand, allowing the gangling footman to help her from the coach.

"Nay, milady, your cousin—"

"Needs you to hand her down from the coach." Mirabelle's cheeks dimpled in a most engaging smile as the footman's mouth gaped open, his gaze leaping to where Cecily sat, hidden by the coach's dim interior.

"My—My Lady Cecily," Alistair squeaked, his Adam's apple bobbing crazily in his skinny throat. "Where—Where in God's name have you—" The choked words died off, his chin dropping nigh to his chest as embarrassment left crimson stains upon his scarce-bearded cheeks. "Your— Your pardon, milady, I—"

"Alistair, you are as worthless as the day Father dragged you in from the fields!"

Cecily winced at the high-pitched whine, her eyes shifting up to where Lavinia stood, framed in the door, a froth of snowy muslin, meadow-green frills, and eager, malicious eyes. "Maman bade you hasten Lady Mira in at once, so—" Lavinia halted her tirade as Cecily leapt lightly down from the coach. Pouting, pink lips tugged into the slumberous smile of a crocodile eyeing a most promising feast.

"Cecily!" The feigned gladness in Lavinia's voice made Cecily want to jam her reticule down the woman's throat. "We had thought you kidnapped by a highwayman, or crushed beneath the wheels of some carriage, or at the very least devoured by—"

"Sorry to have disappointed you," Cecily said with acrid sweetness, starting to push past her, but Lavinia stepped in front of her, blocking her path.

"Oh, I vow 'tis no disappointment," Lavinia crooned. "No one has been awaiting your return more eagerly than I. And Mira—dearest sister, we all know what a hideous gap your absence has left in the London whirl. At every soiree the pots of roses lining the walls have positively *wilted* without your company."

Cecily saw Mira's cheeks whiten a shade, her too-vulnerable mouth trembling just a whisper, and despite Cecily's first instinct to dash into the town house and ease her father's worry, she could not desert her new friend.

Looping one arm protectively about Mirabelle's waist, Cecily fixed Lavinia with a blinding smile. "Strange," she observed, "I thought 'twas your constant sniping that faded the bloom from every flower in the room, and banished the smiles from every gentleman's face as well."

"Of—Of all the—" Lavinia's pale eyes fairly popped from their sockets, her thin chest swelling with indignation. *"Maman!"* The wail made the footman clamp his hands over his ears, the horses yet hitched to the coach skittering in their traces as Lavinia spun in a flurry of skirts and ran up the stairs. One hand was flung dramatically over her brow in a gesture worthy of any actress who had ever trod the boards at Drury Lane, while in her eyes, Cecily knew, glinted a cruel delight she had witnessed far too often in her weeks at Moorston Hall.

Cecily met Mira's gaze, the other girl's lips tipping into an unsteady smile. "Is there yet time for me to have the coachman drive me about London . . . how many times, did you say?"

"Three would not serve nearly enough." Cecily started up the stairway, furious to feel a trembling in Mira's slight frame, knowing that she dared not abandon the girl to face the duchess's wrath alone.

The vaulted ceiling of the entry hall was a mass of plaster carvings—fat-bellied cupids with sly eyes attempting to spear each other with arrows that had more the look of pike staffs. Cecily wished she could pluck one from above to arm herself as she and Mira made their way to the duchess's receiving room. Servants lurked in every shadow, peeking out from behind the balustrades and carved pillars, yet nowhere was there a sign of Charleton Lansdowne's drawn face. Cecily saw Bess skitter through the door leading back toward the kitchen, and could not blame the girl for her cowardice.

"And so, daughter, you've deigned to grace us with your presence at last." The cutting, nasal voice seemed to slash through the open door like a pirate's brandished cutlass. Cecily clenched her teeth in defiance, her eyes narrowing upon where the duchess sat enthroned upon a blue-velvet chair, her considerable bulk resplendent in ecru net and pink satin, a sniveling Lavinia cradled in her arms. But before Cecily could speak, Mira darted through the door in front of her, dropping into an awkward curtsey at the duchess's feet.

"G-Good day, Maman."

There was pain in Mirabelle's gentle voice. The wide gray eyes were timid, eager, with a hinting of hopelessness about them that tugged at Cecily's heart.

Mira fidgeted with the frills upon her gown as she peered pleadingly up at the duchess. "You—You are looking in the peak of health."

"Did you expect to be met by a corpse, girl?"

Bright crimson stained Mira's cheeks. "N-No. 'Twas . . . 'twas but a greeting. I meant no insult."

"Nay, you reserve your insults for poor little Lavvy, here." Honoria Lansdowne smoothed her beringed hand over Lavinia's moon-pale curls. "And your kindnesses for climbing boys and—"

The duchess's watery pale eyes flashed up as though she had suddenly taken note of some vermin infesting her velvet drapings. *"You!"*

Cecily stepped beside Mira, head high, eyes spitting challenge. "Aunt Honoria," she said levelly.

"And where, pray tell, have you been, you wicked girl!" the duchess blazed, her cheeks puffed like a wineskin nigh to bursting. "The whole house has been in an uproar! Darling Lavinia has been beside herself with palpitations, and the duke has every servant he could spare out scouring the streets! Where—"

"Cousin Cecily has been with me," Mira interrupted, her

face pathetic with the forced brightness playing about her false smile. "She—She went out for a walk and lost her way, and—"

"A walk?"

"Aye. To St. James," Cecily jumped in. "I thought—"

"'Tis patent you thought not at all!" Honoria blustered. "Bumbling along on foot like a common beggar—and at such an unseemly hour! My reputation will be quite destroyed!"

"Maman—"

"Mirabelle, you will stifle your tongue before I coat it with vinegar! 'Twas bad enough—that wastrel Charleton forcing the duke to be bound by family obligations, imposing upon me to chaperone the chit all over London. But then to hie off to that godforsaken estate of his, deserting me with—"

"Uncle Harry has returned to the country?" Cecily broke in, confusion and a gray washing of dread seeping through her.

"Of course he hasn't you little witling! Your father. I am speaking of—"

The rest of the duchess's ravings faded to a horrible buzz, as though a thousand stinging hornets were trying to burst Cecily's skull. She swayed, exhaustion, confusion, and disbelief roiling inside her. "Papa . . . Papa on his way to Briarton? I thought . . . thought he would be—"

"Railing about your absence with the rest of us? Oh, nay, he had not even the decency to bid any of us farewell. He just—"

"Why? Why would he just ride off of a sudden? He would never—"

"Don't expect me to decipher the man's eccentricities! What I should question is how you can be so presumptuous as to think that your father owes *you* any explanations whatsoever concerning his whereabouts. You're naught but a silly girl whom he is trying to wash his hands of as speedily as possible."

"Nay! I don't believe you." Cecily hurled the denial back at her aunt's quivering face, pain and a stark sense of betrayal sluicing through her exhausted limbs.

"Don't believe what?" Honoria challenged. "That your father wants to be rid of you? If 'tis not the case, then why did he drag you here to be married off? Pay a fortune for your clothes, jewels, give me free license with his purse for the ball he is forcing me to hostess in your honor? And why would he run sneaking back to his moldering old books before anyone in the house was awake this morn?"

Why? The terrifying question screeched through Cecily's mind, tormented with visions of night-black cloaks, a haunted, gaunt face, and eyes the savage green of a hunting tiger's.

Her fingers clenched beneath Mira's cape, the fingernails cutting deep into soft palms. *Papa would not just desert me!* the little girl inside Cecily wailed. *He would never abandon me to this . . . this misery. . . .*

Her throat felt seared with the tears she would not— *would not*—shed, her chin held rigidly at its accustomed proud angle. "Papa would not leave me without some word, something—" She gritted her teeth in an effort to stem the pain rising inside her as she spun and ran, past the grand twin staircases leading to the duke and duchess's elegant quarters, down the more somber, dark-paneled corridors in the older section of the establishment.

Flinging wide the door to her father's study, Cecily ran to the yet-drawn portiers, ripping wide the moss-shaded velvet drapings. The sunlight pierced the room's shadows, washing all within the chamber in a sickly saffron light.

All vestiges of her father's clothes were gone—the silver-handled razor she had gifted him with upon her fourteenth birthday, the well-worn brocade dressing gown. With a sick knotting in her stomach, Cecily flashed her gaze to the huge expanse of desk. Her fingertips rose to quivering lips, the betrayal she had been feeling moments before blossoming into panic.

The papers, books, and inkstand that Charleton Lansdowne was never without still littered the desktop, abandoned as certainly as Cecily herself was. She scanned the room, searching desperately for some clue as to why or where he had flown. 'Twas upon the delicate porcelain statue of Athena that she found it—a note scribed in her father's precise hand, her name penned at the top of the page.

Cecily,

In spite of herself, she winced at the abrupt greeting.

Have to leave London. Do as your aunt bids you and end the season with the conclusion you know I expect of you. Will return for come-out ball.

Papa

The letters blurred before Cecily's eyes, her already raw emotions waxing even more painful. The pain carried her back thirteen years, feeling again her father's arms about her as he tried to explain about death.

The winter had been long and dark, the cold stealing the rich colors from the land. She had marched up to him like a cavalier entering some fray she alone could see, her chest thrust out beneath her little nightgown, a miniature of Anastasia Lansdowne clutched in her pudgy little hand. "J-Johnny says you'll leave me, Papa," she had choked out, eyeing him solemnly. "Like Mother did."

"Nay, little Cis. Your mother died—she had no choice but to go to heaven. 'Twas not her fault. You mustn't blame—"

"*Do* blame her. C-Could have stayed if she had wanted to badly enough." Her chin had thrust out with the childhood belligerence that knows all things.

He had struggled to explain death to her for hours and well into the next day, yet never could he rid her of the belief that nothing could defeat you if you fought it hard enough —refused to run.

Cecily forced the knot of tears back from her throat, betrayal washing over her in devastating waves, mingled with the sickening disillusionment of that same little girl. Nay, she still refused to run, even if her father had fled halfway across England. She would yet discover what power these close-guarded secrets held over Charleton Lansdowne. But she would no longer—*no longer*—rend herself with desperate worry, when he had not even borne enough concern over her emotions to inform her of this journey.

She bit her lip to stop it from quivering, her hands clenching into fists as she crushed her despair into anger.

Chapter Five

THE TOWN HOUSE OF WINTERSCAPE rose from the center of St. James Place like a fairy-tale castle, its glittering facade garlanded in graceful carvings, openwork spires piercing the star-spangled sky like ice-carved lace. Cecily peered through the coach's window with eyes overbright from lack of sleep, watching as the queue of richly appointed carriages circling the town house's drive spilled out myriad silks and fans, starched cravats and immaculate gloves curved lazily about gilded quizzing glasses.

'Twas as if some wood sprite had splashed Cecily's dreamings across the London night sky, stroking into the vibrant colors all the girlish fancies that had poured from her when her father had first told her she would be gifted with a London season. Yet now she hated the vision silhouetted against the darkness—despised the people sweeping up the broad, curving steps, despised the private palace that dared to weave a dream in the midst of crushing reality.

'Twas but a cunning ruse, the ethereal quality that clung to Winterscape—a bitter herb coated in sparkling sugar. She knew full well the soul sickness that would devastate her afterward if she expected anything of this night except compliments that pained more than they praised, and hearts that delved no deeper into a future spouse than how great a bundle of coin they bore to their marriage bed, or whether a title preceded their name.

But was that not all that held importance? To Aunt Honoria, ensconced in the far side of the coach? To Cecily's own father? All Charleton Lansdowne's avowals of honesty, openness with his daughter, had held no more substance than the confection of delicate spires, diamond-bright glass that rose before her.

. . . end the season with the conclusion you know I expect of you . . . her father had scribed. 'Twas as if he were ordering her to snatch up a wealthy husband in the same fashion Cook bade her underlings to choose a lobster at the fish markets.

Well, if Charleton Lansdowne desired his daughter to be a belle of the haute ton, far be it from Cecily to deny him! Cecily felt the stinging of tears at the back of her throat. Nay, she would not start that infernal weeping again. She would sweep into Lady Lyton-Snow's fanciful mansion and be so excruciatingly charming that not a beau in the ballroom would escape losing his heart to the glittering Lady Cecily Lansdowne. She arched her neck with the studied arrogance of generations of nobility, forcing herself to give over peering out the window like some moonstruck country dairymaid.

But all thought of feigned arrogance vanished when her eyes caught a glimpse of Mirabelle there beside her. The delicate planes of Mira's face were drawn as if she faced a firing squad instead of the grand ball that was touted to be the most smashing success of the season. The ruffled collar of Mira's yellow-satin gown gave the girl's already-wan complexion a sallow cast, emphasizing the dark circles smudged beneath the gentle gray eyes. And her nosegay of overblown roses was so glaringly bright it seemed to mock Mira's trembling hands and bloodless lips.

'Twould be far less cruel to place girls of marriageable age upon a slave-auction block, Cecily thought bitterly, to be sold to the highest bidder, instead of subjecting every girl above the age of fifteen to the gauntlet of scathing eyes and vicious tongues that filled London's most elegant ballrooms.

"My—My sash . . ." Mirabelle's nervous whisper cut into Cecily's grim thoughts as the carriage continued to wend its way slowly toward the glaringly lit entryway. "'Tis—'Tis coming undone again."

"The way you are fidgeting, 'twill be a wonder if you do not appear as crumpled as your father," the duchess snapped. "That is, if he can drive this shiftless coachman to let us down before the ball is over!" She cast a baleful glare out the coach window to the shadow-veiled figure of Duke Harry, blissfully and most improperly astride his cherished hunter. "Mind the way Lavinia has been taking care of her furbelows." Honoria's mouth pursed in a doting smile as she ran a thick finger down her youngest daughter's crisp ribbons. "Fresh as a sprig of Sweet William."

"And pleasant as a fistful of nettles," Cecily muttered. Mira's gray eyes darted toward Cecily's face, the stark terror in their depths lightening not a whit at the attempted jest. "Mira, shift about but a little and let me check . . ." Cecily slipped a hand beneath Mira's cloak, gauging by touch that the bow of pink satin banding her waist was yet intact.

"'Tis fine," Cecily assured her, with a bracing smile.

"Nay, 'tis naught will be fine," Mira whispered, shaking all the harder. "'Twill be but another disaster like all the others."

"Only if you persist in being sullen and unreasonable, you foolish chit!" the duchess said. "You are entirely too discriminating for your own good, and now that you've passed your twenty-first year . . ." The duchess let the sentence trail off, as though that burden in itself was too great to be borne. "The Earl of Larrinbea was asking after you at Mrs. Ambercrombie's musicale a few days past, and if you've a wit hidden somewhere beneath that Friday face of yours, you will press your advantage with the earl before you grow so old even *he* will give over his notice of you."

"'Twould make small odds to the earl if Mira was well past eighty," Cecily interrupted, gritting her teeth as the coach lurched to a halt before Winterscape's huge carved doors. "Even then she would be scarce a babe in arms in comparison to his lordship."

"If he were a hundred, he'd make a grand match for any lady of quality!" Honoria Lansdowne's eyes narrowed upon Cecily, the duchess's infuriatingly prim mouth drawing taut. "Mirabelle would do well to snap the earl up at once, before some other lucky young woman snatches him from beneath her nose. All those titles . . . lands . . . And some of them are not even entailed!"

"Please, Maman." Mira looked quite ill. Cecily's own stomach was churning as she remembered Larrinbea at the musicale three days past, his bulbous nose buried in the punch bowl, his lecherous, ferret eyes seeming to disrobe every woman in view. The very thought of gentle, sweet Mira as Larrinbea's bride made Cecily's skin crawl. And the fact that Mira's own mother would joyously condemn her to such a fate sickened Cecily so hideously she wanted naught but to flee back to the Lancashire countryside, where life was not poisoned by the demands of a society festering within.

Nay, Cecily thought, bitterness sharp in her throat as she thought of Charleton Lansdowne's scholarly countenance, even in Lancashire there would be no sanctuary from this whirl of betrothal rings and dowries, titles and lands. It seems even her father held marriage-mart ideals, demanding of his daughter that she make a suitable match, marry, and bear children to some man she did not love.

Cecily started as a liveried servant flung wide the carriage's door, extending one gloved hand to help them alight. But even the stunned expression on the bewigged lad's face could not still Cecily's tongue.

"The earl should be taking the air in his gardens, or setting his affairs in order with his solicitor," Cecily bit out defiantly, her slipper soles smacking hard into the pebbled carriage circle as she stormed down from the carriage. "Not chasing after a bride young enough to be his great-granddaughter! How could you even think of—"

"Of providing my daughter a grand alliance?" the duchess demanded, sweeping down in a flurry of purple silk and blinding pink feathers. "I vow I'd wed her to Bonaparte himself to keep her from falling into your state—an outcast relation, with naught but moldering bloodlines to gain her entry into polite society. A nobody. A nothing clinging to the coattails of—"

"Please, Maman . . . Cecily . . ." Mira's distress quavered in her voice, her shaking hand clutching at Cecily's arm. "People . . . people are staring, and . . ."

Yet not even Mira's misery could leash the wrath pounding sharp through Cecily's veins. "Papa bears as much wealth as half the earls in England, and he was as much the old duke's son as your husband. I—"

"Yes, *now* Charleton bears wealth, though God knows how he came by it. Poor as a beggar's mouse, he was, when he dragged that Anastasia creature home from his grand tour—cast out by the old duke, and well 'twas his due—"

"Enough, Honoria!"

Cecily started, turning to see the ruddy countenance of her uncle, Duke Harry, glaring down at them from atop his gelding. The cravat his valet had secured with such care was askew beneath the duke's jowls, the irrepressible twinkle in his brown eyes giving his plump face the appearance of one of his beloved hounds out a-bounding in the fields.

"After all," the duke said, swinging down from his mount and casting the reins to a footman, "without those 'moldering old bloodlines' that you are maligning so freely, I much doubt you would have given me the insurmountable joy of becoming my wife."

Cecily caught the glint of irony in the duke's merry gaze as he cast a vague smile toward his offspring. Yet there was about his voice that single threading of steel that could quell Honoria Lansdowne's railings in a pulsebeat if he so chose.

Cecily saw the duchess suck in a deep breath, her bosom swelling nigh to her quivering chin. "Oh, aye, an insurmountable joy, is it? Such a joy that you've not deigned to ride in the carriage with me for five years! Nay, you prefer to cause us to stumble in late, humiliate me by attending all from the Regent's ball to the theater smelling of your infernal stables—looking like a lowly squire—"

"'Twas a spit boy you likened me to the time past," the duke observed, winking at Mira as he took his wife's arm and propelled her toward the door. "Begad, you may be civilizing me at last, my love."

Cecily trailed after them, aware of Mira a-tremble at her left and of Lavinia preening like the cook's own goose to her right. But the outrage, hurt, and anger engendered by the duchess's words seemed to whirl Cecily's surroundings into a blur.

She struggled to draw a deep breath amidst the crush of the crowd that surrounded them the instant they breached Winterscape's huge doors, but the air was stifling, the blaze of countless candles setting perspiration to beading at the nape of her neck. Even the scarlet-liveried footman's booming voice as he announced their party scarce penetrated Cecily's consciousness, and it seemed they had hardly entered the vaulted entry hall before she found herself facing the receiving line and the woman who served mistress to this dream-woven castle.

Lady Aurora Lyton-Snow stood as regal and elegant as a pallas lily, her auburn hair caught up with ropes of pearls and delicate gold ribbon. An ageless beauty graced features that might have adorned the face of a Greek goddess, except that there was some quality so warm, vital, in those sherry-colored eyes that it could never be captured in cold, white marble. 'Twas as though Winterscape had been carved by a goldsmith's hand as a perfect foil for the beauty of Aurora Lyton-Snow, and as if the fairy castle surrounding the countess drew life and breath from her graceful gloved hands.

Cecily watched with reluctant fascination as, all at one time, the woman greeted the Marquess of Northborough, bade a servant to refill the enormous crystal bowl with ratafia, and gave a towheaded page's curls an affectionate tug as the child darted past on some errand.

"Is she not the boldest, most disgusting sight you've yet laid eyes on?" Lavinia's biting whisper rasped across

Cecily's ears as the duke and duchess stepped up for Lady Lyton-Snow's greeting. "Look at her, parading about this absurd monstrosity, wallowing in her husband's wealth now that he is rotting in his grave."

Cecily felt a tug of sympathy for Mira as she saw the girl take a hesitant step toward their elegant hostess, then felt a deep welling of gratitude as Lady Lyton-Snow's face beamed a gracious welcome to the shy young woman.

But though Cecily strained to see what it was her ladyship was saying to bring the dimple to Mira's pale cheeks, Lavinia's fingers kept pulling at Cecily's arm, dragging her back into her biting gossip. "'Twas the talk of London, Maman says, that when her ladyship was five and twenty she ran off with her father's master of the horse to Gretna Green. Married him over the anvil, then paraded the common wretch about London as though he were a crowned prince. I vow her family must have been most relieved when the rogue perished in a stable fire."

"No doubt they held a grand ball to celebrate," Cecily gritted, casting Lavinia a killing glare.

But the chit batted not so much as a stubby eyelash, preening all the more at Cecily's obvious annoyance. "No, they reserved their celebration for two years after, when her ladyship entrapped an earl. Maman said 'twas scandalous, the way her ladyship flung herself at every man in breeches, until at last Lyton-Snow had no choice but to wed—"

"Lady Lavinia, such a pleasure as always."

Cecily started, jerking her gaze up to see a distraught Mira wringing her hands beside her parents a few paces away while the elegant face of Aurora Lyton-Snow turned in icy perfection toward Lavinia's catlike countenance and Cecily's own guilt-flushed one. The countess's smile was yet as gracious as it had been a moment before, but Cecily could see a hard glint in the once-warm eyes, which betrayed the fact that her ladyship had well caught the gist of Lavinia's brainless prattle.

"My Lady Lyton-Snow," Lavinia simpered, and Cecily could have slapped the idiot chit's face for the insolence in her smile. "My cousin, the Lady Cecily, here, was inquiring most pointedly about your husbands." Lavinia accented the suffix. "And I was attempting to enlighten her regarding—"

"I am quite aware of your methods of 'enlightenment,' Lady Lavinia, despite the fact that you've been in London but two weeks." Lady Lyton-Snow fixed Lavinia with a frigid smile. "And now we have a cousin present, cut of the same cloth as you are. How infinitely entertaining for us all."

Cecily dipped into a curtsey, her face yet flaming. She wanted to flee into the blissful anonymity of the ballroom beyond, but she refused either to contribute to Lady Lyton-Snow's well-deserved outrage or to be party to Lavinia's cruelty.

"Your pardon, your ladyship," Cecily said, raising her eyes to the countess's face. "'Twas most ill-bred of me to ask my cousin regarding you, but Winterscape—'tis so intriguing, I suppose I was prying where I had no right."

Cecily detected a softening in the countess's face, as if her thick-lashed gaze were delving beneath the icing of satin ribbons and fine white muslin to Cecily's very heart. Aurora Lyton-Snow bestowed upon Cecily the slightest of smiles. "'Twas a gift from my second husband, built expressly for me—"

The countess stopped, her beautiful mouth touched with some secret pain, and Cecily felt as though somehow, even in the midst of this crushing crowd, she had trespassed upon something very hallowed, private.

"Your ladyship, I—"

Cecily's words were cut off as suddenly Aurora gave a glad cry and, sweeping from her place, dashed past two dukes and an earl toward the doorway. Cecily turned, stunned, Lavinia's gasps, and Honoria Lansdowne's umbrage at her charges being thus snubbed, lost as Cecily watched Aurora Lyton-Snow stretch out her graceful arms, her hands catching those of a newly arrived guest.

The light from the dozen chandeliers seemed to be snared within burnished gold hair, bronzed skin gleaming with a dangerous masculine beauty that seemed to draw the gaze of every woman in the room. Stark black pantaloons clung like a second skin to hard-muscled thighs, the meticulously tailored black evening coat straining against the breadth of shoulders seemingly designed to tempt a woman's fingers. A snowy cravat was knotted in delectable contrast beneath an iron-carved jaw, sensual lips tugged into a mocking, bewitching smile that whispered of promises—dark and honey sweet. Promises Cecily had tasted of but the day before . . .

Her breath snagged in her chest, her fingers rising, unbidden, to her parted lips as she stared into the tiger-green eyes of Ransom Tremayne.

"Oooh! That scar!" Lavinia shrilled into her ear. "Is that gentleman not the most dashing roué you have ever laid eyes upon? I mean to dance with him at least twice this night—enough to give Maman pure apoplexies!"

Cecily heard Lavinia's lips smack as though the girl were eyeing a slab of marchpane, and feared that she, as well, bore the same glazed look to her face. But still, Cecily could not tear her eyes away from where Ransom now bent to brush a kiss across Aurora Lyton-Snow's peach-blushed cheek. An odd, tearing stab jagged through Cecily's breast as Ransom straightened, his incredibly beautiful mouth parting in a heart-stopping grin. Cecily would have sold every trinket in her jewel box to hear what words the two whispered so intimately between them, or, she thought suddenly, unreasonably, she would have dumped the crown jewels themselves into the Thames for the immense pleasure of jamming the pin of one of her brooches into Ransom Tremayne's lazily sensual smile.

What in the name of God was he doing here, at the season's most glittering ball? Ransom Tremayne—street brawler, seafaring rogue, ill-tempered ship's captain—unless . . . Cecily's fingers curled into a fist. Was it possible he had gained some information regarding the *Ninon* and had sought her out here to tell her of it?

Nay. Cecily quelled the budding hope with a sudden tang of bitterness. The scoundrel most obviously bore an invitation. 'Twas far more likely that Lady Lyton-Snow was intending to replace her horse master with a sun-bronzed green-eyed rakehell who, it seemed, was overeager to dispense his kisses.

Cecily's nose turned up in her most disdainful aura, her lips curving in the expression of a queen dismissing a swineherd, and she took the greatest of pleasure in the fact that at that exact moment Tremayne's eyes caught hers in the midst of the crowd.

The grin melted, but the odd, almost indulgent curving that played at the corners of his mouth gave Cecily little pleasure. 'Twas as though he deemed her a child playing at dress-up in her mama's finery, or as though he read the inexplicable sense of hurt that was stealing through her even as he watched.

Cecily caught a glimpse of Lady Lyton-Snow's sherry eyes fixed upon Ransom's face, a single line of perplexity creasing her brow as she followed his gaze. Cecily wanted to hate the older woman, but the smile she turned upon Cecily was not that of a jealous lover, but rather, one filled with . . . what was it? Hope?

"Captain Tremayne." Lady Lyton-Snow's voice brimmed with a bubbling merriment. "You have induced me to be inexcusably rude to my guest, so now you must serve your penance and aid me in asking her pardon." One graceful gloved hand hooked in the curve of Ransom's arm as the countess drew him forward, pointedly cutting Lavinia from her notice. Cecily hardly noticed Lavinia's stark fury, captivated, instead, by the odd reluctance in Ransom's sinewed frame and in the eyes that seemed to weave about her some white-hot snare that she alone could feel.

"Lady Cecily Lansdowne, may I present one of Trafalgar's conquering heroes, and, might I add, the conqueror of a considerable number of feminine hearts as well? Captain Ransom Tremayne."

Trafalgar . . . hero . . . Cecily's mind raced as Ransom's eyes caught hers, an unmistakable twinkle lightening the green-gold depths. Tremayne . . . Vague memories shrouded by childhood lost their hazing of mist as Cecily remembered her father and his friends rejoicing over Lord Admiral Nelson's stunning victory. The gathering at

Briarton had stayed awake until the sunrise pinkened the Lancashire countryside, the men raving about Horatio Nelson and the feats of another sea warrior who had turned the tide of battle upon a ship all had thought surely lost. Tremayne. Ransom Tremayne. But there had then been no title of Captain before his name.

"My Lady Cecily." Ransom's voice whiskey-warm, husky, shook her from her memories as he took her gloved hand, raising it to lips so hot they seemed to sear through the delicate kid. "'Tis most pleasant to see you again." Cecily heard Lavinia's whining protest as Honoria dragged her off in a huff. She forced her own mouth to close, humiliatingly certain it had been gaping open like that of a coster monger.

"Again?" Lady Lyton-Snow's pink lips parted in surprise. "Then you—you have already made each other's acquaintance?"

"At the theater," Ransom supplied, the suppressed humor in his voice stiffening Cecily's spine. "A most diverting spectacle, I assure you."

Aurora Lyton-Snow's gaze flicked from the militant set of Cecily's jaw to the amusement turning Ransom Tremayne's lean face into a veritable study in masculine pleasure.

"Captain Tremayne *adores* making a spectacle of himself," Cecily bit out, tugging her hand from Ransom's strong fingers. "A residual, no doubt, of the laurel leaves weighting his hero's brow."

"Ransom? A spectacle?" Lady Lyton-Snow echoed. "I have found quite the opposite. In all the time I've known him, never once has he allowed anyone to cite his good works, either with Admiral Lord Nelson or with the little ones."

"Aurora," Ransom protested, looking distinctly uncomfortable. "I trust you'll not bore the lady with a recounting of the badges of honor you'd like to bestow upon me. The chest of Colossus would not be broad enough to bear them all, and Lady Cecily has little time or patience for aught but furbelows and waltzing and—"

"Oh, I beg to differ," Cecily interrupted. "I wait with bated breath to hear of all Captain Tremayne's philanthropies. Why, his kindness in setting a man's shattered arm outside Drury Lane nigh stole my breath away."

"You set a man's arm? Ransom, why did you not tell—"

"I fear Lady Cecily has the happenings a bit reversed. I *broke* the man's arm, did I not, your highness?" There was a savage gleam in his eye, hinting of the peril veiled beneath black satin and elegant white lawn.

"You— Oh," Aurora said in a small voice. "Well, I am—am certain the rogue deserved . . ." Suddenly her face lit up, her lips compressing, eyes sparking with anger. "Oh, 'twas *that* man whose arm you broke—the blackguard who crippled little Pip! 'Tis a pity you didn't break the beast's neck!"

"The thought occurred to me," Ransom said with deceptive mildness.

"The man at the theater crippled . . ." Cecily let the words trail off, feeling as though she had awakened in the middle of some very strange dream.

Lady Lyton-Snow's nostrils flared delicately, her face filled with outrage. "Severed every tendon in the poor child's hand, the monster did, to wring people's sympathies when he set the boy out to begging! And if Ransom had not stepped in, the beast would have crippled Pip's other hand as well! 'Tis a pity you didn't thrust the man's own knife into—"

"Aurora, stop, now." There was a tenderness in Ransom's voice that seared Cecily with jealousy. Her mind filled with shifting montages of the night-veiled battle in Drury Lane —the child's stark terror, Ransom's rage, the drunken giant's hand clasping a knife—a knife that had willfully crippled an innocent child, and would have done worse had not Ransom Tremayne interfered.

And had Cecily herself obeyed her first instinct and failed to warn Ransom of the knife aimed at his back, Tremayne would most likely have lain dead, and the child . . . little Pip . . . Cecily closed her eyes against the grisly vision of a blade biting deep into a tiny, helpless hand.

The warm, welcome hardness of a palm cupping her elbow made her open her eyes to see Ransom's face bending near her own. "'Tis a common practice, milady," he said. "Buying children from the poorhouse or from starving parents, and putting them to the knife."

Bile choked her throat. She tried to keep her lips from quivering, failed. "I—I didn't know . . . thought *you* were the one threatening . . . oh, sweet God, I'm sorry. . . ."

The piercing eyes heated beneath their thick fringing of black lashes, and Cecily felt her own pulse trip-hammer. If the ballroom floor had opened in that instant, swallowing every person in the room save her and Ransom Tremayne, they could have been no more alone.

Alone with the white heat, with the danger, with the tug of a tide she could no more evade than that of the seas Ransom challenged.

"Cecily . . ." Her name rasped harsh across his lips, yet soft as a lover's whisper. "I—" Yet whatever words he had been about to say were stayed as his eyes flicked to his right, his face hardening into a bitter mask.

Cecily followed his glare, disappointment and irritation welling within her as she saw the man hastening toward where they stood. Face drawn in his constant smile, Bayard Sutton exuded charm and unshakable confidence, while at his side, his solemn-faced nephew and heir, Arthur, seemed held in his uncle's shadow.

"Cecily, my dear!" Sutton exclaimed, a broad smile pasted across his features, his cravat tied as expertly as a hangman ties his noose. "I have been awaiting your arrival most eagerly."

Cecily felt Ransom stiffen, his hand tightening about her elbow. She saw Sutton's eyes flick down to where Ransom touched her, the politician's smile waxing brittle.

"The orchestra is about to strike up a waltz," Sutton continued, "and you did promise to favor me with your company."

"I am afraid you are to be disappointed," Tremayne's voice cut in, rapier sharp, cold as ice shards. "As *Lady Cecily* and I were about to take the floor."

Cecily stared up at Ransom in astonishment, stunned at the fierce proprietary light in his eyes. 'Twas the same light that had glinted across the night in Drury Lane—feral, primal, menacing. And she could nigh see Ransom dealing with the aristocratic Sutton in the same fashion he had rid the streets of the brutal red-haired giant.

"Cecily?" Sutton gave a laugh tainted with warning. "Surely you cannot mean to renege on your promise. . . ."

Cecily met that bland gaze with a defiance that gave her infinite pleasure. "I recall saying I would dance with you, Lord Sutton. But I do not remember indicating which dance I would *favor* you with. Captain Tremayne?"

The strains of the waltz were lilting, mesmerizing, but no more so than the man who held her as Ransom swept her out onto the floor. Lithe, lean, with a sensual grace that tempted, taunted, he drew her into his arms, and, Cecily thought irrationally, into something far deeper. His gaze seemed to stroke her face like fingers, possessive, exciting, yet tinged with an anger that set blood to pounding deep in her center.

"It—It seems I owe you an apology," Cecily said, attempting to break the intense spell he seemed to hold over her. "About the child. Had I known the truth of it, I might have helped you douse that wretched man in—"

"Shall I tell you what you owe me, Gloriana?" Ransom's muscles were hard, taut, the planes of his face carved with an intensity that intrigued her, terrified her. "A night's sleep, in a feather bed soft as spun clouds, and dreams . . . you owe me such sweet dreamings. . . ."

Cecily swallowed hard, the pulsing rising to the crests of her breasts as they brushed the steely hardness of Ransom's chest. "Dreamings? I—I don't understand. . . ."

"Those you stole from me last night, when I lay abed, thinking of a crowned princess so beautiful I scarce dared to touch her, and a kiss . . ." His eyes dropped to her lips, his own mouth compressing in a white line. Longing . . . was there really such devastating longing in those green eyes that could blaze so fierce? And a hopelessness that made her want to reach up, trace her fingers over the daringly wrought curves of his face, brush her lips across his hard mouth.

"Captain Tremayne, I—"

"Ransom." His voice was rough, compelling, threaded through with scarce-leashed emotion.

"Captain, I hardly think it proper to—"

"After what we shared at the docks a day past, 'tis past time to concern ourselves with what is proper, princess." The long fingers curved at the base of her spine tightened, the feel of his lean-muscled thighs brushing against her own turning Cecily's knees to blanc mange.

She felt her cheeks fire but held his gaze with hers, reveling in the tempest roiling beneath Ransom's dark brows. "About the day past—" She fought to keep her voice brisk. "Have you—have you discovered anything regarding the matter I put before you?"

"Oh, aye, the villain even now awaits in Newgate. After all, I've had forty-eight hours to bring him to justice. I've solved cases for Bow Street in less."

"Don't mock me, Captain Tremayne. I assure you 'tis quite serious to—"

"I know 'tis serious." The bedeviling grin melted from Ransom's lips. "More serious than even you might suspect. But 'twill be passing difficult to gain any information regarding the *Ninon*. Fifteen years I've been searching for something—some clue, some record of that vessel—but there is nothing, Gloriana. 'Tis as though it never existed."

Cecily felt a chill scuttle up her spine as Ransom's hushed voice whispered over her. "But surely there must be something—a ship cannot just disappear. The logs, manifests, must be somewhere."

"If they were, they would have been in my hands years ago." Grim lines etched deeper beside Ransom's mouth. "If you want to discover who is scattering those cards about, princess, you are going to have to trust me." Was there a bitter twist to his lips? "Answer any questions I might put to you, no matter how odd or unrelated they might appear."

"You've already gotten me to tell you the one thing I vowed not to reveal," Cecily snapped, unsettled at the intensity within Ransom's face. "I'll agree to answer your questions, as long as you understand this before you begin. I know nothing about this ship, or the person who has tormented my father. If I did, I wouldn't need you." She saw a flicker in Ransom's eyes, the word *need* seeming to pulse between them, holding a far different meaning from what she had intended. His shoulder stiffened beneath her hand, rippling with steely muscles.

"The first thing I *need,*" he said in a hoarse voice, "is a full explanation as to why a crowned princess the like of you is linked to a bastard like Bayard Sutton."

"Uncle Bayard?" Cecily's slippers faltered in the steps of the dance, and she shook herself mentally, trying to clear the webbings of sensuality from her mind and body as she stared into Ransom's taut face. Loathing for the man who had been such a large part of Cecily's childhood was carved into every sharp-angled plane, the green eyes again as unyielding as granite. Shock swept through Cecily, coupled with anger at the sudden attack directed toward the uncle who, true, was beginning to irritate her, but nonetheless yet held her loyalty.

"Uncle? That man is related to you by blood?" The husky tones that had set wings to fluttering in Cecily's stomach had vanished from Ransom's voice, leaving it cold, analytical.

"No. But he might as well have been. He was constantly at Briarton when I was a child. Read me books, pushed me on the garden swing, even gifted me with a pony cart one summer."

Ransom's hand fairly crushed her fingers, bruised her waist as he guided her about the dance floor. "Cecily, did that bastard ever—" The words seemed torn from him, but he cut the sentence off, his jaw knotting on some rage he alone understood. "Did Sutton ever . . . hurt you?"

"Of course not!" Cecily said, shaken by the ruthless light in Ransom's eyes. "He was my father's dearest friend, until—" She broke off the sentence, suddenly wary. "Captain Tremayne, I did not hire you to—to waste both our time and effort by poking about Lord Sutton's affairs. He bears an impeccable reputation—noted for his liberal policies—"

"Bayard Sutton bears policies that would singe your hair ribbons to ash, Gloriana," Ransom snapped. Cecily stared, her feet suddenly leaden with a dread she could not explain. 'Twas as if he had transformed into some mythical dragon, his face wreathed in an emotion so terrifying, Cecily fought the urge to bolt from his arms.

"Captain Tre— Ransom, what—what is it?"

She could see the effort it took him to crush whatever was roiling inside him, could see his lips battle to form a reassuring smile. He failed, his gaze yet burning into hers, the harsh slash of his mouth only a little gentled. "I don't know, Gloriana, but I damned well intend to find out. Your father has left London for a while. . . ."

'Twas statement not question. The figures of the dance seemed to whirl in Cecily's mind. Mira whisked past, her face almost beautiful as she gazed into the eyes of lanky Arthur Sutton. Lavinia simpered in the arms of a handsome officer, while Honoria Lansdowne glowered from her chair amidst the other chaperones. The duchess's eyes caught Cecily's, but even the fierce disapproval in that broad face could not penetrate the dizziness drowning her as Ransom swept her about the floor, past a blur of garlanded blossoms decked in bright ribbons, past doors flung wide to the cooling breeze.

"How did you know about my father's leaving—"

"You've paid me—and quite handsomely, I might add," —his eyes flashed to her lips—"to know what Lord Lansdowne is about."

"Don't—Don't tell me what I paid you for, Captain Tremayne. Just tell me how you knew."

"It doesn't matter, except that 'tis possibly the most fortuitous break we could have gained. Cecily, I've told you that there are no records regarding the *Ninon* anywhere in London. That means"—his eyes pierced hers—"that the only place we might discover anything that will protect your father is amongst his own things—papers, books, records of his business interests, if he has them."

"My father's things? You are suggesting that I—I paw

through his private records?" Cecily's palms dewed with perspiration, something small closing tight inside her. It blossomed into indignation, then outrage.

"Captain Tremayne, if you think I would break my father's trust by violating his journals, his—his belongings like a common sneak thief, you are sadly mistaken!" She saw Ransom's eyes flash dangerously, but rushed on. "Under no circumstances—"

"Ransom, please." A dulcet yet anxiety-ridden voice quelled Cecily's diatribe, as Aurora Lyton-Snow all but dashed across the room toward them. Her beautiful eyes were wide, her face pinched. "I—I'm sorry to intrude, but—"

"Aurora, what—"

"'Tis Sutton, Ransom." One gloved hand swept out toward the entryway, the other locking about Ransom's forearm. Cecily saw his eyes blaze to where Bayard Sutton stood just within sight, engrossed in angry conversation with a char-smeared figure bearing a peg leg. Even from across the crowded ballroom Cecily could recognize the surly countenance of the man who had plucked her and Bess from the midst of the dock rabble the morn before.

The grizzled Jagger had Bayard all but pinned against a marble statue in the entry, the gnarled hands that had handled pistols with such ease gesticulating wildly, his clothes rippling like faded ribbons about his thin frame. Three footmen scuffled in an effort to draw the old sailor away from the baron, but their hands were not ungentle upon the scrawny Jagger as they urged both the crotchety sailor and the disdainful nobleman out of the view of the rest of the guests.

Aurora's voice broke in yet again, strained, soft. "'Tis the mill, Ransom, the one in Covent Gardens. The roof . . ."

Ransom's face went gray. "Oh, my God!"

He shook free of Aurora's grasp, dodging with lithe grace the dancers circling the floor, his face holding both fear and rage.

As though she were linked to him with some unseen

chain, Cecily trailed in his wake, Lady Lyton-Snow but a step behind her.

"The children," Ransom bit out, "are there any—"

"Six dead that we know of, Ransom, and at least twenty others somewhere—" Lady Lyton-Snow choked. "Somewhere in the rubble."

"Damn that bastard, I'll break every bone in his greedy body!"

"Nay, there's no proof yet, Ransom. You cannot—"

"Sutton, you bloody, goddamned devil!" Ransom charged past the cursing Jagger. "I warned you that roof was faulty, warned you, you son of a—"

"And why should that dung heap of rotted stone and beggars be of any concern to me?" Sutton's gaze raked him with sneering dismissal. "Except that I have to endure the stench when I drive past it on the way to my tailor's?"

"You know goddamned well why the hell—"

"String 'im up by 'is cursed neckcloth, lad," Jagger urged, "else I be tempted t' soil me lady's carpets by slittin' 'is lyin' gullet."

"You'd best leash your dog, there, Tremayne, before I'm forced to dispose of him myself."

Cecily saw Ransom's hand knot, knew in a sickening instant that he intended to plunge it into Sutton's jaw. Yet 'twas Sutton's visage that clutched at her, something veiled, terrifying, lurking within the baron's countenance.

"Ransom, no!" Cecily leapt between the infuriated Ransom and Sutton, uncertain as to why she did so, only knowing she bore no other choice. Jagger's oaths echoed through the entry, Ransom raking her with a scathing glare, filled with disgust, loathing.

"Please, Ransom, listen to her." Lady Lyton-Snow swept to Cecily's side. "The little ones, you have to get to the children. And you *have no proof—*"

"Proof, aye, I'll damn well get my proof," Ransom fairly spat, his fist clenching tighter still. "And when I do—"

"You would do well not to fling such threats about." Sutton's eyes narrowed to slits. "Lest more than a cartload of bricks crashes down upon your head." His lips parted in the patient smile of a sleek barracuda.

Cecily held her breath for a heartbeat, half expecting Ransom to attack the baron. But Tremayne spun toward the servants yet clustered in the room, his gold hair a tangled mane about a face savage with fury. "Lowery!" Ransom yelled to the dour-faced butler. "Have Porter bring my horse around! Hasten! And Aurora—" He spun to face Lady Lyton-Snow. "We'll need shrouds, blankets, bandages. Send Lowery for Doc Townsend, tell them to meet me at the mill—can you spare any servants to aid in the digging?"

"I'll send all I have right away, bearing whatever I can find to give comfort."

"The worst of the injured we'll hie off to the doctor's. The others to Rosetree."

"Please . . ." Cecily laid a hand on Ransom's broad chest. "I'm not certain what is amiss, but can I help?"

Ransom's mouth slashed into a cruel sneer, his eyes flashing to Sutton, then back to her face. "You've already done quite enough, 'Gloriana.' " The nickname that had seemed nigh an endearment moments ago was harsh as the most condemning of oaths. "Go dance with your blasted 'Uncle Bayard,' ply your fan, and don't dirty your cursed hands bothering with lowlings far beneath your notice."

The sound of hoofbeats pounded across the drive, and Ransom bolted out the doorway, followed by the glowering Jagger. A spindly footman flung himself from the back of a magnificent night-black stallion as Cecily and Aurora hastened out behind the two men. The spirited horse reared, pawing the air, but Ransom merely clutched its reins in one strong hand, swinging astride the horse in one graceful movement.

"Run, Satan, fly," Cecily heard Ransom urge as he drove his heels deep into the horse's barrel. She glimpsed Jagger struggling to mount a snaggle-toothed mare, heard him curse as he made to follow Ransom.

Oaths, screeches, and the sounds of snorting horses filled the drive as arriving guests and their equipages struggled to evade the path of the bolting stallion. But Ransom seemed to see them not at all. He only leaned tight against the horse's neck, driving it in a mad rush into the darkness.

"'Twould almost have been worth being involved in this disaster to rid you of that ruffian's company."

Cecily started at the sound of Sutton's voice, turned to find him inches from where she stood.

"Rid you of his company, and, of course, claim the dance you seemed so reluctant to give me," Sutton continued, reaching out, grasping her arm.

She pulled away, feeling somehow tainted by the touch of that immaculate hand. "Worth it to be involved in what?" she demanded, turning her gaze from Bayard's face to Aurora Lyton-Snow's barely leashed fury, desperation and confusion warring inside Cecily. "I don't understand any of this."

"The roof of a cotton mill in Covent Garden collapsed tonight." Lady Lyton-Snow's voice was brittle. "A mill whose laborers consisted mostly of starving children."

"Children? Sweet God!" Cecily's stomach lurched at the hideous image her mind wove of tiny limbs shattered by falling brick, of terror as beams fell, crushed.

"'Tis a common enough state of affairs," Sutton said in bored accents. "The urchins have to work if their parents want gin to swill—"

"Or the luxury of sparing their babes from starvation," Lady Lyton-Snow interrupted. "I think 'tis time for you to leave, Lord Sutton." Cecily was stunned by the frigid tones of Lady Lyton-Snow's voice. "You are no longer welcome here. And you full well know the reason."

Cecily spun, shocked, unable to fathom the undercurrents that seemed to be sucking her deep into some dark madness. The town house that had seemed woven of dream mist but an hour before now seemed wrought of nightmares echoing with the trapped children's screams.

Cecily saw Bayard Sutton's eyes narrow, the slightest edge to his accustomed bland smile. "Your ladyship, you will excuse me, then." His perfect bow mocked the graceful countess before him. "I bear enough intelligence to know when I have been ill-treated." His eyes flicked to Cecily. "And I know full well how to repay in like coin. Until later, *child.*"

His fingers were cold even through their smooth casing of kid as he grasped Cecily's hand, bending to kiss it. She curled her fingers tight, her nails cutting into her palm, but the baron crushed his lips onto her clenched fist, seeming to seal in that instant some dark covenant he alone understood—a covenant Cecily sensed the powerful baron intended to etch in the blood of a golden-maned warrior even now battling in the hell of London's streets.

Chapter Six

Moonlight streamed over the small, lace-curtained bed tucked beneath the eaves of Rosetree Cottage, gilding in silver a motley collection of rag-stuffed animals and dolls so well-loved that their once-lovely curls lay snaggled and torn across the feather pillows. Yet even upon the day Ransom had shoved his coin across the exclusive toy-shop's counter to purchase the most exquisite specimens of their trade, the delicate china-faced figures had held not half the beauty of the child curled now in his arms.

Lacey, his Lacey. Safe.

Ransom tangled his fingers through his daughter's dusky curls, the silky tresses snagging upon myriad cuts and weals he had gained while struggling against murderous fallen brick. But Ransom cared not, only laying his burning eyes against the child's petal-soft cheek, trying desperately to blot out the horror of the past hours. 'Twas always this way after he confronted the cruelty of the London slums—gut-wrenching sickness, helpless rage eating at his very soul, and the desperate need to hold his own little daughter in his arms, to assure himself that she was safe.

Aye, safe and warm, tucked in her own bed, her dimpled hand curled about her nightgown's satin ribbon. Ransom's throat knotted as he thought of other young faces, gray with terror, some cold with death. He had cuddled them deep in downy coverlets, settled them gently into Doc Townsend's infirmary beds, or taken them home to parents so desperately poor they had borne no choice but to cast their children to the mercy of brutal mill life.

And three, three of the battered urchins he had carried with him here, to the haven he had carved in the midst of London. He had sat with them for hours, until Jessamyn had come, her red-gold hair streaming down her back, her plain nightgown making her look nigh a child herself, despite thirty years of the most brutal living fate could offer.

She had chased him from the room, telling him that if the children awoke to see a fright the like of him bending over them, they'd likely flee right back to the streets.

A bitter laugh tore from Ransom's lips as he raked the tangle of tawny-gold hair from his grime-encrusted face. Aye, what he should have done was hie back to Aurora's ball, his finery now a mass of filthy rags, his cravat torn into strips to help splint broken arms and legs. What would the fine gentlemen and their sheltered ladies have thought, had they been able to view the cost of their frippery, coined thus in blood and flesh?

His jaw clenched, bitter fury surging through him anew at the memory of a violet-eyed beauty, leaping between his fist and the taunting countenance of the man Ransom knew— *knew, damn it*—was responsible for the carnage at Silvanus Mill. 'Twas not the supposed master of the mill who had condemned those children to death. Pratt was naught but a puppet through whom the mill's true owners filtered their profits in order to save soiling their aristocratic hands.

'Twas Sutton, Bayard Sutton, who seeped his black poisons through half of London—handling the reins of a score of foul enterprises with the expert ease of a whip driving a high-perch phaeton. Nothing but the subtlest of pressures did Sutton exert over his dealings, but with the merest flick of his hand, he could cast to ruin any man he chose, or assure the death of any enemy who dared attempt to stay him.

And Cecily Lansdowne, with her empress's face and cherry-sweet lips, had leapt to defend the God-cursed bastard. Ransom bit back the unreasonable sense of betrayal that surged through him at the memory of her pleadings, her slender nymph's body defiled by the touch of Bayard Sutton's hand.

From the first, Ransom thought bitterly, he should have known where the society beauty's loyalties would lie, should have known that the heart-wrenching pain he had glimpsed in her face concerning little Pip had been naught but a clever ruse. Oh, aye, 'twas passing pretty, most women knew, to drop diamond-bright tears over some injustice. And most likely the man who caught the fruits of their weepings in his handkerchief would somehow lose his heart as well.

Or could it truly be that Cecily Lansdowne was the innocent she seemed? Trapped in some sort of dream world herself, from which she could not escape? Ransom drew an aching breath into his lungs, remembering the vulnerability touching the corners of her mouth. Sutton's closest friend, she had claimed her father was. If that were true, might not Charleton Lansdowne be elbow deep in the blood of innocents? And if Cecily Lansdowne adored her father with the same unshakable faith Ransom had seen in his own little daughter's eyes, what would happen when she learned the truth . . . the truth she had offered her pitiful little bundle of coins to unearth.

Lacey stirred against him, her rosebud mouth suckling on some imagined treat borne of her four-year-old's dreamings. "Papa . . . angel . . . catched Lacey angel . . ." she mumbled against his torn shirt, her chest rising in a contented sigh.

"Nay, little Lacey," Ransom breathed in a choked voice. "'Twas your mama who gave Papa an angel. My own little—" His throat constricted, eyes searing as he buried his face against the sweet-smelling warmth of Lacey's chubby neck. Surely whatever sins lay upon Corianda Verney's jaded soul would be cleansed from her because of this one precious gift she had laid in Ransom's arms four years ago. The gift of hope after a lifetime of despair, someone to love, shelter, someone who bore complete faith in him and cared naught about a past filled with a pain that had dragged him into hell.

And now he might well be hurling Cecily Lansdowne into a fate as devastating. He brushed parched lips across Lacey's tumbled curls, struggling to hold on to the fury that had boiled in his blood for fifteen long years, struggling to remember every shriek of agony, every clank of irons weighting men down as they fought in crazed terror against the merciless sea.

But even the thrice-cursed hull of the *Ninon* was glossed in his memory, hazed beneath wide, violet eyes, and lips . . . a shiver wracked Ransom's exhausted body . . . lips he bore no right to touch.

He had disposed of the tug in his loins as expediently as possible in the years since he had fled the African sun. Had taken to his bed countless women only too eager to taste of his steel-honed body. Yet always before, the women who had drawn him had borne a weariness beneath their sparkling eyes. Their faces, no matter how beautiful, held the cynicism that twisted Ransom's own heart. He had avoided the pristine young daughters of the ton as though he were contaminated with some deadly miasma. Aye, and mayhap he was . . .

But Cecily, with her innocence and fire, seemed to hold some magical talisman that burst the chains he had bound so carefully about what little remained of his heart. A band of hopelessness seemed to tighten about Ransom's chest, his face burning with a despair he had crushed from his life years past. Nay, Lady Cecily Arabella Anastasia Lansdowne, her perfect body draped in satins, her face etched with the pride of generations of nobility, could be nothing to a man whose heart lay as scarred as the slash marring his face.

She was everything he hated, everything he scorned, everything he had railed against in his helplessness and his pain. And he could no more hope to hold her than a skein of spun moonlight.

"Your papa is a fool, Lacey-love," he whispered against

the child's dewy skin. "Still reaching for things I can never have. But I have you, little one. I have Rosetree, and the children, and enough goddamned money to make certain no one can take them away from me. And as soon as I force Cecily Lansdowne to let me search through her father's papers, I will blasted well gain a means to the revenge I've sought these endless years. 'Tis enough, Lacey. Damn it, 'tis *enough.*"

The moonlight flickered across the little one's face, blessed with a peace Ransom Tremayne had never known. And he wondered why in God's name he suddenly felt so empty.

Cecily raked the ivory-backed brush through the luxuriant mass of her hair, the soft bristles yanking relentlessly at what few tangles yet remained in the raven-hued tresses. Hours since, Bess had scurried off to her own little room, dismissed with far less patience than the fluttery girl deserved. But Cecily could not bear any more of the maid's worried glances, nor the nervousness that set the girl's hands to dropping everything in sight.

Cecily's fingers tightened resolutely about the brush's carved handle as she glared at her reflection in the mirror. Nay, her own hand would not—*would not* go on trembling this way, shaken still by the sensation of Ransom Tremayne's hard palm, her body yet tingling from the primal strength that had been sheathed beneath his skintight trousers, the blaze of desire in those intense eyes.

When she had lunged between Ransom and Bayard she had wanted only to shield Ransom from some menace she alone sensed—a danger somehow tangled in the baron's urbane smile and the careless guise that seemed never to quite reach his eyes. But in that instant she had seen a lightning flash of pain fire in Ransom's gaze, had seen his mouth harden at what he saw as betrayal.

Nay, he bore no right to rage at her, he who had demanded that she violate her beloved father's privacy. The very thought of pawing through Charleton Lansdowne's cherished papers and journals, or allowing a total stranger to do so, made Cecily's stomach churn. But the echoes of Ransom's impatient words tore at her more deeply still.

. . . 'tis as if the Ninon never existed . . . Cecily, the only place we might discover what will protect your father is amongst his own things . . .

She slammed the brush to the dressing table, the candlestick perched atop its polished surface skittering across the shiny wood as she shoved to her feet. How dare the rogue make her name sound so achingly sweet . . . how dare he wax so reasonable against her misgivings. 'Twould be betrayal of the worst sort, to allow Ransom to delve through those things dearest to her father's heart. And yet, could she deny Ransom access to the very things he claimed held the only chance of solving the enigma of what was tormenting Charleton Lansdowne?

She paced to the window, glowering out onto the moon-glossed gardens below. Ransom was right, plague take him. If he was to be of any aid to her beleaguered father, she would have to trust him. Yet in all the questions he had asked her as they circled Lady Lyton-Snow's ballroom, there had been a quality of danger—his probings about Charleton Lansdowne and Bayard Sutton leaving her with the disturbing feeling that 'twas not some nameless villain Ransom intended to drag to justice, but rather, her beloved father and the "uncle" she was just coming to face with a stirring of fear.

"Damn him!" Cecily bit out, padding in bare feet to the closed chamber door. "Even if I did decide 'twould be worth the guilt to let him into Father's rooms, how would I sneak the blackguard up to the chambers with the house crawling with servants? If so much as a spit-boy caught a glimpse of him, Aunt Honoria would drown me to save herself the disgrace. Not to mention the fact that if Father discovered . . ."

Cecily winced inwardly at the image her mind conjured of the pain that would crease her father's face were he ever to suspect her deception. He had always trusted her completely, never banned anything he owned from her hand if she but asked his permission. But now . . . now she was suddenly certain that by tomorrow she would no longer deserve such faith. For somehow she would dump her father's secrets into Ransom's outstretched hands as though the carefully recorded journals were naught but rosy shells.

If she could but wait until the rest of the house was asleep, then creep down to the door leading to the back gardens, she could easily slip Tremayne up into her father's study, help Ransom to gain some information that might aid Charleton Lansdowne.

Providing, a niggling voice whispered inside her, that in his anger Ransom Tremayne would still honor the agreement struck between them.

"Nay, Cecily Lansdowne, do not even think it!" she railed aloud. "He wants to discover the truth of this *Ninon* affair as much as you do—more, it seems." She felt suddenly cold at the remembrance of the piercing determination in those tiger-green eyes. "Think of where you might reach him—tell him you've reconsidered."

Rosetree. The name of the cottage where he had taken the beggar-child Pip swirled into her memory. Twice Tremayne had alluded to the cottage where he must make his home. If he had spent the night clawing through rubble, searching for the children buried in the mill cave-in, most likely the morning would find him collapsed at the place he called Rosetree. She had but to reach him there.

Taking up her candle, Cecily opened the door, padding out into the hall. If she could somehow enlist Mirabelle's help, the two of them could make their way to the cottage buried somewhere amidst London town. But 'twould have to be as soon as possible, before Charleton Lansdowne returned, and, Cecily thought grimly, before the conscience even now clamoring inside her made her change her mind.

She shivered, the chill of the floor seeping into the bare soles of her feet as she slipped through the corridors into the new wing of the town house. A single candle flickered in each of the hallway's sconces, dribbling inky shadows across the portraits of generations of Lansdownes that lined the walls like solemn-faced ghosts. Ghosts that even now seemed to be whispering of sorrows lifetimes past.

Cecily shook herself, trying to drive back the morbid fancies as she hastened toward the chamber where she knew Mira slept. But the nearer she drew to the shadow-pooled door, the deeper the shrouding of sorrow drew around her. Cecily paused, holding her breath, her heart twisting at the sounds she heard within Mirabelle's darkened chamber.

Mira was crying.

Cecily's fingers gripped the candlestick so hard the brass carvings cut deep into her palm. Her cousin was crying not in healing, cleansing sobs, or in the ragings that steeled one's spine, but rather, whimpering, muffled soft into a pillow, as though she felt she bore no right to trouble anyone even with her tears.

Of their own volition, Cecily's fingers clasped the door latch, eased it open. The room beyond was as scathingly formal as Honoria Lansdowne herself, stiff, proper, and unrelentingly oppressive. The Georgian bed with its heavy damask curtains seemed to dare anyone to be insolent enough to seek repose upon its regal expanse, the birds embroidered into its draperies peering out at the world with sly black eyes. Burl-oak chairs stood at attention along the wall, their elegant lines and hard-cushioned seats as inviting as the faces of soldiers in battle.

Only a small bowl of gillyflowers tucked upon the daunting dressing table seemed to belong in a room where gentle Mira sought haven.

Cecily felt her own throat tighten in empathy as the light of her candle trickled across the pathetic figure tangled in the bed's tumbled sheets. Pale hair straggled across pillows stiff with embroidery, Mira's thin, almost childlike figure was lost amidst the folds of a prim white nightgown, while the girl's narrow shoulders shook with a woe she battled desperately to suppress.

"Mira?" Cecily said gently, making her way to the side of the monstrous bed. "Mira, 'tis Cecily." She set the candle upon an ornately carved table and climbed up the high side of the bed, curling up beside the girl who even now seemed oblivious to her presence.

Cecily reached out, smoothing the tangle away from her

cousin's feverish face, her hand coming away wet with Mira's tears. "Mira, what is amiss?"

The sob that choked the other girl's throat tore at Cecily, and when Mira lifted her face from the pillows, the despair in those reddened eyes made Cecily catch her lip between her teeth. "'Tis—'Tis naught," Mira protested, her gaze darting in fright toward the door. "You didn't—please tell me you couldn't hear—hear me."

"Nay. I was but coming to ask you something. I heard naught until I opened the door." Cecily ached over the stark relief in Mirabelle's gray eyes.

"Maman . . . she . . . she gets so angry when I cry. 'A—A lady does not indulge in dis-displays of ill-bred emotion.' " Mirabelle gave a wild, watery little laugh. "D-Darling Lavinia w-would never—"

"Lavinia has no emotions to display!" Cecily snapped out in protective fury, her arms encircling the trembling Mirabelle. "Mira, what . . ." The question she had been about to ask died on her lips, a small, gilded volume tumbling from Mira's hands into Cecily's lap. Cecily reached down, picking up the book, its new leather cover splotched with tears. Her fingers slipped it open. The flyleaf inside, printed with twining roses, bore a carefully penned inscription.

Forever.

Mira's slender fingers caressed the inked word as though it contained every hope she had ever dared to hold. Cecily looked up to see her cousin's face soften into an expression of painful longing.

"'Tis—'Tis from Arthur Sutton," Mira whispered. "Sonnets. He always gives me sonnets. . . . " Mira closed the little book tenderly, cradling it in her hands. "He doesn't even dare to write his name upon the pages, for fear Mother would burn the book if she found it. But 'tis as if he is giving—" Her voice caught. "Giving me a part of himself. The only part I will ever have."

Cecily closed her eyes, remembering Mira whirling about the ballroom with the solemn Arthur. The love Mira felt must have been plain upon her face, yet no hint of it had penetrated Cecily's consciousness, caught up as she had been in the currents roiling about herself and the green-eyed rakehell who had held her in his arms.

"Why *can't* you have Arthur Sutton?" Cecily demanded. "He obviously loves you, and you love him—and he is by far a more suitable husband than that detestable Earl of Larrinbea."

"Not—Not as far as Maman is concerned. She says Arthur is scarce a match for the—the daughter of a duke, and—"

"Suttons have served the crown longer even than the Lansdownes," Cecily objected. "Arthur stands to inherit Uncle Bayard's titles some day. Who knows, if matters continue as they are, Arthur may well be the heir to England's next prime minister."

"And if your Uncle Bayard marries, Cecily, and gets himself a direct heir, Arthur will hold no claim even to what Maman calls a paltry baroncy."

"And you are afraid of life without a grand title? Estates?"

"Of course not!" Mira cried, her face suffused with passion. "I would not care if Arthur were a country squire, tending his flocks and his crops. I vow, I'd like it better than—than being paraded about London. I hate crowds, and noise, and love wandering amongst the farmers' children with baskets of apples and ginger nuts and—" Mira tore away from Cecily's grasp and slid down from the bed. In silence, the girl paced to the window. "But it does not matter," Mira said dully. "None of it matters. The Duchess of Moorston full intends to see her eldest daughter wed according to her rank. And I—I refuse to take any husband save Arthur."

Cecily stood, walking over to lay a gentle hand upon Mira's suddenly squared shoulders. Memories stirred of Bayard Sutton's sneering words concerning Mirabelle's failure in two London seasons, combined with memories of Honoria Lansdowne's ragings.

"God knows, I bear not much courage," Mirabelle said

achingly, "but I'll not barter myself off to some rich husband for the sole purpose of giving my mother the opportunity to gloat over her success with Mrs. Ambercrombie."

"Talk to your father. Surely Uncle Harry would not be so cruel as to forbid the match."

"Papa is not like your father, Cecily." A sad smile touched Mirabelle's lips. "The Duke of Moorston has no use for girl-children. From the time we were little he has scarce paused to pat us on the head before dashing out to play with his hounds, or hie the neighboring lords' sons off to a hunt. He has never bothered to interfere with Maman's plans for us, and he'd not begin now."

"Mira, how can you be certain—"

"The day Maman had my puppy drowned for puddling on the carpets, I ran to beg Father to stop her. He gave me this vague smile, as if he didn't even hear me, tugged at my hair ribbons and said, 'Fetch the groom, child. This mare has picked up a stone in its hoof.'"

Cecily swallowed, tasting Mira's despair.

"You could elope," Cecily protested. "Dash off to Gretna Green. There would be a scandal, but 'twould be worth it if the two of you gained marriage."

"Nay, *you* could elope," Mira said, her tear-swollen face bearing a look of affection. "You could run off like a Minerva Press heroine, thrown over the saddle of some glorious hero's steed. You could snub society, your parents, your friends. But I—I cannot.

"Once I am a confirmed spinster, 'twill be easier, I suspect," Mira said. "Maman will leave me alone, and I can stay in the country. 'Twill not be so awful a life. Except . . . except I will never have a babe to love. And I would have taken such joy in—in bearing Arthur's child."

The words trailed to silence, the two standing long minutes, shrouded in sorrow.

"So."

Cecily started at the overbright tone in Mira's voice as the girl turned to face her, her chin lifting with an inner pride not so different from Cecily's own.

"You obviously did not brave the drafts in the hallways in

the middle of the night to listen to my sniveling. What drew you here to begin with?"

Cecily twisted the ribbon tie of her nightgown about her finger, staring down at the bit of rose silk. She had come to ask Mirabelle's help, embroil her cousin in her own troubles. Yet after having listened to the girl pour out her heart, Cecily had not the will to cast more weight onto Mira's already burdened shoulders. "'Twas nothing. I just wanted to ask you to accompany me on some errand. But it will keep until another time."

"Nay, tell me. I would love to get out of this—this house. Away from Maman and Lavinia and the servants."

Cecily looked into Mira's earnest features, recalling the longing in the girl's tones when she had spoken of carrying baskets to the farm children on her father's country estates. A plan took form in Cecily's mind, and she felt the first stirring of happiness she had known in her weeks at Moorston. Why had she not thought of it before?

"There was an accident at a mill in Covent Gardens last night," Cecily began. "Some children were hurt. I thought that if you and I could rummage about, find some things to amuse them while they are ill, we could go entertain them and spend some time away from calling cards and fans and being proper young ladies." Cecily pinched her nose, saying the last in Mrs. Ambercrombie's irritating nasal drawl.

"Oh, Cecily!" There was genuine happiness in Mira's voice. "That would be heavenly! I've been knitting some mittens in secret for the children about our country estate. But I would have plenty of time to work more before the season is over. And books. I've been painting cloth books. . . ." Mirabelle turned, rummaging in the bottom of a drawer. The sadness that had been in her face faded to but a dusting of tears upon her lashes as she spilled out a fistful of the most cunning little volumes Cecily had ever seen. Plump rabbits and clever foxes romped across leaves fashioned of cambric squares stitched together, while a comical toad bearing a turban suspiciously like that of Mrs. Ambercrombie sat enthroned upon a lilypad whose stem was being feasted upon by three very jovial goldfish.

The Misadventures of Dame Rubblestone, the title proudly proclaimed.

"Mira, these are incredible!" Cecily gasped, running her fingertips over the painted images. "The children will adore them."

Mira's cheeks colored prettily. "If I start painting now, I might be able to finish the one I've been working on. . . ."

"Have you ever shown them to anyone? Anyone besides the children, I mean?"

"No." Mira shifted uncomfortably on her bare feet. "I doubt Maman would be pleased to see to what use I've put all those French painting lessons she gave me."

"Then Aunt Honoria is a fool." Cecily turned the pages, delighted as she scanned a painting depicting the haughty Mrs. Rubblestone, facefirst in the mud, her purple turban adorning her considerable behind.

"Maman is not so much a fool that she will not question where we are off to," Mira said dubiously. "And if she were to discover what we were about, she would be furious. She does not hold much truck with doling out what she terms 'charity to disease-ridden beasts.'"

Taken with a need to see Mirabelle smile, Cecily jutted her chin up in a mime of Lavinia at her best, flinging one hand across her breast.

"'Why, Mirabelle, *darling,*'" Cecily crooned in a sickening voice. "'We would not dream of tainting ourselves with the dirt of that rabble. 'Tis just that I've suddenly developed a most decided aversion to that new ball gown Papa had the seamstress stitch up for me! And I will simply *perish* unless I can hurl it in that overpriced Frenchwoman's face.'"

Instead of the smile she had hoped for, Cecily saw Mira's lips tremble, the girl stepping toward her, encircling her in a grateful hug. "Thank you, Cecily, for coming to Moorston," Mira said in a broken voice. "You—You are so very special."

Cecily kissed her cousin's pale cheek, her own arms tightening about Mira's slight form. "So are you, Mirabelle Lansdowne," she whispered, feeling as though she had found a treasure.

She closed her eyes, reveling in the feel of friendship blossoming between them. Nay, she would not spoil Mirabelle's enjoyment of the outing to Rosetree Cottage by confiding her own dread to her cousin. Let Mira gather her picture books, her mittens, and her spirits, while Cecily alone tilted with fierce green-eyed dragons and secrets that whispered of doom.

Chapter Seven

THE AFTERNOON SUN MELTED like honey over the streets banding the outskirts of the city. Cecily lifted her face to the kiss of the warm golden rays, drawing deep into her lungs the tantalizing scents of fresh-baked gingerbread, savory meat pies, and bright-faced blossoms newly picked by the flower sellers in the hours before dawn.

She patted the basket hanging heavy on her arm. Even the thought of confronting Ransom Tremayne did nothing to dull the glow of anticipation wreathed around her at the prospect of spilling the split-oak container's treasures into the laps of the injured children.

It had taken every one of her purseful of guineas, and Mirabelle's pitiful allowance as well, to stuff the baskets with the myriad treats they now contained, but the soft smile shaping Mira's pale lips and the exhilarating sense of freedom flowing to the tips of Cecily's fingers made the small, homely objects more valuable than a troughful of gold.

"Oh bother!" Mirabelle giggled, her hand flashing out to capture in midair the lead-painted soldier who seemed wont to dive from her basket's safe haven to seek adventure in the gutter. "'Twill be pure relief to turn this ill-trained rogue over to his new general. I vow he has tried to bolt ranks at least a dozen times, and if we do not reach your Rosetree

Cottage soon, I'll be tempted to let him. My arm aches so abominably I'll not be able to pick up a sable brush for a week!"

Cecily peered past the apple-cheeked Bess to cast Mira an affectionate look. "More like you've managed to rob yourself of the last of your paints, and the money you would have used to purchase more."

"It matters not at all!" Mirabelle said, shoving the brim of her bonnet back until the confection of dove-gray satin tumbled from her head to dangle down her back by its pink ribbons. "'Twas worth the royal mint just to see the expression upon Maman's face during your little performance at breakfast. You are fortunate she did not decide to come along with us to beat your nonexistent French seamstress over the head with her fan."

"'Twas when Lavinia started hinting that she *adored* the gown we were to return that I thought we were done for." Cecily shook her tumbled curls. "If you had not been so quick to claim Lavinia would look dashing in my castoffs, I vow she would have snatched it right out of my hands!"

"Small chance! Maman had a passel of older sisters, and when the family was in reduced circumstances, she had to wear their old gowns. Despite her faults, she has never once permitted either Lavvy or I to wear so much as a ribbon worn by someone else."

"You—You're both courtin' disaster," Bess moaned, glancing yet again over her shoulder. "'Twas close enough to the axe you came the last time you went bolting off, milady. But now, wandering about the streets searching for some—some house—"

"A *cottage,* Bess. Rosetree *Cottage.* And the orange seller swore 'twas just around the bend."

"The orange seller." Bess sniffled, rolling her eyes heavenward. "And when the hackney driver stopped to ask the tinker where it was an hour past, he said 'twas but a hop and a step down the lane. 'Fine,' says you, 'stretch our legs a bit.' Well, my legs are so stretched they may snap at any minute. And I'd wager my grandmammy's wake money that there is no *cottage* within a crow's flight of—"

"Avast, me hearty! Dare a step farther and I'll pierce your heart with my trusty saber!" Cecily started at the sinister shout carried on the breeze, her heart racing at the unseen threat.

Her gaze swept the row of neat rambling houses with their perfectly tended gardens, but no pirate lurked behind the cabbages that lined the dooryards, no sword-brandishing ruffians dangled from the apple trees. Yet the crow of delight from nearby left no doubt that a battle of some sort was being fought upon the little lane.

"Jimmie, 'tis your turn now," a most disgruntled little voice piped up with grisly relish. "Tell 'im you'll feed 'is liver t' a big fat whale!"

A giggle bubbled in Cecily's throat, and she scooped up her skirts, fairly skipping toward the sound, feeling again the delight she had known when she had played at such games as a child. She rounded the street corner, nigh bumping her nose on the corner of a sturdy wooden fence, the spaces betwixt its whitewashed boards revealing glimpses of red-painted swings cradled in an oak's spreading branches and barrel hoops being batted merrily about by tousle-haired boys.

But the most astonishing thing, there before the homey rose-brick house, was a ship's mast, plunged deep into the ground. A child's most cherished fantasy, it was, dominating the generous dooryard, its thick length a-tangle with masses of rigging and a genuine ship's wheel. Soaring high above the ground, a crow's nest promised a glorious gateway to whimsy, and Cecily could almost picture the battle the bright-faced imp of a girl perched within must be painting in her imagination. In the clear, high-pitched voice of an empress, the engaging child called out orders to a stout lad of ten and a tall, golden-haired man, dangling from the ropes in most dashing pirate fashion.

"Jimmie, you're s'pose to be savin' me!" The black-curled child's lips pursed in disgust. "De-tangle your buttons from the rigging an— God's teef, he'd've fed *my* liver to the whale by now!"

Cecily stifled a laugh behind her palm, heard Mira's

answering giggle as the girl's tiny foot stomped down, baby lips muttering an oath as the boy fumbled with where his waistcoat was snared.

"Take a hun-dret years for him to save me," Cecily heard the fairy child grouse. Cecily shielded her eyes from the sun, peering up to catch a glimpse of the girl bending down to grab something just as the gold-haired mock pirate reached into the crow's nest with a most terrifying snarl.

"Bad pirate!"

Cecily put her hand on the fence, her mouth gaping open as she saw the child's hand arc through the air. Something grasped in her fist collided with the blond man's wooden sword. Cecily saw a tiny Morocco-leather slipper fly through the air, saw the "pirate's" weapon tumble from a hand achingly familiar.

Nay, 'twas impossible. The "pirate" could not be . . .

Ransom Tremayne.

Cecily stifled a tiny cry of disbelief as she caught a glimpse of bronzed face, a scar ice white across a cheekbone of masculine perfection, green eyes wide with sparkling amusement as they fastened upon the girl-child. Then the pirate gave a bloodcurdling scream of defeat, his hand releasing its hold on the play rigging.

A scream snagged in Cecily's own throat, and she watched in horror as Ransom's tall frame plummeted the six feet to the ground, his broad shoulders thumping into the earth with a resounding crack.

"Papa!" the little girl cried, almost tumbling out of the crow's nest herself as her nemesis hit the ground. "Papa!"

Papa? This green-eyed rakehell was this little nymph's father? A hundred emotions roiled to life in Cecily's breast, but she bore no time to assimilate any of them as the child clambered up on the edge of her small wooden perch, stretching out her arms. The basket flew from Cecily's hand, her palm tearing on the gate latch as she tried desparately to reach the girl.

"Nay, don't!" she cried, but 'twas too late.

Pushing off with one stockinged foot, the imp flew through the air, her ruffled skirts flying about her chubby legs. In a mad dash, Cecily hurled herself across the small space that separated them, her arms outstretched in a futile attempt to catch the winsome cherub.

Cecily felt her slipper catch upon the hem of her skirt, saw a boy's barrel hoop careening crazily toward her. She gave a shove with her other foot, using her momentum in a last effort to get beneath the girl.

"Sweet Jesus!" Ransom's bellow mingled with the sickening sound of fabric rending as her gown tore, grass and stones raking elbows and knees as she skidded wildly toward him and the child.

Her chin cracked into solid muscle, her eyes smarting as the curve of Ransom's rib banged hard into her nose. Through a blur of tears she saw a flash of movement as, at the last possible instant, the slain "pirate's" strong arms swept up, catching about the child's ribbon-sashed waist. A string of curses burst from Ransom Tremayne's lips, but the pixie cradled in his arms scarce seemed to notice either her father's blusterings or the young woman struggling up from a tangled heap of grass-stained muslin and wounded pride.

"Feeded your liver to the whales!" the girl chortled with blood-thirsty glee. "Feeded your liver to the whales, Papa!"

"Bloody hands of God, woman!" Cecily heard Ransom sputter as she tried to shove the mass of grass-spangled hair from her face.

She clawed at the clumps of grass stuck to her chin, caught a flash of gray skirts as Mira dashed to her side.

"Cecily, are you hurt? Did you—"

"Cecily!" Ransom exploded. "What the—"

She heard the child give a cry of protest, felt hard, strong hands close just beneath her breasts. How Ransom had gained his feet she had no idea, but in an instant he was dragging her up, her body raking against the hard plane of his chest.

"How dare you frighten me that way, Ransom Tremayne!" Cecily burst out, whapping one graceful hand against a hard curve of shoulder. "Diving out of crow's nests, flopping about like you've snapped your blasted neck!" She shook back her hair, trying to gather the tattered fragments of her pride about her, but the leaf curled under her nose like a green mustache made any attempt at hauteur impossible.

"I've fallen out of that rigging a hundred times, and never once have I broken—" Suddenly he stopped, splotches of color darkening his cheeks, the eyes that had ever met her gaze with such unrelenting intensity flashing to the ground, the fence, anywhere except her face.

He was embarrassed, Cecily knew with sudden certainty. Nay, shy. Shy because here, in this garden, surrounded by raucous children, she had seen the walls he built about himself completely breached. Captain Ransom Tremayne, hero of Trafalgar, street brawler, rogue with the charm of the devil himself, was blushing, and never in all the times she had seen him had his handsome face entranced her more.

"So, Captain Tremayne," she managed, choked with laughter, "are you going to feed my body parts to the sharks as well?"

The green gaze that caught hers glinted with a humor so warm she drowned in it, the grin widening across Ransom's tanned face stealing away what little breath she was yet able to draw.

"To a very large shark," Ransom said, his eyes skimming down to where the ruffle scooping over her bosom twisted askew. "And . . ." He let the word hang, warm as mulled wine. "A very hungry one."

Cecily felt a flush warm on her flesh where his gaze had touched, his thumbs skimming up a breath to brush against the ripe swells above.

"Now, Gloriana, what in the name of Saint Michael are you doing, flinging yourself into respectful citizens' gardens? The shopping districts are to the north, the theaters are at Covent Gardens, and if you are searching for a ballroom, Mayfair is the most likely—"

"Look, Papa! Look!" A warm little body shoved its way between Cecily's ruined skirts and Ransom's lean-muscled thighs, one Morocco heel biting pointedly into Cecily's instep. Cecily stumbled back with a laugh as the little girl jammed a fistful of broken gingerbread into Ransom's taut stomach.

Cecily's eyes swept the ground, her lighthearted mood vanishing as she stared at the fallen basket, its treasures strewn across the ground. "Perdition!" she blustered, thumping down onto her knees to scoop the treats back into the container. "Look at this mess! Half of them are ruined, and—"

"Leaden soldiers . . ." Ransom's voice held a sweet wondering that made Cecily's heart slam against her ribs. She looked up to see Tremayne turning the little figure over musingly in his rope-scarred palm. "Tell me, Gloriana, are these all the fashion in the ton this season? Perched atop a bonnet perhaps, or nestled amidst ruffles?"

"Of course not." Cecily snatched the toy away from him, suddenly self-conscious. "Mira and I . . . we thought they might help pass the hours for the children you brought here . . . the ones that were hurt last night. . . ."

Her cheeks burned as she watched him hunker down beside her feet, retrieving first a rag-stuffed princess, then one of Mirabelle's cambric books. The sounds of the other children who had been frolicking in the yard grew louder as they drew near, gathering about the scattered treats. But their delighted cries seemed to fade to a faint humming as Cecily met Ransom's tiger-wild gaze, felt it caress her as certainly as his hands had the evening before.

"Papa? Papa!" The indignant voice pierced the spell weaving around them, the girl-child struggling to climb Ransom's lean leg as though it were the mast. "I asted you a twestion. Me. Lacey."

Ransom's gaze flashed down to the curly-topped child, and the piercing love in his eyes tugged at something deep in Cecily's heart.

"Lacey? Lacey?" Ransom said the name as though he had never heard it before, scooping the child high in his arms. "And all this time I thought your name was Mergatroit."

"Nay, Papa. Lacey! Tell the pretty ladies Lacey."

"Lady Cecily, Lady Mirabelle." Ransom sketched them

an elegant bow. "May I present my daughter, her royal highness, the princess of disaster."

"Nay, you're the dis-bastard!" The swear word rang crystalline clear from the babe's mouth. "Jagger said—"

"Lacey Tremayne!" Scarlet stained Ransom's lean cheeks, his voice choked with despairing laughter as he clapped one palm over the child's mouth. "I said 'disaster'! *Disaster!* And I have no desire whatever to hear what that damned old sea spawn said! God's teeth, he's done enough damage, stuffing your mouth with bloody swear words!"

"Oh, aye, I can see 'tis all Mr. Jagger's doing." Cecily couldn't stay the laughter bubbling to her lips as she impulsively swept the child from her father's arms. "Although, I must say, upon more than one occasion I have heartily agreed with Jagger's estimation of your papa's dis*as*trous temperament."

The bundle of ruffles and giggles squirmed with delight, twining arms around Cecily's neck with surprising strength. "Papa talks naughty!" Lacey whispered breezily, her black eyes sparkling. "But Lacey doesn't care. Lacey loves Papa."

Cecily raised her gaze from the child's glowing face, feeling as though something soul deep had been torn from her own heart. It raged in a tempest but an arm's length away, entrapped in the scarred, bewitching visage that stared into her eyes. Cecily knew a fleeting pain, as, unbidden, her mind conjured images of a woman's face holding the dark beauty of little Lacey, of eyes like liquid onyx, fair, rose-kissed cheeks, and lips that had known the tender fury of Ransom Tremayne's loving.

Was the child's mother even now bustling about the homey cottage a few steps away? Was she pulling fresh-baked currant buns from their pans, icing them to delight her little daughter?

Cecily caught her lip between her teeth, suddenly touched with a sick stirring in her stomach at the thought of the kiss she had shared with Ransom—nay, gloried in. If he were truly wed . . .

The child wriggled down, plopping beside the fallen basket in a flurry of ribbons and petticoats, and Cecily fixed her gaze upon the mass of dark curls, unable to stop the words upon her lips.

"She is beautiful, your little girl. Her mother . . ."

"She has no mother. Has no need of one." There was no sorrow in the words, no grief, only a threading of belligerence, as though Ransom dared anyone, even himself, to suggest that his cherished child had not all she could desire. Cecily looked down at Lacey, the pixie's lips bowed in a rosy smile as she held up yet another found treasure for her father to see.

Cecily lowered her eyes, furious with herself for her prying, terrified that Ransom might understand the reason for her curiosity far too well. "She is spoilt to the core with loving," Cecily said in a soft voice, trailing her fingers over Lacey's silky curls. Cecily could feel Ransom's whole body stiffen, sensed his face whiten with anger.

"Your opinion of my daughter is of no concern to—"

"I was, too, you know," she interrupted, her lashes sparkling with unshed tears. "My father . . ." The words trailed off, an aching lump in her throat, slips of an enchanted childhood dancing like will o' wisps beyond her reach.

One finger, callused, infinitely gentle, hooked beneath her chin, a slight pressure urging her face to turn upward. His eyes had darkened to ebony, his lips a harsh slash, unyielding, as if he were battling the need to crush them down upon her own.

"'Twas the most important thing in my life . . . my father's love. . . ." She pulled away from the compelling snare of Ransom's finger, pulled away from emotions yet too raw to confront. She felt a sudden need to escape, escape her doubts about her father's love, flee the throbbings of tension between her and the bronzed man before her.

"I—We are sorry to have intruded upon your play." Even to her own ears her voice was cool, stiff. "If you would but show us the way to the children's chambers, we will trouble you no longer."

"Children?" Ransom said, his tones touched with confusion.

"The children from the mill. So we can bring them the treats we collected."

Ransom seemed to shake himself mentally, his hand returning to one narrow, black-breeched hip. "Of course. Lacey, while I am gone, do not—"

"Don't worry, Papa. Lacey won't climb up the damned crow's nest. Lacey promise."

"Damn it, Lacey, don't say damn!" Ransom snapped. Cecily's eyes flicked to the little girl, blissfully attempting to feed the broken foot of a gingerbread man to Mira's cambric rendition of Mrs. Rubblestone. But the child seemed well used to the vagaries of her father's temper and utterly secure in the love Ransom bore her.

Cecily saw his glossy boot heel dig sharply into the ground as he spun toward the white-painted door, his long strides leaving Mira, Bess, and Cecily as well, running to keep pace as he strode into the cottage's dim interior.

The hall beyond was sunny yellow, a rainbow of rag rugs covering most of a scarred wooden floor. To the left sprawled a great room, complete with pianoforte and a score of huge stuffed pillows a-scatter with letter blocks and patty pans and a magnificent Noah's Ark, the paint upon its animal passengers worn away by small, loving fingers. Bits of charcoal lay abandoned by some miniature artist's hand, while curled in the corner sat a lone child of eight or nine, his haunted, thin face turned to peer out a shiny glass window.

"Tea is not ready yet, Ransom Tremayne." A feminine voice drifted from another room. "And if you plunder a one of my scones, I'll—"

The sound of spritely footsteps came toward them, a saucy, apple-cheeked woman appearing in the wide-flung door at the end of the corridor. Cecily felt jealousy claw within her as she met the gaze of a pair of the bluest eyes she had ever seen. Hair the color of new copper rippled in glorious disarray about a heart-shaped face, a smile bracketed by faint lines dancing upon ripe lips. The woman looked to be well past the blush of youth. Yet the openly adoring expression that glowed upon her face as she fixed her gaze upon Ransom made her appear more like a girl in the first flush of love than a woman, frazzled and weary from the care of dozens of waifs. Cecily's hands knotted into fists.

Lacey has no mother . . . She remembered Ransom's words with a sudden sharp bitterness. *Has no need of one* . . . Nay, the thought goaded her, this woman, with her blue eyes and her lushly curved figure, most like provides all the mothering that Lacey Tremayne could ask—as well as serving the needs of her father. . . .

"Your scones are safe, Jessamyn, I swear it." Ransom plucked a piece of dried apple from a wooden bowl on a table and popped it into his mouth. "I only came tramping inside to show these ladies the way to the infirmary."

Blue eyes, far wiser than their years, swept Mira and Bess, then lingered long seconds on Cecily's glowering face with the intensity of a patron of Gentleman Jackson's sizing up an opponent. Cecily ground her teeth as the pretty older woman swept up to Ransom, her slender fingers seeming infuriatingly intimate as she explored the grass stains he had crushed into his shirt in his fall from the mock rigging.

"Well, Ransom, the instant after you direct the ladies where to distribute their charity"—did Cecily imagine the slight bite to that word?—"I want you to strip off that shirt and bring it down to me to soak." Jessamyn's flattened palm lingered upon Ransom's chest. "And those underdrawers you ripped the night past—cart them down as well. 'Tis unforgivable, the way you have me ever dashing up and down the stair to your bedchamber."

"'Tis common knowledge I take advantage of you shamelessly." Ransom chuckled. "But I hardly think the ladies came all the way to Rosetree to hear a listing of what garments I hold in disrepair."

"Nay." Jessamyn leveled a shrewd stare upon Cecily. "'Tis patent they did not."

"Perhaps, if you would give them greeting . . . ?" Ransom's prodding made Cecily want to yank the woman's lace cap over her face.

"Of course. Forgive me." Jessamyn cast a challenging smile at the three women. "Taking care of Ransom and the babes has left me lax on my manners. He is such a demanding sort, but then, you ladies—unmarried as you are—you would know naught of the masculine sex's failings."

"A simple good morrow would have sufficed," Ransom said, a threading of much-tried patience running through his tone.

"Good morrow." The woman bobbed a curtsey shaded with impudence as Ransom introduced them each in turn.

"Jessamyn is my housekeeper, cook, and plays mother to the little ones," Ransom said, giving the woman's lace cap an exasperated tug. "I don't know what I would do without her." 'Twas as if something unseen had passed between the two in that instant, and when she again turned toward Cecily, the woman had blushed so prettily, it made Cecily's stomach sour.

"Most like you'd find some other woman eager to patch your breeches," Jessamyn said airily, her hand smacking playfully at the taut curve of Ransom's buttock.

"I much doubt Captain Tremayne has any trouble at all with his breeches with you about." The brittle words were out before Cecily could stop them, and she clenched her teeth, horrified as she saw Jessamyn's face blanch.

Cecily heard Mira's stunned gasp, but even her own self-loathing was eclipsed by what fired deep in Ransom's face. She had seen his eyes blaze with murderous rage, seen them glitter with passion, but even the night he had dueled with his fists in Drury Lane had not prepared her for the gale raging in his lean visage at that moment.

The hand that had been so gentle in the cottage yard clamped around her arm with bruising force, his teeth bared in unleashed fury. "You will damned well say you are sorry, *Lady Cecily,* or I vow you'll regret it."

"Nay, Ransom," Jessamyn broke in, but the hard edge to her voice had shattered. "I've heard far worse. Take the ladies up to distribute their largesse. I'll be up in a little to bring the babes their tea."

"Blast it, Jess, you don't have to endure insults from any—"

"Ransom, just go!" The woman gave him a soft shove, turning to go back into the other room. With an oath, Ransom jerked Cecily in front of him, propelling her up a set of narrow stairs as though he would much like to launch her from the open window at the risers' head.

Cecily could hear Mira and Bess scurrying after them like frightened mice, could hear the angry thump of Ransom's boot heels inches from her own slippers, but in spite of the guilt chafing her at every step, she arched her neck at a haughty angle, glowering in defiance.

"The infirmary is at the end of the hall," Ransom snapped out. "The children's names are on cards mounted above the beds, to make them feel like they bear a place of their own in Rosetree."

Cecily started to pull free of his proprietary grasp, to hurry with Mirabelle and Bess as they started to skitter past him.

"Oh, nay, Gloriana, not you." His voice was low, dangerous, as he yanked the basket from Cecily's hand, thrusting it at the round-eyed Bess. "*You* and I have severe need of a discussion on the finer points of manners."

"I bear no need of a lecture from a—a dock ruffian the likes of you!" Cecily sputtered.

"Captain Tremayne," Mira's timid voice piped up, "my cousin—"

"Into the infirmary, Lady Mira. Now. I vow I'll not put your cousin under a physician's care unless she tries my temper further." The tone that had ordered sailors into battle was no match for Mira's flagging courage, and Cecily could scarce blame the other two women as they bolted into what looked to be a cheery, light-filled chamber.

Then, yet again, the daunting seafarer was dragging Cecily forward, into a chamber but a few paces away. The door shut with a resounding crack, and Cecily felt him fling her down, hard onto a fluffy feather tick.

"You brute!" she blazed, struggling upright, her knotted fists digging deep into the worn quilt. "You cursed ruffian! Don't you ever—"

"Don't play the princess with me, madam, or you might

well find yourself turned over my knee, while I take the greatest of pleasure in applying a willow switch to your backside!" Ransom's hands splayed on his hips. "Never in my life have I struck a child. In your case I might well make an exception."

"Child?" Cecily hated the burning flush rising to her cheeks. The sensations of guilt, jealousy, anger, and the unbearable knowledge that she deserved some measure of Ransom's scorn set her temper snapping like a brush fire. "You—You insolent, ill-mannered, dolt of a—"

"Aye, you are right, I am an insolent dolt. 'Tis totally unjust to lump innocent children into the same category with someone as blatantly cruel as you. Jessamyn Smythe bears one of the most generous hearts I've ever encountered, and I'll be damned if anyone will come into my house—*my house*—and flay away from her what little confidence she has managed to gain."

"She seemed to have an overabundance of confidence to me," Cecily flung back. "And if you are so all-fired concerned about your precious Jessamyn being insulted, you should tell her not to sweep about your house pawing you like—like a—lovesick ewe. Her reputation—"

"Her reputation was destroyed years ago, left in ruin by the lecherous society bucks who do not dare to kiss your sacred feet, *Lady Cecily*."

"Ruined? I—I don't understand. . . ."

"Neither did Jessamyn, when she came to London, desperate to gain some coin to support her starving brothers and sisters and drunkard father. She was a total innocent when an old crone took her in to work in the kitchen of her supposed boardinghouse—a house that ended up being naught but a brothel."

Cecily felt the blood drain from her cheeks. "Nay."

"Oh, aye, Gloriana." The slashing scorn in Ransom's voice made Cecily battle to keep her chin jutting proudly, the spark of anger in her eye. Yet despite the niggling certainty that she had wronged the pretty older woman, something disturbingly like jealousy gnawed at Cecily ever more deeply.

"She—Jessamyn could have left," Cecily said defensively. "Could have found a position as a chambermaid or—"

"Without a character from some former employer? Hardly, princess. Think you your grandaunt the duchess would allow a girl the like of Jessamyn within reach of all that Lansdowne silverplate? And besides, the crone, she was most skilled at twisting an innocent's will to her own. Never once did she rail at Jessamyn, lock the girl in a room, force her to service a customer. Nay, she bore one 'regular' she reserved most especially for reluctant flowers like Jessamyn. Cultured, elegant, handsome as sin, with a pair of the most cursed-sincere eyes ever slapped upon the face of a man— aye, and with a special taste for virgins."

"I don't want to hear—"

"Well, you are damned well going to! The bastard made a game of getting Jessamyn, and God knows how many before her, to believe that he loved them. Wooed them into one of the back rooms, stole not only their maidenhead, but every wisp of self-worth they had. Then, once he had taken his fill, cast a bag of coin upon the table and turned the girl over to whichever of his friends happened to be gathered—"

"I don't want to hear this!" Cecily choked back the bile rising in her throat.

"'You're a whore already,' the bastard would say. 'Three more men will scarce make any difference'—"

"I didn't know! Damn you—"

"Don't waste your curses, princess." His voice was bitter, broken. "I've been damned to a depth farther than you can even imagine."

Cecily felt iron-hard hands manacle her arms, Ransom starting to haul her to her feet, but the instant his palms abraded the delicate skin upon the underside of her arms, something exploded within her, something raw, wild, full of pain, of promise. Her hands delved deep into the tumbled gold of his hair, his name a hoarse cry upon her lips as she sought his mouth with her own.

Eyes like molten emerald darkened, night black, passion raging through them with the force of a stark sea gale. Ransom's curse was hot upon her lips, scented of cinnamon, apple, and desire. She could sense him war to pull back from her, felt him throw all caution to Hades.

"Damn . . . damn you . . ." Ransom's mouth opened over hers, his lean, hard body bearing hers back into the warmth of the quilts. Cecily struggled to draw breath, failed, her heart pounding like that of a wolf-trapped doe as the honed-muscle plane of Ransom's chest crushed the softness of her breasts. 'Twas wicked, shameful, more wonderful than anything she had ever imagined—the sensation of his hardness molding tight to her soft curves, his muscles rigid, fire hot, his mouth wet and drugging as he kissed her.

Jealous . . . aye, she had been sick with jealousy at seeing the lovely Jessamyn's hands upon Ransom, terrified that the woman indeed played mother to Ransom's child, served as wife to a man who fascinated Cecily, tempted her beyond all reason. Because despite the danger in him, despite the agony scarce hidden behind his arrogant smile, he touched something deep in the core of her—this warrior who championed the defenseless, this man whose eyes burned with pain he would allow no one to share. He was hers for this moment, linked to her body and soul by some primal destiny, already etched in the stars. And Cecily sensed that even if she were to choose to run from this room at this instant, flee Ransom Tremayne, never see him again, she would never escape the storms he had loosed in her, never satisfy the fierce questing even now tearing at her vitals.

"Ransom . . ." She whimpered his name into his mouth, and was stunned again at the melting pleasure as the sleek wetness of his tongue entered her parted lips. Before the morn in the shipping office she had never suspected that people kissed this way—tongues twining, exploring, seeking out every recess of someone else's soul, while hands . . .

She could not gain enough of the feel of him, his back, hot through the thin layer of his shirt; the muscles a rippling, delicious contrast to his tumbled mane of hair. She shivered in raw pleasure, the warm roughness of Ransom's palm skimming down over the curve of her slender hip, then up past the slight indentation of her waist to where her breasts trembled against his hard flesh. His thumbs paused there, just a whisper away from the tingling swells, long seconds seemingly designed to heighten the tension coiling tighter and tighter low in Cecily's stomach. Then he gently withdrew his lips from her swollen ones, trailing a series of butterfly-soft kisses down her throat, along the delicate curve of her collarbone.

Cecily clenched her teeth against a moan, arching her head back into the feather tick as Ransom shifted his long, lean body, uncovering the thin layer of cloth shielding her straining nipple from his gaze.

"Ah, Gloriana . . ." Nothing but his breath heated the hardening bud, yet 'twas so excruciatingly pleasurable, the whisper of moistness dampening her skin, that a whimper escaped Cecily's lips.

"Gloriana, you make me so cursed mad. . . ." His golden head leaned closer to the delicate icing of fabric. "Mad to touch you . . . taste you . . . mad to try . . ."

Cecily's lungs threatened to burst, her fingers digging deep into the muscle sheathing Ransom's shoulders as he blew gently upon the pebble-hard tip. Then, with agonizing languor, his tongue parted his lips, touched the place his breath had just heated.

Cecily cried out, shaken to her core as jagged bolts of sensation tore through her center, piercing deep into the heart of her womb. "Ransom . . ." His name was broken on her lips, a plea for him to stop, a plea for him to spiral her on into the magic his touch promised, regardless the cost.

"Aye, princess, I want you too." He sucked in a ragged breath, his eyelids closing, face tight with emotion, need. "Want you more than I've ever wanted a woman in my life."

Cecily knew his words should incense her, hurt her, rife as they were with the certainty that Ransom Tremayne had wanted countless women . . . and no doubt drunk deep of their charms. But instead she felt a soaring triumph, a rush of joy thundering sweet through her heart. 'Twas her he vowed he wanted most of all, mayhap with the same clawing hunger Cecily felt in her own body.

"I want to bury myself inside you, princess, want to kiss every inch of your satin-pale skin. But if I did . . . if we did . . ." His mouth twisted in an ironic smile, his scar standing out white against his passion-flushed cheek. Cecily choked back a protest, strangely hurt as he levered himself away from her, rolling onto his back amidst the tumbled quilt, one wrist flung over his eyes.

"Christ." A chuckle rumbled low in Ransom's throat. "If I did, you'd most like claw my eyes out, and I would end up exacting a revenge of my own. You are exactly the cut of woman who drives me to fury, and I . . ." His mouth widened into a self-deprecating grin. "You've never made any attempt to conceal your estimation of me. Yet here we lay, rolling about the covers like a milkmaid and her beau, while at any moment the door could burst open upon us. . . ."

He let the sentence trail off, but Cecily was excruciatingly aware of what would have been revealed had anyone intruded upon them a few moments past. She bit the inside of her lip, tormented by images of that tumbled-gold head at her breast, of those strong hands molding to her body, of his hot mouth slanting over hers.

Bury myself inside you . . . The words, so sensual, rasped in his husky, passion-roughened voice, echoed now in her mind blatantly sexual, as coarse as the matings of the heifers upon Briarton's meadows. Cecily tasted blood, humiliation. She had tumbled upon the bed with a man who was scarce but a stranger, kissing him, urging him to work shameful pleasures upon her. And now . . . now he lay there, laughing. . . .

"You bastard!" Cecily jammed her hands into the feather tick, shoving herself upright as she battled to recapture the shattered bits of her pride. "How—How dare you—you paw at me—"

"How dare *you* enjoy it." Ransom pushed himself up on his elbows, his hair glorious gold about his lean cheeks, his smile so bewitching it was a stake in Cecily's heart. "Come now, princess, 'tis my laughing that is setting that bloody temper of yours to blazing, but even you must see the humor in the situation. Every moment we are cursed with one another's company becomes a contest as to which of us is going to murder the other first. But the moment we are alone . . ." A sudden tempest roiled to life in his emerald-hued eyes. *"Christ,* all I can think about is how soft your skin feels beneath my hands, how your lips taste, hungry, on my own, and how I don't give a damn if I have to barter my soul to the devil to possess you for just one night."

"'Twould take a bargain with the devil for you to ever touch me again!" Cecily struggled to straighten her mussed clothes, fighting desperately to convince herself of the truth of her words.

But the throbbing passion in Ransom's voice seemed to thicken her tongue until she could do nothing but sputter, the room falling into silence suddenly, deafeningly shattered by the creak of the bedchamber door.

"Blast it, who is it?" Ransom's voice roared out, honed by frustration, exasperation, and a dark, wry amusement.

Whoever stood behind the door moved not a whisper, and Cecily drew a sudden clear image of a giant mouse, standing, frozen in fear upon the other side of the portal. Embarrassment flamed in her cheeks, and she stalked to the door with the aura of a queen, nearly ripping the portal from its hinges as she flung it against the chamber's inner wall.

But instead of finding herself glaring at Jessamyn's face, or Mira's, or that of Bess, nothing met her gaze at eye level except the blue-painted wall. She muttered a curse, half thinking whoever had been outside the room had fled. But as she started to wheel to confront the yet-reclining Ransom, she caught a glimpse of white-blond hair, a ghost-pale face turned up to hers. A boy-child it was, so small he looked to be of Lacey Tremayne's age. But there was none of Lacey's sparkle in the sharp-boned features and soft brown eyes turned up to Cecily's own. Rather there was wariness, hopelessness, as though, within the lad's narrow chest, something lay broken that could not even be mended by Ransom Tremayne's fierce loving.

"Nicky?" All passion was gone from Ransom's voice, only tenderness remaining in its deep tones as Tremayne caught sight of the child. The bed ropes creaked, Ransom rising from the tumbled counterpane as slowly as though the child were a skittish fawn with an arrow in its breast.

"Nicky, lad, what is it?" Ransom knelt down before the boy, and Cecily stared, transfixed, as those carnal lips formed a reassuring smile.

"J-Jessamyn. T-Tea boiling," Nicky whispered, his little fists clenched before him as his wide eyes flicked to the rumpled bedcovers, then to Ransom.

"Did Jessie send you up to tell me 'tis time for tea?"

"A-Aye. T-Tea."

"And I'm so hungry, I could eat a hull full of barnacles. You've saved me from starvation, you have," Ransom joked gently. "Can I give you a hug to thank you?" He reached out one tender hand to the boy's sallow cheek, and the genuine love emanating from every muscle in the big man's body brought a tightness to Cecily's throat. But Ransom's finger had scarce brushed the child when Nicky flinched back, raw terror rounding the whites of his eyes.

Ransom did not jerk his hand away from the lad. He but let it drift slowly to bent knee, and there was no hint of the sting of rejection in those black-fringed green eyes. "Well, young sir, if a hug is not to your liking, mayhap this will suffice."

Cecily saw Ransom dig into one of his pockets, Nicky's eyes lighting with reluctant fascination. "'Tis the best Lorimer has to offer—carved of pure agate." Ransom's voice reminded Cecily of tales of magicians of genii conjured from mystical lamps. And she felt the same eagerness as the boy when Ransom's rope-toughened hand opened, displaying upon its callused surface a marble the color of amber.

Cecily could scarcely stop herself from scooping the beautiful plaything into her own hand, so tempting was the object glowing warm in the sunlight melting through the open windows.

But though Nicky stared at the marble, his thin lips parted in wonder, he made no move to touch it.

"'Tis yours, Nicky," Cecily found herself urging. "Captain Tremayne means for you to take it."

"Pretty." Nicky touched the marble with his finger. "M-Master Ransom . . . is it truly for—for me?"

"Aye, Nicholas Dolan. 'Tis yours to do with whatever you choose."

"I never . . . had a marble of my own. Even when . . . when Father was alive."

Cecily felt her hackles rise, her mind conjuring remembrances of the brute in Drury Lane who had so abused another small boy. But the loathing budding in her breast toward Nicky Dolan's absent father was crushed in the next instant, left instead in a whirling confusion.

"M-Master Ransom," the child began again. "Think you . . . think you Rat's Castle would trade this—" Bonethin fingers took up the agate sphere.

"Trade it?" Ransom's brow crinkled in confusion.

"For a—a biolin. Jew Isaac had an old one and—"

Cecily started at the slight thinning of Ransom's lips, the only betrayal his patience was frayed.

"Do you not fancy marbles?" Ransom said, still gentle. "Mayhap I could find some other trinket to please you."

"Nay!" There was a desperation in the child's voice, his transparent fingers trembling. "Love marbles. So pretty. But my father . . . 'tis just that he—he played biolin. Played on the street corners. People would throw coins."

"You needn't worry anymore about money, Nicky. The night I brought you to Rosetree, I promised I would take care of you. You've not been hungry since I showed you the way to Jessamyn's kitchen, have you?"

Nicky shook his head.

"And you've been warm, Nicky, and safe, with a soft bed to sleep in, and clothes that won't let in the bite of the wind?"

"Aye."

"You'll never have to fiddle for your supper on the streets again, little man. You bear my word."

Cecily watched the child's face, yet instead of the relief she expected to come out of Ransom's soothing words, the child's face grew paler, tauter still, the small feet shifting uncomfortably upon the rag rug.

"Nicky, did you *like* to watch your father fiddle in the squares?" she asked, ignoring the hard look Ransom shot her over the boy's head.

"Oh, y-yes, milady. Father . . . he taught me how to—to make the bow dance crost the strings. And we'd sing and play and—and I loved him so much before the dandy-buck crashed him."

"Crashed him?" Cecily echoed.

"In one o' them high things. Phaetons. The dandy he was racin', an' he went up on the boardwalk, tryin' t' win. I'm glad he lost. He didn't—didn't even stop when he—"

"I think 'tis time we favored Jessamyn with our presence," Ransom interrupted, his tones brisk, yet Cecily could sense his irritation with her. Even the set of his shoulders proclaimed that Nicky Dolan's woes were none of her concern.

"But the—the biolin . . ." Nicky dared. "Will—will you let me—"

"Nicky, 'tis best to put your past life behind you. Go on from here, from Rosetree, and don't chase after long-ago memories that will hurt you."

"But—" The child started to object, then stopped, swallowing hard what Cecily sensed was disappointment.

She looked up at Ransom, full intending to argue in behalf of the timid waif, but something in the seafarer's scarred face halted her.

Don't chase after long-ago memories that will hurt you . . . Ransom had said, his voice raw, his expression etched with tightly coiled pain. And before, when their mouths had locked, loved, *Don't waste your curses, princess, I've been damned to a far greater depth than you could ever imagine. . . .*

Cecily probed the haunted countenance of Ransom Tremayne as they gathered a laughing Mirabelle and merry Bess, taking them down to Jessamyn's domain.

If you knew the truth, you would run from me, Ransom had once warned Cecily, *run screaming in horror . . .*

But even in spite of Ransom's churlish behavior in the aftermath of their kiss, even despite the clear challenge in

Jessamyn's face as she served the small party scones dripping with honey, Cecily doubted there was anything Ransom could reveal to her that would steal from her the need of his mouth, his hands, the need to ease the haunted expression that never left the handsome planes of his face.

She had nigh shamed herself in the tiny homely chamber at the head of Rosetree's stairs, had nearly given herself to Ransom in a way only a harlot would allow.

Why?

Cecily's gaze skimmed, soft over the jagged scar slashing Ransom's cheekbone. So much pain. So much love. So much passion. And yet, underneath the facade of the gallant captain, the naval hero, protector of the helpless, was there a hazy image of the one person Ransom Tremayne's strength could not heal?

The chipped tea dishes had been cleared from the table before she shook off the web of emotions Ransom had woven about her, and she remembered the true reason she had risked stealing off to Rosetree.

She bent close to that tousled golden hair, her pulses hammering a jerky rhythm as she whispered, "Three nights hence Aunt Honoria is repairing to a theater party. I'll plead sickness, wait for you at the door cut into the garden wall."

Ransom's gaze slashed to hers, piercing, sparking with a triumph that set her nerves on edge yet tantalized her as well. For in those eyes she felt the pull of something deeper even than her father's trouble or her own confusion. Something marvelous, perilous.

Her fingers curled into tight balls as she willed herself not to reach out to the man, so tormented, tempting before her—the man who, in but three nights, would slip into her family's private chambers, a heartbeat away from her own velvet-draped bed.

Chapter Eight

Ransom GLOWERED down at the crumpled mass of brown paper, divested hours past of its burden of honey-shaded wood, and was not at all certain he would not wring Cecily Lansdowne's beautiful neck when next he saw her. "For Master Nicholas Dolan," the footman had decried as he had delivered the mysterious bundle, the servant nigh frightening the awestruck lad into a trance with the blinding gilt trim rimming every inch of his livery.

It had taken Jessamyn a quarter of an hour to coax Nicky into tugging free the wrapping's string, folding the crackling paper away from a case of ebony. But the joy in the child's face as he fumbled eagerly with the catch had twisted an unexpected pang of jealousy in Ransom's chest. And when Nicky raised the polished black lid to reveal below a child-sized violin, Ransom's jaw had clenched as the child's eyes brimmed with wonder.

Ransom stalked to the table and bolted down the glass of brandy he had poured a moment ago. His hand clenched tight upon the cut-glass snifter. Never had he realized how cursed selfish he could be—with his gratitude. With his children. But the knowledge that it had been someone else who had brought stark happiness into Nicky's sorrow-dulled eyes ate at Ransom, the liquor burning a fiery path down his throat, searing him not half so much as the memory of Nicky's face turned up to his, pleading to be allowed to trade his precious marble for the one thing Ransom had forbidden him.

Out of love, Ransom brought himself up sharply. He had wanted the child free of hauntings, wanted him to begin fresh, with all the old pain washed away. Yet despite fierce reluctance, Ransom was forced to admit even now that there had been no pain in Nicky Dolan's face when the child had reverently slipped the small instrument from the case's printed paper lining and cradled it against his sunken little belly. Rather, his peaked features had been wreathed in joy, such as Ransom had seen painted into the faces of the cherubs wreathing the dome of the cathedral in Cannes.

'Twas as if Cecily Lansdowne had gifted Nicky Dolan with the single thing Ransom had been battling so long to give him. Hope.

You were wrong, Tremayne, a voice battered him from within. *Wrong. About Nicky's needs, aye, and about the careless, haughty princess you've spent most of your hours lambasting for her selfishness.*

And you were wrong for what you did to her when you tumbled her back onto the bed. Ransom jammed his fingers back through the unruly waves of his hair, blood pulsing painfully in his loins. Wrong. Aye, it had been inexcusable, the way he had kissed her, touched her, the way he had exacted from her body sensations that had made her writhe beneath him in need.

'Twas none of Cecily's doing, the lust that had raged between them. She had but offered her lips for a child's kiss—the kind obsequious princes offered their chaste maidens at the end of the fairy tales he read to Lacey. But he had deepened the meshing of their mouths into something far more potent, branded her with his lips, his tongue, his hands.

He ground his fingertips into his eyes, wishing that the brandy would dull the pain throbbing beneath his temples. A mistress had once told him he could wring sobs of passion from a fire iron. 'Twas nigh true, he thought, self-loathing a bitter knot in his throat. God knew, he had been taught the arts of the body by masters. Cecily Lansdowne, for all her outward elegance and bravado, was scarce a match for a man who had—

"Nay," Ransom berated himself inwardly. "The past can hold no power over you unless you let it."

But the bracing words he had spoken to every child who had ever crossed Rosetree's threshold were brittle on his tongue, tainted by memories of a cherubic face the color of coffee swirled in thick cream, black ringlets framing fine-boned cheeks, huge eyes bordered by the thickest, most sweetly curling lashes Ransom had ever seen.

Will.

The stab of pain in Ransom's vitals was as sharp-edged and fierce as it had been fifteen years ago when he had burst into the opulent chamber in Satan's Well. Ransom's nostrils flared, assaulted in his memory yet again by the carnage that had confronted him. Even the ever-present stench of violet water had been driven back into the gold-painted wallpaper, the whole room reeking with the sickly sweetness of fresh-spilled blood.

Blood matted in dark, curling hair, congealing upon Will's death-paled brow. But even eternity had not held the power to give the eight-year-old Will peace. The horror the boy had endured had been etched deep into Will's beloved face. The horror that by rights should have been Ransom's own.

Ransom felt the biting sting of tears he had banished years ago, guilt and fury surging through him as though he were once again entrapped in that nightmare room.

God, how he had wanted to draw blood himself. He had been crazed with the need. Snatching up a heavy candlestick, he had charged toward the man sprawled in a drunken sleep across the silken sheetings, crimson stains smearing his beringed fingers.

But he had never reached Will's murderer, had never seen the man's face. Tuxford Wolden's beefy fist had cut Ransom down from behind, driving him into unconsciousness.

Ransom shut his eyes, trying desperately to drag himself

from the past, from the hell that had driven him nigh to madness, but the faceless image of the man in the haunted chamber burned deep behind Ransom's closed lids, his only clear memory that of the huge seal ring that had winked evilly upon one bloodied finger.

A quatrefoil, the seal had been, pierced by a serpent. But never in all his searching had Ransom been able to link the heraldic crest with any family on England's shores. The man had disappeared as certainly as the *Ninon* had, leaving but one legacy. . . .

Ransom's shaking fingers drifted up to the ridge of white flesh raised across his cheek, his stomach churning with the same sick despair that had gripped him when he had awakened that long-ago evening, his hands bound so tight they felt dead, his whole body throbbing as though 'twere one solid mass of bruises. Cackles, hideous cackles, had whirled nauseatingly about him, seeming to thrust shards of crazed grief into the very marrow of his bones. But even those satanic sounds had held not half the terror of the object he had seen glowing in Tuxford Wolden's fist.

Ransom had seen it used only once before—the most vicious means of punishment at the brothel master's disposal—a fleur-de-lis wrought of iron, white hot from the flames.

Compliments o' your sweeting's bedmate, Wolden had chortled, weaving the instrument in a hellish path before Ransom's eyes. *An' a partin' symbol o' me own regard.*

Ransom had not screamed, even as Wolden jeered at him, even as the brand seared deep into flesh. Will's death was an agony too deep for railings, so deep that even physical pain bore no power to pierce it. Which of the brothel-spawned urchins had cut his bonds, freeing him when the rest of the house lay asleep, Ransom did not know.

He bore no memory at all of the hours he must have spent, fighting the ocean's fierce current to reach the cluster of vessels anchored in the small harbor, no memory of gaining the deck of the ship called the *Ninon*. He remembered nothing except the numb agony crushing his soul. That and the sticky flow of blood running down his cheek, the crimson rivulets splashing the knife clutched in his own hand.

Yet despite the fact that he had carved the brand from his cheek, rid himself of Wolden's evil marking, he had but traded one disfigurement for another, both symbols of scars that twisted far deeper—a legacy Ransom could never escape, carved into his features anew each time he glimpsed himself in the shimmering surface of the sea or the silvery plane of a stray mirror.

A dozen perfumed ladies had whispered in husky, bed-chamber tones how dashing the scar made him appear—a pirate, a highwayman, a rogue of the night come to seduce them. But to Ransom's eyes the slash of white teemed with poisons he could not cut out of his soul, though the devil knew he had tried. . . .

"Ransom?" The soft voice from the door made him start, and he felt naked, vulnerable, his emotions as thinly veiled as the curves of Jessamyn's body. The folds of a virginal nightgown flowed over her full breasts, the candlelight outlining the dark circles of her aureoles and catching a dull glint from the thick-iron sides of a stove-battered skillet she was wielding as a makeshift weapon. Ransom averted his eyes even as she pressed one hand to her heart.

"You frightened me half to death, Ransom Tremayne," she accused. "I thought you had said you were taking Lacey back to Tradewinds tonight, and I had conjured at least a dozen cutthroats in the noises you made."

"I was—I mean, I am leaving soon," Ransom allowed wearily, the miles to the separate home he kept for Lacey and himself seeming interminable, burdened as he was this night by the past. He turned his eyes to the thunderheads gathering close about the moon. "'Twas just that Lacey was worried about Nicky—wanted to snuggle up with him until he fell asleep, in case the storm broke."

Jessamyn glided over to the child-worn settee, curling her feet beneath her as she sank down upon it. "He seemed better today, after the package came." She eased the pan to the floor with a dull thud. "I doubt Nicky would have even heard the thunder if—"

"Damn it, you *know* how terrified he gets," Ransom snapped, hating the temper flaring within him.

"Yes. I know how terrified he gets."

The quiet words seemed to hang in the air, echoing with Ransom's own angry tones.

He stalked to the open window, bracing one arm above its cherrywood frame, leaning his aching head upon his lawn-clad bicep. "I'm sorry. I've been a bastard of the first water tonight. 'Tis just . . ." He let the words trail off, unable to cause hurt to well in Jessamyn's blue eyes by telling her that his peace was haunted not only by his past this night, but by the memory of soft lips opening beneath his, of eyes like slumberous violets heavy with the need of him.

Even though Jessamyn had attempted to hide it, Ransom had felt her attachment to him growing; spawned, he was certain, by gratitude that he had helped her escape the life of the streets. It was that growing dependence that had spurred him to purchase a house for Lacey and himself away from Rosetree.

And in the year that had passed since his wide, oak-carved bed had been hauled from Rosetree's chambers, he was certain 'twas the wisest of courses to choose. Sometimes the nights were passing empty, the solitude a screaming pain he wanted to forget. And he was certain Jessamyn, with her lost innocence and loving heart, oft tilted with the same demons. 'Twas best if they were miles apart, unable to breach their loneliness with an impulsive mistake that could only hurt them both the more deeply.

"'Tis that fine lady that has you so troubled. Lady . . ."

"Cecily." Her name sounded so right upon his lips, Ransom caught the flash of hurt within Jessamyn's eyes. "Nay, 'tis a score of other things," he said quickly. "Jagger had a difference of opinion with a customs officer this morn, the *Lacey* was due back from Brazil three weeks ago. And Nicky . . ." Ransom's mouth twisted in self-disgust. "Damn it, Jessie, 'tis absurd how much it bothered me when he got that blasted violin. The lad was sparkling with joy, so stunned with happiness he could not even manage to play the cursed thing. And 'twas all I could do not to scowl when he brought it over to show me."

"You've worked hard with the boy," Jessamyn defended. "'Tis only natural that you should feel some twinge of irritation when a careless butterfly of the ton casts crumbs before the child and he lights up like Lady Aurora's chandeliers."

Nay, a voice inside Ransom whispered, *'twas not a careless gesture, the gift Cecily sent . . . and she is no more a shallow butterfly of the ton than Aurora Lyton-Snow or the woman who placed the coin in your child-hand an eternity ago in Baytown. And you want her, Tremayne . . . want Cecily Lansdowne with the same desperation that has driven moon-drunk sailors to dive from the prows of ships in search of Odysseus' sirens.*

Ransom rolled his aching shoulders back, an emptiness yawning inside him—the emptiness that had spurred him more than once in his nights at Rosetree to walk to Jessamyn's chamber door, even sometimes to curl his fingers about the brass handle. But he had never entered her room, her bed. Just as he would never enter Cecily's.

He stiffened, feeling as if Lucifer's own fingers trailed soft across his spine. *Three nights hence . . .* He could hear Cecily's tense whisper. *Everyone will be gone to the theater . . . I'll plead sickness, wait for you. . . .*

"She is beautiful." Jessamyn's wistful voice shook him from his musings.

Ransom turned to see her regarding him with a longing not quite veiled. "So are you, Jessamyn Smythe," he said, wanting to bring a smile to her face. "And you—"

A sudden muffled thump on the ceiling above them made Ransom stop, turning his gaze upward.

"Lacey." Both he and Jessamyn said the child's name at the same time, their voices tinted with amusement and exasperation, the dangerous currents flowing between them receding for the moment.

"I vow, I'm going to nail the hem of her nightgown to the bed." Ransom shook his head with a smile. "The feather tick has not been stuffed that can keep that child in bed the night through. I still say 'twould be simpler to drag the tick down onto the floor in the first place and let her sleep—"

"Don't even think it! The floor is full of drafts, and besides, a young lady does not—"

"Sleep on the floor like a starving hound." Ransom finished Jessamyn's oft-repeated lecture as he took up a candle and started into the corridor. "Oh well, at least I'll not need to wake Nicky, trying to drag her out from the covers."

"Ransom . . ." The voice was but a whisper, the fingers touching his arm achingly tentative. "We could—could tuck her back into bed, and—and you could stay. . . ."

Jessamyn's fingers reached up, skimming his lips. Ransom looked down at her, tempted. The old crone had tutored her well, and his loins were yet full of wanting . . . wanting another woman, not the one standing before him, her heart in her eyes.

"Lacey's cloak is on the hall peg," was all he said, reaching up to take Jessamyn's hand in his, squeeze it gently before he turned to mount the stairs.

"Ransom."

He paused on the third riser, turning to see her face wreathed in candle shine.

"I know you don't love me. It wouldn't matter."

"Yes it would, Jessie." His voice was rough, tired. "You and I know that better even than most."

But as he turned, continued up the narrow stairs, his heart hurt, not from the expression on Jessamyn's face, but rather, with the memory of violet eyes, wide with wonder as he kissed Cecily's berry-sweet lips.

Love . . .

A knife thrust seemed to twist in his chest, Cecily's features, so beautiful, innocent, mingling in his memory with shadings of Will's coffee-dark eyes. Aye, love mattered. Ransom bit back the welling of despair in his throat. But oft times 'twas not enough.

Chapter Nine

MOORSTON'S ROSES WERE GREENING, twining pale shoots from the tough, thorn-sparred wood deadened over winter. Cecily drifted her fingers over the tender April-kissed leaves, imagining the blossoms that would droop heavy from their stems when summer blew hot upon the city. She would not be there to see them. Long before July she would be carted off to Briarton, or, if her father intended her to sample more of the social whirl, to Brighton-upon-the-Sea's balmy shores. And by the time Cecily returned, either to endure London's season yet again or to culminate preparations for a wedding, the promise in the green sprigs would be already frozen by winter's breath.

She tucked her feet more tightly beneath her, shifting the volume of Byron upon her lap as she stared moodily into the tangle of rose vines. She had stolen out the garden door to escape the niggling fears and doubts that yapped about her peace like fractious pups, yet even here, with the sweet spring breezes toying with her curls, she could not escape the presence of Ransom Tremayne.

He was like this garden, holding the promise of incredible beauty within a rough shell of stone, only to snatch it away, leaving nothing but a bittersweet longing, an emptiness that seeped into her very core.

From the night she had first seen him, he had loosed in her

emotions so potent, devastating, she had never experienced anything like them in her life. Loathing, rage, then respect, admiration, jealousy, and now . . . passion, aye, and something more.

Cecily closed her eyes, her pulse racing at the memory of his mouth upon hers. It had been so strange, the lulling power he exerted over her, the draining of all that she was into his body. Never once had he seemed out of control, yet in the very leashing of his passion, the very skill with which he blended his lean frame with hers, there had been a desperation far greater than her own.

What would it be like to break the chains he had bound about himself? Shatter the leash he held over the passion that had blazed in his eyes? A tingle of anticipation shivered up her spine. 'Twould be the stuff of dreamings, Ransom Tremayne's lovemaking. And to gain his heart—

She caught her lip between her teeth, her stomach trembling. Nay, 'twould be impossible—a love between a seafaring rogue and the daughter of one of England's most honored families. Even if she offered to defy her aunt, her father, and dash with her Ransom to the anvil at Gretna Green, the proud Tremayne would never go. *If you knew the truth, you would run from me in horror. . . .*

His words echoed in her mind. Yet she sensed 'twould not be she who fled if Ransom ever chose to reveal the agony locked in his past. 'Twas Ransom who was running . . . fleeing some pain too great for even his daunting inner strength to bear. What phantom from his past could fill his eyes with such anguish, self-loathing . . . fear? She had seen it, just a whisper, the slightest hint of some secret terror in his lean, sun-bronzed face. And it had been that shading of fear in the countenance that seemed hewn of raw courage that had clutched Cecily's heart in a fist of loving.

Aye, *loving.*

The realization struck her with the warm, welling glow of molten sunlight. How could she *not* love Ransom Tremayne? A man who bore the wistful quality of a knight-errant bent on some impossible quest, tilting with windmills, aye, but with very real dragons as well, in a world that had long since stopped believing in the power of a single man.

She loved him. And yet, what of that other side to the man she scarce knew, the dark side she had glimpsed the night in Drury Lane and again at Lady Lyton-Snow's ball? If Ransom Tremayne were truly all that he seemed, why did she sense he was secreting something away from the world? 'Twas as though his face were cast in shadow and in sunlight, and the blending of dark enigmas and shining kindness disturbed even as it intrigued.

The warmth that had enveloped her faded to the slightest chill, her memory suddenly conjuring the nigh predatory expression that had hardened his face when she had mentioned the hell-ship *Ninon.*

Why did she not swirl a midnight cape about Ransom and be done with it? she thought in self-disgust. 'Twas absurd, to allow unfounded suspicions to run wild. He had given her no reason to doubt him, even his spates of anger having been grounded in his fierce sense of honor. And he had agreed to aid her in extricating her father from whatever difficulty he was embroiled in.

Her father.

A twinge of guilt shot through Cecily, and she shifted uncomfortably upon the marble bench. Since her father had deserted her at Moorston, she had spared precious little thought to the troubles that had so lately consumed her peace of mind. 'Twas as though she were Cook's little girl Emmie, flouncing off to pout when she was denied a taste of the icing spoon. But the sense of betrayal ran far deeper than being deprived of a fingerful of frosting.

"Father cared not enough to even speak to me before he ran off," Cecily grumbled aloud, her mouth set in belligerence. "'Twould be folly for me to worry myself to a shade over him. Tonight Ransom will come, delve through Father's journals, and by the morrow we should bear some idea of who is tormenting—"

"Tormenting?" The velvety purr behind her made Cecily

nigh jump from her skin. She spun from the bench, the book in her lap flying to the ground, her skirts tangling immodestly above trim ankles.

Her hands unconsciously knotted into fists as she stared into the face of Lord Bayard Sutton, the aggravation that had been besetting her whenever she was in his presence swelling into sudden and definite dislike.

"Thunder in Hades!" The words were out before she could stop them. "Have you nothing better to do than creep about, frightening—" She bit off the sentence, appalled at her lack of manners yet fuming at the expression upon Sutton's urbane features. There was a slyness about his heavy-lidded eyes, as if he had been watching her for far too long, mayhap knew far too much, yet hid his cunning beneath a veneer of brittle charm.

"Frightening, my pet? I would not dream of attempting to frighten you. However, there are those who are so addled as to . . ." A laugh rippled low from his throat. *"Fear* me."

Cecily gave her rumpled skirts an angry tug. "Mayhap if you were not always popping out of corners—"

"The footman announced me from the garden door, but you were so lost in thought, it seems you failed to hear him. Come now, dearest, 'twas hardly my fault. Be a good girl and beg pardon as you did when a child."

"I am not a child anymore." She clenched her teeth against a flaring of irritation, remembering the stricken look upon Jessamyn Smythe's face when temper had last taken the place of common courtesy. "I'm passing old enough to know when I have been unforgivably rude. I am sorry, Uncle Bayard."

"Nay, child, think no more of it. 'Tis obvious you are not yourself."

A sudden wariness stole through Cecily, her fingers curling into the primrose cambric of her gown as her mind raced back to the moments before she had realized she was not alone in the garden. She had been muttering her thoughts aloud as she had when a girl, and, she was certain, she had spoken Ransom's name, mayhap even betrayed their plan for tomorrow night. She bent down with a strained laugh to retrieve her book, hoping 'twould allow time for the guilty flush to leave her cheeks.

"The season has not quite been what I expected," she said, trying to deflect the probing questions in Sutton's countenance before he verbalized them.

"Not what you expected?" Was there a subtle edge to Sutton's voice? "How not? From all appearances, you are the toast of London, with the most eligible beaus in England battling for your favors. Stake me, but at the last entertainment you could spare not even one dance for me. A dance you had promised . . ."

Cecily searched his features for some sign of anger, remembering well the threat that had been in his silken tones the day at the market when he had exacted her word. A dance in exchange for not telling her father about her outrageous behavior. *Blackmail.* The word reared a face far too horrible to be linked with the suave, smiling visage before her.

"As I remember, you left the ball somewhat early," Cecily said, examining a smudge of dirt on her palm. "I was . . . quite disappointed."

Small white teeth showed in a tight smile. "Oh, aye. 'Twas most evident. But there will be many more balls in our future." Sutton reached out his hand, his gaze meeting hers. Cecily started inwardly at the power that lurked within the brown depths of his eyes, a ruthless strength of will she had not imagined.

"Come." Sutton gave a laugh laced with an aura of unsettling pleasure, as though he sensed the prickling of nervousness working through her. "You may make amends by allowing me the privilege of walking through this garden with the most sought-after belle in London upon my arm."

Cecily's gaze flicked down to the crook of his sleeve. She hesitated a moment, again feeling as though she had been silkily maneuvered into a spider's web. But 'twas such an innocuous request—to show an old family friend about the garden. And the past times they had met, she *had* acted like a spoiled wretch. She forced her lips to curve in a polite smile and let the fingers of one hand drift down lightly upon

Sutton's arm. "If you would like to start down this path, Aunt Honoria has placed some lovely Grecian statues amidst the shrubbery."

"You know well the nooks and grottoes hidden away from prying eyes, do you? I trust you've had no swains sneaking in through the side gate to tryst with you?"

Cecily looked quickly up to Sutton's face, surprised that anyone else, especially the elegant Baron of Wythe, knew of the vine-obscured door. Yet in the next instant she was filled with puzzlement and a colder feeling crept about the edges of her mind. Of course Sutton knew the garden intimately. Had he not been there with her father the night she had first seen the black-caped figure?

Sutton had claimed that his own fate was linked to her father's secret misery—the bearer of the cards with the unfamiliar words scrawled upon them as dangerous to the prominent politician as they were to Lord Lansdowne. Would it not prove most logical—aye, and far more honorable—to reveal her fears for her father to Bayard Sutton rather than stealing about like a sneak thief, rooting through her father's belongings? Ask the baron to explain the agony that was driving her father to the brink of collapse? 'Twas lunacy, these dark humors that seemed to beset her whenever Lord Sutton was about. Naught but her imagination run a-maying.

She tipped her face toward the baron, her lips parted to speak.

"Perdition!" She squeaked the oath as the corner of another marble bench caught her thigh, making her stumble against the elegantly clothed shoulder of Lord Sutton. The feel of his hand tightening about her to steady her made her feel vaguely unclean, and the unreadable expression upon his thin face drove away all thought of confiding in him.

"I fear the influence of the company you have been keeping is showing, my dear," Bayard observed, giving his head a grave shake. "You never cast out oaths at Briarton."

You never heard me, Cecily thought, the beginning of a headache knotting at the base of her skull. "Annie and Cook used to pepper my tongue when I was little," she said airily, "so I merely saved all of my cursing until I grew too fast for them to catch."

"Nay, I yet avow 'tis the fault of the low individuals you favor with your smiles. I know full well what *soaring value* you hold upon politeness, but 'tis most unwise for an heiress of impeccable family, the like of you, to be seen with a brawling fortune hunter of most questionable birth."

"Ransom Tremayne is no fortune hunter," Cecily burst out with passion, "and when he was fighting outside Drury Lane, 'twas because—"

"So 'tis as I feared," Sutton interrupted with a solemn expression. "This Tremayne person has insinuated himself into your good opinion?"

Cecily's cheeks burned and she felt as vulnerable as a fear-frozen rabbit at the jaws of the canniest of wolves. She swallowed, her gaze skittering away, suddenly aware of the veiled threats Sutton had made toward Ransom in the entry at Winterscape. And the accusations Ransom had flung out in return.

"Of course I have a good opinion of Captain Tremayne. Most of London does. Why, Lady Lyton-Snow—"

"Has never been the wisest of women, as I am certain you must have heard. It seems she ran off with her father's master of the horse when she was—"

"Lavinia has already raked that old scandal over the coals," Cecily said. "I have no interest in hearing it again."

"Well, then, my dear, mayhap you *would* bear an interest in hearing a bit of truth about your Captain Tremayne? You cannot help but be aware that he and I are . . . shall we say, not on the most intimate of terms."

Cecily brushed a wayward curl from her cheek, feeling distinctly uncomfortable at the memory of Ransom's bronzed hand knotted into a fist, a fist only her own interference had saved from landing the baron against Winterscape's entry wall. "I think 'twould be best if you kept whatever quarrel the two of you hold between yourselves."

"Impossible, when the bold wretch makes to seduce you beneath my very—I mean, your father's very nose."

"Seduce? Captain Tremayne has made no attempt to seduce me! He has been the soul of honor and—"

"A man of Tremayne's ilk has no honor. Witness the child he drags about with him in the guise of his legal daughter."

Cecily wanted desperately to turn on Sutton, rise to Lacey's defense, but wariness had spun about Cecily with the certainty that already she had revealed to Sutton far too much.

She forced herself to feign disinterest, pointing to a small alcove cut in the garden wall wherein reposed a headless mock-Greek goddess. "This is Aunt Honoria's most especial favorite." Cecily tried to adopt a careless tone to avert the subject of Ransom and his child. "A French artist copied it outside the Parthenon and—"

"Cecily, Lacey Tremayne is bastard born. The fruit of Tremayne's *grande passion* for a vulgar French dancer, by the name of Corianda Verney."

Cecily fought back the twisting of pain in her chest at the sound of that beautiful name . . . a name that lilted like tiny, tinkling bells on a frost-rimed night. She could picture every feature of the unknown woman's face, Lacey's pert countenance matured to a sable and ivory beauty totally opposite from the bronze and gold rough-hewn perfection of the child's father.

Lacey, little Lacey with her dusky curls and melting dark eyes stained with a shame not of her own making. Bastardy. And for Sutton in his supercilious arrogance to be using that faultless stain in order to horrify Cecily—hoping to offend her sensibilities so that she would turn away not only from Ransom, but from the bright-eyed child who had so enchanted her from the crow's nest of a play mast . . .

Cecily's lips compressed in a white line, her fingers withdrawing from the baron's spotless sleeve. "A dancer, you say. And French." Cecily fetched a dramatic sigh. "Well, then, that must be why the child is so graceful and bears such a sharp wit. Or mayhap 'tis because of the loving way in which her father is seeing to her care. Now, if you will excuse me, Uncle—"

"Her 'father' should not be 'seeing to her care' at all."

Sutton startled her by cutting through her words. "There are scores of estimable nannies about London, and governesses well schooled in dealing with the taming of children. Tremayne's dragging about of his . . . side-slip of a child is but one more example of his ill-breeding."

Cecily was stunned at the force of the anger that snapped within her, the need to rise to the defense of Ransom and his daughter surging fiercely along every nerve in her body. "And so, you have now become an expert upon the raising up of children, as well as upon the Poor Law?" She let a hard laugh trip off of her tongue, and tossed her head in ill-concealed scorn. "May I make so bold as to suggest that you tend to your legislating and leave the nurturing of babes to men like Ransom, seeing as you bear no children of your own."

"Yet." The single word thudded through Cecily's indignation like a chill stone.

Her gaze darted to Sutton's, and she misliked the expression veiled in those bland brown eyes. "I . . . don't understand."

"Don't you? At three and forty years of age 'tis hardly startling that I should be considering founding a family, getting myself an heir."

"I . . . I suppose not. 'Tis just that you've ne'er shown the least inclination in, er . . . wooing . . . in all the years I've known you."

"Aye, but at that time I was not a prominent member of the Whig party, in need of a hostess." Sutton ran his tongue over his thin upper lip, his nostrils pinched with smugness. "A political hostess possessed of great beauty, impeccable lineage, and the ability to bewitch any man or woman who passes the threshold of Wythe House."

Cecily felt his gaze travel an appraising path from the crown of her head to the toes of her slippers. She shifted in crawling discomfort beneath his regard, and turned, ostensibly to examine a small rose thorn. "I am certain that there are any number of most intelligent older women, well versed in the ways of court, who will be honored with your attentions."

"And well versed in expressing their own opinions? Nay, I want no woman embarrassing me or my guests with feminine drivel concerning the affairs of men. I like my ladies younger . . ." Sutton reached out his fingers, touching her ebony curls. "With soft smiles and winning ways, to be molded as I see fit."

Cecily felt a sour twisting in the pit of her stomach at what Sutton was insinuating, the headache threatening a moment before becoming stark reality as the blood pounded in her temples. "Molded?" Cecily echoed in an acid-sweet voice, sickened by the expression upon Bayard Sutton's face. "I fear you are mistaken, Uncle Bayard. You do not need a wife—what you seek is month-old bread."

With a toss of her head, she jerked her curls from beneath the man's fingers and started to run lightly down the garden path.

"My Lady Cecily—"

The low menace in the voice stopped her, and she turned, letting the defiance blaze openly in her face.

"You have grown into a beautiful woman." The brown eyes roved dispassionately over the curves thinly concealed beneath the layer of fine cambric. But there was no fire in Bayard Sutton's gaze, only a cold disinterest that unnerved Cecily more than any absurd protestation of devotion she had ever received. "I need a beautiful woman. And you . . . I fear your father has not appeared in the best of health of late. You might well need a protector, sooner than you think."

"What do you mean, need a protector? I am quite capable of looking after myself, and Father will be back in but a few weeks to attend my ball. He would not miss—"

"Of course he would not, my dear, unless circumstances beyond his control prevented him. But unfortunately ill-health and emotional strain do not oft pick the most opportune times to assert themselves."

Cecily felt the waves of her darkest fears wash over her, Sutton's hintings at her father's misery, mayhap even his death, driving the bravado from her with the force of a fist being driven into her stomach. "You think—think Papa is unwell?"

She watched, nails digging deep into her palms as a smile oozed over Sutton's features. "Who can say?" he purred. "I can only trust you will do nothing to, say . . . cause him further pain." The baron's eyes shifted up to the glistening window set in the wall of Charleton Lansdowne's abandoned chambers.

Cecily followed Sutton's gaze to the room she and Ransom would search when night had twice again darkened the city, well certain she had been most silkily warned.

Chapter Ten

THE WIND CREPT with chill fingers under the hem of Cecily's nightgown, the breezes nipping at her ankles and setting her knees a-tremble. She shivered beneath the shielding of her dark sapphire cloak, her eyes darting nervously to the hulking form of Moorston silhouetted against the night sky. The windows in the new section of the town house glimmered with a sly aura, as though the house itself bore eyes with which to watch her. But the chambers in the far wing remained thankfully dark, even the loyal Bess having been bustled off to pass the evening with the other servants about the warm kitchen fire.

Pray God the girl stayed there long enough for Ransom to gain the clues that they so desperately needed, Cecily thought, wetting parched lips. And pray God that Aunt Honoria found the entertainments at this night's theater diverting enough to hold her fickle attentions, lest the whole of Duke Harry's party descend upon the quiet house too soon. . . .

Then again, it might well be that she was out here in the night air courting lung fever for naught. Cecily wrapped her arms tight about her ribs, glaring at the narrow slice of street visible through the partially opened garden door. What if, indeed, Ransom did not come—if he had forgotten he was to meet her here, or was delayed, or failed to find the garden gate. Glory knew, 'twas difficult enough to see in the dark-stone wall even when the sun was high over London's innumerable chimneys. And in the night, 'twas all but impossible.

Cecily squinted her eyes, trying to pierce the inky shadows. But the winding tendrils of vines that had appeared so innocuous in the afternoon sun now seemed to clutch with skeletal fingers at the rough stone, clawing their way up from the dark king's domain. Even the wind had taken up an evil, hissing sound, as it tangled around the gnarled branches of the trees.

Cecily's gaze skimmed yet again about the garden, her heart thudding dully in her chest, her pulse light, where it beat near the delicate hollow of her throat. 'Twas a night for the dead, old Cook would have said, a night for those wronged to go a-stalking their tormentors. A night for secrets.

Nay, not secrets, Cecily upbraided herself sharply. A night to gain answers. A night to grasp some measure of control over a life that seemed to be careening like a whirlwind, frightening in its uncertainty and intensity. Cecily tried to stifle the shiver that prickled along her nape, one particular distant shadow seeming to take on a shape that chilled her more certainly than the brisk night wind.

She could almost see a huge beast in the inky darkness where she knew a sculptured yew bush resided, the light from the distant window twinkling through the trimmed branches giving the nightmarish image eyes of glittering yellow.

Eyes . . . Cecily battled to quell the fluttering of panic in her stomach. 'Twas as if the whole garden seethed with them, borne, no doubt, of Sutton's suspicious words two days past. Yet 'twas absurd even to consider the possibility of the Whigs' brightest hope skulking about rose trees, playing at Bow Street with a spy glass.

'Twas naught but guilt that goaded her so. But why, then, could she feel the hostile eyes boring into her back, then in a few heartbeats more could feel them search her face, feel in her imagination whatever foe lurked in the shadows grappling for her dark secrets. 'Twas insanity, Cecily knew, the creations of a vivid imagination that more than once had cast her into the deep, smothering terror only a child can know. Yet even the adult logic she now held claim to could not dispel the foreboding that lay like a heavy cold stone upon her chest.

"Blackguard!" Cecily hissed between clenched teeth. "Curse the man for forcing me to sit here, half freezing, waiting. 'Twould serve him right if I threw the bolt across the door and left *him* stranded in the chill till dawn." She thrust her fingers deeper into the warming velvet of her cloak. "If he does not arrive in the next five minutes, I'll go into Father's rooms, rake through them myself."

The crack of a twig nearby made Cecily start, her palms dampening with sweat, heart bounding.

"Alone? How fortunate." Warm as brandy, and more drugging, the rich voice wisped from the night. Cecily spun toward the sound, despising the quavering of her knees.

"Who is there?" she demanded in her most regal tones, gauging the distance from where she stood to the door, judging the likelihood that any of the servants would hear her if she screamed.

"You were expecting yet another caller? Tell me, Lady Cecily, do you make it a habit to invite more than one man to your bedchambers in a night?"

Cecily felt the fury rise high in her cheekbones, scarce noticing the barely leashed tension in Ransom as he strode toward her at a leisurely gait. She did not know whether to fling her arms about the broad-shouldered form emerging from the darkness or to bash her fist into the glinting white flash of his smile.

"You—you—"

"Blackguard?" Ransom supplied with the slightest shading of bitterness. "Rogue? Rakehell is always an epithet that can be most effective, or—"

"Don't you dare make jest of me, you dolt! I'm chilled to my marrow, in danger of being disowned by my family— should they ever discover what I am about this night—and

I've been nigh in the state of a Bedlamite, conjuring terrors out of mist."

"The world has enough real dragons without you stitching together new ones, princess." His voice was a caress, so achingly tender it drained the anger from her, and a measure of the foreboding as well. One bronzed finger reached out, tracing a curl of her unbound hair with a reverence that made Cecily's throat constrict with emotion. "Pretty," he breathed, lifting the silken skein to his lips, rubbing them gently against the dark tresses. "'Tis so pretty this way, tumbled loose about you. I wish I could see it lying soft against your skin . . . dusk and roses and honey sweet. . . ."

"I'm not sweet. I'm angry." Cecily warred against the tremor in her voice and against the welling of relief stealing through her at his presence. But even her pride could not bar her from the strong arms offering such a wondrous haven. She closed the space between them, burying her face in the spice-scented warmth of his shirtfront, reveling in the slightly unsteady thrumming of his heart, the tenderness in the hand that whispered over her face.

"I know how hard this is for you, love," he said, resting his lips against the crown of her head. "If there were any other way . . ." He let the words trail off, and Cecily burrowed more closely against his hard frame, feeling warm, protected . . . loved, for the first time since she had jolted into London in her father's traveling coach. Bitter-sweet joy seemed to crush her chest. Ransom Tremayne had called her "love." . . .

"I vow I—" Ransom's voice cracked. "I almost did not come. Was afraid of what—" He stopped, but Cecily could feel the war waging within him still. "God, I don't want to hurt you."

She pulled away slightly, struggling to make out the features night obscured, the brief feeling of refuge she had known in Ransom's arms palling at the tension rife within his sharp-chiseled face.

"You came here to *help* me, like you help everyone around you," she said softly, her fingers reaching up, smoothing the lines that creased his forehead, the night-wing satin of his eyebrow, the raised ridge of scar upon his left cheek. "Ransom Tremayne, you are—are the most truly *good* person I have ever met. Noble and loving. I know you would never hurt me on purpose."

The choked sound that came from his chest seemed born of some unbearable pain. "Don't, Cecily," he rasped out, his whole body stiffening against her. "Don't weave me into Robin of the Hood, or one of Byron's imaginings. You'll be sadly disappointed." He gently eased her from his arms, turning, the faint glow from one of Moorston's windows catching his face in dark-gold light.

"I've done . . . done more things that I am ashamed of than I can count. I'm capable of a cruelty deeper than you can imagine. And of betrayal . . ." He raked one hand wearily through the rich waves of his hair. "God, I never knew I was capable of betrayal."

Cecily lay one palm gently on his shoulder, the shudder she felt coursing through him pricking at her own unease. "Ransom, what is it?"

The sound that tore from his lips was harsh. "Guilt. By Christ, I've felt it oft enough to know its less subtle shadings. But it doesn't matter. I cannot stop—*damn.*" The oath grated from his lips. "Let's just get it over with."

Cecily stood, her feet feeling woven into the garden floor as she watched Ransom spin away from her, stalking in a taut stride toward the dark wing of the town house. Betrayal. Guilt. The anguish in Ransom's strong features terrified her, confused her, made her want to draw him back into her arms, drive away whatever demons bedeviled him this night.

But she scooped up the hem of her gown, hastening after the rigid set of Ransom's shoulders as he strode to the heavy oak door she had slipped out of an hour before.

"I left a candle lit just inside the door," she said as she caught up with him. "I didn't dare bring a lamp, for fear the servant might see it and come to investigate."

"'Twill be enough." Ransom opened the portal. The single flame from the taper gilded the unyielding square of his jaw, a hinting of ruthlessness, pain evident in the lips that had wooed Cecily's own so sweetly.

Cecily tried to quell the hurt that rose inside her as Ransom grasped the candlestick in one hand, his eyes hard. All traces of the tenderness he had shown her but moments before had vanished, as if he suddenly despised her, or was it—the thought flitted dark across Cecily's consciousness— that he despised himself?

"Your father's rooms . . ." Ransom said. "We'll have to hasten, unless you want the whole house to discover you are running about in your nightgown with a man."

"I—'Tis this way." Cecily brushed past him, blinking tears from her eyes. 'Twas as if he had meant to humiliate her, anger her, as if he were trying valiantly to erect some kind of wall between them now. She was the one about to act out the most loathsome betrayal she could imagine, and she needed desperately the warmth Ransom had wrapped about her while he had held her in the night-shaded garden.

The candle flame's reflection flickered upon high-polished cuirasses, gorgets, and fierce-visored helms as she and Ransom stole quickly up the corridor, even the door to Charleton Lansdowne's chambers seeming to yawn black, somehow frightening. But had it been a freshly dug grave, Cecily would have plunged into it without a glance, fired by her battered pride. She swept the cloak from her shoulders and tossed it upon a chair, her head high as a queen on the gallows as Ransom stepped into the room behind her.

The candle holder made a muffled rasp as Ransom settled it upon the desktop, the circle of candlelight limning the contents of the chamber. Cecily could see his face darken with impatience, his eyes hard and cold as ice-cast emeralds. "Journals." Ransom's voice was that of a stranger. "You said something once about your father having journals."

"Aye. Since before I was born. He loves to scribble down notes, press things between the pages to save. And then, when he can't sleep at night, he pores through them—" She stopped, hating the whispering of longing in her voice, as she fingered the memories of wondrous security like a strand of elusive pearls, the quiet beauty of the past, well-loved and warm in her hand. Remembrances far too precious to cast before the hard, icy-visaged man before her. She stiffened, suddenly feeling vulnerable, somehow betrayed, as the reality of this night swept away the sensations of safety, the love she had relied on her whole life leaving only bitterness.

"And your father . . ." The hard slash of Ransom's mouth made her want to strike him. "He fit all these scribblings into one cursed volume?"

"Of course not! He filled one nigh every year." Cecily stalked over to where the leatherbound volumes lined a cherrywood shelf. "He never travels anywhere without them. When he disappeared, 'twas that which frightened me most of all. He left them. All of them, here at Moorston. I've known Papa to forget his cravats and nightshirts. Once he even forgot me when he was in the midst of dissecting Machiavelli with one of his friends." She drew out one of the heavy journals, her tones ragged with a pain she could not disguise. "But never these."

She saw a flash of something in Ransom's eyes, his strong hand seeming to strain toward her, then halt, the fingers curling into a fist as he turned toward the shelf.

"'Tis fair providence he left them behind this time, wherever the blazes he's hied off to." Cecily couldn't bear the sarcasm biting deep in Ransom's voice. Detached. He sounded so detached, as though her father were no more real to him than the brass-work dolphins writhing up the fire irons in the chamber's cold grate. As though *she* were nothing to him . . . less than nothing.

"Damn you, Ransom Tremayne." The room blurred before eyes dewed with tears. "Do not dare—"

"Dare what?" He wheeled on her, his eyes spitting a fury she did not understand, mingled in the emerald depths with stark despair.

Dare to promise haven with your lips, your hands, her heart screamed, *dare to mesmerize me with eyes that can be so haunting, so alive with passion, only to snatch it away, leaving me even more empty than before.*

"Don't you dare lash at my father with your cursed sharp

tongue," Cecily spat back. "Else you can get the blazes out of here and go—go *play pirate.*" She fought to make the last words drip with scorn, saw Ransom's face pale, his lips twisting as though she had dealt him a well-aimed blow.

Her fingers dug deep into the leather binding of the journal she held as she spun away, wanting to block out the flash of hurt she detected in Ransom's lean visage, needing to place distance between herself and the man she hated . . . loved?

Nay. She heard Ransom's muttered oath, heard the thunk of volumes being shifted against the wooden shelving as he tore through the pages with a vengeance. A vengeance she did not understand. Would never understand, because he would not allow it. Sickened by falsehoods, weary of half truths, secrets, she paced to the mullioned glass panes revealing the night. The leaded frame even still lay bolted heavily from the inside, as all the windows had been in the long-past days when Londoners feared the Mohocks, bands of roving ruffians reveling in plundering any homes left unprotected. That cruel society had long since died, Cecily thought numbly, yet Moorston had not yet shed the reminders of that past peril.

Oblivious to Ransom's mutterings behind her, Cecily ran one finger over the iron latch, tears knotting in a lump in her chest. Aye, when this horror was over, for her father, for herself, would she not be a little like the panes now reflecting her pinched, pale face? Never be able to totally unbar the emotions she had once taken so for granted? Would she ever bear that former unshakable confidence in Charleton Lansdowne? In herself?

When in God's name had she grown so cursed weak? Tears knotted in a hot lump in her chest. She had always seen herself as fiercely independent, shunning any who wished to coddle her, shelter her, ever ready to confront any adversity with naught but her own wits to shield her. Yet until this moment she had never realized how deeply she had depended upon that wellspring of security that was her childhood. She had wrapped that pristine sense of safety about herself like a cavalier girding on his armor.

And Ransom Tremayne . . . had she not flung her heart open to him with the wild abandon of that headstrong child she had once been, only to have it crushed?

"Damnation!" She started at his frustrated oath as yet another thick book joined its fellows in a pile of rejection. "Not one of these blasted things bears a date even close to the time the *Ninon* sailed. Is that thing you are clutching to your bosom, by any chance, the year—"

Cecily yanked open the book in her hand, her eyes flitting over the page. "'Tis from when I was seven," she hissed back at him in a harsh whisper, taking an absurd pleasure in his irritation, glad he was floundering amongst the pages, despite the fact that she herself had brought him here in hopes of aiding her father. "Unless you have the desire to read about when I got my first pony and how I held a fete for my dolls 'neath a cedar tree, there would be naught here of interest to you."

"Blast it, Cecily, you know damned well what I'm searching for! If you'd give me some cursed help . . ."

Cecily felt the challenge in his voice despite its hushed tones, his savage need for a verbal battle, but she bore precious little energy for anything, losing herself in a melancholy that before had so rarely beset her. Crooking one arm about the thick journal, she walked to the velvet-covered feather tick of her father's great bed, curling up on its lush softness. Candlelight played in flickering circles upon pages ivoried with age as she opened the volume.

Grief, dull gray numbing stole over her as her fingers skimmed over a crumbling, lovingly dried crown of daisies, a faded blue ribbon, a child's glove, impossibly tiny, exquisitely embroidered. Lost. All lost. Moments vanished along with the little girl who had woven the sticky green stems of the flowerets together one long-vanished summer morn.

Cecily's gaze drifted over bits of her past, fragments of a time that seemed now nigh as misty as the fantasy worlds she had once read of . . . *took my sunshine to the booksellers today for book I promised her . . . would have none of fairy tales. Naught but a volume of Chaucer would satisfy her highness, though I tried to bribe her with peppermint drops. . . .*

A stab of pain went through her as she remembered her father's long-suffering expression, and the wondrous anticipation she had felt that long-ago day with the beloved book clutched in her seven-year-old hands. Simple. It had all been so simple then. Or had the beauty of those days been but a lie as well?

She traced her thumb over the carefully scribed lines, fighting the sense of disillusionment, the weariness. God, she was so tired . . . She started to close the book, her lids sliding over gritty eyes. But in a heartbeat her hand froze, catching the page she held open, her eyes widening in a sick, twisting dread as she battled to focus them upon the single phrase that had leapt out at her in that instant, grasping her throat in talons of fear from the midst of the myriad scrawled lines.

. . . Nigh murdered my own child this day . . . tenant cast sack full of kittens into lake . . . though could not swim, Cecily plunged in after . . . rescued . . . Child . . . willful, spoiled, wonderful child . . . Ninon, if you had but lived to see her grow, you would be so proud of our little daughter. . . .

Ninon.

The name seemed to scream through Cecily's consciousness, icing her skin with chill sweat, wrenching her stomach with stunned terror. Her father had called her mother Ninon, in place of the formal Anastasia. A pet name, Ninon, brimming with love, affection, its tones apparently so painful after her death that Charleton Lansdowne had not been able to utter it aloud, even to his daughter. And that loving name had been given to the ship that had sailed into a legend of darkness, hell.

"Blast it." Ransom's curse made Cecily bound from the bed, the journal clattering to her feet, her breath caught, hard, in her chest. "'Tis gone. That one thrice-cursed year, vanished as if it never exist— Cecily." The hushed word clutched about Cecily's throat, and she could feel her guilt, fear, betraying her to Ransom's piercing gaze.

Slowly, so slowly, he eased the journal he had held back into place, his eyes never leaving hers as he paced toward her. "Cecily, what the devil did you—"

"Nothing! I found nothing!" She couldn't stop herself from snatching up the fallen volume and skittering back before Ransom's whip-taut visage. "I want you to leave now. Get out of here before—"

"I'm not taking a step from this chamber until you bloody well give me that book."

"Nay, damn you, I—"

"Don't make me tear it out of your hands, lady. I vow I will if you force me to— Christ!" The sudden oath made Cecily jump, every nerve in her body snapping like wildfire with the stark sense of danger. Voices. In the hall there were voices. . . .

She and Ransom both froze, their battle of wills over the journal lost in a far more immediate peril. If anyone should find her here, alone, with a man . . .

"Go! You have to—"

She sensed, rather than heard, Ransom swear savagely as he lunged for the window, throwing back the stiff bolt. "Damn you, Cecily Lansdowne, this isn't finished yet," he ground out, flinging his lean-muscled body over the marble windowsill and gazing back. "Will never be finished unless you bear the courage to make it so. If you don't show yourself at Tradewinds by tomorrow eve, I vow I'll crawl into your cursed bed and lie in wait until you're forced to face me."

"Tradewinds?"

"'Tis the house I share with Lacey, near St. James. Damn it, Cecily, be there or—"

His eyes blazed for an instant on the leatherbound journal clutched against her, his gaze flicking over its gilt edge to where her breasts swelled against the thin fabric of her nightgown, lacing his threat with a darker meaning that tingled over the skin he had brushed with his hard palm, his hot mouth. Muffled, indistinct, the voices in the hallway carried through the hallway, one shrill, belligerent, the other with tones of most definite distress. Lavinia. Mirabelle.

Cecily felt the blood drain from her face. "Sweet God, Ransom," she choked. "Go!"

In what seemed a heartbeat, the burnished gold of his hair vanished into moonlight, the rough iron bolt scraping Cecily's knuckles as she hastened to refasten the window. She darted over to her father's desk, snatching up the candle with one hand while she clutched the binding of the betraying journal in her other. Her fingers trembled, stung by the certainty that guilt was emblazoned across her face and by the certainty that Lavinia's sly eyes would close upon any hint of weakness with the benign savagery of a silk-garbed barracuda.

Cecily started to the chamber door, battling to school her features into an expression of sleepy indifference, but the sudden clarity of the words her cousins were speaking made her pause, listen.

"Lavinia, nay!" Mira's voice crept through the small aperture. "Do not you dare . . . barging in . . . blasting poor Cec . . . such hideous tidings . . ."

"'Tis our duty to break the news to her ourselves, sister. Just think . . ."

Tidings. Hideous tidings. Confusion stirred in Cecily, died as her blood turned to ice, her mind whirling with black-cloaked figures, secrets laced in evil, her father's sudden flight. There was but one person tied so deeply to Cecily's heart 'twould bring that strained hush to Mira's gentle voice.

Cecily flung wide the heavy door, bolting out to where the two sisters confronted each other, yet garbed in their theater-going finery. Lavinia squeaked, Mirabelle's features washing gray with fright at the apparition that had descended upon them in a whirl of pale nightgown and eyes that Cecily knew must be dark with anxiety.

"Merciful goodness." Mira pressed her hands to her chest. "Cecily, you frightened us to death. We thought—"

"My father, Mira, is he . . ."

Cecily saw Mirabelle's cheeks pale. "How—How did you know 'twas—"

"Have you been listening at windows, cousin?"

Cecily's nostrils were assailed by the reek of lavender water and new-sewn muslin as Lavinia swept between Cecily and the waxen Mira.

"Nay, tell me—"

"What Mira was attempting to babble out is that it seems there was a carriage accident." Lavinia feigned the aura of a Minerva Press heroine. "And Uncle Charleton—"

"Accident?" Cecily felt all the strength drain from her knees. "Father—"

"He's all right, Cecily!" Mirabelle's voice cut through Cecily's budding panic. "Shame on you, Lavvy, making it sound worse than it was! He's all right."

"Aye," Lavinia trilled. "Mayhap the messenger was exaggerating, too, claiming as he did 'twas fair miracle anyone escaped the wreckage alive. Even the horses broke their necks. And the harness, 'twas sliced clean away, as though someone with a knife—"

"Lavinia!" Mirabelle's elbow flashed out, gouging deep into her sister's stomach.

Cecily barely heard Lavinia's outraged grunt, could scarce breathe as she leaned against the door for support, images of shattered wood, horses screaming in pain, tormenting her. The harness had been cut. . . . "But he wasn't hurt," she said, as if only half believing it. "He wasn't . . ."

"Naught but a few bruises. The messenger said Uncle Charleton would continue on here to London as soon as he could make arrangements for one of his other equipages to be sent. 'Twill most likely take a few days. . . ."

"Yes, from—from Briarton. 'Twill take a few days," Cecily echoed. "But he is all right."

"Yes, but are you, dearest?" Lavinia trilled. "I vow you look nigh fit for Bedlam, the way you are gaping about."

"Of course she's stunned, you dolt!" Mira's voice cut in, its usually sweet tones blade sharp. "She's borne a shock—"

"Nay. 'Tis . . . 'tis well enough now . . . I'm fine." Cecily forced the words through stiff lips, hating the feel of Lavinia's eager eyes upon her, devouring her misery. Her fingers tightened upon the journal, her chin jutting high. "I but want to be alone."

"Alone? Cecily, do you think that wise? Let me bring you something to soothe you. Some milk warmed with cinnamon, or rosehip tea." Mira's hand was gentle on Cecily's cold cheek. "I'll stay with you until you sleep."

"I want to be alone!"

Lavinia jumped at the fierce cry, Mira's eyes rounding with hurt and distress as Cecily jerked from beneath her hand.

"I—I only—if—if you need anything . . ." Mirabelle stepped away, and Cecily felt sick from the hurt in her cousin's gentle eyes.

"I'm sorry," Cecily choked out. "I just need some time. Please." She buried her face in her hands, a torturous sob wrenching from her throat. "Please!"

She heard a slight scuffling sound, heard Lavinia's whinings as Mirabelle all but dragged the girl down the hall. But she did not care if they both thought her mad . . . and maybe she was touched, somehow, by the same terror that had all but broken her father's sanity—all but ended his life.

Her skin felt like ice, deadened, the shell of numbness around her pierced only by what now was total silence. The candleflame wavered atop its wick, quaking with the tremors in her hand, carving in the rows of armor yellow eyes, mouths gaping where the visors lay open, spaces where faces were supposed to be, framing now naught but emptiness. "Papa . . . dear God, Papa, what is happening to you? To me? What . . ."

She shuddered, the words echoing back to her like the cries of an abandoned child, mingled with the harsh rasp of Ransom's parting promise. *'Tis not finished yet, Cecily . . . not finished . . .* Sweet God, would it ever be? Would it ever end, or would she be lost in this maze of doubt and danger for eternity?

"Nay, Papa, I won't let . . ." Her mouth formed the denial, but she could not force it past her lips as silence closed about her, scraping nails in bloody tracks across her nerves.

Evil . . .

Why had she not sensed it before? A pervasive mixture of

163

jasmine, orange flowers, and danger. It seemed to wisp through the corridor on wings woven of nightmare.

Cecily straightened her sagging shoulders, her gaze darting about the shadowed hall, half believing some horror conjured of a child's most agonizing dreamings would appear. Her scalp prickled, self-loathing born of what she deemed cowardice building inside her as she hastened the steps to her own bedchamber.

'Twas the same sensation she had sometimes known as a child, that bittersweet certainty that if she could but shut the door behind her, she could bar whatever demons lurked from beyond the silent room.

The fire lit earlier to ward off the night chill struggled in the old chimney, the logs scattering embers to the stone hearth. Cecily shivered as she placed the candle on the piecrust table, remembering her cloak yet abandoned in her father's rooms. Cold . . . the room was so cold. . . .

Mayhap Bess had failed to close the drapes that blocked the drafts from the tightly barred window. Cecily dragged her eyes up to where moss-shaded velvet dripped from heavy brass rods. A chill not born of the drafts iced her very blood. The heavy bolt that had locked the window had been thrown back, the mullioned glass panes swung open, swallowed by the veilings of night. She spun around, her gaze raking the room, her pulse hammering in her throat as she searched the shadows melting from the armoire, the writing table, the gown draped over a chair.

As though by some sorcerer's spell, she felt her eyes drawn to where the deepest pools of darkness lurked, curling in macabre shapes over the huge silhouette of the bed she had lain upon before Bess had left her. The rich curtains draping from the bedposts to the floor had been tied back then, at Cecily's own orders, knotted by thick gold cord. But now velvet rippled like a witch-woman's hair, spilling night blue to hide the face of whatever evil lurked behind.

Cecily's breath caught heavy in her lungs, her bounding heart threatening to burst her chest as she stared at the bedcurtains whiffling softly in the drafts from the window.

Beckoning . . . beckoning . . . she could feel ethereal fingers goading her forward, a heartbeat at a time—taunting her.

She bit her lip, fighting to block out the sound that seemed to rage in the silence . . . laughter, hideous laughter tinged with cruelty, madness. She wanted to scream, refused, her eyes burning deep into the velvet as she steeled herself, reached out to catch the curtain in her fingertips. Holding her breath, she nigh ripped the velvet from its moorings, tearing back the veiling from the bed where she had lain but hours before, defenseless in sleep.

Candlelight flooded over the white sheetings like gold-tinged blood, driving back the shadows, leaving in their wake something more terrifying still.

Cecily's hand caught at her throat, stifling the scream threatening to choke her, horror pouring through her like molten acid as her gaze locked upon the pillow.

A card, exactly the like of the ones that had terrorized her father, lay against the pristine sheetings, the white paper scrawled with an eerie, charcoaled symbol. But though Cecily bore no notion of what meaning the strange markings might hold, there could be little doubt about the intruder's intentions. Blue, silver, the candlelight raced down a length of glistening steel, the blade of an elegant dagger driven deep into the very place yet hollowed from Cecily's head.

Chapter Eleven

"Lacey, ANGEL, the toweling, give Papa the toweling." Ransom fought to keep his voice level, disguising the alarm rushing through him as he hurled one bloodstained hank of linen into a basin and grasped for the other that lay just out of his reach. He couldn't quite catch the corner betwixt his fingers, and did not dare release the pressure he held on the split lip of the battered woman before him, but even still, the stark terror in his daughter's face tore at something inside him.

All morn he had snapped at her, his temper stung past the breaking point as he waited for some sign of Cecily. Lacey had been hurt, aye, and pensive even then, her dark eyes filling him with gnawing guilt. But from the moment the strange woman had collapsed outside the door at Tradewinds, Lacey had washed pale as new cream, her eyes huge in her pixie face.

'Twas hardly surprising, the child's fear, considering the condition of the woman's beautiful features, and the fact that, though Lacey had seen all sorts of people in her four years in London, she had seen but few bearing the ebony hue of those torn from Africa's jungles. But it seemed there was something deeper haunting the child's black-fringed eyes, some misty-dark fear even Ransom could not explain.

"Lacey, *give me the towel!*" Ransom hated the sharpness

in his voice, hated the hurt that rose to join the confusion and fear in his daughter's face as the usually dauntless child skittered forward to thrust the length of linen into his hand. But he bore little choice. Bruises mottled the burnt-sugar skin of the strange woman who now lay curled upon the settee in Tradewinds' generous great room, the purpling marks driven into the lithe body by some crazed brute's fists. Blood from the cut lip splattered over apple-green satin and silver lace, staining the lush swells of breasts half exposed between the torn edges of cloth.

"Good angel." Ransom tried to soothe the child, his hand deftly replacing the clean cloth upon the vicious cut marring the sensual perfection of the woman's full lip. "That is Papa's good angel." Ransom clenched his teeth in empathy as the woman beneath his hands gave a muffled groan, the fabric paining her torn flesh despite his best efforts to be gentle.

"Jagger. Damn him!" Ransom grated to himself. "If he were here . . . but nay. Late. Always cursed late."

"Some—Someone is coming here?" The woman shrank back, her slender fingers clutching at her bodice, her heavy-lidded eyes round as Lacey's had been but a moment before. "Please . . . do not . . . tell anyone I came. He . . . he'll kill me if he finds me. Promised he would."

"Who promised?" Ransom coaxed, casting a furious glare at the yet-empty door. "Who did this to you?"

"A man . . . a most important man. Kept a—a house with me and some others, would . . . come . . . whenever he wanted to . . . Swore . . . he would kill me if ever left . . . He could kill the devil if he wanted to." Hate and terror twisted the battered face. "Help me . . . They said on the streets you would help me to hide."

"Aye, I'll help you." Ransom felt outrage hammer through his own veins, his memory filling with a dozen like cases of humbly bred mistresses, lightskirts, abused once their "protectors" had wearied of them. The fashionable impures, beauties bred and raised in Europe's glittering courts most often bore shieldings of rank and social standing to protect them from the brutalities of the men who patronized them. But stationless girls the like of Jessamyn and this injured woman were at the mercy not only of men's lusts, but of their cruelties as well.

Ransom's jaw clenched and he battled to keep his rage from showing in his voice and further frightening the broken woman before him. "What is your name? If I'm to help you I need to know—"

"Khadija." Sultry, rich as a jungle flower, the name stirred in him memories of scorching, wet heat, relentless rain.

"Khadija," he repeated, trying to frame the correct words to ease the woman's agitation. "I understand that you are afraid. Know that whoever did this to you terrorized you into thinking he bore the power to kill you if he chose. But the king himself bears no right to do this to you—to anyone."

"You don't understand . . . know him. You—"

"Acquaint me with him." Ransom could not stem the feral anticipation in his tones, his fists fair aching to drive themselves into the flesh of whoever had brutalized this woman.

"Nay. I cannot . . . dare not."

"You *can.*" Ransom carefully removed the cloth from the gash in her lip, examining it to see if the blood flow had been checked. The ripped flesh oozed but a little, yet he sensed it was in bad need of Doc Townsend's able needle. "If you will but tell me who hurt you, threatened you, I promise you I'll see to it the bastard bears no chance of doing such harm again. But if you refuse to tell me, he'll go on hurting others the way he has you."

"Nay, don't . . . ask me," Khadija pleaded, great tears coming to her eyes. "Please do not force me."

Frustration stung deep into Ransom's temper, blending with the rage he ever felt when he witnessed the marks of cruelty upon some innocent's body. But he bit back his angry need to demand the truth of the woman, knowing it would only make her afraid of him as well. And God knew, the woman had obviously been plagued by enough terror of late. He reached out a gentle hand, smoothing back a wispy tendril escaping the heavy crown of braids about her head, the dark curls making her seem incredibly fragile despite her unusual height. He could feel her stiffen beneath his hand, understood too well her aversion to the touch of a man—any man.

He let his fingers fall away, for the moment conceding defeat. Hunkering down, he met the woman's gaze with his own. "Let it be as you wish, for now. I'll not press you for any more information. What you need is a great deal of rest and the arts of a fine physician. Mayhap once you feel more secure, you will trust me." He forced his lips to curve into a reassuring smile.

"I will pay you back for your kindness. I be most accomplished at—at what he retained me for."

Ransom's stomach turned at the eagerness with which the beautiful woman was willing to cast her body to him in lieu of coins. Fear . . . aye, of being without a protector, without someone from whom to gain shelter, clothing, food, that was the greatest terror of all to the women who bore the life of paid lover. For the moment beauty faded along with youth, the relentless misery of the streets became the woman's fate—the alleys but littered with one more hag, babbling of beauty and old lovers over bottles of Blue Ruin.

A knock on the door gave Ransom something to vent his temper upon, and he latched on to it with savage relish. "Don't stand out there like a cursed idiot, get your blasted arse in h—"

He spun to glare at the opened portal, but the oaths he had been about to utter tumbled over each other in his throat, nigh choking him as he confronted not the grizzled countenance of Jagger Wace, but rather a fragile angel's features near lost in the hood of a sapphire cloak.

"C-Cecily," he stammered, the shaft of pleasure jolting through him at the sight of her lost immediately to dread and wariness as the light caught the waxen planes of her face. "What the devil are you doing—"

"I—I'm getting my 'arse' in here." A laugh tore from her

lips, the sound, bordered with sharp-edged hysteria, prickling the nape of Ransom's neck. "Last night you told me to—to come, or—"

"Blast it, princess, what is it?" He hastened toward her, gripping hands cold as winter. The sound of something crumpling came from beneath his fingers, but at that instant he would not have given a damn if every clue to the fate of the *Ninon* were vanishing beneath his hand. She looked as though a hundred specters had battled for her soul, stealing all but the slightest whisperings of the indomitable spirit that had captured his heart. He struggled to speak, couldn't, stunned as he was by the anguish reeling through him at the sight of her stark pain. Sweet God, what had he forced her to confront in her father's cursed journal? Some truth so hideous it had left her thus broken?

In that instant he wanted to drag her to his bedchamber, demand whatever truths she might hold, to make right whatever was haunting those melting violet eyes. But before he could force aught past the knotting in his throat, a tiny cry burst through her lips, her fingers jerking from his, pressing against her throat.

"Dear God, what happened?" Whatever she had been grasping fluttered to the floor as she dodged around Ransom, eyes raking the bloodied cloths, the beaten woman upon the settee.

"Don't . . . tell her. Go . . . tell her to go!" Khadija's cries were pathetic, her face half hidden amidst the torn folds of her gown.

A surprising irritation stung sharp through Ransom, the patience he had lavished upon the people of the streets for once eclipsed by his own driving need—the need to seek out what had so stricken the violet-eyed woman he loved. Yet a lifetime of placing the needs of others first surged to the fore, Khadija's alarmed cry tearing him back to the realities of abuse and duty.

"Nay, 'tis all right." Ransom hurried to the woman's side, peeling the silk from her fingers. "I promise you—"

"Looks like a bloody mess t' me!" The gruff voice from

the doorway made Ransom start, the sound of Khadija's choked gasp grating across his nerves. "Not one blasted woman litterin' up the place, but *three.*" Ransom caught a glimpse of Cecily wheeling toward a figure silhouetted in the door, heard Lacey's glad cry as the child hurtled past him to fling herself into Jagger Wace's arms. The crabbed sailor's peg leg thunked into the rich carpets in blatant disapproval as he attempted to keep his balance beneath the weight of the clinging child. "Here, now, ye little hoyden! Ye be crumplin' me fancies, an' me jest havin' 'em washed two weeks past!"

Ransom's eyes shot daggers at the grizzled countenance of his erstwhile first mate.

"'Tis damned well time you got here!" Ransom snarled. "I need the cursed doctor, Lacey is half terrified, and—"

"An' the duchess 'as come a-callin'."

Ransom nigh wished there was the accustomed rancor in the sailor's tone so that he could blast the old sea dog for sniping at Cecily or Lacey, but the strip-muscled arms cradled his daughter with all the tenderness of a mother, the gap-toothed mouth that had ever spouted naught but scorn for the fairer sex curving in what seemed—sweet mercy, was it possible?—almost a smile as the sailor raked his gaze down Cecily's cloaked form.

Yet any sense of good humor in the crotchety old sailor vanished as Jagger's keen eyes caught a glimpse of Cecily's face beneath the deep sapphire hood. "What the devil . . . " He lanced Ransom with his eyes, and had the old sailor had a hand free, Ransom sensed it would have been knotted into a fist. "Well, ye great gudgeon, are ye goin' t' tell me what the blazes happened 'ere, or just stand there glarin'?"

"I vow I'm damned well not certain myself anymore. I heard a knock on the door and found Khadija, here, so battered up, Lacey was terrified of her. Then Cecily—Lady Cecily—barged in, and you— Damn you, if you had been on time—"

"Ye know full well I never be in time. Ye should plan on 't. If ye tell me t' meet ye at eight o' the clock, don't bother hangin' about till past nine. Now, if ye want me 'pinion . . ." Jagger jerked his head toward Khadija. "That 'un there be in need o' ol' Townsend's needles 'n' gut."

"Brilliant deduction!" Ransom snapped.

"An' the duchess, 'ere, must o' descended from 'er gilded carriage at yer doorstep fer some reason. I got me gig jest outside, if ye want me t' take Kha—whatever 'er name be—t' the doc's place."

"He's supposed to be at Rosetree right now. If you'd but take her there—"

"Want—Want to stay with you!" Khadija pleaded. "A-Afraid—"

"'Tis impossible for you to stay here." Ransom turned, bending over her, his hand soothing upon her arm. "Half the time no one is even about at Tradewinds. 'Twill be better, far, for you to stay at Rosetree. 'Tis a hostel I keep for children, women, anyone who has been hurt, has nowhere to go. There are medical facilities, and—"

"Nay! Want to—"

"You'll be much safer amongst many people, people who can be certain your . . . former protector cannot reach you. And I promise I will come to see you often."

The woman appeared to be ready to argue, but Ransom shook his head, his arm encircling her waist, helping her to gain her feet. "Jagger will allow naught to befall you on the way, and once you are in Rosetree, no one will dare to—"

"Nay! Nay!" Khadija's sudden cries startled Ransom, the woman battling in his arms as though some fearsome monster had reared its head before her. One bloodstained finger jabbed toward the carpets, her eyes wild, terrified. "Obeah!" she whimpered. "Obeah!"

Ransom followed the path her finger directed, saw Cecily snatch up the bit of paper that had been lying forgotten upon the thick carpet.

"What the hell?" He grabbed the stiff card from Cecily's shaking fingers, recognizing at once the same unique gilt edging that had bordered the notes of blackmail Cecily had entrusted to him that first day at Defiance Enterprises. But there was no boldly scrawled word slashed across this card—rather, another figure had been etched onto the rich paper, a figure Ransom recognized far too clearly.

Faces flashed before him, seen in countless ports, on countless slave blocks in the Indies—faces bred with deadly pride, their features, be they comely or hideous, seemingly wrought by the black arts they practiced. The obeah. Scourge of the rich cane planters, terror even to the other blacks that dwelt in the meager huts provided for their shelter. A society woven of healing, fierce arrogance, yet also magic, curses, stealthy, secret deaths. Deaths . . .

Ransom's hand crumpled the edge of the card he held as he stared at the symbol scrawled across the pale surface like some gaping, hungry python but waiting to devour . . .

"Ransom, what is it?" The stark terror in Cecily's face dragged white-hot claws down Ransom's chest, but he could not look at her, dared not as fury, fear for her, ripped through him.

"Jagger." Ransom dragged his gaze from the card, meeting the all-too-aware eyes of his first mate. "Take Lacey with you to Rosetree. And Khadija. Tell Jessie I'll be over later to—"

Ransom saw Jagger's eyes flick to Cecily, his face lined with worry. "Ransom, lad, I—"

"I'll take care of her, Jagger."

"Aye."

"Damn both of you, what is it?" Cecily's voice was ragged, a half sob, but neither man would answer her as Ransom bore the softly whimpering Khadija out into the dooryard, Jagger with Lacey bare steps behind them.

The richly appointed room, decorated with treasures and curiosities gained in a hundred mystical ports, seemed to shift in slow, sickening patterns around Cecily, an eternity seeming to pass in the minutes before she again heard Ransom's footsteps in the chamber. 'Twas as though the grave-chill fear that had wrapped about her heart from the moment she yanked back the bedcurtains had never left her, as though the eyes she had felt watching her yet delved her innermost secrets.

"Princess?" Gentle, so gentle, she felt Ransom's hands

upon her, but she whirled on him, knocking away the fingers that offered comfort.

"Tell me!" she fairly screamed. "Damn you, what—"

"'Tis a symbol born in Africa, Cecily. A symbol witch-women, women of the obeah, sometimes used to mark their next victim."

"V-Victim?" Cecily felt like she was going to be sick, the strain that had been fraying at her nerves the night past threatening to snap. "Obeah . . . I—I never heard of—"

"Of course you haven't. They were a society in Africa, and now in the slave colonies, that hold incredible power, inspire terror and murderous loyalties in any black man or woman who knows them for what they are."

"I don't understand."

"Magic, Cecily, black arts. They are said to be able to murder without leaving so much as a mark on the body. . . . Even those of their own race fear them, so deeply that if a master suspects an obeah is practicing upon his plantation and tries to torture the name from one of his innocent slaves, that person will die a hideous, tormented death, rather than expose one he fears more than the horrors of hell."

"How—How do you know? It might be naught but a sick jest. An attempt to—to frighten—"

"I grew up on the Gold Coast and sailed every port charted on any map you can find. And this much I can tell you: there is not a man born who has had any contact with the obeah who would dare pilfer one of their symbols for a jest, not even to terrorize his most hated enemy."

Cecily felt her knees going weak, and she grasped the edge of a whimsically carved sandalwood trunk to keep from sinking to the floor.

"Cecily, where did you find this card?" Ransom's hand reached out to steady her, and when she looked into his face, she had never seen such solemn fear.

"'Twas after you left last evening," she said faintly. "The window in my bedchamber was open, and this . . . was on my pillow." She reached into the reticule looped over one arm, drawing out the slender, deadly dagger, placing its hilt in his palm. "The card was on my pillow, with this driven through."

What little color had remained in Ransom's tanned cheeks drained, leaving him white as new tallow. Cecily cried out as his fingers clamped with bone-crushing force about her arm. "Your pillow! Sweet Christ!" He hurled the dagger to the floor, and in a pulsebeat she was in his arms, unable to draw breath as he clutched her against him, cursing, biting out fragments that might be prayer.

"Ransom, there—there is more . . . about the ship . . ."

"Blast it, I don't give a damn about—"

"'Tis about what I discovered last evening," Cecily insisted, grateful of the arms that held her, strengthened her with . . . could it be love? "In the journal. There was a pet name my—my father christened my mother with."

Ransom stilled against Cecily, and she could feel his breath go shallow. "Pet name?"

"Aye. Her Christian name was Anastasia. She died when I was born, and I—I had never heard her called anything else. But in his journals, sometimes, Papa longed so to talk to her that he wrote . . ." Her voice trailed off, her eyes rising to his with stark despair.

"Ninon, Ransom. He called my mother Ninon."

It was as if the room had suddenly plunged into the confines of a fresh-dug tomb. Silence. Deafening silence. Cecily struggled to fight her way through it, shatter it, but the expression upon Ransom Tremayne's sharp-carved features slashed away her ability to speak.

A thousand tempests roiled in his eyes, tortures of the damned seeming to twist the muscles in his beautiful mouth. The pieces of some macabre puzzle whirled in Cecily's exhausted mind—the hell ship, the *Ninon*—an African obeah tormenting a man who had spent nigh his whole life on an English country estate, the fury in Ransom Tremayne.

"Tell me. Damn you, Ransom, you tell me what in blazes this all means!" Her voice was shrill, anguished, lost as she grasped a handful of his shirtfront, the sinews of his chest rigid as iron against her knuckles. *"Tell me!"*

His fingers manacled her wrists, tugging them away with such a look of emptiness in his eyes, Cecily's stomach lurched. "Do you really want to know about the ship your father named after your mother? Do you?" he demanded.

"Aye! I have to know! Need to—"

"Christ!" He spun away from her, pacing, a wild jungle cat caught in a huntsman's trap, a trap he could never escape.

"I stowed away on it—the *Ninon*—after . . . after a friend died." His voice was a single thread of agony. "I did not know what cargo it bore . . . would have gladly shipped onto a vessel bound for hell. Hell would have seemed like paradise after where I had been. But the *Ninon*, it was a misery far worse than any Lucifer could have conjured." Ransom's eyes were hazed, distant. "Slaves. The holds were crammed with them. Layers of them, jammed into narrow shelvings like fishes in a smokehouse. Not enough room to move, sit up, stand. Chains dragging at their ankles, throats. The ship's holds bore as much treasure as the diamond mines in the south of the continent, only the coin they traded in was flesh."

Cecily fought to dispel the images Ransom painted, denial, disbelief roiling inside her. A mistake. It must all be some hideous mistake. Her father would never . . .

"The *Ninon*—a slave ship?" Her voice was pleading, begging Ransom to draw back truths too lashingly painful to bear, but he only stared deeper into the fire, his voice ragged, face pale.

"Aye. Little wonder the poor wretches lying in their own filth in the hold sickened, died like dogs—worse than dogs." Ransom jammed his fingers through his hair, as though to drive out hideous images he alone could see. "Ship fever, it was, turning their bodies into putrid masses of infection, until finally . . . finally one night . . ."

Ransom's gaze lockd with hers, and Cecily wanted to run from it, stop up her ears so she would not hear the horror his eyes now held.

"Three days' sail from our destination, the captain and five of his men took torches while the rest of the crew slept.

They lowered the launches. Lowered them and then set the ship afire."

Cecily's hands pressed to her mouth, bile rising in her throat as she pictured with agonizing clarity the wooden-hulled ship being eaten by hungry flame, pitch, tar crackling as red-orange tongues of death lapped at them, the hold turning fierce with heat, and helpless victims below lying in chains that seared their skin. Screams. Dear God, she could almost hear their screams.

"Why? Why would a captain burn his own vessel?"

"Profit," Ransom bit out. "Had the *Ninon* reached port with such a sickened and meager cargo, her owner would have suffered enormous losses. But in the event of a catastrophe, there were options that might salvage—"

"Nay! My father would have nothing to do with such horrible things! He would not—" She tried to cry out the words but her stomach threatened to betray her.

A bitter laugh tore from Ransom's lips. "Even if it had been your father, I could prove nothing. Whoever lay behind the affair was cunning enough to shield himself completely. Had I not stowed away on that ship, no one—not one man—destined to be murdered upon it would have survived that night to avenge the others who died.

"A sailmaker named Tremayne had discovered me trying to pilfer food a few days out of port, but the sailor vowed the captain bore a heart more weevily than the biscuit and pork in the ship's stores. Tremayne—I think he feared the captain would put me over the side if he discovered me. Most likely he would have, and flogged the sailmaker as well. But in the end the risk Tremayne took to protect me bore him good luck. He had crept out of his berth to slip me part of his rations the night of the fire. Had he not . . ."

Cecily saw Ransom's lips curl back in a savage snarl, his eyes haunted. "They fired the crew's quarters first. Burned the poor bastards they had worked alongside. Tremayne and I, we couldn't help them. But we tried—tried to free what few slaves we could before the deck caved in. Even those we managed to loose . . . their iron collars dragged them down into the sea. Christ, I was only fifteen. But I still hear their screams, can still feel them clawing at us, helpless as we clung to the wreckage."

Cecily saw Ransom's hands knot, as though he were still battling to grasp at shattered wood, to keep the brine from filling his throat.

"Tremayne, he had been burned so badly that after the fourth day we were adrift, he couldn't hold on any longer."

"Sweet God," Cecily breathed, reeling from the horror, imagining a golden-haired youth possessing none of the tensile strength that now banded Ransom's strong arms.

"Is that where you—you—" Her fingers reached out, touching her own smooth cheek. Ransom gave a harsh laugh, his fingers digging into the raised flesh scarring his face.

"Nay. 'Twas before the *Ninon*. The sailmaker but stitched it after—" He stopped, suddenly wary, and Cecily was certain there was something he was yet shielding from her, something he would never betray. He spun away, pacing over to the window, staring blankly through its glistening panes. "'Twas Jagger who spotted me two days later, dragged me aboard the Welsh trader he served upon," Ransom said at last. "Nursed me until I was sane again. As sane as possible after all that had befallen me." He faced her, the eyes blazing into hers, pits of despair. "I vowed then I would find whoever was responsible for torching the *Ninon*. Find them and destroy them."

Cecily took a step backward, her hip cracking into a sharp-cornered table. Pain shot to the center of her body, driving deeper still into the core of her soul.

"'Tis not—not my father! He scarce stepped foot off of Briarton the whole time I was growing up. He never captained a ship—"

"I've not sought the *captain* of the *Ninon* since three months from the day the ship sank. By that time I had tracked the survivors to Port Royal, only to discover that the man who had commanded the *Ninon* was dead. Killed, rumor had it, at the order of the Englishman who had sponsored the voyage."

"Nay! 'Tis some horrible mistake! My father is the most gentle man who e'er breathed. I don't believe—"

"You don't believe?"

She cried out at the savagery in Ransom's voice, alarm jolting through her as he turned on her, catching her roughly by the arm. "Then why the hell is someone trying to drive him insane with hintings of that ship? The port it sailed from? Why is an obeah creeping into your goddamned room? Sweet Jesus, if she had touched you—" Ransom's hand shot out, knotting in Cecily's hair, a few delicate strands ripping in his fingers.

She felt his anguish as his lips crashed down upon hers. There was madness in the kiss, savagery, the roughness of his mouth upon hers tearing from her a cry of denial, of an inner agony so great it seemed to rend her very soul. She fought to break his hold upon her, nails clawing at the yielding flesh of his cheeks, fists pounding on his chest.

"Stop, blast you!" she cried as she broke free, her hand flashing out, cracking with all her strength into Ransom's scarred cheek. "My father would never have involved himself in something so loathesome as slaving! Never!" Her fist thunked hard into Ransom's chest. "A mistake . . . it must be—"

His hand caught hers in a bruising grip and he shook her hard. "Damn you, Cecily, listen! I've spent half my life searching for answers about the *Ninon*. Let it devour me like some cursed poison. I know—"

"You know nothing! Nothing! You—"

"I know that I love you, damn it. *Love you.*" The hopelessness in his eyes seared her. "I don't want to see you hurt, dead. We have to do someth—"

"I *hate* you! You vile, vile liar! Cozening me into allowing you to rake through the journals—plotting to use them against him—conjuring lies—*lies!*" A ragged sob tore at her chest. "If you ever so much as breathe my father's name again, I vow I'll find a way to destroy you! I vow it, Ransom Tremayne, if I have to plunge a dagger into your cursed heart with my own hand!"

Tears flooded Cecily's cheeks, searing her as she turned and ran. But even as she fled, Ransom's words twined about her soul like murderous vines, crushing trust, hope. She wanted to scream, sob, rail at the world, but she knew not who she mourned for—the scarred fifteen-year-old boy who had suffered the flames, the terror, the pampered girl-child, whose fantasy world lay shattered . . . or for the death of a love that might have served salvation for them both.

Chapter Twelve

THE GOWN SHIMMERED in hues of twilight—lavender, dusky rose, heathery blue that melted into gold. Even the mirror's reflection could not fully capture the beauty of the fabric, the slightest shifting of the silk over Cecily's body sending ripples of opalescent color to accent the creamy tones of her skin, the sweet swell of breasts curving enticingly from wreathings of silver gauze. Yet neither the magnificent cloth that had been her father's gift the evening he had announced she was to have a London season, nor the magical skill of the dressmaker who had fashioned humble woven fibers into what now seemed the petals of some magnificent, exotic flower, could hide the tithings of misery from Cecily's wan face.

Dark purple smudgings marred the delicate skin beneath eyes that had aged a lifetime in the eight days since she had run from the great room at Tradewinds. The sparkling color that had always blushed her cheeks and lips had faded to the frail pink of autumn's last rose. Even the lush sable of her hair seemed only to accentuate the waxen tinting of skin drained by exhaustion and heartache.

Eight days, eight endless, sleepless nights haunted by Ransom Tremayne's ravaged face and her father's specterlike misery, and still Charleton Lansdowne did not come.

"Perfect! Is it not perfect?" The sound of Mira's voice, eager, tentative, seemed to well to a deafening roar in Cecily's aching head, driving away all possibility of glum musings. "Maman, will she not be the most glorious belle to grace London in an era?"

"Humpf!" Honoria Lansdowne grumbled, giving Cecily's bodice a censorious tug. "'Tis acceptable—barely. Such a muddle of colors 'twill fair make the gentlemen giddy. And the notion of allowing a child the like of this to don such a vulgar set of amethysts . . ." The duchess's eyes flashed haughtily to the rich violet stones pooled upon Cecily's skin, and she could almost feel the older woman fight the urge to snatch the jewels from about her neck.

"Shocking. Most shocking."

"Because they are the one thing Papa was gifted with from his mother's dower?" Cecily's eyes met Honoria's shocked ones with deliberate belligerence, exhaustion having drained away any will she had held to control her tongue. "Or is it only because you would never think of giving up one of your precious trinkets in order to garb your own daughters?"

The puffing of Honoria's cheeks in outrage gave Cecily not so much as a wisp of her accustomed wicked pleasure. But there was the barest stirring of relief as she shrugged off the guise of pretty manners and petty hypocrisy like a sodden cloak.

"Of all the impertinent—" Honoria Lansdowne's raised-dough cheeks seemed in a fair way to burst. "After all I have done for you—for your ungrateful father—laboring my nerves to a frazzle with the details of planning your introduction into society, clasping to my bosom a viper who stands in my own home, insulting—"

"'Tis heinous, Maman!" Lavinia sniffed, her long nose poking into the air. "The most detestable bad manners. You should be ashamed of yourself, cousin!" One plump finger wagged at Cecily's face. "Maman would be only too happy to give me any piece of jewelry I might crave!" Cecily gritted her teeth as a sly light stole into Lavinia's eyes, the girl going up to clasp her mother in a theatrical embrace. "Why that—that gold and garnet ensemble Grandmama gave you last Christmas would be exquisite with my parchment satin. Give it to me, Maman, and show this country upstart that you are the most generous of parents."

Cecily caught the inside of her cheek between her teeth to keep from breaking out into wild, weary laughter. 'Twas a performance to rival any actress at the Royal Theater, and the cunning chit had spun her spider's web of fierce compliments so tightly about Honoria Lansdowne's wrinkled throat that the duchess was choking on it.

"The—The garnets . . ." Honoria said faintly. "Why, heart's dearest, you cannot mean—" For an instant Cecily thought her aunt might finally thwart Lavinia's machinations, but after a moment the older woman pursed her lips, glaring at Cecily as though it were she who was stealing the cherished jewels. "Of course you may have them, treasure," Honoria pronounced more firmly than was necessary. "'Twould be most improper for the *daughter of a duke* to be outshone by a mere lord's child."

"The duke has two daughters." Even through her own misery, Cecily was not adverse to a bit of manipulating herself.

"Pearls. I'll give the chit pearls," Honoria snapped. "At least 'twill not give the beaus stomach complaints by assaulting their eyes with such waggglety-tag colors! Merciful heavens, I hope Charleton gets himself to London before the ball he has spent a king's fee for. If his grace and I are forced to serve as hostess . . ."

She pressed the back of her hand to her fish-white brow. "Now get yourself out of those—those trappings before Mirabelle steps on the hem and destroys it somehow."

A discreet knock upon the chamber door drew the duchess's glare. "What in the name of mercy is it now!" Her irritated cry pierced the door.

"Your pardon, your grace," Bess said as she skittered into the room. "'Tis just that his lordship—Master Charleton, I mean—I thought my lady Cecily would want to know he was just let down by Lord Sutton's phaeton."

"Papa?" The word was ragged in Cecily's throat. She

heard the duchess's railings about the dress, heard Mirabelle's glad cry, but she was already running from the chamber, bolting down the staircase three at a time, as she had when a child.

She glimpsed her father in the entryway, solemnly handing his top hat and great coat to William the footman, and the familiarity of the scene she had witnessed a thousand times warmed the cold shell that had been hardening about her heart. The thin, scholarly face tipped up to see what was making the commotion, and when those achingly gentle blue eyes caught Cecily, she was certain—death certain—that the Virgin Mary herself would have commissioned a slave ship before her loving father.

With a glad cry she hurled herself down the last few risers, catapulting herself against Charleton Lansdowne's narrow chest. His arms circled about her, the early-spring chill clinging to rumpled pantaloons and the untidy folds of his cravat. But a cold far deeper than the bite of the night wind seemed to emanate from somewhere inside the weary man.

"Papa, I was so afraid! When I—I heard you had been in that horrible accident—"

The welcome of the arms that had held her seemed to fade, her father easing his stiff body from her embrace with a weak laugh. "The accident . . . ah yes, 'twas naught but a bit of carelessness on a stable lad's part. A touch of paint to the coach wheels, a few nails, and all should be well."

"A touch of paint?" Cecily's joy in seeing her father dissipated, abandoning her again to bewilderment and hurt. "The messenger made it sound as though 'twas far more serious than that—the horses—he said they broke their—"

"Blast it! I did not want him to worry you with—with paltry details—"

"Of how you were almost killed? *Murdered,* Papa?"

"Hush, girl! Are you mad?" Charleton's hand grasped hers hard, his voice a rough whisper. "Do you want every servant in Moorston to hear you?"

One inkstained hand grasped the door to the salon, thrusting it open impatiently. Cecily hastened through the door before her father could yank her in like a disobedient child. She turned to face him as the door latch clicked closed behind them, the noise echoing on the gold and cream damask-covered walls.

"For God's sake, girl, I thought you bore more sense!" The harsh words seemed those of a stranger, worlds away from the father Cecily had always known. Hurt seared across her exhausted senses, leaving her raw.

"Aye, Papa, I have sense, enough to know that you are in some sort of trouble."

What little color remained in Charleton Lansdowne's features faded to gray. "Cecily, your imagination never ceases to amaze me!" He gave a stiff laugh. "Trouble? I am supposedly in trouble, am I? With brigands no doubt waylaying my coach? Mayhap stealing through my chamber window with poisons—"

"Nay, *my* bedchamber window, Papa."

"Your—" His voice cracked, his eyes pools of anguish, confusion. "Cecily . . . what—what in God's name . . ."

"'Twas a few days after you left London—I was out walking . . . at night." She struggled with evasions. "To the library. I went down to find a book, fell asleep in the chair there. When I came back to my room, the windows were flung wide and someone had—" She steadied her voice. "Someone had graced my pillow with a card scribed with a strange symbol. Then, so there would be no confusion as to the missive's meaning, whoever had planted it there drove a knife into the ticking."

"Nay! Oh, dear God." She darted forward, half expecting her father to sag to the floor. He looked beaten. Old. Unutterably old. His hands caught her cheeks, and she could feel in him a trembling. "Child. You didn't see them . . . they didn't hurt—"

"Not that night, Papa. But ever since, I've felt something . . . someone watching me. I've caught glimpses of shadows on the grounds. Haven't slept. Please, Papa, please." Cecily felt tears sting her eyelids. "Tell me what is happening. I know a little—the *Ninon*—I—"

"You *what?*" The quiet savagery in his voice stunned her, and Cecily stared into eyes suddenly glassy, cold.

"I said I . . . I know it bears something to do with a ship, the—"

"And how, pray tell, did you discover this wealth of information? Have you spent your time in London perfecting the art of a sneak thief? Listening at doors?"

Cecily took a step backward, stunned by the fury that whitened Charleton Lansdowne's face. "Papa, stop. I only want to aid you. You ever said there was naught we couldn't share, no trouble we couldn't defeat if we only worked together—"

"And you believed it?" His laugh raked Cecily's soul as he buried his face in one quavering hand. "Dear God, I believed it, too, once. 'Tis laughable! Sickening. Life traps you, Cecily, child. Wraps its sinews around you like some cursed serpent while you aren't looking. And then—then it crushes . . ."

"Papa." Cecily's words were scarce a whisper. "Papa, tell me you know nothing of this slave ship. Tell me 'tis all a mistake—"

"Aye. A mistake. I did not know—did not—"

Cecily wanted to shriek at him, plead for a denial, but the expression on his face burned into her breast. Guilt. Maiming guilt.

"Papa—"

"You want to hear that I knew nothing of the cursed *Ninon,*" Charleton Lansdowne blazed suddenly, his face contorted with an anguish she was only beginning to understand. "Well, I'm telling you—'tis all misunderstanding. I will right it, unsnarl it somehow. I did not know—did not give the orders to—"

Cecily stared at him, recalling in searing clarity the hell Ransom had described—men burning alive, chains dragging bodies into the sea. She wanted to vomit, purge herself of the horror, wanted to rip from her shoulders the glorious gown she knew with a certainty had been bought with human suffering.

Charleton Lansdowne raised a face carved with torment, his eyes slits glistening with tears. "Cecily . . . child . . ." He reached out his hand, and she could feel the despair in him, but layers of stinking, searing flesh and terrorized screams yawned in a chasm between them.

"I am not a child anymore, Papa." Dull, her voice sounded so dull as she caught her fists, tight against her churning stomach. She turned, exiting the room on leaden feet, leaving behind her the last vestiges of the carefree princess who had plaited wildflower crowns at Briarton, leaving behind as well the father that child had woven with snippets of Galahads, Arthurs, Launcelots, and dreams.

Bayard Sutton crossed Wythe House's vast study with a measured stride, surveying the ruin of his friend's once-handsome face with the detached interest of a spectator at Tyburn Tree. The once-serene eyes that had been the delight of half the women in London were veined with scarlet, the irises pooled in a devastation that was repulsive in its depths. Shrunken flesh clung to cheekbones like parchment, gray-peppered hair in inexcusable disarray, while narrow shoulders, devoid of any cloaking despite the cold, trembled so violently 'twas a miracle the griffin-carved chair's legs were not rattling upon the floor.

"Charleton, drink," Bayard said in his most commiserating tones as he placed a crystal goblet brimming with Madeira into the man's stiff fingers. "'Twas mad for you to ride all this way in this cold. Surely, after your accident, you should yet take better care of yourself. After all, Cecily—"

"Cecily is the very reason I had to come. I didn't know where to turn, what to do when she—" Charleton's hand flashed out, catching Sutton's in a desperate grasp, and he could feel the grime of the road against his skin. "Bayard, dear God, she knows."

"Knows? The girl has ever 'known' more than was good for her, in my estimation. Surely—"

"She knows about the ship, its . . . its cargo. . . ."

"Impossible!" Sutton cursed, yanking his hand from Lansdowne's grip, battling the urge to fling the Madeira into that weak, despair-ridden face. "Every shred of evidence was destroyed years ago. Unless you poured out your guilt to her, there is no way she could have linked you with the ship.

I made certain that no one—*no one*—could e'er use it against me. For the love of God, you did not admit to her . . ."

"Nay, I denied it, but—while I was gone, she must have pried about . . . discovered—" A sob choked Charleton, and Bayard fought the urge to slap that haggard face. "I'll ne'er—ne'er forget the look in her eyes. She knew I was lying . . . loathed me . . ." Charleton buried his face in hands the color of old tallow. "Sweet God . . . my little girl . . ."

Teeth on edge, Bayard yielded to his first impulse, grasping the sobbing man's shoulders, shaking him with a force that made Charleton's teeth chatter. "Stop this, for God's sake, man! Of course the chit judged you guilty if you shattered in front of her, the way you are here. No one can prove anything against us, unless your interfering daughter does something more foolhardy than that of which she is already guilty."

Charleton yanked from his grasp, obviously bearing a better hold upon his emotions. "Cecily? Guilty? I don't understand—"

"I vow I do—more clearly than I would like. While you have been recovering from your most unfortunate accident, I have managed to trace the inquiries about the ship to their source here in London—a ruffian upstart by the name of Tremayne. Ransom Tremayne."

Lansdowne stared with a dazed expression. "Not the Tremayne who battled so nobly at Trafalgar?"

"Nobly?" Sutton snorted. "The blackguard was but saving his own lowling skin, and now he bears access to any salon in the city."

"But you were speaking of Cecily . . . what possible connection . . ."

"I regret to inform you that she cherishes a most ill-advised *tendre* for this rakehell."

"Cecily, involved with the man who is seeking to destroy me? I do not believe—".

"Charleton, you are my dearest friend." Bayard affected an injured aura. "Think you I would cast accusations lightly, knowing how upset you have been of late? I realize sometimes your adoration for Cecily drives you to be a bit . . . unwise in your judgments. But I assure you, I am most certain that the girl has not only been casting calf's-eyes at the rogue, but has been slipping off to his household unescorted."

Bayard nigh laughed aloud at the fire that blazed in Charleton's rheumy eyes. "My daughter would ne'er—"

"Oh, but I assure you she has. You see, I have managed to infiltrate one of my own staff into Tremayne's household. Thus far I have been unable to . . . shall we say, 'obliterate' the problem as I would wish." Sutton's eyes narrowed. "But the single thing I *have* managed to discover for certain is that the principal source of Ransom Tremayne's information is a sable-haired, violet-eyed woman by the name of Lady Cecily Lansdowne."

"Nay . . . 'tis not possible," Charleton moaned, shoulders sagging. "She would not ally herself against me."

"Come, she could scarce have suspected Tremayne's true designs when he first set out to seduce her. No doubt the blackguard but used her innocence to deceive—"

"Seduce?" Lansdowne bolted up from his chair. "Dear God, think you the bastard has ruined her? I'll murder him with my own hands!"

"That is one detail you shall not have to trouble yourself about, I assure you." Sutton waved his fingers in blasé dismissal. A faint amusement stirred within him as, despite the firing of anger in Lansdowne's visage, the scholarly man blanched. "And about the girl . . ."

Sutton drowned his triumphant smile in a delicate sip of dark wine. "I would be most pleased if you would allow me to be of assistance to you in that matter as well."

"Assistance? How . . . ?"

"Well, as you know, should the information regarding the *Ninon* become public knowledge, there will be some most unpleasant repercussions—repercussions that will bear dire consequences upon your daughter's marriage prospects. Add to that chance the danger of someone discovering her clandestine dealings with a noted libertine the like of

Tremayne, and I fear it combines to form a most dismal picture."

"I will forbid her to go near him again! And you vowed that Tremayne will . . . will prove no further trouble in the matter of the ship."

Bayard fetched a deep sigh. "If only 'twere that simple, my friend. You know what a deep fondness I've ever cherished for your Cecily. From the time she was in short skirts she has been . . . most especial to me. At the risk of sounding like a pompous buffoon, I would like to point out that I am a member of impeccable standing in London society—many claim I will be the next man to fill the prime ministry. If I were to ally myself with your daughter . . ."

"Of course. You are most kind. You have always proved her friend."

"I am not offering to be her friend now, Charleton. I am offering myself to be her husband."

Thick as the stench of death upon a battlefield, silence fell. Bayard watched as Charleton Lansdowne floundered in emotions written all too clearly on that bookish face. Bewilderment and revulsion were poorly masked as Charleton stammered, "You—you are too—I could not ask you to—to sacrifice—"

"'Twould be no sacrifice. The girl is most comely, despite her sharp tongue, and her willful ways will be curbed easily enough once she gets with child. Of course, there is always the danger that Tremayne has already . . ." Sutton let the sentence trail off with great effect, watching as Lansdowne's face waxed green.

"I hadn't—hadn't thought of—"

"Stake me, man, there is no need for you to lash yourself with that possibility. You are like a brother to me, and I would be more than willing to give my name to any child Cecily bore, if in so doing I could protect the girl from harm."

"Perhaps you are wrong, and she and that Tremayne have—have not—"

"Of course, 'tis possible she stole away, unescorted, to his home to, er . . . dissect one of the tracts you were so fond of

examining with her. Pericles, or Aristotle, or Shakespeare."
Bayard let his doubt show in his voice. "However, Tremayne
does not strike me as the sort to spend time poring over stale
writings in the company of a woman as beautiful as Cecily."

Lansdowne started to protest, but Sutton merely encir-
cled the man's stiff shoulders with his arm, giving him a
bracing squeeze. "I am not expecting you to commit yourself now, old friend. I only ask that as you consider my suit,
you recall my many efforts in your behalf these past years."

Sutton's lips curved in the slightest of smiles. "Now, go
home, Charleton. Have your valet mix you some rum and
lemon, and drown in sleep. I fear you are looking quite pale,
and 'twould be most unfortunate to worry poor Cecily
further."

"Aye . . . I—I am passing tired," Charleton murmured.
"The accident . . . I've not fully recovered. . . ."

"A plea for your full return to vigor will be in my prayers
this night, I promise you," Bayard said, escorting Charleton
to the door. "'Twould be most devastating to me, if anything
should befall . . . ah, there is the footman. Aloysius, if you
would fetch my Lord Lansdowne one of my capes. He was
so eager to see me that I fear he forgot his own."

"Very good, sir. Is there any in particular you would have
me get for his lordship?" the pretty-faced lad asked with an
intimate smile.

"Any except the ebony-tiered. I favor it by far the most.
Now, farewell, Charleton. I fear I bear a daunting amount of
business to deal with before the evening is done. Consider
my offer, old friend."

"I will—will think about it," Charleton said in a weak
voice, yet beneath the layering of gray-tinged skin and
swollen eyes, Bayard could see the man's fierce reluctance.
Sketching Lansdowne a bow, Sutton turned on one heel,
returning to the sanctuary of his study.

The instant the door was closed behind him, Bayard
leaned back against the heavy panel and let go a harsh laugh,
a sense of triumph building in his chest. So Charleton
thought he could keep his nubile young beauty from the
jaded grasp of Bayard Sutton, did he? Resolved to be

191

strong—hold firm. Well, 'twould not be the first time the two had locked wills, and despite Charleton's occasional balking, Sutton had always been able to bring the mewling dolt to heel. In the end, the matter of the headstrong Cecily would prove no different.

Everything was coming together with the precision his orderly soul always craved—a dozen tiny details, each, in itself, unrelated to the less cautious eye, yet in truth woven together into a perfect, unassailable whole—a magnificent vision that would send the name of Sutton soaring into the annals of England's most revered sons and bring the Whig party back into the station of supremacy it so richly deserved.

Sutton reached out, fingering the African statue he had carried away with him from the dark continent more than a decade ago, taking delight in the way each separate image was carved into the smooth ebony. Wise-eyed snakes twined about the necks of exotic birds, jungle vines weaving about trees they would one day kill, a tribal chieftain—was he Ashanti?—with spear and war club raised high was held back from some unseen battle by the graceful hands of a woman, her lithe-carved body bared to his eyes.

Astonishing, Sutton mused dryly, how perfectly some native savage had captured the essence of the jungle in that one piece of wood—had captured the essence of life, if one but had the wit to see it. The chieftain, charging off to confront his foes openly with weapons and battle cry, gave them fair warning, time to raise their own spears in defense. Even the snake, in its struggle to subdue its prey, might well draw the attention of some predator eager to devour it. But the vine . . . ah, the vine . . . embracing the object of its intent with soft tendrils, creeping about it slowly to drain away will, life.

Sutton reverently traced one perfectly manicured nail over the twining carved leaflets, his lips curling back from white teeth. His idiot opponent for the lead position in the Whig party was already helpless to stay the powerful baron. Chains of ugly rumor bound Overton already, hammered of policies held in secret—that he bore in his home rosaries, trappings of idolatry, papistry. And while the witling, Overton, buried himself in honest effort to bring about Catholic emancipation and erect strictures protecting children caught in crushing factory work, Bayard Sutton was constructing speeches so brilliant, his statesmanship was being touted from the shores of Cornwall to far-off Edinburgh.

He needed but little to rocket him into the position of prime minister. More wealth. Aye, it had cost him most dear over the years to gain the power he now held. And an alliance with one of England's foremost families. A woman so beautiful, young, that even his most avowed enemies, should they learn the truth about him, would not be able to convince the ton of his darkest secret. . . .

The smile on his lips stiffened into a half snarl, his fingers falling away from the statue. If only the "snakes" in his employ had rid him of the single obstacle blocking him from the wealth he so deserved. Wealth he had gleaned with his cunning, his daring, and the paltry seeding of funds from a man he had claimed as friend.

It had been but a simple errand Sutton had charged Gibbon with—a few quick slashes of a knife upon leather, a shot fired from the roadside to make the horses bolt—and then not only the heiress, but her entire estate, would have landed most comfortably in her grieving Uncle Bayard's hands.

Sutton's brow puckered. Nay, he had grown too greedy, eager, driven by the growing sense that someone was battling to tear the veilings from his secret with most dangerous tenacity. Someone by the name of Ransom Tremayne.

Gritting his teeth, Bayard poured out another draught of Madeira, downing the fiery liquor in one gulp. Tremayne . . . Nay, there was no need to fear that dockside ruffian. Despite the fact that his heart yet beat, the man was already marked for death . . . as soon as the single difficulty Sutton's minion had reported was dispatched. A difficulty in the guise of a single child with a memory far too keen for its own continued health.

Sutton's fingers closed caressingly over the African carving, his mind filling with images of tiny hands as they made a bow dance across the strings of a fiddle. Hands he, Bayard Sutton, had begun to school in other skills. It had proved infuriating, the effort he had wasted in teaching the boy the arts of pleasuring. For the moment the waif had suspected what would culminate the "games" they were playing, the ingrate had bolted, leaving Sutton frustrated, with a niggling sense of unease. Yet before the week was out he would need worry no more, for those fingers would lie forever stilled.

And before the year had waned, the baron thought with grim satisfaction, he himself would realize his own highest aspirations. Aye, the tendrils he had been weaving about the throats of his enemies were driving deep into their veins, twining, crushing. 'Twould be worth it in the end, what deaths he had to effect to gain the seat in government he craved. In fifty years, a hundred years, if historians should discover the truth concerning how the Baron of Wythe rose to power, even they would claim that a few paltry lives were of no consequence when compared with the glorious leadership the baron had effected.

Sutton strode to where a carved ivory casket sat upon his desk, opening the tiny chest's lid with crushing satisfaction.

Glorious . . . aye, he would show them—show all England the meaning of strength, of nobility, even if he were forced to clamber over the bodies of Ransom Tremayne, Charleton Lansdowne, and that whey-faced fiddler urchin to do so. And when he stood before them, Baron of Wythe, the most powerful man in the realm, *she* would be beside him, she whose haughty beauty and violet eyes could drive any man to his knees.

Any man, Sutton thought with a sardonic smile, except the man who would serve as her husband. Bayard reached into the ivory box's velvet-lined interior, taking from its depths a ring bearing the seal that had belonged to his family two centuries before, before they had lost their lands in a gamble with the Stuarts, only to regain them under the plodding Hanover cows. Aye, the Suttons had been wise enough to conceal their less savory dealings, even then adopting a crest unsullied by the taint of former treason.

He turned the ring over in his soft palm. Cecily Lansdowne . . . she, too, would be a shield, obscuring that part of him which must be hidden. Stiff-necked, proud, the chit would serve as his wife—*his wife*—powerless, with none to protect her from whatever fate he might choose to bind her with. There was something tantalizing in that . . . some small wisp of allure in the prospect of taming the arrogant chit to his hand. He had done so before, had he not? Broken the will of countless others. He savored the memory, fingering in his mind the images of small, pinched faces, eyes wide with most especial terrors.

It was building again inside him. The twisted need he could never quench. Jamming the ring on his smallest finger, the baron strode out the study door. She could wait, Cecily Lansdowne, Ransom Tremayne, even the glorious future. This night he had fiercer fires to embrace—fires that consumed with dark forbidden pleasures. Scarce pausing to grab his hat and tiered cloak, he hastened out Wythe House's massive doors to seek the flame.

Chapter Thirteen

Cecily curled her feet beneath her on the brocaded stool, pillowing her aching head in the crook of her arms. The windowsill was scented with the light spring breeze, the night a-spangle with stars casting the same subtle hue as the gown that was now crumpled upon the bedchamber floor.

She blinked gritty eyes, her mouth twisting bitterly in memory of the stark horror upon Bess's plain face when she had seen it hours ago. The maid had bustled in, a flurry of disapproval at the condition of the magnificent dress, but had fled, white-faced, when her usually kind mistress had spun on her in fury.

"Be glad I don't cast it into the fire!" Cecily had half sobbed. "'Tis where it belongs! Where everything he bought me with his blood money belongs! Away! Go away, damn you!" *Damn you!* The words had echoed back through the corridor, striking Cecily herself like a slap in the face. Yet she knew not who she had been casting to the devil—the father who had betrayed her, or the gold-maned rogue who had turned her blood to fire with his passion, then seared her with a truth so agonizing it seemed to shatter her very soul.

I love you . . . Ransom had vowed, his voice hoarse with hopelessness, fury, shaded by the words he had uttered before . . . *vowed to find the man responsible for the* Ninon . . . *destroy him* . . . A day ago, a week ago, Cecily would have been proud to stand at Ransom's side, demanding retribution from any man black-hearted enough to condemn hundreds of human beings to a torment far worse than a quick, clean death.

But despite the revulsion she felt, despite the childhood faith that lay crushed at her feet, Charleton Lansdowne was yet her father—the father who had rocked her nights on end when the measles had wracked her body with fever, the father who had helped hold a mock funeral that grief-stricken night her most cherished kitten had died.

And Ransom had vowed to destroy him.

Cecily's fingers dug deep into the flesh of her arms, the nails driving painful crescents into her skin. She wanted to tear at the agony swelling in her breast, wanted to hurl it away from her—hurl both her father and Ransom from her heart forever.

"I hate both of you!" she cried aloud in a broken voice. "I—"

She lurched upright, a knock at the door making her bolt to her feet, wheel toward the sound blazing defiance. "Blast it, leave me alone!" she shrilled at the closed panel. "I told you—"

Had she been able to reach the portal, throw the latch before it had turned, she would have, but the old iron gave a squeaky protest, the door easing open with infinite slowness. Cecily glared at it, tempted to hurl a vase at the head of whoever lurked without.

A fleeting sense of unease struck her stomach, born of the obeah missive she had found upon her pillow. But as the portal swung open on its hinges, Cecily felt she would have preferred any demon Ransom's black sorceress could have conjured to the figure who stood framed in the doorway.

Lamplight wavered over the stony features of Charleton Lansdowne, the cloak straggling about his shoulders making him appear like some bedraggled voyager from the gates of Hades. The smell of fine Madeira mingled upon his breath with the sharper tang of gin. But whatever liquor her father had been attempting to drown himself in had only served to exacerbate the anguish on his pale face.

Cecily turned away quickly, trying to block the haunted image from her mind, trying to cling to her horror, her fury, her pain, and cast away from her the clamoring memories of a thousand actions that had been steeped in love. "I did not think I had to lock my door," Cecily said, struggling to keep her voice level as she brushed the last traces of tears from her lashes.

The portal shut with a dull, melancholy sound, and Cecily could hear the muffled thud of her father's pumps as he crossed the floor to where the gown lay in a heap of disillusionment and broken dreams. Out of the corner of her eye she saw him bend down, lift the shimmery folds in one thin hand. "I did not know I had to lock doors against you, either, child," he said in a weary voice. "It seems we were both mistaken."

Cecily turned, refusing to acknowledge the flushing of guilt staining her cheeks as she recalled her own dishonesty. "I—I don't know what you mean."

"I think you do, little Cis . . ." Charleton skimmed the silk against his stubbled jaw, his countenance so broken it crushed Cecily's heart. "I have just come from Wythe House, and it seems that a man has been making extensive inquiries into my business dealings while I was indisposed. From what Bayard has been able to glean, this . . . interloper has been making an incredible amount of progress in his search."

Cecily couldn't stay the alarm singing through her at his words. "Papa, who—"

"Don't, Cecily. At least spare me the hurt of more lies between us. The man has a name. A name, from what I am told, of which you are quite aware. Tremayne."

"Ransom . . ." Cecily faced her father, biting her lip to still the quavering in her voice.

"So you *do* know the bastard rogue."

Cecily winced at the pain in her father's tone, wanted to scream at him, cry. But she held her head high. " 'Tis I who convinced him to make inquiry into your affairs," she admitted, twining her fingers in the folds of her nightdress. "I knew something was amiss, wanted to help you. But you would not give me so much as a clue as to what, or who was . . . was haunting you. I was desperate. Afraid—" She gave a harsh laugh. "Afraid that some evil ruffian was somehow terrorizing an innocent, loving man. . . ."

"But now you think me the evil ruffian, do you not, child?" Charleton Lansdowne's face crumpled as though she had dealt him a thrust with a white-hot rapier.

"I don't know what I think. You tell me nothing, you dash off without a word—"

"And what was I to tell you? Look at your reaction even now—the dress . . . the dress I scoured half of England to find for you, nigh ruined, while you act as though you loathe me. Fifteen years—nay, nigh twenty now, I have battled to shield you from harm. I owe you no accounting, Cecily, except for the certainty that everything I have done since the day you were born I did for your good."

Cecily stiffened, the words raking her with guilt. "Do not you dare to use my welfare as an excuse for—"

"Excuse? 'Tis no cursed excuse! I am your father. 'Tis my duty—my *right* to do whatever I see as being in your best interests. From the day your mother died, I have devoted my life to you and—"

"All I ever needed was your love! I never asked for satins, silks, never asked for this whole hateful London season!"

"*I* needed to give it to you. Needed to know that despite my father's miserly ways, despite the fact that I could not give you a mother, you would bear the upbringing of a princess. Just as now I need to see you safe—with a husband to guard you if I—if I should—should be unable to protect you."

"I don't want anyone to protect me! What I want is to strangle these popinjays strutting about, touting their family lineage and the vastness of their estates—half of which have no doubt been bought by money as tainted as yours! Not one of them would bother to so much as step over a beggar-child fallen in the street or—"

"And this ruffian Tremayne would? The man is no Sir Galahad. He has nothing to recommend him except that he was idiot enough to embroil himself in battle, and fortunate enough to keep from being blown to bits there."

Cecily felt the blood drain from her face, her knees rubbery, but she did not allow her gaze to falter as it met her father's. "Ransom Tremayne is the most noble, honorable—"

"Sweet God, Cecily, this Tremayne is nothing, no one. And you are the daughter of a lord, granddaughter of the Duke of Moorston. You bear beauty and intelligence and wealth enough to tempt the baser instincts of men far more honorable than a rogue the like of Tremayne."

"Papa, you know nothing of him. Nothing!"

"I know that he used the affections of an innocent girl, twisting them to his own purposes! That he is most likely battling to extort monies from—"

"Nay!" Cecily blanched at the voicing of her most tormented fears. "Ransom would never—"

"How can you be so certain of that?"

"I know him! He—"

"Do you? Do you know him as well as you thought you knew me?" Charleton ran trembling fingers over his clammy brow. "'Tis not that I blame you. If you have been a shade foolish—well, the saints know Tremayne has borne a reputation for coaxing even experienced women from wiser paths. But for that brigand to lure you off unescorted to his household knowing full well 'tis the most serious crime an unmarried girl can be accused of—"

The censure in her father's voice made Cecily laugh wildly. "Aye, 'tis a far more serious offense than cramming hundreds of innocents ripped from their homeland into the hold of a ship, binding them in chains and—"

"Cecily!"

"Then setting the ship afire. Ransom said the captain even burned his crew alive—blocked the door so they were seared—" Hysteria welled up inside her, her voice shrill, cracking, terrifyingly broken.

"Cecily, enough!"

She heard the warning in her father's voice, heard the alarm, but 'twas as though she were tearing at some lance buried deep in her flesh, as though she could not stay herself. "How many died, Papa?" she shrieked. "Do you know? Do you even care?"

"Child . . ." Charleton's voice was a ragged plea.

"How many did you murder?"

Cecily jerked back, but not quickly enough to evade the stunning arc of her father's open hand. Surprise and pain shot through her as his palm cracked into her cheek with a force that snapped her head around. Charleton Lansdowne's first blow to his daughter reverberated through the chamber, slicing ruthlessly at the deadly silence shrouding them both.

Cecily saw the horror upon her father's face. He reached out toward her, attempting to draw her into his arms, his eyes brimming with tears. "Cecily . . . forgive . . ."

"Don't, Papa." She flinched away, as though his touch would defile her.

"Dear God, Cecily, what did this Tremayne tell you? Do to you? Did he—" The question was bladed with a hundred tearing spikes.

"He told me the truth!" Cecily choked out a laugh. "The truth about the *Ninon* . . . He said he loved me. . . . Nay, he lied to me from the first day I met him, lied just as you did—"

"Love? The bastard claimed he—" Charleton lunged at her, gripping her arms desperately. "Tell me you bear no feelings for this hell raker, this—"

"I wish to God I didn't!" Cecily blazed. "I wish I could hate both of you!" The words bit like the lash of a whip, and Cecily saw her father flinch. "But I can't—damn you both to hell, I—" A sob raked her chest, and Cecily buried her face in her trembling hands.

"My God," her father breathed in a rasped whisper.

"Aye, pray for me, Papa! In my *great sin*. Set me to confess to some huge assemblage of judges—mayhap cast me into

Newgate! Or—Or Briarton. Sweet Jesus, there is naught that would give me more joy than if you would hurl me back to Briarton."

"Damn it, I cannot take you to Briarton! The world is crashing down upon us, and all I can do is see that you are sheltered when it lies in ruin. But Tremayne—" Charleton squared thin shoulders, a steely glint in his blue eyes penetrating even the haze of pain yet engulfing Cecily. "I can damn well assure he'll not drive his bloody talons into you any longer."

"Papa—"

"No, Cecily. You will never speak that man's name again." She saw her father's mouth twist in a snarl of hate, aye, and resolve. "For if Ransom Tremayne ever dares to try to come near you . . . hurt you . . . again, I vow the lowling bastard will wish to Christ that the cannon fire at Trafalgar had sent him to eternity."

The swan skimmed the sapphire water, her neck arched in regal dismissal of the awkward creatures clustering about the bright lake's shore. Ransom's gaze dragged wearily in the lovely bird's wake, his heart throbbing dully as the swan circled in a scornful path around a ragglety-tag toy boat a lad was attempting to launch from the far shore.

He could almost feel the boy's longing as one pudgy arm reached out toward the snowy grace gliding just out of reach. For just a glimpse of such perfection bore the power to take things that one had imagined perfect and shift them into crude sticks and strings, stripping them of illusion.

"Lacey—Lacey, nay!"

At the sound of the high-pitched voice, he turned burning eyes toward the bank sloping toward the pool of blue and gazed at the sight before him. Tumbled midnight curls and dark Gypsy-babe eyes brimmed with mischief in his daughter's face, her rosy-cheeked happiness a jolting contrast to the pallid, somber set of Nicky Dolan's features.

"You'll stain your petticoats, an' Jessamyn will scold!" the lad called in warning, but his face was as resigned as that of a soldier being ordered off to battle.

" 'Ware, Nicky! 'Ware!" Ransom heard his child cry. "The red In-di-jans are comin' an' they'll tomahawk off your hat!"

Ransom felt a reluctant smile tug at the corner of his mouth as he watched Lacey hurl herself down the little hill, rolling pell-mell down the slope with a battle cry that would make an Iroquois proud. Skirts and petticoats fluffed in wild abandon about tiny lilac-pink stockings. The hole in one woven knee already attested to a day filled with many more pleasures than Jessamyn Smythe had anticipated when he had carried off the two children that morning. Yet, though he had intended to drown his own miseries in a full dose of childhood joys, for once the laughter of his daughter left him even more melancholy than before.

He sat upon the chill ground, leaning back against a willow tree, the waving fronds dripping from its great trunk brushing against his arms. Always before when with the children, he had been able to yank his dark moods into perspective, force himself to acknowledge how very rich he was in all that mattered. Yet in the eternity since Cecily Lansdowne had fled Tradewinds, her spirit savaged by truths too brutal to bear, Ransom had had to face truths of his own about a life, a love that tore at him with relentless power.

Happy . . . nay, he had never allowed himself to be happy. Even when he had been Lacey's age, trapped on the shore of a town founded for the sole purpose of furthering human misery, he had been caught up in filling some huge emptiness inside him. He had jammed countless rages into the gaping hole, along with fierce protectiveness. And at a time when most boys were wielding cricket bats or hying off to Oxford, he had been shouldering a hundred responsibilities that had left him crushed beneath their weight. And now, no matter how much happiness he had tried to sweep into that yawning chasm that was his heart, he had ever been empty. Alone.

He longed for someone to share in his daughter's antics, revel with him in her independence and her courage. Yet there was no one with whom he could whisper late at night in the bed he had held alone for fifteen years. There was no one who could tease him when he fussed over the child too much, or to reassure him when he tried to curb her streaks of wildness.

He plucked a snippet of willow bough, twirling it between two fingers as he watched Lacey and Nicky frolic in the sun. Nay, he had never needed anyone to guide him in giving his daughter an atmosphere crafted to make her thrive. Yet never once had he stopped to think of his own spirit.

Until he had glanced up from a street brawl and drowned in Cecily Lansdowne's wild-violet eyes.

A laugh tore from his lips, bitter. Cecily Lansdowne . . . nay, what was that monstrosity of a name her father had christened her with? Lady Cecily Arabella Anastasia . . . He could see the line of the dour-faced portraits of ancestors she had been named for—legacies of noble relatives honored in monarchs' households for three generations. While he . . .

He was naught but the spawn of some nameless slaver, and a girl far too young to have borne the agonies of childbirth. When he had been growing up, at Satan's Well, it had been a jest, the tale of how he had come by his name. Ransom. Yes, he had served as his mother's ransom, freeing her from shacklings more hideous than any iron-hewn chains could offer. She had offered her infant son up to the diabolical Tuxford Wolden like some sort of pagan sacrifice. A life for a life . . .

Yet even as a child, clawing through refuse heaps, Ransom had understood far too clearly the shattering reality of life in Satan's Well. And he had never come to blame the child who had given birth to him for gaining her freedom in the only way she could.

He shifted his gaze back to the swan, sweeping across the ripples like some enchantress. Pure, untouchable, the graceful bird was trapped in its own beauty, bound as certainly by fate as Ransom himself was.

But 'twas no longer the swan he saw, but rather, the sable-tressed spitfire who had buried herself in his heart.

I hate you! Sweet God, she had meant those words when she had thrown them at him in half-crazed fury. And that verbal lashing had cut him more deeply than any physical abuse he had ever endured. Yet even as she had stormed from his house, from his life, he had welcomed the shattering anguish. 'Twas safer this way, with her loathing him. Safer. For if she hated him, he would ne'er again be raked with the temptation to touch her, to kiss her, to take her to his huge oak bedstead and tumble her back into ecstasy.

Ecstasy? Ransom ground his fingertips into his burning eyes. Aye, that he could give her. Such skillful lovemaking she would cry out beneath him, toss her glorious dark hair, writhe with pleasure. Mayhap she would not even know that he had defiled her. But he would know. He would always know.

He felt bile rise in his throat, his gaze fixing upon his rope-callused hands. The cruelest twist the fates had ever served him was that they had drifted within his reach a haughty princess with skin like new cream and a smile like a shy madonna's. He could almost hear them laughing at him—the devils that had chained him all these years—jeering at that part of him that wanted to hurl himself, reckless, into Cecily Lansdowne's arms, despite the cost.

His wife . . . aye, he would make her that in an instant if some magical waterfall could cleanse him of his past. If they could be whisked into a world where it did not matter that she bore four names of ancient lineage, and the only surname he could give her was one stolen from the first man who had e'er shown him kindness.

But now, even if he could capture that mystical world, she would not have him. She hated him. He had seen it countless times now, in the pallor of her face at her bedchamber window as she peered out into the night. He had searched her distant, obscured features every chance he could while secreted below, keeping watch upon her. But just as there had been no other sign of the intruder who had breached her bedchamber, there had also been no sense of forgiveness in the pale shade of a woman whose candles burned nigh until dawn.

"Papa! Papa, watch!" Lacey's shrill cry made him drag his gaze to where she was scaling a gnarled cherry tree, the trusty Nicky standing below, his arms outstretched as if he meant to catch her should she take a tumble. 'Twas ludicrous, the idea that the lad's stick-thin arms could hold the dimpled, energetic bundle that was Ransom's daughter. Yet watching the boy wrenched at something buried in Ransom's heart. He could remember another lad, flesh barely covering his lanky bones, green eyes more savage than civilized, battling to save a child from a fall promising far more dangerous results than a sprained ankle or bumped head. And now, as a man, Ransom knew the task had been equally hopeless.

Was it that aura of fragility about Nicky Dolan that raked Ransom so deeply—the stark adoration the child held for little Lacey? Or was it rather the hopelessness in the child's pinched face, the shattered innocence that made Nicky shrink back in revulsion any time anyone save Lacey touched him?

From the first moments Ransom had freed the boy from the rubble—his frail body miraculously unscathed, his eyes empty of all save some hideous shame—Ransom had sensed that the abuses to this child went deeper than bruisings and batterings. And the knowledge had eaten like poison inside Ransom, robbing him of the patience with which he usually handled the children he found. He had wanted to take Nicky, shake him if all else failed, force him to reveal who had abused him—and once Ransom had discovered the name . . . His mouth twisted in an ugly smile. Aye, *that* would be a murder worth hanging for.

He had tried so cursed hard to win the child's trust, to gain his confidence, to help him heal. But both Ransom and Jessamyn had made scant progress, until Lady Cecily Lansdowne had breezed in, scattering her largesse of violins and ginger cakes.

And when he had seen the breachings in Nicky's carefully constructed defenses, what had Ransom Tremayne, the great champion of wronged children, done? He had had a blasted temper tantrum more worthy of his four-year-old daughter than a man past his thirtieth year.

Wincing inwardly, Ransom glanced at where Nicky's

treasured violin lay ensconced in the crook of a tree root, its honey-hued wood protected by a nest of grass. Only once had the lad offered to play it for the daunting man who had rescued him—offered on a morning after Ransom had sensed Cecily sobbing during her vigil at the mullioned glass pane. Ransom had snapped at the child—not cruelly, Lacey would have scarce batted an eye—but to Nicky it had been the most painful of rejections.

Ransom had tried to mend things between them, coax the child to weave for him a song, but the thread of trust Nicky had offered had proved too fragile, and the child had drawn back into his secret world of pain.

No, Ransom chastised himself, he had been handling nothing in his life with much success of late. Jagger had threatened to set fire to Defiance Enterprises, to see if the shipping company could gain a bit of Ransom's attention. Jessamyn and he had had an argument that had threatened to blast the roof from Rosetree. Khadija was threatening his very sanity with her constant harpings to be taken to Tradewinds. And Lacey . . . she had loftily informed him that "Nicky was takin' tare of her now, 'cause Papa never laughed anymore."

It had been Lacey's pronouncement that had wounded most deeply, her blunt little tongue slicing to the crux of the matter with childish ruthlessness. He never laughed anymore. Christ, it tore his heart out to force a smile. But after each endless, sleepless night of keeping guard outside the window of the woman he loved—a night of seeing her silhouetted in the window, the lamplight behind her shadowing the sweet curves of her body against the thin cloth of her nightgown—it had been torment even to breathe.

Need of her was like a clawing inside of him, never ceasing, only slashing him deeper, deeper, until he was certain that if he did not taste of her sweetness, he would go mad. And to see Cecily, so unattainable yet so broken, had been the most exquisite of tortures Ransom had ever known.

He gave a bitter laugh. No wonder Jessamyn had nigh broken a crock over his head. Every morn, when he had returned to retrieve Lacey from where she had slept at Rosetree, he had been fair aching to battle with somebody —anybody. And Jessamyn's own temper had been stretched to its limits from the moment the sultry African beauty, Khadija, had stepped into Rosetree's domain. He had heard the bickerings of both women until he had nigh wished that it were possible to cast the two of them into the ring at Gentleman Jackson's to fight out their differences.

When Jessamyn had dared to venture the opinion that Lady Cecily's powerful relatives could damned well protect her without Ransom driving himself into the grave, Ransom had exploded, ranting, raving, furious. It had been a horrible purging, a dizzying relief. And when the dust had settled around him and Jessie, they had sagged down onto the child-worn chairs in the great room and held each other. Just held each other.

You have to make an end to this, Ransom. . . . I—I care about you. Need you, she had said softly into his shirtfront. *The babes need you.*

And Cecily Lansdowne doesn't. She had not made that final statement, but it had been written across her honest features with wrenching clarity, mingled with such a pleading that Ransom's throat had constricted.

"Nay, she doesn't need me," Ransom murmured aloud, watching the swan lift off of the lake, take to wing in the cloud-starred sky. "But I—I need . . ."

With an oath he drove his fist hard against the turf, levering himself to his feet. Aye, he needed to make an end to it, but not until he had seen her one last time . . . to make certain that she was going to be all right.

Once he was sure of that, he could turn over the surveillance of her window to a handful of his most trusted men. Then, mayhap he could give Jessamyn peace. The moment he returned Nicky and Lacey to Rosetree, he would hasten over to Winterscape, ask Aurora to hire Khadija as a laundress or a seamstress—anything that would remove the African from Rosetree.

And after . . . His eyes tracked to where Lacey and Nicky now curled beneath the shade of a tree, Nicky cradling beneath his chin the violin he so cherished. With a rapt expression Lacey watched the pale boy make his bow dance across the strings, a crown of willow leaflets Nicky had woven earlier perched askew upon a wealth of dark curls.

And after . . . maybe now was the time to cast away the dreamings Ransom had not even suspected he had cherished somewhere beneath his cynical exterior. The time to take up permanent residence at Rosetree, to be father to the brood he was gathering upon the streets. Jessamyn . . . she loved him. Aye, he had seen it in her eyes, known it, mayhap longer than he cared to admit. Would it be such a horrible thing, then, to give the girl one thing she wanted out of life? Would it be such a crime to take up that warm, caring relationship, sharing the children they both loved? Mayhap filling their arms with babes of their own bodies as well?

A year ago . . . a month ago it would have seemed a fate rich in the things Ransom truly cared about. But then Ransom had not felt this need to bury himself in one special woman's heart, to carve a home, sire children. . . .

Yet even when he closed his eyes, the children he envisioned bore eyes the hue of Lancashire violets, haughty little noses and fiery courage.

"Curse it, I *will* make an end to it," he bit out, feeling something tear deep in his chest. "I'll find a way to see her, and—"

Winterscape . . . the memory of his last visit to the Lyton-Snow town house rose with startling clarity. Aurora had had on her desk an invitation engraved with the Lansdowne crest. *'Tis your Lady Cecily's come-out ball,* Aurora had said, her gaze unsettlingly sharp as she met his thunderous eyes. *It does become most tiresome, attending fetes on my own. If I but had someone to accompany me . . .*

Blast it to hell, he would take Aurora up on her none-too-subtle offer—would storm Moorston's ballroom on Lady Lyton-Snow's arm and discern for himself how Cecily fared. 'Twould be safe—so damned safe. Hundreds of people would be crammed into the town house, the spacious dance floor ringed with sour-faced chaperones.

And Cecily . . . Ransom felt an odd catching in his throat.

Even if the ball was not given in her honor, there could be little doubt that the eyes of every man in the place would be fastened upon her.

Ransom tried to fight back the raking excitement that rose inside him, battling with a need so fierce it defied him to leash it. With an oath he started down the hill to where the two children sat. Nicky's hand faltered, the bow skittering from his fingers at the sight of the man stalking toward them, and Ransom's jaw knotted in self-deprecation at the guilty flush that spread on the little boy's cheeks.

"Papa, go 'way!" Lacey's treble was rife with annoyance. "Nicky's playin' pretty music, an' you don't like it."

"Nay, Lacey, I do like it," Ransom offered, hunkering down to retrieve the fallen bow. "'Twould be special, so special, if Nicky would play a tune for me."

He saw Nicky's eyes widen in disbelief, a kind of timid hope creeping about the sallow face that made Ransom want to take a horsewhip to himself. "Nicky, have you ever heard the song 'So Early, Early in the Spring'? 'Tis an old sea tune . . ."

A smile dawned upon the boy's pinched face. "'Tis . . . 'tis a sad song . . . the sailor . . . he loses his love . . ."

"Aye. He loses his love." Ransom folded long legs beneath him, reaching one hand out to touch the boy's cheek. "Play it for me, Nicky. Please."

Tentatively, the boy took the bow, and the plaintive tones he coaxed from the instrument seemed wrenched from Ransom's very soul—bittersweet, full of pain, yet cherished. Yes, 'twas worth the pain he had known just to feel the wonder he had experienced at Cecily Lansdowne's kiss, her smile. 'Twould be enough to last him a lifetime.

He would cling to it, years hence, when he sat at the fire at Rosetree, surrounded by children, with Jessamyn's bluff scoldings ringing in his ears. He would take out the memory of his forbidden angel and touch his own sea dreams.

Chapter Fourteen

LIKE GLOSSY-WINGED LOCUSTS, society's elite descended upon Moorston's ballroom, swarming over any man or woman of fortune as though they would lief devour them. For two hours Cecily had struggled to endure them—endure what was supposed to have been the pinnacle of her London season. But the constant glare of smiles and the incessant rasp of bows across the orchestra's stringed instruments seemed instead to serve as some ingenious form of torture, designed to punish her for loving two men. Two men now avowed to destroy each other.

Cecily drew farther into the shadows of a tiny curtained alcove, praying for but a breath of peace. Her hand yet knotted in the beauteous cloth of her gown, to prevent her from clawing the eyes out of the next simpering miss or obsequious dandy who dared to coo praise over the glorious silk. Her mouth ached with returning a forced smile to lips that seemed to have forgotten what it was to show joy. And her eyes . . . they stung with the effort of avoiding the one person who seemed most desperate to seek her out with his resolved but infinitely sad gaze.

Against her will, Cecily caught a glimpse of that long, solemn face, the cravat for once knotted with some precision on a scrawny neck as Charleton Lansdowne engaged in conversation with the blustery Duke Harry. It seemed her father had been shedding weight in the time since the altercation in her bedchamber. But though the wistful expression upon Charleton Lansdowne's face twisted dull pain inside her, it could not batter through the shell of misery that seemed even now to isolate her from the rest of the world.

Cecily could not stifle a bitter laugh. She herself had been scarce able to keep any food down since the night the obeah had stolen into her room.

And if Ransom Tremayne and she had taken their tumblings upon the bed at Rosetree to the conclusions both their bodies had seemed to demand, she might well have suspected she was being tormented by the morning sickness she had heard the farmers' wives at Briarton bemoan.

Yet Cecily knew full well 'twas not the burgeoning of life that clawed at her stomach, but rather, the welling of guilt, hurt, shame.

She closed her eyes, seeing again the great room at Tradewinds, rich wood, thick carpets, a thousand curiosities gathered from exotic ports. But most clearly of all she could see dark brows slashed low over intense green eyes, eyes burning with emotion, with hopelessness, love—such desperate love. . . .

"He lied to me," Cecily hissed under her breath. "Used me from that first day."

To find the butcher who had murdered hundreds of innocents, a nagging voice within her cried. *Just as he battles in London to save those too weak to help themselves. 'Twas that which made you love him from the moment you discovered the truth at Winterscape. . . .*

"But then he was not trying to destroy my father! *My father!*" Cecily hated the stirring of tears in her eyes, and willed them away. Her heart ached for Ransom, her hands burned to cradle the slashing of scar that was mute testament to the hell he had survived. But at the same time, the broken little girl buried inside her longed to run to the gaunt man so miserable across the floor and fling herself into his arms.

If Ransom Tremayne had not battered his way into her

life . . . if she had never seen that mysterious cloaked figure . . . if they had never come to London, she would yet be roving the meadows at Briarton in blissful ignorance, certain no evil could e'er touch her.

But instead she was struggling to evade the clinging of the ton's darlings, struggling against the clamorings of viciously divided loyalties and stark pain. Fighting to deny the truth that was far more agonizing than anything she had ever known.

If her father had sent every person on the continent of Europe to the bottom of the sea, he was yet the "Papa" whom she had adored as blindly as little Lacey adored Ransom. And despite the horror of what Charleton Lansdowne had been involved in, despite threats cast out in his pain, she loved him. Loved him, aye, and loved the daring, temperamental rogue who had buried her in such torment.

Cecily felt the stiffness in her neck relax but a whisper as she noted the burly arm of her uncle slung across her father's shoulder, the duke obviously maneuvering his brother off on some vital errand fashioned as an excuse to escape the crush of people. Sweet Mary, 'twould be a relief to escape her father's brooding gaze for even a quarter of an hour. And if she could but also evade the notice of the hovering dandies who had been fair smothering her with their attentions . . .

Her gaze roved longingly to the ornate gilded entryway leading from the ballroom—*from* or *to,* Cecily realized with a jolt, surprised to see the bustle of late-arriving guests. 'Twas naught but a flurry of cape and wisps of gown visible from a distance, yet with a sick, sinking feeling in her stomach, Cecily realized that with the duke and her father absent, and the duchess off fussing about Lavinia's supposed migraine, there was no one save herself to receive whoever belonged to the silver-gauze gown and lean, tight-molded pantaloons.

The footman's scarlet livery was a bright splash against the newcomers, and as Cecily left her hiding place, gliding purposefully across the room, she noted with relief that he was seeing to the needs of whoever was yet in the entry.

The gold-topped cane the dapper young servant held cracked smartly into the marble flooring, his sweet tenor ringing out above the din of voices, dancing, and music. "My Lady Aurora Lyton-Snow, Countess Winterscape." Cecily's eyes had scarce had time to focus upon Aurora's serenely beautiful countenance before the footman intoned, "Captain Ransom Tremayne."

She stumbled, the lightheadedness that had been plaguing her threatening to send her pitching to the feet of the Honorable Miss Danhurst as the ebony-clad figure that had been partially obscured by the countess's gown stepped into the frame of the doorway.

Burnished gold hair, untamed by a brush that had obviously battled with its stubborn waves, skimmed over a frothy white cravat, while shoulders hardened in years of warring sea gales filled out an immaculately tailored coat.

How could the barest glimpse of a single person's face be so devastating? The expression of stubbornly veiled agony in Ransom's visage made her want to scream, made her want to cry. The ruggedly carved features that had branded themselves into Cecily's heart were honed sharper still by what she knew was pain, loss, and a raw frustration.

Cecily glanced hastily toward the direction in which Charleton Lansdowne had disappeared, gratitude to some unnamed deity surging through her. Yet she hastened toward the gilded archway, aware that in a heartbeat her father could return to the fete. And if he were to see the very man he thought had defiled his daughter—the man who threatened to reveal his complicity in the *Ninon* affair . . .

Dodging about the rotund, waistcoated belly of the Earl of Larrinbea, Cecily darted up the few stairs leading down into the ballroom, all but crashing into the broad chest of Ransom as he and Aurora began to descend.

Ransom's green eyes snapped away from Aurora's face, his stormy gaze locking with Cecily's own in a belligerence that froze Cecily's heart and at the same time touched something deep, maternal inside her; as though he were a little boy, not invited to a birthday celebration, who had darted in to filch a bit of cake. Or as though he were the hero of an old sea ballad coming to bid his lady-fair farewell before he set sail to disaster. She scarce noticed as Aurora Lyton-Snow drifted past them like a gauzy silver butterfly, disappearing into the crowd.

"Ransom." A thousand longings were in that name, and a thousand clamoring fears. Cecily felt the pull of his eyes, drawing her in, deeper, deeper, until Lady Lyton-Snow, the absent Charleton Lansdowne, and the whole glittering ballroom seemed to swirl madly into a rainbow of bright colors splashed upon some canvas.

"Gloriana." He couldn't help himself as his tapered, gloved fingers took up her trembling hand. He bowed low over it, his lips lingering upon her knuckles. "You—" His voice caught in his throat. "You look like the princess I named you. Beautiful . . . so . . . beautiful." His mouth twisted as though in pain, his lips set with a grim, gray resolve.

The same type of resolve she had seen on her father's pale face. The fleeting reminder of Charleton Lansdowne's anguish, the threat of his anger, broke through the raging sensations in Cecily's blood, the alarm of moments before crashing over her again in an icy, drenching wave.

"I have read that the ancient Aztecs garbed virgins in their finest raiment before they sacrificed them as well." Cecily gave a cynical laugh, brushing her gown with a dismissing hand.

"And your father intends to sacrifice you this night?" Ransom's eyes, flint hard, swept the dancers.

"Nay, I . . . My father . . ." Cecily cast a worried glance over her shoulder, aware of an uncomfortable number of curious eyes fixed upon them, there, beneath a huge crystalline chandelier. The place where her father had stood sentinel over the proceedings was yet empty, but shadows moved in the night-dimmed doors opening out onto the terrace—shadows that could well be her father and the duke.

"Please! If I could but talk to you for a moment . . . alone . . ." Cecily caught Ransom's hand, tugging him with scarce concealed anxiety toward where one of

Honoria's grotesque imitation Grecian statues dangled grapes the size of cricket balls over a sly-faced cherub.

A spasm of something akin to hurt flashed across Ransom's features, and Cecily was certain that he sensed he was being hidden, that he thought she was ashamed.

"So," he said, his voice tinged with bitterness. "We dare not sully Charleton Lansdowne's pet lamb by allowing it too near the wolf. Of course, I seem to recall that lamb exceedingly eager for the . . . sacrifice a while past."

"Ransom . . . please, don't." Pulsings of hurt throbbed in Cecily's very core. "I—'Tis not what you—"

Ransom snorted a harsh laugh. "'Tis my fault. I hoped . . . thought . . . I don't know—thought you might be a little glad to see me. Or angry. Christ's blood, I'd rather see you spitting fury at me than have you hustle me off behind a statue as though I bore the pox."

"I have been sick with wanting to see you, speak to you, but—"

"But you hate me, still, 'cursed liar' that I am, eh, Gloriana?"

Cecily dragged her gaze to his, needing to trust him, to soothe the hurt pride that formed a brittle shell around him. But even as she stared into his eyes, she could not betray the haunted man yet wandering off somewhere on Moorston's grounds. "Ransom, I could never hate you." She turned her face away, but Ransom's finger crooked warm, gentle beneath the chin she was struggling to keep from quivering.

His hand carefully urged her face upward, and through a blur of tears she saw his own lips, a tight, trembling line of anguish. "What the hell have they done to you?"

"Done? No one has done anything to me—I'm the envy of every girl in London this night, Mirabelle says, the envy of every girl in England. Can you not—not see how *happy* I—"

"Shhh, shhh." Callused fingertips swept up her cheeks, gathering the diamond tears welling over her lashes. "Dear God, Cecily," he rasped, "what have *I* done to you. Those lost-waif eyes, and so thin . . ."

She heard Ransom's breath hiss between his teeth, the scent of bay rum washing over her as his arms eased about her, attempting to draw her against the hard-muscled plane of his chest. But she stiffened, her gaze darting nervously behind her as she drew away. His muscles went taut with the rejection, his tones so soft, full of aching; the tears flowed free down Cecily's cheeks.

"I never wanted to hurt you," he said. "You must believe that! Never intended to . . ."

She battled to force out the words that would devastate him further. "Please, if you do not want to hurt me, leave now. Ransom, my father . . . he knows. Knows about our pryings into the *Ninon*. About my seeing you at Tradewinds. About my . . . my love for you." She saw quicksilver joy and disbelief clash with agony in Ransom's face, such fierce need flashing into his eyes she could scarce force herself to continue. She tore her gaze from his but an instant, trying to steady her voice. "Ransom, he forbade me to ever see you—speak with you again. And I—"

The dauntingly broad shoulders sagged a whisper with what appeared to be acceptance, but the words that came from that beautifully carved mouth stunned her. "I don't blame Lord Charleton, Cecily. But I'll not leave. I cannot rest another night without talking to you—attempting to untangle this mess between us."

She started to protest, but he lay his fingers across her lips, swallowing hard, his eyes flickering away, their usual blinding bright green misted. "I'll not make a scene here, I vow it. But you have to see me . . . tonight, Cecily, please. . . ." He drove fingers restlessly through the tumbled gold of his hair. "Jagger is threatening to ship off to Brazil, Jessamyn is a breath from taking her frying pan to my skull, and Lacey . . . she prefers Nicky Dolan's company to mine. I'm going crazy, Cecily, watching you every night . . . seeing you so pale. . . . Damn it, I—"

She turned eyes washed with bittersweet love to his haggard face. "You. 'Tis you who has been lurking outside at night. Because of that dagger." Her voice quivered, her fingertips whispering up over the full curve of his lips, her throat choked by a lump of emotion.

Ransom turned his head away from her, as though somehow the gentle touch of her hand was torment too great to be borne. But the plea that remained in those arrogant, aquiline features wrung Cecily's soul.

"Aye. I'll see you," she said. "Tonight. But I know not how. . . ."

"Your window. Leave a candle upon the sill after you rid yourself of your maid. Unlatch the window bolt and I'll come to you."

"The window? Are you crazed? There is scarce any grooving betwixt the stone, and no tree to scale to——"

"Gloriana, I've been roving about rigging since I was fifteen. If any man born can gain your bedchamber, 'twill be me." His face was suddenly solemn, and Cecily could see the reflection of the death symbol in his eyes. Aye, they both knew full well 'twas possible to make one's way through her window.

"Let me come to you." His voice was scarce a breath, but it hypnotized her, shattered her with its longing.

She let her hand skim down to his chest, the uneven thrumming of his heart making her want to cry. "Aye. 'Twill . . . 'twill be best to unsnarl all that has happened," Cecily said, hating the tiny demon whispering in her heart. *Unsnarl it all so we can make an end . . .*

The single taper melted fire into the mullioned glass panes. Cecily watched the reflected flame dance, doubled and redoubled in the diamond-shaped pieces of glass, the orange glow skimming along the window bolt that even now was thrown wide. She drew deeper into the ripples of the nightgown Bess had garbed her in earlier, the feel of the exquisite fabric somehow soothing despite the nerves that were drawn taut as bow strings through Cecily's body. But still, she was uncomfortable with the impulse that had made her stay the maid from rummaging out one of her more practical, warm nightdresses. It had been pure, unsullied folly to bid the maid to withdraw from the highboy instead a whimsical confection of lawn so delicate it was near transparent, lace finely spun as an enchanted spider's web, and countless satin ribbons of rose, blue, lavender, and gold.

'Twas not that the nightgown was some cherished relic, to grow aged and discolored wrapped in crackly paper, Cecily had rationalized. She had worn it before. Yet then it had been mere chance—Bess, indulging in a fanciful mood, or somehow sensing her mistress was in need of something to lift her spirits. But this night Cecily herself had requested that Bess swirl the gossamer folds about her body, touch the tiniest brushings of lavender scent to her throat, wrists.

For Ransom was coming.

Not that her dashing rogue would even so much as glimpse the nightgown, she thought wryly, buried as it was 'neath layers of velvet wrapper. But knowing she had worn the beautiful gown in his presence this last time would lend just a hinting of dreams to the night that would end the magic between them.

She hazarded a glance toward the doorway that led to the corridor and to her father's chambers, battling again the childish urge that made her want to hasten over to the portal to assure herself for the dozenth time that the latch was thrown home. But she gritted her teeth, turning instead to where her silver-backed brush lay amidst the clutter of her dressing table. Grasping the handle the silversmith had wrought in the image of a lily, she shook back the ebony waves of hair that tumbled well past her slim hips. The heavy tresses were brushed even now to the sheen of the finest of silks, but she dragged the stiff bristles through the dark curls anyway, longing to fill the interminable minutes since she had set the candle upon the sill. It seemed it had been forever since she had signaled him 'twas safe.

Aye, as "safe" as it could be, she thought with a nervous laugh, what with the house brimming with not only the duke's servants, but scores borrowed from his friends as well. As safe as it could be with Charleton Lansdowne pacing in his chambers scarce a cart length away, and with the threat of the obeah shrouding the room. But the biggest danger, Cecily knew, lay beneath the velvet folds of her bedrobe, in the wild, sea-dream wings battering at her heart.

"Perdition!" She hissed, biting her lip as the brush skittered from clumsy fingers and clattered down upon the table with what seemed a deafening sound. But whatever other oaths had been rising to her tongue choked her as she caught a glimpse of the window behind her reflected in the mirror's face. Hungry eyes were dark-shadowed in night-hazed features, the stark white scar slashing down one arrogant cheekbone but accenting the masculine beauty in Ransom Tremayne's bronzed face.

"And you bid *me* to mind *my* swearings?" The low, raspy tones struck through her.

Cecily spun toward that voice, so beloved, yet edged with the same despairing tension she herself was prey to. The candle holder caught loosely in one large hand, his body enveloped within the night-black fall of a cloak, Ransom sat upon the windowsill, his eyes hot and dark upon her unbound hair.

Cecily struggled to swallow, but her throat was suddenly dry.

"There is nothing to fear, princess," he said in that whiskey-warm voice as he slid lithely down from his perch, the candlelight gilding every tantalizing plane of his face, shading it in mystery. "I'll not put pepper on your tongue."

"Pepper?" Cecily managed to squeeze from her frozen throat as he angled away from her a moment, unfastening the heavy portiers to cover the window's revealing expanse. "How . . . how did you know they used to . . ."

"Pepper your tongue? Ah, so your illustrious governesses did attempt to curb your wicked ways." There was a touch of humor in his voice. "'Tis Jessamyn's cure as well for mouths that, shall we say, bear too tart a vocabulary." The hinting of smile that curved the corners of his lips made Cecily's heart slam hard against her ribcage.

"You—You must run up an enormous tally at the spice merchant's." Her voice sounded fuzzy, somehow detached from her, whisked away from the real Cecily Lansdowne by the woman who stood before the man she loved in shieldings of velvet, petaled over gossamer lawn.

"Nay. I developed a penchant for pepper long ago, and—sweet Mary, princess . . ." He turned toward her, the light striking full upon his face, and the breath left her body in one crushing gasp. "You look so damned pale. But beautiful . . . dear God."

Hunger. She had never seen such hunger. Felt such a grinding sense of loss. He was like the sleek tigers from the jungle where he had been bred—never tamed, yet so wildly beautiful, she wanted to risk any danger to embrace what he promised with those devouring eyes. And she would have— would have cast all to the winds for her rogue of the sea—had it not been for the haggard man who was no doubt tossing restlessly in the bedchamber across the broad hallway.

"Ransom . . ." She took a hesitant step toward him— moth to flame—heard his rasped groan as he closed the space between them. Hard, so hard and warm his arms crushed her to him, his face buried deep in her hair.

"Damn it, I've been crazed, certain 'twas my idiocy that had turned you into this pale little waif. After you left Tradewinds that morn, I wanted to kill somebody—your father, whoever left that blasted dagger. But mostly myself for casting out those God-cursed accusations."

"I—I wanted to murder you myself," Cecily replied. "But I know now that you did what you had to. That you feared for me, and . . ." Her voice dropped to a hushed whisper. "That you *loved* me. I wanted to hate you. But all I could think of was how you looked tumbling from that silly mock rigging. Or with Lacey in your arms. Or giving a marble to Nicky. I couldn't drive away the image of your smile, or the feel of you when you . . . you kiss me."

She felt his groan rumble deep in his chest, felt a shudder work through his lean body. "Princess . . ." He dragged his face from her hair, drawing his body back so only the tips of her breasts brushed against him.

"This is not—not fair!" she railed. "From the time I was a babe I've been lavished with everything life could offer. My slightest whim. . . . Now, for the first time, *I* want something . . . want you so much, and I can't . . . because of the *Ninon* . . . because of my father. . . ."

She tried to break his grasp, wanting to laugh at the irony of it all, but the only thing that would emerge from her lips was a choked, hopeless sound as she framed Ransom's cheeks in trembling hands. "I can't have you, Ransom Tremayne . . . can never have you."

She was stunned to see his piercing emerald eyes glisten with a welling of . . . could it be tears? Saw the harsh slash of his mouth contort in anguish.

She willed that mouth to crash down upon her own, willed Ransom to drown her in his bone-melting kiss. But he only reached up his own hands, curving his long fingers about the fragile skin of her throat, his thumbs circling upon her pulsepoints.

"Cecily, 'tis far more than the ghost of the *Ninon* that is keeping us apart, more even than your father. There are things . . . things about me so hideous I cannot even tell you. Things that would horrify you more deeply even than the truths about the *Ninon* did—more deeply than you could imagine. You're so innocent." His fingertips trailed across her lips, his voice catching in his throat. "So brave, and—and loving. An angel after a lifetime of hell. And I . . . will never willingly taint you."

"Ransom—"

"I love you, Lady Cecily Arabella Anastasia Lansdowne." His fingers threaded gently through her hair, his voice a broken caress. "Love you too much to saddle you with a man who . . . who bears not even a surname he can rightfully claim as his own, and a past—"

"I don't give a tinker's damn about—"

"Don't." He lay his fingertips upon her lips, his gaze flicking away from hers, lingering long seconds upon the delicate ribbon ties of her wrapper. She saw his shoulders straighten, hated the steely resolve, the shadings of loss in his eyes as he raised them again to her face. "This is the most difficult thing I've ever done, leaving you now. But before I walk out of your life, I will at least gift you with the few comforts that lay within my power."

Cecily caught her lip between her teeth, not wanting to hear about the "gifts" he was offering, not wanting to acknowledge the agonizing finality in his voice.

She pulled away from his touch, squeezing her arms tight about her waist in an effort to stay the wracking chill enveloping her heart.

"I—I've heard some girls slip their beaus a glove as a remembrance," she said, struggling to keep her tone even, light. "Mayhap you could give your cravat into my keeping. God knows, you're ever ripping it off in a temper, or letting the little ones pull it all awry." The last words came out in a quavery whisper. "Or your hair. You could let me snip a lock of your hair. I've never seen any quite so gold. . . ."

"Cecily." Ragged, raw, she felt his anguish pierce her, mingling with her own. "If I could, I would give you everything—my heart, my life, all that I am. But—" He turned, and she saw a shudder wrack through his taut-muscled frame. "But all I can give you is this. I promise you that there will be no accusations leveled against your father until—*unless*—I gain hard evidence against him. And even then, you will be the first person to know. I'll come here, confront Lord Charleton openly, long before 'tis—'tis fodder for the scandal mongers."

Cecily struggled to drag air into her burning lungs, her hands knotting in her wrapper. "Thank you. I know how much 'tis costing you to leash your temper . . . to be . . ." She let the words trail off. To be what? Kind? Loving? To bury his own fury to battle to shield her?

"And the one other thing I swear to you, Cecily, is that no one—" He wheeled to face her, his visage a mask of savage protectiveness. *"No one* will hurt you. Not the obeah who left the dagger. Not whoever is bedeviling your father. Someone will be keeping watch over you every moment."

"You cannot stand guard endlessly."

"'Twill not be me, angel. I want you too much. Need you." His hand rose to his face, his fingers pressing against his eyes. "And 'tis time we both let go of dreams that are as ephemeral as sirens in the sea, else both our lives be lured onto the rocks. You belong here, amidst satins, laces, ballrooms dripping in diamonds. I belong in the gutter, cracking my knuckles into some dolt's face."

Cecily turned, taking up that beloved, rope-toughened hand, her fingers caressing hard palm, scarred knuckles. "You have such gentle hands, Ransom Tremayne," she breathed, her tears blinding her. She lifted his fingers to her lips, kissed the bronzed, callused flesh. "Such gentle . . ."

She bit back a sob, forced herself to look into his face this last time. "Be happy. You—you deserve to be happy."

"And you, Gloriana . . . don't take the first titled dolt who offers for you. Make certain he . . . he bears a heart to go with all his fancy carriages."

The words twisted like a knife blade deep in Cecily's chest. She wanted to tear her gaze away from him, wanted to look at his face forever. She gritted her teeth, the coldness around her heart seeming to ice her very skin. She shivered, hating the tear that trickled down her cheek.

"If I had been able to wed you, I would have loved you looking just as you are now." Ransom's fingers brushed a path of anguish down one pallid cheek, tangling his fingers in her curls. "I would have sent your maid to the devil, would have brushed this spun silk for hours. Then . . . then I would have carried you to our bed, tucked you deep 'neath mounds of coverlets." She could sense him battle the longings inside him. "Let me, just this one night." This night she would have allowed him anything he might have asked, longed for him to seek more.

She nodded, wild hope pulsing in her center as Ransom's fingers slipped the satin bow of her wrapper, tugged it free. As though she were something sacred, infinitely precious, he eased the garment down her shoulders, letting it fall away to reveal the gossamer folds of lace and the pastel ribbons. She stood before him, not caring that the light from the candle cast a rosy glow over the skin so thinly veiled from Ransom's gaze; proud that she was able to spark the inferno of desire that raged into his eyes, tempered there with such love.

"Ahh, Gloriana. I knew you would look like this—roses and cream and silken ebony." He threaded a single curl through his fingers, pressing it to his lips but a moment. Then he skimmed the tress, warm, moist from his mouth across where the crest of one breast shaded a darker hue against the thin fabric.

Cecily stifled a moan, swayed toward him, drugged with the need to have him touch her as he had during those desire-hazed moments at Rosetree. But he only caught his strong arm beneath her knees, the other about her shoulders, and scooped her into his arms as though she were no more than a child.

Cecily burrowed against the hard heat of his chest, her fingers knotting in his shirt as she tried not to cry. Soft as mists on a moor, he drifted her down into the haven of coverlets, smoothing them about her with an innate tenderness astonishing in such large, hard-callused hands.

"Ransom," Cecily whispered. "I cannot bear you to—to go . . . cannot imagine a forever without seeing you . . . touching you. . . ."

"You'll have a beautiful forever, princess," he said, the cajoling, comforting tones edged with bitter reluctance.

"Nay. I love you. When things are resolved . . . with Papa . . . with the ship . . . it could work out for us as well."

"There is no *us*, love. Never can be."

She saw him wince, knew he read the hurt in her eyes.

"By the time the *Ninon* affair is left to die in peace, I will—" He looked away, and she sensed he was unable to meet her eyes. "I will be giving the babes at Rosetree a permanent father—be wed to Jessamyn."

The words ripped a jagged hole deep in Cecily's soul, and she could not stifle the tiny cry of pain. She scarce felt the heat of Ransom's lips upon hers as he bent over her, taking her mouth in a long, agonizing kiss.

Cecily stretched out her hand, her fingers skimming the burnished gold wave tumbling over his brow, the lines life had carved in his brow. Unable to speak, unable to cry, she leaned toward the man who had stolen her soul, brushing quivering lips across the stark white scar.

"Forget me, angel," he rasped, and she could feel the searing heat of his tears upon her cheek. "Be . . . happy." There was a shuffling of his boot soles as he strode toward the window, the echoing emptiness of the window latch clicking closed.

Cecily shut her eyes in the silence, feeling as though she were shattering into a thousand tiny fragments of despair.

Chapter Fifteen

The first wisps of the coming morn wreathed ribbons of deep mauve, slate blue, and palest rose about the cottage nestled amidst its yard full of hand-built playthings. Ransom trudged toward the heavy oak door, skimming his weary gaze across the fenced enclosure, searching for an elusive peace among the accoutrements of the childhood he had never had. An abandoned hoop sprawled, forgotten, against the ship's mast, while an overturned wagon laden with wood-carved soldiers besieged a bedraggled bed of the springtime's first snowdrops.

In his mind's eye he attempted to fill the yard with the little ones he loved, their whoopings and antics driving back the darkness ever smothering his soul. But even this haven he had carved for them gave him small comfort. For this dawning 'twas as though the cottage yard were filled with cowering shadows of the countless battered children he had not yet found and those he had found too late.

He dragged his feet up the stairs leading to the cottage door, bitterness crushing heavy on his heart. A thousand times he had seen it, in the faces of the sophisticated beauties he had taken to his bed—thrill at the danger in him, a kind of catlike fascination with a renegade who defied society. Ransom Tremayne—the accomplished rakehell who served as champion to guttersnipes. Ransom

Tremayne, a blackguard just far enough beyond the bounds of polite society to titillate.

Those women he would allow himself to sample—experienced, cynical ladies with eyes as chill and hard as their diamonds—had reveled in his body and in the aura of mystery about him. And the simpering little misses in their first ball gowns and their brittle governess-schooled smiles had fair purred like sated kittens whenever he had graced them with so much as a glance.

Yet not one of the lot of them would have cast a moment's thought to babes yet screaming in hunger in some filthy hole while their mothers swilled gin.

But in Cecily Lansdowne's exquisite eyes, he *had* been some sort of knight-errant, questing amidst dragons woven of cruel factory masters and the abusive beasts supposedly charged with children's care. Blast it, when he had seen himself reflected in those dark-lashed, innocent depths, he could almost imagine himself cleansed of the hell of Satan's Well, could almost release the pain of the boy who had defied the brutal Tuxford Wolden, then paid for that defiance more hideously than a woman the like of Cecily Lansdowne could ever imagine.

Almost . . . but only *almost* . . .

And so now I am going to marry Jessamyn . . .

Even now the raw pain in Cecily's pale features drove like talons into Ransom's belly. He loved her. Ransom's face twisted with the pain of it and the far greater agony that *she*, Lady Cecily Arabella Anastasia Lansdowne, loved *him*, a scarred, explosive-tempered blackguard who bore not even the right to touch her hand to aid her down from a carriage.

He leaned his pounding head against the cool plane of the door, shutting his eyes against the vision of slender, long legs, slim curves of hip, a waist he could span with his hands, all veiled from his hungering eyes by naught but a wisp of lawn delicate as a dragonfly's wing. His hands had trembled with the need to cup the sweet swells of her breasts, worship her with his mouth, his hands. Had he ever felt the rushing need that had assailed him in her arms? Had his body ever shaken with desire? Love?

No, always he had been controlled—his mouth twisted in irony—every whisper of his lips over eager flesh, every path his hands charted, designed specifically to glean the most devastatingly erotic effect.

But with his angel . . . in her arms, would he have been able to release himself from the iron grip of a hundred lessons learned while wandering the hallways of Tuxford Wolden's brothel or in the beds of countless bored beauties? Sweet Christ, in the haven of Cecily's love would he have at last been able to *feel?*

"You vowed to make an end to it, Tremayne," Ransom gritted, grasping the door handle in a crushing grip. "For her sake. For your own." And here he stood, dreaming of her yet, his body hard with the want of her, battling the fearsome temptation to sprint to where his gelding was tied, hie back neck-or-nothing to Moorston to claim his princess, devil take the cost.

Fighting the urge to smash something, Ransom unlocked the cottage door, entering the hall beyond. The lamp awaiting him on a sturdy oaken table sent warm-gold patterns shifting about the walls, the scent of bread drawn from Jessamyn's oven that evening filling the cottage with the aura of home. The type of home he would have bartered his soul for as a child. The home he would soon be father in.

But not tonight. Tonight the pain was too fresh in him. Ransom curled numb fingers about the lamp base, his eyes catching a glimpse of Jessamyn curled upon the settee in the great room, a quilt cuddled around her practical nightgown, a nightcap covering her hair as she slept. He knew he should wake her—sensed that she had attempted to wait up for him, perhaps in order to make certain their argument of the other afternoon was healed. Or, he grimaced, to rail at him yet again over some supposed insult perpetrated by the statuesque Khadija. He sighed, kneading his stiff neck muscles with his fingers. At least the conflict between the two women would be put to rest on the morrow, thanks to Aurora's generosity.

If for no other reason than to ease Jessie's mind on that account, he should speak with her now. Yet he bore not the will to wake her. For if it was the raw emotions roiling between the two of them that clouded Jessamyn's brow even in sleep, Ransom knew he could not comfort her—could not face soothing anyone else when within his own soul there was no comfort to give. He would bundle Lacey into layers of quilts, take her to Tradewinds, and rock her in the big pinewood chair he had dragged home from a long-ago voyage to the Carolinas.

So as not to waken Jessamyn or Khadija, he kept his boot tread whisper soft upon the old staircase, gritting his teeth at every squeak and creak of the much-abused risers. On the landing he paused, listening, assuring himself that the dark-skinned beauty behind the closed door of his former bedroom yet slept before he started toward the room Lacey had been settled in earlier. Letting the lamp glow shine through the open door, he grimaced at the tumbled sheets, as usual, devoid of the active little bundle that was his daughter. His mouth twisted in a wry smile as he scanned the bright-rag rugs on both sides of the bed. Empty. His smile softened with love as he turned toward the room where Nicky Dolan slept.

Ransom could almost see the dark-curled imp's little nightgown trailing behind her as she scampered into Nicky's room, soothing the boy when he cried out at night, terrified of visions he alone could see.

The bedchamber door was open, the cheery red curtain Jessamyn had strung up to separate the room into two sections rippling in the draft from the fireplace. A tiny bit of privacy, Jessamyn had claimed the timid Nicky needed. Just a corner of the house to call his own, to retire to when the other children grew too boisterous or his own fears clamored too great.

Beyond the curtain Ransom could hear little Pip snuffling in his sleep, could hear one of the other boys shift restlessly amongst the quilts. Ransom felt a smile tug at his mouth, some small sense of satisfaction warming the misery in his heart. After the day at the park, he hoped he would soon be able to delve to the bottom of Nicky's hauntings, and then throw back the curtain to let Nicky revel in the rompings of the other lads, or at least share the shelter of the comradery that drove away the darkness.

But until then . . . Turning down the lamp wick as low as it would go without extinguishing completely, Ransom entered the chamber, the dim light falling across Nicky's tousled hair, his skinny nightshirted body outlined in the quilts. Only the extra pillow there, beside the lad, attested to Lacey's nighttime trek to the room, its whimsically embroidered case hollowed yet from the girl's curly head. Ransom gave a smile touched with a bittersweet love. Aye, even angels needed a few comforts when they whisked off on their missions of mercy. But the pillow would no doubt have served Lacey better had she settled it on the floor.

Ransom took a step toward the opposite side of the bed, certain that the lamplight would reveal a sturdy lawn-clad Lacey burrowing contentedly into the soft rug. But the circle of gold thrown from the lamp shone on naught but emptiness.

In that frozen instant Ransom's whole body stiffened, foreboding pulsing through his veins, his eyes darting up to where the window stood, closed, aye, but unlatched. . . .

'Twas as though the ominous symbol of the obeah danced amongst the shadows with sinister glee. "Nay," Ransom told himself. "They wanted Lansdowne, to terrify *him* through *his* daughter." In that moment the thought seared through him with sickening clarity. "Sweet God . . . if they deduced 'twas I who was rooting around about the *Ninon* . . .

"Lacey? Nicky, where the devil is Lacey?" Ransom reached out, grasping the child's thin arms to jar him awake, but the moment his hands curled around the boy's flesh, Ransom's own heart stopped. The child was cold, so damned cold . . . Merciful Jesus, the certainty struck Ransom like a dagger thrust to his soul, the candle glow dripping over Nicky's features, stilled forever beneath a mask of gray. Dead . . .

Blind terror, panic, burst Ransom's lungs, thundered against his ribcage, mingled with unreleased screams of denial. "Nicky! Dear God . . . *Lacey!*"

He tore the bedcovers back, not certain what he had expected to see, tore back the cherry-hued curtain like a madman, unaware of the wide-eyed fear in the children behind it as they bolted upright in bed, unaware of the scuffling sounds of alarm running through the rest of the household, unaware of anything but the need to find his daughter.

"Ransom?" Jessamyn's voice carried through the corridor. "What is it? What—" He saw a flurry of white fabric, a face paled more from shock than from terror.

"Damn it, where's Lacey?"

"Ransom, for saint's sake—"

Her words scarce penetrated the stark panic rising within him, his eyes catching a fleeting bit of movement as Jessamyn hastened over to where an applewood sea chest stood, not quite flush against the chamber's corner. Lamplight wisped over black curls, horrified eyes. And the cries of the child huddled behind the chest drove stakes edged with relief and yet-raw fear through Ransom's vitals as Jessamyn straightened, clutching the half-wild Lacey in her arms.

"Stop, babe! For the love of heaven." Jessamyn's protests were cut short as Ransom charged across the room, nigh hurling the lamp onto the trunk lid, to sweep Lacey from Jessamyn's arms.

But instead of the fierce joy his daughter had ever taken in seeing him, he felt Lacey recoil from his touch, her tiny fingers digging into Jessamyn's neck, chubby legs twining about the housekeeper's body as though she were the only safe port in some unexpected gale.

The hurt that cut through Ransom was jagged, deep, as though a cutlass had split wide his chest. "Lacey, 'tis all right, 'tis Papa . . . Papa . . ." Ransom battled to soothe her, mad with the need to hold her in his arms, assure himself she was truly safe. "Let me—"

"No!" The dark eyes were huge in the child's round face, their accustomed innocence and mischief veiled instead with very real fear and . . . *accusation?*

Ransom stumbled back a step, stunned.

"Lacey, enough, now," Jessamyn said in a tone that

brooked no nonsense. "Betwixt you and your father, you've awakened the whole house, except, thank God, Nicky, who must be sleeping like the—"

"Dead." Ransom supplied the word in a tone rife with grief, guilt, and the starkest of pain. He saw Jessamyn's gaze snap up to his face, her eyes locking with his. Had not Lacey been clinging so desperately to the woman, Ransom was certain Jessamyn would have dropped her.

He could see Jessamyn try to form the word, but her lips were suddenly too stiff, her voice too choked.

"Nicky . . . my Nicky won't wake up." Lacey sobbed, burying her face in Jessamyn's breast. "My Nicky . . ."

Jessamyn laughed, the sound sending shivers scuttling down Ransom's spine. "Nicky always sleeps deeply . . . takes half the morn to grow truly awake. When he is stronger—" She dragged the panic-stricken Lacey off of her, hastening to the big bed.

"Jessie—" Ransom tried to catch Jessamyn's arm, but she jerked away from him.

"Nicky's sleeping!" Jessamyn hissed, hysteria lacing her own voice. "He's just . . . Nicky!" She shook the child's thin shoulder. "You've given us all a fright, now *wake up* this instant, or I—I'll douse you with water from the ice house."

"Jessie?" Timid voices crackling with nervousness came from the doorway and from the other side of the chamber, their tones full of the same fearful questions. "Jessie?" "What . . . what happened?" "Is Nicky—"

"Nay!" Jessamyn cried. "Nicky is fine, he just . . . he'll wake in just a—"

"Get back to your rooms!" Ransom snapped, hating the shocked fear that shone in the children's eyes as he turned on them. "Pip, you and the others go into my chamber— Charles, ride to Doc Townsend's. My horse, 'tis outside."

"Aye, Captain." The strapping fifteen-year-old bolted from the room, the sound of his feet clomping down the stairs reverberating through the house like hammerings of coffin nails.

"Captain Tremayne . . ." Lisette quavered with a six-year-old's infinite faith. "Fix—Fix Nicky—"

"Get out!" Ransom flinched as Lisette skittered backward, crashing into the tall, silent silhouette of Khadija. Like an apparition she stood in the shadows, her face half veiled in the dimness, her body swathed in silk the color of blood. In that instant he hated her, hated her impassive features, the brittle, emotionless expression in her eyes. "Khadija!" Ransom barked. "Get the babes out of here!"

"Death walks in this house." Her voice was whisper quiet, yet pierced the children's murmurs with tones of stealing phantoms. "Walks in this house still . . ."

Ransom heard a sharp, tearful sob from the room's dim corner. He wheeled toward the scarlet-clad Khadija, feeling as if he wanted to strangle her for frightening the children further with her cursed mysticism. "Get the hell back to your rooms, all of you!" he blazed. *"Now!"*

As though he were some flame-breathing dragon, the little ones fled before his anger, skittering down the hallway. He turned toward Lacey, needing to hold her, comfort her, but her fear-chilled eyes met his just an instant before she, too, bolted from the room.

Ransom took a step after her, but the sounds in the corridor as Lacey disappeared were lost in the sob Jessamyn muffled against a work-reddened fist.

Khadija's voice rippled through the room like cool silk. "I will tend to the little miss, while *she"*—there were tones of scorn in the African woman's voice as she curled her full lips disdainfully at Jessamyn—"while she rids herself of her wailings."

Ransom started to fling out a biting retort, but before he could form the words, he caught a glimpse of Jessamyn, curled upon the bedclothes, the lifeless form of Nicky in her arms, her fingers stroking at a lank tendril of hair falling over the boy's chill forehead as though 'twas the only thing of any importance in the world.

Far more important than clashes in personality, more important even than harsh words. He would deal with Khadija later—aye, if 'twas the only thing he accomplished before the sun set, he would pack the woman off to

Winterscape. Jessie would have enough misery to confront without the other woman's presence.

Ransom raised his eyes to Khadija's, his voice filled with quiet promise. "Don't you ever speak to Jessie that way again, if you value being sheltered under my care. Now go tend to the other children, and if you say aught to upset Lacey further, 'twill be *my* 'wailings' you will have to deal with."

Khadija lowered her eyes, the light falling across her features to show them schooled into an expression of insincere obedience as, without a word, she turned and glided from the doorway. The hush that fell over the chamber was agonizing, and Ransom cursed, torn between going after Lacey himself or attempting to aid Jessamyn. Lacey would be safe enough with Khadija and the other children, and Christ knew his daughter wanted none of him at the moment anyway. 'Twas Nicky . . . Nicky's death and the thousand clamoring details surrounding it that needed his attention first.

"He—he can't be dead," Jessamyn said brokenly. "He went to bed so happy, practicing some—some cursed sad song about the spring. . . ."

Ransom's throat seemed swollen shut with grief as he sank down beside her. Ever so gently, he curved his own large hand about the small, still fingers that had danced for him that day upon the violin's sweet strings, feeling as though he had lost some vital part of himself.

Ransom's gaze tangled once again in the dark folds of Hiram Townsend's cloak as though somehow that familiar garment held the power to banish the shadows of death that clung about the house. The afternoon sun was only now daring to peek through the cottage windows, the noises of the children in the dooryard subdued. Lacey was amongst them, bruised circles about eyes that screamed of betrayal, her lips pale and trembling. Thrice since she had fled Nicky's chamber, Ransom had attempted to go to her. But each time she had run away. Ransom bit back a despairing oath. From the time she had been but a wee little bundle, gurgling up at him from downy blankets, he had tried to protect her from the harsh realities of life he had been forced to witness. Even the victims of brutality he brought to Rosetree had borne for the little girl the aura of a bold pirate's rescue, holding the certainty that no matter what the coil, her father would be able to unsnarl it, make it right. But Lacey had made the same jolting discovery Cecily had endured but a while before—that fathers were not God, that some things cannot be fixed, that no one can hold death at bay when it swirled its grim veilings about you.

Ransom ground his fingertips against his burning eyes, unable to banish the unsettling aura of accusation in his daughter's small face. Jesu', what did the child expect him to do? Raise Nicky from the dead for her? Aye, Ransom had seen it in her eyes, had seen, too, the shadings of betrayal. Damn it, if he only *could* breathe life back into the boy's cold lips . . .

"Saint Stephen's arrows, when will he make an end?"

He started at the sound of Jessamyn's voice, his gaze sweeping up to where she yet paced the roomy kitchen.

"'Tis past an hour the doctor's been up there, poking and—and prodding at the poor child," she said in a broken voice. "And all for naught. Naught." Her glare fastened with accusation upon Ransom. "All this will do naught to bring Nicky back."

"'Twill give us some idea as to why the boy died," Ransom reasoned, his own patience drowned by stark misery. "Mayhap he had some sickness the other babes could catch, or mayhap . . ."

Ransom let his musings drift into silence, unable to voice the other, far darker fear that yet gnawed within him. He closed his eyes, picturing again the window, its latch unhooked. He hesitated, then shifted his gaze to Jessamyn's chestnut curls. "Jessie, did you—you didn't, perchance, leave the window in the bedchamber open last night?"

She spun toward him. "Are you suggesting I let that child catch a draft?"

"I didn't mean to suggest aught of the sort. I just noticed the window unlatched."

"Oh, aye, so you noticed the window, did you?" A sneering laugh tore from her lips. "The window I've been pleading with you to fix for the past four days?"

"Jessie . . ." Ransom tried to deflect her anger with weary-edged patience. "'Twas naught but a question. I didn't think that you—"

"Nay, you didn't think!"

Ransom was stunned by the sudden raging of grief-spawned fury in Jessamyn's voice.

"You didn't think about me, about Nicky—you didn't think of anyone except your precious Lady Cecily. Nicky . . . he must have been sick, there must have been some sign. If it hadn't been for your cursed fascination with that—that spoiled witch, he might still be—"

"Nicky is dead, Jess. And Cecily Lansdowne had naught to do with it."

"She has half an army of 'Lords' and 'Honorables' to defend her! She damned well doesn't need you!"

Ransom clenched his jaw, fighting the rage his grief threatened to unleash, but Jessamyn would not let it rest. Fierce as a tigress guarding her slaughtered cub, she stalked toward him.

"You haven't given a farthing about Rosetree, about the children, about *me* these past weeks! If I hadn't practically bound and gagged you, you'd not even have taken Lacey and Nicky to the park yesterday."

Ransom felt the welling of guilt bear him down, smothering him beneath the weight of responsibilities suddenly so great they seemed to crush him. "You don't own me, and neither do the babes, no matter how much I love them. I have a right to—"

"Serve as Cecily Lansdowne's lap dog? Some cursed pet for her to bear around on a pillow like Aurora Lyton-Snow's pug? I thought you more a man than—"

"Damn it, Jess, *enough!*" Ransom bolted to his feet, sending the chair he had been sitting in clattering against the floor. With an oath, he kicked it, enraged by the cutting truths in Jessamyn's words.

"Captain Tremayne? Miss Smythe?" Dr. Hiram Townsend's voice cut through the hostility blazing between them. They both turned, wary, but desperate as well, to find some answer to the madness that had been borne in the bedchamber above them.

Ransom struggled to keep his voice level, restrain the fury yet vibrating through him. He righted the chair he had overturned, gesturing for the doctor to be seated. "Dr. Townsend, forgive us. 'Tis the strain of Nicky."

"Don't concern yourself. 'Tis normal in the face of tragedy. They say that adversity brings out the best in people. I've oft found that death stirs so many fears within us that it draws out the worst."

"Doctor, please," Jessamyn broke in, her eyes wide with sick dread. "About . . . about Nicky . . . did you discover . . ."

A face shriveled with encroaching years crinkled further in perplexity, a pair of compassionate eyes peering out at them from folds of crepelike skin. "Damned if I can say what took the boy. Not a fever, or any other kind of sickness that I can find. No sign of internal bleeding. I thought at first I must have missed some injury to the lad's vitals when I examined him after the factory cave-in. Mayhap a timber had driven a rib through a lung, or—"

"I pulled Nicky from the rubble myself," Ransom snapped. "He was sheltered from the wreckage from one of the machines. He scarce bore a scratch."

"Captain." Hiram rubbed one hand through a shock of ice-white hair. "I said *at first* I suspected an internal injury. But upon examining the lad, I could find no evidence of any swelling, no discolorations of the skin."

"But you must have some idea . . . must be able to give some . . . some reason . . ." Jessamyn's tremulous pleading drove away the fury Ransom had felt toward her moments ago.

"I'm sure there is, Miss Smythe. But only God will ever know it." Townsend forced himself to his feet, regarding them both with empathetic eyes. "I understand 'tis hard, but sometimes things like this just happen—a weakness in the blood, mayhap, a sudden shock, the heart merely stops beating."

"Are you suggesting that Nicky could have been . . ." Ransom paused, trying to frame the horrible thought into words. *"Frightened* to death?"

"I'm not saying anything of the sort, Captain Tremayne. I'm merely attempting to explain that any one of a score of things could have happened to Nicky Dolan. The child is dead. That is the only certainty I can give you."

Ransom bit back a bitter laugh.

"Captain, you've seen death enough times to know that God sometimes works in mysterious ways. The child had obviously endured a"—the doctor licked his lips—"a most distressing life before you found him. Perhaps 'tis for the best—"

"That he never know joy? That he finds his home in a coffin because no one would offer him one here? Don't tell me the boy is better off with some God who abandoned him when the child was no more than a babe! Don't tell me—"

"Ransom . . ." The sob from Jessamyn made Ransom swear, slamming his fist into the scarred wood of the table. Silence settled over the kitchen, heavy, stifling.

At length the doctor cleared his throat. "Well, I . . . I vow I'd best be going. I can be of no use here." He walked to the peg, removing his rain-wet cloak, dragging it tiredly about his shoulders. "Captain Tremayne, Miss Smythe." He turned toward them, and there was compassion in his voice. "I know it does not serve to heal any of the pain you are feeling now, but I can set your hearts at rest on one account. The other children—they are perfectly safe from . . . from whatever took the unfortunate boy."

Safe . . . Ransom wanted to laugh aloud, couldn't as he heard the door shut quietly behind the doctor. The witling had as much as said that Nicky Dolan had no reason to die . . . that the fates had merely plucked him as some sort of random sacrifice, unless . . .

A sudden shock . . . Townsend's voice reechoed in Ransom's mind. *The heart stops beating* . . .

"No." Ransom hissed the word aloud, unable to face that most wrenching possibility of all. He closed his eyes, picturing Lacey's face when he had first entered the bedchamber, seeing her again cowering behind the sea chest, the haunted expression in her eyes each time he drew near her.

Frightened to death . . .

With an oath, Ransom wheeled, stalking toward the door, but before he could reach it, Jessamyn barred his way. "Where are you going? What—"

"I'm going out to get Lacey, find out what the devil happened last night before it drives me mad."

Jessamyn's chin stuck out stubbornly, the tiniest spark of her old fire returning to her eyes. "You'll have to battle your way through me first."

"What the hell?" Ransom blazed, taking a step toward her. "Damn it, I'm going out to get my daughter and—"

"And traumatize her further? Ransom, the child is half crazed with terror. Her dearest friend died—*died* right there beside her."

"For God's sake, I know—"

"You *don't* know what she is feeling. Neither do I. But if you go storming out into the dooryard, drag her in here and force her to slash open all that happened last night, you could well lose her trust forever."

"Something is wrong, Jess. I sense it. Christ, she's terrified. And the way she looks at me . . ." Ransom's voice broke, his hand raking back through the tangled mass of his hair.

"Of course she's terrified. Death is enough to freeze the courage of grown men in battle. To a four-year-old who has known naught but love and security, it must be the most frightening thing imaginable. And as for . . ." Jessamyn paused, and Ransom could see her battle to choose her words with the greatest of care. "As for the way she reacted to you . . . it hurts you, Ransom. I know it. But Lacey has never seen you so . . . angry, fearful."

"Then I have to make her understand—have to find out

what . . . what is driving her away from me. Fix it." He spun on Jessamyn, defiant.

"There are some things even you cannot repair." Jessamyn's voice was soothing, laced with grief as she stepped toward him, her hands comforting, warm upon his face. "And Lacey . . . she has to learn that, painful as it is. I know you're half mad with needing to heal things. But you have to give her a little time."

"Time," Ransom repeated bitterly. "The one thing I failed to give Nicky. The only thing that really matters."

The sound of the door creaking open made Ransom's jaw clench against the hot welling of grief choking his throat. He did not turn his gaze toward the portal, but could feel hostility crackle within Jessamyn as she gazed at whoever had entered. Musk and silk, the scent permeated the room, spiced with an incongruous aura of a world mere mortals could ne'er tread.

Khadija. He knew 'twas she even before that husky-dark voice rippled across the silent room, and he wanted to hurl her out of the private agonies he and Jessie were both suffering.

"The doctor—I saw him leave," Khadija said, the sound of her footsteps shushing across the floor as she neared them. "Did he discover anything? Any . . . sickness in the child, or—"

"He said 'twas most likely the boy's heart." Ransom tried to control the unreasonable anger in his voice. "He said it just . . . stopped beating."

He turned his gaze toward her in time to see the woman shrug, her delicate brown fingers readjusting the pin anchoring the turban of scarlet that bound up her hair. "To be sure, 'tis most heart-wrenching, to see the boy dead." Ransom felt her gaze sharpen, a strange, weighing light penetrating the guise of concern in her eyes. "I know he was quite . . . close to you."

"Not close enough, damn it." Ransom's hands clenched into fists, frustration and sorrow seething in his chest. "Another day . . . one more day, and he would have . . . God damn it to hell!" He slammed his fist into a pewter bowl, sending it careening off of the table, the sound as it crashed to the floor deafening.

A cry of surprise breached Jessamyn's lips, her hands pressing to her throat, but Khadija merely stood, regarding him with those strange eyes, her silence eating like a thin layer of acid upon his flesh. He rammed his fingers through his hair, feeling upon his knuckles a warm wetness where the skin had split.

"Mayhap instead of damning your god you should be thanking him," Khadija said with a stony calm. "'Twas but a sickly boy who died, not your daughter."

"Every child at Rosetree is as much Ransom's babe as Lacey is!" Jessamyn stormed. "Even the sickly—"

"The sickly boy you let waste away before your eyes?" Khadija said mildly. "Had you not been scheming to gain your own children by Captain Tremayne, mayhap you would have seen—"

"Damn it, stop!" Ransom roared, but already Jessamyn's face was crumpling with such grief and humiliation he wanted to slam the pewter bowl into Khadija's compressed lips. "I think you've said enough," he said, fighting the unsettling feeling that Khadija was battling a smile. "I think we've all said enough."

He glared at Khadija, suddenly, savagely glad he could rid the cottage of her presence with a clear conscience, yet knowing, with stunning certainty, that even if Aurora had not agreed to give the woman work, he would have rid Rosetree of Khadija this day. His fingers curled tight into his palms so that he would not physically dash her out of the door. "I had planned to tell you this morn anyway, thought to have you on your way off to Winterscape before breakfast, but what with Nicky . . . the doctor . . ."

"Winterscape?" Khadija arched one fine dark brow in inquiry. "I'm sure I bear no idea as to what . . . where—"

"'Tis a town house nigh St. James," Ransom cut in. "Owned by Countess Lyton-Snow. She has need of a laundress."

The haughty Khadija's nostrils flared. "I'm sure I do not understand."

"You will. I told Lady Lyton-Snow that I had a woman most anxious to gain honest employment. And I asked that she take you on as—"

"Nay! I—I need . . . want to be with you at Tradewinds!" He was shocked to see the genuine shadings of alarm in that darkly beautiful face as she stammered. "I fear—"

"Winterscape boasts scores of servants. There is no way your former protector could harm you in its confines."

"Let me . . . at least let me remain here. I—"

"Nay." Ransom's eyes flicked to Jessamyn's strained, ashen face, the shame and raw sorrow upon her features feeding his fury with the turbaned Khadija, his voice hard as he looked again at the woman who had so grated against the housekeeper's nerves. "I promised Lady Lyton-Snow that you would arrive first thing this morn, so you are already tardy."

Khadija swept up the train of her gown in her hand, her eyes narrowing. "I'll not—"

"You'll take the position I've gained you, or you'll sleep in the streets this night," Ransom said, his voice holding a sharp edge. "Now gather the things I had Jessie buy you and go."

"Go? Oh, aye, I'll go." The berry-dark lips parted, some secret hidden away beneath their ripe curves. "I'll go. But not to play drudge to some aristocratic witch."

She turned, gliding from the room with the majesty of a sorceress and an odd, lazy menace. She paused just outside the door, turning. "My condolences upon the boy," she said, her moist lips glistening. "What was his name?"

"Nicky! His name was Nicky," Jessamyn fairly sobbed, but already the door was closing behind Khadija, making her vanish as silently, suddenly, as she had appeared.

Jessamyn sagged against the table, one fist pressed to her brow, but Ransom was unable to offer her succor. He was tired, so damned tired, and felt so cursed old. Slowly he paced to the window, pulling back the curtain of cheery gingham, leaning his brow wearily against the pane. His eyes found within the crowd of children the pale little waif who appeared but a ghost of his vivacious Lacey, her face cast in shadow as the rest of the babes ringed protectively about her.

Ransom felt a burning beneath his lashes, felt the soul-wrenching need to bury his pain in the haven of Cecily's love. Bracing his arm against the window frame, he leaned his head against his bicep, winding through a cruel labyrinth of grief he alone could see—a labyrinth as dark and terrifying as the twisting corridors of Satan's Well.

"Ransom." He felt Jessamyn's fingers brush light against his shoulder blade, her voice hesitant.

"I'm sorry, Jess. Sorry I dragged Khadija here. Forced you to deal with—"

"Nay, 'tis all right. At least a . . . a part of what she said was true. I've not been scheming, Ransom, to gain your bed. But . . . mayhap if I hadn't loved you so much, hoped . . . mayhap I would have seen. You'll never come to Rosetree, take me as wife. Because you love Cecily Lansdowne. And now, naught else will ever be enough."

"Jess . . ." Ransom closed his eyes, her words ripping wide truths too painful to bear. And all the reasonable, logical plannings he had made the day before suddenly seemed the blind rationalizations of a child. "I can never . . . never marry."

"I know. But I do need to ask one boon of you. Just one thing, Ransom, because I . . . I love you."

She paused, and Ransom forced his gritty eyelids to open, his gaze focusing upon the earnest, loving curves of Jessamyn's face.

"Vow to me, Ransom, that you will . . . will give Lacey time before you confront her about last night. Say, until at least after the burial."

"I'd not confront her . . . I only—"

"You wouldn't intend to," Jessamyn interrupted, the love in her eyes wrenching Ransom's heart. "But I know your temper. You have such a foul temper when you . . ." Her words trailed off, her fingers falling away from where they had rested upon his skin. "Please, Ransom."

He tried to speak, couldn't, his gaze roving out to the yard beyond, to where Lacey huddled at the base of the play mast. Time . . . the child needed time . . .

But he . . . he needed . . .

Ransom closed his eyes, the urge to bury his face in Cecily's soft hair, pour his grief into her graceful hands, raking through him with savage intensity.

Damn it, angel, I need you, he cried inside. *Jesus, God, I need you.* His eyes burned, a shudder wracking his shoulders as he battled the sorrow bearing him down. Nay, she too was beyond his grasp now, the comfort of her beauty, her courage—her *love*—as far from the reach of his sullied hands as windflowers on the sea.

Chapter Sixteen

T RADEWINDS LAY SILENT as a sea-struck maid, peering out across the ocean in search of a lover who would never come. Ransom tugged the black armband free from one bicep, dropping the symbol of mourning upon the squat-legged table he had brought from Cathay. If only 'twere as easy to uncinch the grief crushing his heart. Grief for the child in whose stiff, folded fingers he had tucked a violin that morn, and for the little girl who even now whimpered in her pillows in the chamber at the head of the stairs.

It had been Lacey who had tremulously asked Jessamyn if Nicky could take his "biolin" with him to make music for the angels, and it seemed to give the girl some comfort to see it tucked amidst the soft-woven shroud. But when Ransom had attempted to scoop Lacey into his arms, to hold her as the grief rent through her, the raw terror that haunted his dreams had returned to that pale little face.

He closed his eyes, a shuddering sigh burning his lungs. Every night, he had offered the child the "time" Jessie had claimed Lacey needed. He hadn't attempted to touch his daughter, hold her, soothe away the tears he had ever been able to banish. He had drawn none of the surcease he had needed so desperately, the peace he found only in the big rocking chair in her rose-painted room, her trusting, little body nestled warm against his chest.

No, he had done nothing to fray the fragile healing he prayed was taking hold in her. Yet as the last of the mourners left Rosetree, Jessamyn herself had been forced to admit that instead of easing, the pain in Lacey Tremayne had grown until her eyes were twin mirrors of fear.

Ransom sucked in a bracing breath, his shoulders steeling against the pain of the confrontation to come. Never in all his years of fatherhood had he ever felt so blasted inept— aye, and so cursed terrified. Even when Corianda had plopped the wee bundle that was his daughter into his arms four years past, he had borne faith in himself, a fierce knowledge that he had enough love to overcome anything that could threaten his child. But this nebulous threat, this enemy he could not touch or fight, made the link that bound him to his daughter seem suddenly tenuous as a single strand of silk, and more precious than the lifeblood that pulsed in his veins.

The sound of muffled footsteps coming down the stairway made Ransom raise his eyes to the black-garbed form of Jessamyn, her nose reddened with crying, her serviceable gray shawl drooping over sagging shoulders. And despite the chasm of hurt that yawned between them, Ransom was glad she had come to slip Lacey into her own small bed this first time since the eve of Nicky's death.

"She's exhausted with weeping, poor mite," Jessamyn said, her voice thick yet with her own tears. "'Tis so hard for her to understand." She stopped, her eyes seeking Ransom's, and he felt as though she were delving too deep into a fresh-slashed wound. "I—I . . . know how hard it has been for you. But mayhap 'twould be best to let her . . . let her sleep . . . then tomorrow . . ."

"Rake it all open again?" Ransom turned away, unable to bear the pleading in Jessamyn's eyes. "Nay, Jessie. 'Tis not healing, whatever it is that is hurting her. We both hoped that a little time, space, would help, but she is doing nothing but withdrawing further into some—some prison her fears are weaving around her. Tonight I'll tear down the walls she's raised between us, or by Christ 'twill drive me mad."

Long seconds drifted into silence, heavy with words

neither could say. At last Jessamyn tugged her shawl more tightly about her. "Well . . ." she said uncertainly, "I had best be on my way back to Rosetree. Jagger should have the babes in bed by now, but what with . . . with the funeral and all . . ."

"Thank you for coming," Ransom offered quietly. "I know it meant the world to Lacey."

"And to you?" Soft, so soft were the words, tinged by the slightest of hope despite her claim of understanding there could be no future between them—a hope 'twould be cruel to nurture. Iron bands seemed to fuse about his chest.

"'Bye, Jessie." He shut his eyes, hearing her footsteps upon the rugs, hearing the muffled greeting of the trusted dockhand Ransom had assigned to escort her home.

The door clicked shut, the empty sound washing over Ransom in a stark loneliness that made him want to go to the bottles of brandy, Madeira, and claret on a stand nearby, to drink them until his mind was too hazed to be victim to such pain. But he only straightened his spine, mounting the stairs as though he were going to face his own execution.

He paused outside the door to Lacey's room, his eyes skimming the beloved, familiar furnishings, the hearth with its unicorn fire irons, a merry blaze burning upon the grate, the plump feather bed, its curtains done up in ribbons and dried flowers. Nestled cozily in an alcove under the slope of the eaves stood miniature chairs, and a child-sized table set with a tea service even Aurora Lyton-Snow would envy.

Wiping palms damp with sweat upon his thighs, Ransom stepped into the room that had ever brought him such a sense of joy. He trailed his fingertips with a bittersweet longing over the back of the rocking chair where he and his daughter had spent so many dream-touched hours.

"Lacey." He said the name softly, excruciatingly aware that the muffled sobs he had heard but a heartbeat ago had now been crushed into silence—a silence that clawed at his heart. He walked to the bed, watching as the firelight flickered over eyes shut so tightly her whole face was crinkled with the effort, while tiny white teeth caught nervously at a still-quivering lower lip. She was attempting to escape him even now.

He sat down beside where she lay, felt her body stiffen beneath the coverlets even before a shuddery little breath betrayed her. His hands knotted helplessly at his side as he searched for the right words to soothe her, a fragment of prayer gleaned from a holy man on his way to America's red Indians flitting across Ransom's mind: *In your infinite mercy, Father* . . . Please give my child back to me. . . .

"I think your unicorns have missed you," Ransom said at last, pointing toward the gleaming fire irons. "And just think, Lord Nelson, here, has been waiting for his tea nigh on five days." Ransom picked up what had once been a fashionable French doll, its golden curls shorn a long-ago afternoon by busy little hands. A most dashing eyepatch adorned one glass eye, while the dainty pink frock in which the dollmaker had garbed the diminutive figure had been exchanged for a clumsily stitched uniform fashioned from Ransom's cast-off gloves. He held the favored plaything toward Lacey's hand, close enough to tempt her, yet far enough beyond her fingertips that she would have to break her pretense of sleeping to take it from him.

He was nigh about to concede defeat, attempt another tack, when Lacey snatched it from him, the slightest glint of her dark eyes showing against her white face. "Mine!" she flung at him, scuffling over to the far side of the bed with a baleful glare.

"Aye, 'tis yours. You love it, don't you, Lacey-babe."

She said naught, only glowered at him with huge, pain-filled eyes.

"I know you do," he continued as though she had answered. "Do you remember the time we filled the washtub with water and made one of Jessamyn's hat boxes the HMS *Victory?*"

"The big boys, they took it an'—an' Lord Nelson," Lacey lisped with wounded dignity.

"They went to the park to sail it. They were going to bring it back before you awakened from your nap, but the string snapped."

"They were de-test-able naughty," Lacey said warily.

"Aye. But they could have just tripped back to Rosetree and never mentioned that they took Lord Nelson. No one would ever have suspected the truth, and Jimmie, Alexander, and Christopher would never have gotten in trouble."

Lacey said nothing, merely regarding her father with distrustful eyes.

"But they were honest lads. They came to me, and I was able to hie off to the park, retrieve Lord Nelson before his vessel was sunk."

"You swimmed an' the ladies laughed."

Ransom forced a half smile to his lips at the memory of the ton beauties who had observed his daring rescue. "I didn't care about their laughing, didn't even mind so much about the boys taking Lord Nelson. The thing that was important was that the boys had the courage to tell me the truth . . . in spite of the fact that they were afraid. And because of that, Papa was able to help . . . help mend what was the matter."

Lacey made a tiny sound in her throat, and the expression on her face struck Ransom like the blow of a headsman's axe. The lips that had blessed him with a thousand baby kisses were set fierce against tears, the dark eyes spitting confusion and accusation far too wrenching for one tiny girl-child to bear.

"Can't fix! Go 'way, Papa! Go 'way!"

Ransom clenched his teeth, struggling to hold on to patience already frayed by the strain of burying a child who had captured his heart, the loss of relinquishing the woman he loved. He swallowed hard, his fingers digging into the muscle of his thigh. "I'm not going to go away until you tell me what is the matter. Damn it, Lacey, I know you miss Nicky. I miss him too. Talk to me, sweeting. Tell me—"

"Nay! Can't! You can't make me! Won't—" A jolt of pure fear shot down Ransom's spine at Lacey's cry. The sound was shrill with panic as her arm drew back, flinging the doll against the hearth stone with a force that split the delicate head.

The whole chamber seemed to echo with her terror,

snapping the iron control Ransom had struggled to impose upon himself, baring emotions raw as flesh laid open by a surgeon's knife.

His hands flashed out, spanning the child's sturdy waist, dragging her, kicking, screaming, into his arms. "Damn it, Lacey, stop this!" He gave her a shake. "What the hell is the—"

He nigh leapt from his skin as a sudden flurry of violet cloak whisked into the room. "Ransom, what—what is—"

He looked up into eyes the hue of amethysts.

Cecily.

'Twas as if she were some cruel jest, a phantom his mind had conjured. But she hastened over to where Lacey yet struggled against him, and the cloaked arms were warm, tender, wrenchingly real as she reached them about the hysterical child.

Ransom bit his lip until he tasted blood, as Lacey tore from his grasp, clawing at Cecily to escape him.

"What the hell are you doing here?" The words were rough-edged with anguish and a despairing kind of joy. "Was there sign of the obeah? Is your father—"

"No, 'tis nothing to do with me." Cecily cradled the sobbing child against her, the sight of his daughter snuggled against her somehow so natural, so right, it tore at Ransom's heart. "Lady Lyton-Snow called after the burial. The instant she told Lavinia and I what had happened, I dashed out of the house. I didn't care if they both raised the alarm to all of Moorston. The thought of you here, alone . . ."

"I wasn't alone. I had Lace—"

In a gesture he had indulged in countless times, he reached out his lean fingers to smooth them over his daughter's dark mop of curls, but the child thrust her feet against Cecily's lap, trying to drive herself farther out of her father's reach as she broke into shuddering sobs.

"Dear God, Ransom, what—" Cecily didn't finish the sentence as she struggled to maintain her grip on the hysterical child.

"Don't—Don't let him make me!" the child wailed. "Don't let him—"

Ransom drove his fingers through his hair, wanting to smash something, to cry out with the same hopelessness as his daughter. "Damn it, Lacey, I love you!" Ransom's voice broke. "I'd never let anything happen to you . . . never."

"Don't want you here, Papa! Don't want you!"

"'Tis not my fault Nicky died, blast it. 'Tis not my . . ." Agony threatened to burst Ransom's chest. He spun from the room, realizing his own anguish would but terrorize his daughter further.

Outside, in the dim corridor, he watched as Cecily curled in the rocking chair, crooning to the child, whispering bits of soothing nonsense until the quavering in Lacey stopped and she snuffled against Cecily's breast.

Snippets of singing, melancholy, gentle, drifted through the door, lilting over Ransom until he could no longer bear it. With leaden feet he dragged himself to the chamber just across from Lacey's, lighting a single oil lamp to drive away the shadows. It seemed as if in that instant he heard again icy iron gates slam shut, excluding him once more from all that was warm, sheltered. He dragged a chair back from the desk abutting a corner of the room and sagged down into the leathery hardness. Then he buried his face in his hands.

Cecily nestled the coverlets about Lacey, the child's tear-streaked face at last blushed with the peace of slumber. Exhausted, the babe had been, her curly, dark head drooping wearily against Cecily's shoulder moments after Ransom had left the room. 'Twas heartbreaking, the expression that had slashed across Ransom's features, the vulnerability in a man so strong touching Cecily soul deep. But only after Ransom's daunting presence was gone had Lacey shuddered, releasing the coiled tension that was preying upon her.

Cecily bent down, brushing Lacey's dewy cheek with a kiss, her own throat tight with tears. "All will be made well, little one," she whispered. "I promise you. Your Papa . . . he loves you so much . . . needs you . . ."

She stopped, unable to continue, her eyes stinging. Straightening, she picked up the lamp, tiptoeing from the room in search of the man who had left it a quarter hour ago, his proud shoulders slumped in a way she had never seen before. Would he ever forgive her for seeing him so shattered? For the way his beloved daughter had clung to her?

She paused in the corridor, listening, trying to gauge where Ransom might be. But Tradewinds lay quiet, only the crackling of the fires upon the grates audible. She waited but a moment, then heard it—a muffled sound just across the hall.

Feeling as if she were intruding upon some pain too great to share, but unable to stop herself from doing so, Cecily crossed the corridor, slowly easing open the half-closed door.

The room was as spartan as Lacey's was whimsical—a starkly plain bed, a chest devoid of carvings, the walls as barren as Ransom's own heart.

He sat at a heavy oaken desk, his hands curved about two objects Cecily could not see. He didn't look up, but she could hear his pain in the rasping of his voice.

"Thank you for . . . getting her to sleep. Jessie said I shouldn't press the child about . . . the night Nicky died. But 'tis driving me insane, not knowing. . . ."

Cecily started toward him, wanting to smooth her hands over his stiff shoulders. But she stopped a few steps away from him, not wanting to breach the pride she sensed he was battling to cling to, certain if she did, what little hold he had on his grief would shatter him. "Not knowing what?" she asked softly.

"The doctor wasn't sure what Nicky died of, but thought . . . said 'twas mayhap a weakness in the heart—that a sudden shock—"

"But what has that to do with Lacey?"

Ransom sucked in a deep breath, loosed it. "Lacey was with Nicky the night he died."

"Dear God, then whatever terrified Nicky . . ."

"Terrified Lacey as well." Ransom laid the objects he had been holding on the desk's scarred surface, running one rough-skinned finger across what looked to be a delicate porcelain oval. "I've been trying to find out what happened for days. But Lacey won't even talk to me. She screams whenever I come near."

Unable to bear the cracking of his voice, Cecily closed the distance between them, her hand drifting soft over the tousled waves of his hair. Over his shoulder she caught a glimpse of the objects upon the desktop, one, an exquisitely wrought likeness of Lacey, and the other, a smaller, chipped miniature of a woman with silver-gilt hair and eyes the palest blue of a wintery sky.

Cecily's gaze clung to the two portraits, an odd fascination holding her stare. What was it about the two that so mesmerized her? As though the portraits somehow belonged together, were a pair, despite the stark contrast of straight, moon-pale hair to Lacey's dark, wildly curled tresses, despite the pale, nigh colorless eyes, set against melting brown, sparkling mischief. 'Twas the woman's mouth—the certainty jolted through Cecily suddenly—soft, rosy lips shaped exactly like Lacey's own winsome smile.

"'Tis Lacey's mother." The words were dull, emotionless, and Cecily looked to see the slashes of Ransom's brows dark against his pale face, his mouth set in a harsh line. "She left that portrait when she thrust Lacey into my arms, in case the child ever grew curious about the woman who bore her. What think you, princess? Would I not almost rival Corianda's parenting skills this night?"

Cecily's gaze snapped to Ransom's own tawny-gold hair, intense emerald eyes, also so at odds with his daughter's dark beauty, and the sudden wrenching truth made tears well in her eyes.

"Lacey . . . she is not . . . you are not truly her . . ."

"Father?" Ransom gave a raking laugh. "I could have been. God knew, Corianda and I had indulged our mutual lust oft enough. But our *grande passion* had burned itself out months before Lacey was conceived. Corianda . . . I guess she took me for a fool, thought a man the like of me would be too ignorant to gauge the age of an infant closely enough to know that 'twas impossible the babe was mine. But I knew."

He arched his head back, tormented eyes fixed upon the shadows dancing on the ceiling. "I knew the instant I drew back the little blanket covering Lacey's face. But I didn't care, damn it. I didn't . . ."

He levered himself to his feet, pacing the room, restless, hurting. "Corianda but wanted to give the child a decent life. God knew, she was not fashioned to—how did she put it?—spend the rest of her days swabbing disgusting messes off of her satins. She was a dancer, and the places she frequented were of a certainty no place to drag a babe. And one night when I was particularly drunk," he laughed bitterly, "or foolish, I had betrayed to her how desperately I wanted a child. Betrayed to her the truth of why I could never marry, have one of my own body."

"So she gave Lacey to you." She couldn't prevent her gaze from running down the lean, virile length of Ransom's frame, her body burning with the memory of the hard heat of his masculinity pressing against her . . . the sweet, savage lovemaking it had promised.

"Ransom, think you I care at all if you can't . . . won't . . ."

"Nay, princess, 'tis not that." There was black humor in his voice. "God's wounds, I wish I was impotent of late. 'Twould be blessed relief compared to the hell of wanting you and never being able to—"

"To what, damn you?" She caught his scarred face in her hands, wishing she could soothe his battered heart as well. "Ransom, I love you . . . I don't care who or—or what this 'hideous secret' is that you are bearing around with you. It matters naught. All that matters is the love I bear you. I want . . . want you to show me what it means to make love, just as you've shown me what it means to give love."

With a choked cry, she caught his lips with hers, infusing her kiss with all the aching love within her. She heard him groan, his arms crushing her against him, his mouth hungry, seeking, his hands wild upon her body.

Whether 'twas he or she who eased them to the bed, Cecily never knew, lost as she was in the savage splendor of Ransom Tremayne's kiss. But as he covered her body with his own, their clothes the only small barrier betwixt the ragings besetting their bodies, Ransom braced himself on his elbows above her, his chest vibrating with a choked sound akin to a sob.

"Nay, princess. Nay. I've failed Lacey this night. I'll not fail you as well. . . ."

"Fail me? You could never—"

"I already have." Ransom tore himself away from her, grinding his fingertips into his eyes. "I lost any right I had to you before I ever met you, before I sailed from Baytown. Before—"

"Nay," Cecily said fiercely, kneeling behind him upon the bed, leaning her tear-wet cheek against his back. "You're all I want, Ransom. Everything—"

She jumped as Ransom turned, grasping her chin between fingers far from gentle, his eyes burning. "Look at me, princess. Look. This is what you think you want? This fantasy of half pirate captain, half Sir Galahad you've woven about me? I'm none of the things you think I am, none of the things anyone in London thinks I am. Aye, I saved my own cursed neck at Trafalgar, and managed to drag the rest of the ship along with me. But before that . . ."

Cecily felt some small part of her freeze, afraid of whatever it was that had so broken him, yet at the same time wanting to take his pain into herself, to make it hers.

He must have seen her fear in her eyes. His own darkened. "Before that I lived in a place called Satan's Well. A brothel in Baytown, on the Gold Coast."

"A brothel? You lived in a—"

"My mother was a prostitute." As though to spare her the trouble of shrinking away from him, Ransom shifted a distance from her upon the bed. She drowned in his eyes. "Tuxford Wolden, the animal who owned the Well, told me once that she was incredibly beautiful. She had been the sole survivor of a ship set upon by pirates. The captain, it seems, sailed into Baytown in need of supplies, and my mother . . . she was his coin."

Cecily pressed quivering fingers to her lips. "Ransom, how—"

"Ransom." The grim laugh from his lips frightened her. "That's what I was. The price for her freedom. She plied the trade Wolden forced her into, then, after I was born, gave me to Wolden and fled Africa."

Rage and fury erupted in Cecily, mingled with fierce protectiveness toward the helpless child Ransom had been. "She abandoned you? In the care of . . . of some monster! How could she—"

"She was almost a child herself. Terrified. Alone."

"But what did this Wolden man . . . do with you?" Cecily whispered. "Do with a baby . . ."

Ransom's mouth twisted in a smile that broke her heart. "He had a most lucrative use for the side-slips born of his trade. From the time we were small, he schooled us in thieving—robbing sailors in drunken stupors, or slitting the purse strings of those few prosperous families that dared live on the far side of town. By the age of six we were even housebreakers. 'Twas nothing to loosen a window, then squeeze inside. I swear to God, we would have climbed into those houses even if they had been ablaze, we were that afraid of Wolden's fury."

"He . . . hurt you?"

Ransom jammed his fingers through tumbled hair, his face contorting. "Tuxford Wolden was a master at dealing pain."

Cecily couldn't keep the slow tears from streaming down her face, caught up as she was in that boy-child's hell. That child who had become this man fierce with honor, roving the streets to crush the very type of beast who had victimized him so long ago. She reached out a hand, feathering it across burnished gold waves. "So while I had a hundred servants seeing to my every wish, cartloads of presents, and so many gowns I could ne'er wear them all, you were—"

"Hungry, half savage. Sometimes I think I could have

torn out a babe's throat with my bare hands if it were hiding a crust of bread. Wolden, he played all the brothel's spawn like a master—building the hate between us, lashing us, beating us. And I . . . I was the worst of the lot. I loathed everything, everyone." Ransom paused, his voice hushed. "Until Will came."

"Will?"

"A boy Wolden had bought from one of the African chieftains. A slaver had gotten some black woman with child, and Will . . . he was a symbol of her shame to the tribe. When his mother died, the chieftain wanted to be rid of Will—would have killed him, if greedy traders hadn't happened by. The traders knew—knew Wolden used children for thieving—brought Will to Satan's Well. He was so damned scared. I can still remember the first time I saw him. Christ, we were more beasts than humans, the other brothel urchins and I—and Will, I vow they would have eaten him alive. But he touched something in me. Some protective instinct I hadn't even known I possessed until that day." Ransom's eyes grew misty with sorrow, pain.

"Stealing terrified Will. Christ, he couldn't have filched a dipper of water if he'd been dying of thirst. I knew what would happen when he returned to Satan's Well empty-handed. Will was so small, and even gangly as I was, when Wolden brought out his lash—"

"You shielded him." Of course he had shielded him, Cecily's heart cried. Even then his own peace had counted for nothing against the needs of someone else.

"I sheltered him as much as I could," Ransom said, kneading the stiff muscles in his neck. "Stole enough for both of us. But even that didn't drive the raw fear from Will's face. It tore me apart to see it there, day after day. But though I devised a score of wild plans for us to escape the Well, in the end I knew they were futile. Even if I could have stowed away with Will on one of the ships, taken him away from Satan's Well, he could never have survived the swim to a boat, and if, by some miracle, he had made it, he would have died within a week under the conditions aboard a ship like that. Me, they would have most likely found some job for. But 'twas patently evident that Will bore African blood, and I would have been casting him into a slavery nigh as hideous as the one we served at Satan's Well."

"Ransom," Cecily breathed, savage pride in the child who had sacrificed his own bid for freedom to protect a weaker lad burning inside her. "My bold, brave—" Her voice failed her. She smoothed her fingertips over Ransom's lips, and he shut his eyes, his teeth clenching in remembered pain.

"A year later *he* came." The eyes that had been misty opened, roiling now, black with hate.

"He?"

"I don't know his name, only that he was some high and mighty Englishman, owner of one of the ships in the harbor. It seems he wasn't interested in any of the women Wolden kept in the rooms upstairs." Ransom looked away from her, and she could see a shudder course through his body. "This nobleman had . . . most especial appetites."

Cecily reached trembling fingers toward him, but it was as if Ransom couldn't bear to be touched. He forced himself to his feet. "Wolden ordered me to his quarters. There was a scented bath there, silken clothes. Christ, I'd never had anything but filthy rags before. And as for a bath . . ." Ransom gave a sharp laugh. "I couldn't understand why Wolden had flung open his finest chambers to me. Couldn't understand any of it. The clothes—God, I'll never forget how sweet they smelled, like the ocean—and the cloth, it was so soft upon my skin."

Cecily's fingers knotted, and she could almost feel the wonderment the child Ransom must have known at the fresh garments. She wanted to draw his head to her breast, comfort him, but the torment in that beautifully carved mouth cut too deep to be soothed away.

"It was then that Wolden revealed his plans," Ransom bit out. "He came in, all but drowning me in violet water, raking a brush through my hair. And he said . . . said that the Englishman was coming to the room in just a moment. I was to get into that silk-sheeted bed and do anything . . . *anything* the man required of me."

"Nay," she choked out, "Ransom—"

"I was far from innocent, angel. But I couldn't . . . Damn, if Wolden had beaten me to death, I couldn't." Ransom shuddered, and Cecily could sense the sickness eating within him. "When I heard the nobleman's footsteps in the hall, I bolted out the window. Figured Wolden would beat me when he found me, but most of the ships were to leave the harbor with the turning of the tide. I was certain that by then the wretch who wanted me would be gone."

"Thank God," Cecily rasped. "Thank God you escaped that evil—"

Ransom wheeled on her, his face contorting with anguish. "Oh, aye, I escaped. Thought I was being so clever—so *damned* clever, outwitting them all. But when I got back to Satan's Well, the perverted bastard was still in the room I had run from."

Cecily leapt to her feet, terror fresh in her soul. "He had waited?"

"Nay, the sonofabitch hadn't waited. When I opened the chamber door . . . Christ, there was blood all over. Blood . . . and Will . . ." Tears were coursing Ransom's cheeks, his face ravaged. "It should have been *me,* damn it! *Me!* But the bastard—the *goddamned bastard*—had raped Will, then bludgeoned him to death."

Cecily bit her lip until she tasted the brassy tang of blood, her stomach churning at the agonies Ransom must have suffered, the soul-crushing guilt, shame, and the searing hopelessness. "Ransom, you couldn't have known that the man would attack Will. 'Twas not your fault."

"That Will died? I was twice Will's size, and strong. If I had stayed, maybe I could have gotten away from the man, maybe the beating wouldn't have killed— I was supposed to take care of Will. I promised him nothing would hurt him while I was near. I promised him, angel."

"You were a child, Ransom! There was nothing you could have done."

"I could have stopped it. Could have. When I saw the murdering bastard lying there in a drunken stupor . . . I went mad. Meant to kill him. Wanted to. But before I could do it, Wolden knocked me unconscious. Bound me. He knew I would never work for him again, so he decided to take whatever was left of my life and twist it as well. He branded me, angel. Seared a fleur-de-lis into my cheek so that the world would know me for the thief Wolden had made me."

A cry tore from Cecily, soft, wounded, her hand curving about the scar that slashed his cheek as if somehow she could heal the torment it signified.

"I don't even know how I gained the *Ninon*." He gave a sick laugh. "Don't remember anything except standing with a knife in my hand, my cheek bleeding." He closed his eyes as if to blot out the memory. "A sailmaker named Tremayne found me, stitched up my cheek. He hid me from the captain, aye, and risked his own life to do it. . . ."

"So after . . . after the ship burned, you took his name?" Cecily trailed her fingertips gently across the life-savaged planes of Ransom's face.

"Aye."

"This man . . . this Tremayne . . ." Cecily said in a quavery voice. "He would have been so proud."

She saw Ransom's mouth whiten with taut, bittersweet pain. "Now, do you understand, angel?" His fingers clenched in the silken waves of hair, his eyes pools of hopelessness. "Do you see why I can never take these hands and touch you . . . love you . . . when they . . ."

"When they've dragged scores of children away from brutes that would cripple them? When they battled for some poor, innocent boy who—" A choked sound escaped from her lips, her mouth trailing kisses over the scar slashing his cheekbone, over the chin that yet bespoke the courage of the boy he had been, the pain in the man. "I thought 'twas impossible for me to love you more than I did the night we said farewell in my bedchamber . . . to want you more than I wanted you then. But I was wrong. . . ."

"Cecily, you cannot—"

"Don't you dare to tell me what I can and cannot do, Ransom Tremayne!" A half sob broke through the defiance in her voice. "I'm the spoiled . . . haughty granddaughter of a duke, and I'm selfish enough to damn well get my way!"

"Not when it will hurt you—destroy any chance you might have of—"

"Of wedding an old man like the Earl of Larrinbea? Or some fop who flings away all he owns upon the turn of a single card? Or mayhap you would prefer to see me as a prime minister's wife? Uncle Bayard has made it more than plain that he'd not take objection to that."

Ransom grasped her shoulders, eyes blazing green fire. "If that bastard ever so much as touches you, I'll murder him with my own hands!" The echoes of her own father's threat sent a chill down Cecily's spine.

She lifted her chin, her eyes spitting challenge. "I don't want Sutton's hands upon me. I want yours, damn you!" She took rope-scarred fingers in a crushing grip, pulling them down the ridge of her collarbone, down to where the softness of her breast trembled beneath a thin layer of fabric. The instant that hard palm brushed it, the rosy-hued crest strained against the softness of her chemise, hardened against his hand. Ransom's mouth twisted in something akin to pain, but she would not let him draw his hand away.

"Feel, Ransom . . ." Cecily's lips parted, and she opened herself to the vulnerability of laying all her vast love into Ransom's reluctant grasp. "Feel how much I want you . . . how much I love you. . . . I need . . . please." She whispered the last word, rising up on the tips of her slippered toes.

Her fingers released their grasp on the hand so warm against her breast, and eased up to the column of his throat where his cravat was knotted. She caught her lip between her teeth, the gesture achingly childlike, hesitant, as she unloosed the starched neckcloth. It fell away, baring flesh the warm sun brown of spice cake. A pulse struggled to beat its way from his body at the base of his throat, his jaw cast in granite.

She raised her gaze to his eyes, and what she saw there stole her very soul. There was nothing of the dashing rogue who had danced with her in Winterscape's ballroom, nothing even of the fierce-eyed defender of London's wretched.

Instead there was a boy, frightened to grasp even at the

merest wisping of happiness, terrified that it would vanish in his hands. 'Twas as though, even now, Ransom thought her some fragile dream beyond the reach of the fingers he saw as tainted, as though he expected her to melt away, leaving him more bereft than ever before.

"Love . . ." she breathed, humbled by the power she held over this beautiful man. "My own gentle Launcelot . . ." Her lips parted as she raised them to the hard line of his jaw, trailed kisses to the corner of his mouth. She felt a tremor shoot through his lean, honed body, heard a tortured groan escape him as she opened the rumpled fabric of his shirt.

"If I were a cursed Launcelot, I'd bind and gag you. Drag you away from this room. Away from me." His hands dropped to his side, knotted there, and Cecily sensed that he was warring desperately with the desire stormy in his eyes, struggling to give her every chance to see the enormity of what she was doing, to stop, think of consequences.

Yet even as he reined the raging emotions evident in his hot eyes, flushed face, Cecily could sense that part of him, hidden deep in his soul, pleading with her, begging her to love him. Love him . . . She unfastened the final stud upon his cuff, letting the bits of jet fall from her palm onto the table beside the bed.

She closed her eyes, skimming the shirt from shoulders of rippling bronze, reveling in the feel of that daunting strength beneath her soft palms. The garment drifted to the floor with a gentle, shushing sound, and she opened her eyes, skimming them over the defined planes of muscle, sinew darkened by the sun's rays, the dusting of dark-gold hair roughening his chest. Her mouth went dry, her voice a harsh whisper. "Beautiful . . ." She raised her eyes to his and saw her own wonder reflected in the hue of shattered emeralds. "I never knew a man could be so beautiful."

Ransom's lip curled in a despairing, self-mocking sneer, laced with a soul-deep pain. "The cursed nobleman, he must have thought I was comely enough to—"

"Nay, Ransom Tremayne. The word *comely* doesn't describe half the wonder of you." Cecily forced back the heated anger that rose in her, at his allowing an animal the like of Wolden to steal away his pride in the joy his body brought her. She could sense that he wanted to spur her to anger, wanted to ruthlessly remind her of the past he thought should make her flee from touching him. But his words only made her love him more, want to give him such infinite pleasure that even *he* would be able to lay to rest the brothel urchin that had scavenged in Baytown's streets.

"Cecily . . ."

"Nay, Ransom. Let me. I want to see all of you, touch . . ." Her cheeks burned at her boldness, her finger-tips drifting down over the taut plane of his stomach to where the dusting of hair upon his chest narrowed, then slipped in a silken ribbon past the waistband of his skin-tight pantaloons. The black fabric strained against Cecily's hand, the proof of Ransom's raging need seeming to sear a path straight to her heart. He wanted her. Fierce pride swept through her. Aye, he wanted her. "Hard . . . hot . . . you feel so—"

"Damn!"

The fragile thread of control he had held so ruthlessly snapped, and Cecily felt the force of it sizzle through the chamber. With a groan of surrender, he crushed her against his bared chest, his mouth searing, hungry upon hers, his hands cupping the curves of her buttocks, pulling her tight against his arousal. Cecily couldn't breathe, couldn't think, so mind-shattering were the sensations he was evoking in her body. But then breathing ceased to matter.

'Twas as though for the briefest of instants she could see through some dark passageway into the life he had endured as a youth—could feel in his hands a practiced expertise gained through his observations in the brothel's hallways, and in the beds of jaded ton beauties as he skimmed away the layers of her clothes. But then she shoved the thought away, hating the phantoms that had dared steal even a fragment of her joy.

Her fingers roved hungrily over smooth, bronzed shoulders, delved deep into the satiny thickness of his tumbled-gold hair as he rid her of her chemise, his lips stringing agonizingly sweet kisses across the skin he bared. Cecily shivered, the room chill as Ransom discarded the last of her garments onto the rug. And then she was warm, nay, on fire, pillowed in the angel softness of Ransom's bed, her body shielded from the tempest of his gaze only by the luxuriant waves of her own dark hair.

And Ransom . . . her heart caught in her throat. Ransom's muscular frame was there beside her, hard, hot, insistent, the black breeches that had clung to his powerful thighs crumpled now amidst the folds of her cast-off gown.

Like a warm sea breeze his callused fingertips wisped over her, trailing soul-spinning patterns across her breasts, the slight swell of her belly, his eyes following the paths his hands charted. Cecily whimpered, wanting to sob aloud at the white heat he stirred in her, wanting to cry at the intensity in the harsh planes of his face. 'Twas as though he were trying to infuse every brush of his fingers upon her with the most devastatingly erotic effect he could, and she sensed he felt that the skill gained in countless, empty liaisons was the only gift he could bring to her.

She wanted to comfort him, tell him all that he meant to her, but his lips stole away all control as he blew gently across her straining nipples, taunted them with a lightning flick of his hot tongue. Cecily's hips arched against him, seeking something she could not fully understand, her whole body dissolving into an aching emptiness yearning to be filled.

She clutched at his shoulders, wanting to draw him up to the fierce hunger in her lips, but he resisted her urgings, his mouth opening upon her breast. Never in her wildest dreams had she imagined a man would want to suckle like a babe, and the contact of his lips and tongue as he drew her nipple deep into his mouth shot spikes of raw passion to the center of her womb. She shuddered, melted, a wet heat dampening the dewy curls at the apex of her thighs as his tongue wove magic about her.

"Ransom . . ." She groaned his name, felt the answering tremor in his body. "Ransom, I love . . ."

Her words trailed off in a gasp, her head arching back into the pillow as his hand brushed a fiery path down the gentle curve of one hip, the slender length of her thigh. "Sweet God, angel . . . taste . . . you taste like summer . . . hot and so damn sweet. . . ."

She started to squirm away from him, embarrassed by the moisture that clung to her most intimate places, but before she could will her desire-drugged limbs to move, Ransom's strong fingers found her. A low groan vibrated deep in his throat, and she could see his face contort in a pleasure so tumultuous it nigh frightened her.

"You're damp for me," he rasped, burying his face against her stomach, his voice rough with wonder. "For *me.*"

The stirring of unease Cecily had felt fluttered away like some jewel-hued butterfly, Ransom's hand gentle, so achingly gentle as it toyed with the dusting of spun silk curling about his fingertips. Then he caught her tight against him, every hard muscle in his body imprinting itself on the soft curves of hers, his lips seeking her mouth with a tender fury that made her clutch at him. His lips opened wide, feasting upon hers, his tongue mating with her own deep in her mouth. 'Twas as if he were struggling to wring from her the very essense of her being, yet she sensed him holding back the essence of his own.

Pain . . . the thought wisped for an instant across her hazed senses . . . he held so much pain.

Her own hands grew bolder with the need to loose the chains that yet bound him, the chains she could see in his eyes, feel in the desperate ecstasy of his mouth as it pleasured her. The fingers that had touched her moments before delved between their sweat-sheened bodies, and Cecily felt a low scream tear from her as Ransom unerringly found a point she had not even realized existed. She stiffened with a pleasure so intense 'twas akin to pain.

"Hush, love . . . open . . . open for me . . ."

She could no more have disobeyed that husky voice than stay the tide, and she arched against his hand, her thighs parting to allow his stroking fingers freedom to explore.

"Ransom, I want . . ."

She tried to speak, couldn't through the tumult of sensation besieging her very soul. His mouth was everywhere, his tongue dampening the inside of her elbow, the pulse at her throat, the underside of one pale breast.

"I know, angel," he breathed against her fevered skin. "I'll take you there . . . I promise. . . ."

Take her where? Cecily wondered in a haze, the tension in her body building until she clawed at Ransom's sleek shoulders, her body tossing, writhing upon the bed. 'Twas as though the love in her were growing, expanding, pressing against every inch of her until it threatened to shatter her into a thousand tiny pieces, all of them belonging to the man who was making love to her with such savage tenderness.

She felt the moist heat of Ransom's kisses sweep a scandalous path down her stomach, felt his lips press, hard, against the triangle of curls. In some distant part of herself she knew she should be shocked, but she wasn't . . . was only tossed free upon a maelstrom of desire as the burnished-gold silk of his hair brushed the fragile skin of her inner thighs.

She whimpered his name, her hands clutching at handfuls of the coverlet, her eyes wide with wonder as his lips touched, ever so gently, that part of her swollen and damp with the need of him. A giant's hand seemed to crush all the air from her lungs, her whole body rigid.

"I love you, Cecily Lansdowne." He breathed the vow against her. "So damned much . . ." His lips parted, the wet heat of his tongue touching her with such delicate passion, Cecily nigh bolted off of the bed. And then he was loving her with his mouth, suckling her, swirling the hot roughness of his tongue upon her until she writhed against him. His hands framed her slender hips, his fingers gripping her with a force that should have hurt but didn't as he hurtled her toward some fantasy-borne land he alone could give to her.

Cecily rushed toward it, blindly, plummeting through a thousand brilliant-hued rainbows. She fought to grasp at them, clutched them in her hand, and then she was bursting into flames gold with the silk of Ransom's hair, the emerald of his eyes, the bronzed wonder of his skin. She cried out, wracked with a shimmering earthquake of sensation, bursting until all that she was, all she would ever be, drifted like stardust into Ransom Tremayne's heart.

She dragged at his shoulders, urging him upward as the tremors subsided, even still wanting some undefinable wholeness he had denied her. But he drew back a little, his whole body rigid with the effort, his eyes twin pools of dark, swirling passions, unfulfilled needs. His knuckles skimmed gently across her quivering lips, his eyes seeming to drink in the sight of her, tousled and flushed from his lovemaking. 'Twas as if, somehow, he were trying to conceal from her the fact that he had not reached that pinnacle of ecstasy with her, as though he were, even now, trying to spare her from being "defiled" by him.

Sweet God, how could he look so vulnerable, so cursed lost, when he had just given her the most shattering pleasure she had ever experienced?

"Look at you, angel," he said, his gaze blessing her features with infinite love. "This . . . this is what I promised you."

"Nay," Cecily whispered, bracing herself on one elbow, her hair tumbling silky soft over her breasts as she leaned toward him. "You promised to make love to me."

There was a fleeting confusion beneath Ransom's dark brows. "But I—"

"I want you, Ransom Tremayne . . . all of you." Her fingers skimmed down to that part of him yet throbbing, hard with need.

"Damn it, once I do—bury myself inside you—" His eyes shut, fierce. "Once I do, there is no—no going back. You cannot—"

Cecily forced his shoulders back onto the pillow, shifted her body partly atop him. "I never want to go back, Ransom, never want any life without you. I feel . . ." Her eyes flitted away from his, a hot flush stinging her cheeks as she took his hardness into her hand. "I feel so empty inside. Fill me."

The world seemed to career off its axis as Ransom rolled himself above her, his hands knotting in the midnight mass of her hair, his body bearing her down into the feather tick. Her thighs opened to cradle his hips, his engorged manhood hot and hard against her belly.

"Damn it, angel, I don't—don't want to hurt you."

His shoulders shaking with the effort it cost him, he probed the opening, pressed himself against it so tenderly, Cecily felt slow tears well at the corners of her eyes. A sharp twinge stung her as the last barrier between them gave way, but she reveled in it as Ransom buried himself deep, the groan rumbling through him rife with a thousand raging emotions. She opened her eyes, to see him staring down at her, his eyes bright with . . . dear God, could it be tears? His fingers traced her cheeks with reverence, sweeping up the droplets upon her skin, carrying them to his own lips.

"Never has any man been given a gift so . . . precious." He kissed her, long, deep. "Christ, I don't deserve . . ." He nuzzled his face against her throat, and she knew he was battling to hide his pain as he set himself against her with smooth thrusts that set her pulses to racing again, her hands to clutching at him. The urgency was so much different now—the abrading of sweat-sheened skin, the rough mat of hair upon his chest teasing her nipples, his lean hips driving her higher, ever higher, as the throbbing she had felt in him when she had curled her fingers about his manhood spread through her own body like the compelling, inexorable beat of a thousand primal drums—wild, wondrous.

The rainbow came to her again, yet with Ransom buried deep inside her, it was thrice as brilliant, thrice as shattering. And when she felt him shudder, his head arching back, face contorted as he hurtled into his own release, she cried out, embracing ecstasy.

She whimpered in protest as he shifted some of his weight from her, but he drew her tight against him, as though he were yet afraid she would melt into dream.

"I hurt you." The words were gruff, yet more moving than any tender whisperings could have been, the eyes peering down at her with a mixture of self-loathing, wonder, and regret.

She turned her lips against him, fighting the sudden

shyness that rose into her cheeks as she remembered her wantonness, her pleadings. She stiffened her spine, refusing to hold even the slightest embarrassment in the act that had been so beautiful. "Nay. You were so gentle . . . even before you . . . you made me your own, I knew you would be."

She felt rather than saw the bitter twisting in his mouth. "I was raised in a brothel. The place reeked of skills in pleasuring—"

"Oh, nay, Ransom Tremayne." Cecily sat up, the sheet pooling about her thighs, her hair draping in a soft ebony fall across her breasts. "What happened between us had nothing to do with skill. No secrets you overheard from the women who worked at Satan's Well could ever have schooled such tenderness into these hands, this mouth." She ran her fingertips over his lips. "I love you . . . love you so much. . . ."

She saw Ransom lean toward her, felt his hand urging her toward his chest, but she splayed her palms against that plane of flesh, needing desperately to see that tender, vulnerable mouth tip into a hint of his bedeviling smile. Ransom's eyes widened in solemn inquiry as he levered himself up on his elbows. "Gloriana, what—"

"Do not disturb me," Cecily said with mock severity. "I am trying to recall the correct procedure for challenging you to a duel."

"A duel?"

"Aye. You have compromised me. Quite destroyed my glorious plan of riding off with the Earl of Larrinbea astride a white charger. I bear no other choice except to meet you upon the field of honor, unless, of course, you make amends for your despicable behavior at once."

"My despicable . . . Damn it, Cecily, what—"

"You needn't try to wangle your way out of the noose, my lord captain, else I be forced to put a pistol ball through your black heart." Cecily teasingly thrust her nose inches from Ransom's face. "I demand that you marry me, Captain Tremayne. At once."

"M-Marry you?"

The forced merriment within Cecily faded to a glow so

warm, so deep, it enveloped her, heart and soul. Had a real angel dropped its silvery wings into Ransom Tremayne's big hands, the seafarer could not have looked more stunned. "Aye." Cecily struggled to keep her tones light but failed as she traced circles across Ransom's broad chest with her fingertip. "Unless you offer for me at once, sir, you shall face pistols at dawn." She tucked her chin upon her bent knees, peering down upon the stunned Ransom with smug satisfaction.

"Princess, by all the saints, you know I want you! Christ, if I could but take you to wife . . . never in my boldest imaginings did I think that you . . . you could e'er be wed to the likes of me. Your father would most like see me dead first, and before God, I'd not blame him."

Her hand stilled upon Ransom's chest. The rosy glow that had seemed unbreachable was tainted with shadings of gray as Cecily's mind filled with images of Charleton Lansdowne's thin face, the savage protectiveness in his eyes when he had vowed to kill Ransom Tremayne himself rather than allow the rogue captain to touch her again. . . . She pushed away the shudder of foreboding resolutely, tilting her head with all too evident stubbornness.

"'Twill be done long before Papa can object. In the morn we can take Lacey and dash off to Gretna Green, and after . . ." She couldn't meet Ransom's eyes. "After, when Papa knows how much I love you, he'll bear no choice but to accept our marriage."

Ransom gave a short laugh. "Aye, or make you a very young widow. 'Twill give the noble Lord Lansdowne the greatest of pleasure, no doubt, to entertain as his son-in-law the very man determined to bring him to justice over the *Ninon* affair."

Cecily battled against the cold, insidious twinings of doubt, and drew the sheet closer about her naked shoulders. She turned her face away from Ransom, attempting to hide the hurt sluicing through her, harsh realities grappling with rainbow-shaded dreams.

"Damn it, angel, I *am* a heartless bastard, bringing that cursed ship up now, after . . . after our loving." Ransom shoved himself up to a sitting position, drawing her into his arms. "But I can't just bundle you up in my bedsheets and whisk you off to some blacksmith's shop in Scotland, no matter how much I'd like to."

"So you don't . . . don't want to wed."

"Christ, I'd cast everything I own into the ocean just for one day of having you as my wife. Sell my very soul." The hard strength of his palms cupped her cheeks, gently urging her to look at him. "But, Cecily, I can't cast to the devil the souls of the men who died on the *Ninon*. Not even for you."

Cecily swallowed hard, a numbness stealing over her, a sorrow. "I know that. 'Tis something I have to face. But I know when all is out in the open, you'll find that Father could never be the kind of monster you paint—"

"You don't know that for certain." Ransom forced himself to go ruthlessly on. "I don't know that. And I can't risk chaining you to me with marriage—letting you throw away a lifetime of rank and privilege for one impulsive night, when in a week's time you might well hate me."

"I won't hate you, could never—"

He brushed his fingertips across her lips, hushing her. "If you don't, princess . . . if you can still say you love me when this is all over, I'll make you my bride. But not in some hovel reeking of hot iron and horses. I'll marry you before the whole of London, grande dames and scandal mongers be damned."

Cecily clung to the fierce need in his voice, clung to the certainty that he did love her, want her, and the certainty that she would never be able to hate her restless, questing knight.

She allowed herself to melt against him, snuggling against his powerful chest. " 'Twill all come right in the end," she whispered, trying to brace herself against her own niggling fear. "You'll see, Ransom. Because I—" She couldn't keep the catch from her voice. "Because I love both you and my father, and I'll not desert you, either one."

Ransom tightened his arms around her soft, sweet body, the need to protect, defend this violet-eyed angel, rending his soul. With every sinew he willed her prophecy to come true, pleaded with some half-pagan, half-Christian deity to wash away the disaster even now threatening to destroy this single wondrous miracle in an eternity of bleakness.

Innocent . . . she was so innocent . . . so certain that life was good and that her love could triumph over anything that befell her. But there were some things even angels could not mend. Some souls whose feet were destined to carry them to Hades before they were even born.

Ransom brushed her rose-tinted cheek with his lips in the tenderest of kisses, wishing he could grasp at just a little of the faith Cecily had. He lay awake, watching her, babe soft in sleep, until the oil lamp upon the desk struggled to drain the last fuel from its tin stand, flickered, then went out.

'Twould be the only time he would ever cradle her thus, in his arms, Ransom thought, his chest constricting with bittersweet love. But 'twas more than most men ever bore—one dream-kissed night to touch an angel.

Chapter Seventeen

Cecily snuggled closer to the warmth beside her, reveling in the feel of hard-toned muscle, delicious, hair-roughened skin scented of spice, bay rum and the tiniest tang of sweat. Ransom . . . he held her even in sleep, his hand tangled in the ebony fall of her hair, one powerful leg flung over her thighs, as though he feared she would somehow escape him while he dreamed. Dreamed the sweetest of dreams, Cecily thought, tenderness welling painfully in her chest as she regarded the man beside her with drowsy eyes.

His life-savaged face was softened in slumber, a vulnerability, contentment, totally foreign to his warring-king features squeezing a tight fist of love about her heart. Even his scar was hidden, buried in the downy softness of the pillow they had shared, and the first rays of sunlight melting through the glistening window touched his face with a nigh boyish sweetness that made her eyes sting with tears.

Pain . . . he had known so much pain, had emptied his very soul into the hands of any who had need of him, never taking time to fill the emptiness in his own heart. Cecily brushed a tender, trembling finger across his parted lips, touched the rich, dark curls of the lashes sweeping his high cheekbone. She would fill the emptiness within him, gift him with peace, if it took her a lifetime. And nothing—not

her father, not the *Ninon,* not Ransom's own fierce pride—
would stay her from doing so.

"Thought . . . thought I was dreaming again. . . ."

She smiled at the deep, groggy tones of his voice as
Ransom's lashes fluttered, opened, revealed eyes smoky
green as a misty moor.

"'Twas no dream," Cecily whispered, her throat constricted with emotion. "No mere imaginings could e'er have
been so . . . so wondrous."

"Angel . . ."

Cecily closed her eyes as his fingertips skimmed her
cheek, the calluses roughening his palms snagging in her
hair.

His voice was thick, ragged. "I wanted it to be wondrous
for you, wanted to gift you with every joy 'twas within my
power to give." She saw his gaze slide away from hers, the
lines about his mouth already beginning to tighten, the dark
shades of reality drawing his features into their restless,
questing aura.

She could see his inner torment fall about him like a
well-worn mantle, and she wanted to snatch it away from
him, thrust it into the fires to regain the beguiling, endearing
boyishness that had graced his countenance moments before.

Yet even as he forced himself to a sitting position,
reaching over to take his dressing gown from a brass hook
beside the bed, Cecily well knew that the fantasy world they
had spun about themselves was melting away with the last
trailings of dawn, leaving a daunting tangle of problems they
had yet to unsnarl.

The slash of his scar seemed whiter still, in the clinging
shadows of the room, a symbol of the far-deeper wounds
within him, as yet unhealed—wounds that nurtured the
guilt in his face, aye, and the self-loathing she sensed gripped
him whenever his gaze touched her.

"I love you, Ransom." She whispered the words as a
talisman, pressing them against the spicy-warm skin behind
his ear as he slipped his arm into one sleeve.

"I know." Rough-edged with a patient suffering, the

syllables seemed to catch in his throat. But he angled his face toward her as he slid the garment over his shoulders, his visage contorting with a savage, hopeless longing as he stroked her tumbled hair. "Still, 'tis morning now." He gave a strained, aching laugh. "Time for guardian angels to take wing to their clouds."

"I'm no untouchable angel, Ransom." Cecily could not bear the resigned tone in his voice.

"Shh." Ransom hushed her, drifting his fingers gently upon her lips, at the slightest stirring of sound beyond the bedchamber door. He swooped up his discarded shirt, pressing it into her hand. "I think that Lacey is—"

Crash! The sudden, slamming wide of the door tore a half scream from Cecily's throat, Ransom instinctively leaping to his feet beside the bed as the figure silhouetted within the doorway seared into Cecily's gaze.

In that hideous second she knew she would never banish that stoop-shouldered specter from her memory—knew that those haggard, frozen features would haunt her for eternity. Straggled graying hair wisped about a face frozen, as though in death. Only the gentle blue eyes Cecily had adored since she was but a babe held anything resembling life—and they, too, seemed possessed by some dark demon, their depths wild, roiling with anguish and half-crazed fury.

"P-Papa . . ." she gasped, clutching Ransom's shirt against her breasts, shame, humiliation, splashing over her like boiling water.

She heard Ransom curse, saw him lunge to shield her scarce-covered body with his own broad shoulders. "Lord Lansdowne," he grated, jamming his fingers through hair obviously tousled by loveplay. "I know how this appears, but I—"

"Bastard!" The sickened, strange tones in her father's voice sent shafts of alarm through Cecily, as he seemed to clutch at his stomach beneath the open front of his frock coat. She shoved her arms into the shirt Ransom had given her, wanting to cover herself, to place herself between these two men she loved, her father's mad babble striking a kind of raw terror within her.

"You bastard! Ruined . . . my babe . . . Kill you, damn you, I'll—"

"Papa, he— *No!*" Cecily screamed as she saw her father's hand flash free from the folds of his coat and something silver, glinting deadly, appear in his wildly shaking hand.

A pistol.

"Papa!" She hurled herself from the coverlets as the weapon exploded, spitting death. She bore scarce a heartbeat to register that the window beyond Ransom's head shattered. She was aware of nothing but Ransom's powerful body lunging at the smaller body of her father, Charleton Lansdowne's thin frame thudding, hard, against the chamber's wall.

Like a rabbit in the jaws of a wolf, Lansdowne struggled, insane with rage, helpless in the unyielding grasp of his captor. Ransom's hands manacled the older man's wrists, forcing Lansdowne's fingers to loose their hold upon the useless pistol.

"R-Ransom." A half sob snagged in Cecily's throat as she ran to him, her fingers clutching at his arm. "Dear God, are you hurt? Did he—"

"Don't touch him, Cecily!" Her father's shrill made her skin crawl. "You're an innocent, he used—"

"I came to him, damn it! I love him!"

"Hush, princess, 'tis all right." Ransom's voice was low, taut, yet soothing. "Now we're all—all going to calm down, and discuss—"

"Calm down?" Cecily felt bile rise in her throat, feared she would be sick. "He almost . . . almost murdered . . . in cold blood. . . ." She pressed her palm to her mouth, her senses reeling at the glimpse she had gained of a darker side of Charleton Lansdowne. A side she had ne'er suspected. That of a man capable of any horror, capable of cutting down an unarmed foe.

"Child, he's scum! Naught but a lowling animal who—"

"An animal?" Cecily cried, her voice catching in her throat. "You are the animal! He saves people, shelters them, while you—"

"Angel!" Ransom's voice cut in, harsh, warning, but she

plunged on, caring nothing about the devastation in her father's parchment-shaded face.

"—you not only murdered the slaves upon the *Ninon,* but came here to kill—"

"I did it for you!" Charleton flung back, attempting to wrench his wrists from Ransom's grasp. "My whole life I—"

"I love him, Papa!" Cecily saw the light in Charleton Lansdowne's blue eyes shatter into soul-numbing defeat, his pale fingers twisting in the sleeve of Ransom's dressing gown as though to support the weight of a burden too great for the aged nobleman to bear. Slowly, with aching compassion, Ransom eased his hold on Lansdowne's bony wrists, releasing the man to sag against the wall.

In that instant, all three within the chamber sensed someone's gaze upon them, heard the shallow, terrified breaths wisping from within the door's wide frame. They all turned, their eyes locking upon the small figure peering up at them with round, dark eyes.

Like a diminutive ghost Lacey stood in her white nightgown, frozen by some terror she alone could see. Dark moppet curls clung to her ashen cheeks, her hands desperately clutching her bedraggled doll to her chest.

"G-Go 'way!" Her fear-laden voice tore at Cecily's heart, the child staring at Charleton Lansdowne's face, transfixed as though she were confronted by some hideous monster. "I didn't—didn't tell."

"Lacey?" Ransom's voice was painfully gentle, questioning, yet edged with a shading of alarm as he stepped toward the child. She shrank back, her round eyes never leaving the strange man beside the wall.

"I didn't tell. You can't kill my Papa. Nicky . . . Nicky promised." 'Twas as though the babe were bartering with the devil, and the sight of her, so wary, battling to be brave, chilled Cecily's blood, driving away the anger of moments before.

"Sweetheart, 'tis naught but—"

"He comed to kill Papa, like the witch-woman killed-ed

Nicky," Lacey accused, her eyes filling with tears as they flicked in horror to the gun lying upon the floor. Her lower lip trembled. "Not—Not fair. Nicky promised."

"This is *my* father." Cecily nigh choked upon the words.

"Shooted *gun*. Heard bang," Lacey quavered. "But I *didn't tell!*" Huge tears welled in her eyes, a horrible, wracking sob tearing through her small body. "Make him go 'way! Witch-woman . . . don't let her . . ."

"What the hell?" Despite the child's cowering, Ransom closed the space between them, catching his daughter in his arms, holding her. "What the devil are you talking about?"

"Nay! Can't—"

The maddening strain of Nicky's death, the battle with Charleton Lansdowne, the tearing pain of Lacey's rejection, exploded in Ransom, and Cecily could see the raging desperation in his lean, bronzed face. "Tell me, damn it!" His voice was harsh, and Cecily herself would not have dared defy the blaze in those intense eyes. "Now!" The child flinched, the fear in her face shifting to blind terror.

"But the White man, he'll kill you like they . . . killed-ed my Nicky!"

"Nicky?" Cecily laid a hand on Ransom's iron-taut arm, trying to calm him, feeling her own sense of foreboding clench about her. "Sweetheart, what has this to do with Nicky?"

"My fault. 'Twas my fault they maked him dead. Nicky said—said bad man would come if we ever told. But I promised Papa wouldn't let the White man hurt Nicky. But the witch, she came, an' Nicky—"

"Lacey, there is no such thing as a witch," Ransom bit out.

"Is! Saw snake hair. Scared Nicky!"

Frightened to death . . .

A gasp escaped Cecily's lips, a sudden chill skittering like rat's claws across the back of her neck as the child's terrified ramblings mingled with the physician's haunting words. "Ransom . . . what if—" Cecily hesitated, reluctant to put her fears into words. "What if something really . . ." She didn't finish the sentence, her gaze locking with his over Lacey's head. The bronzed, lean visage was chalky, his mouth compressed with white-lipped denial.

"'Tis impossible. Absurd. Nicky's death has but frightened her."

"Lacey," Cecily interrupted softly, "'tis most important for you to tell Papa and I everything you remember about whoever hurt Nicky. Then your papa will make certain that this person can never harm any little girl or little boy again."

The child wavered, torn between her fear, the father she loved, and the "pretty lady" she had come to trust. Cecily held her breath, not daring to break contact with the child's melting-dark eyes as Lacey regarded her.

Ransom started to speak, but Cecily clenched her fingers tighter about his arm, warning him to stay his tongue, give the child time. Cecily thought her gambit had failed, when Lacey whispered, "'Twas the White man. He—He tried to make Nicky do things. Bad things that hurted Nicky. Said he would give Nicky guineas. But Nicky ran away before . . .

The child's faint words trailed off, and Cecily could see Lacey cringe at the darkening in Ransom's eyes. Yet his voice was incredibly gentle, nigh cajoling as he forcibly calmed himself. "This White man, you say he tried to give Nicky money?"

Lacey nodded. "He said if Nicky ever tol' anyone, he'd send a witch t' make Nicky dead—" The child's voice broke. "He did, Papa. An' I was 'fraid if I told you, Aaron White would make you dead like Nicky. . . ."

Her little arms twined about her father's neck and she buried her pale, moppet face against Ransom's bronzed cheek. "Lacey has been bad to you, Papa. Mean. But I love 'Papa, most in the—the whole world. If you got dead . . ."

Cecily saw Ransom's face contort with a bittersweet joy, saw his dark lashes glisten with unshed tears. "Papa loves you, too, Lacey-babe." He tangled his fingers in his child's dusky curls with fierce tenderness. "Most in the whole world." His eyes caught Cecily's gaze, their green so intense, so full of love and strength, she pressed her knuckles to her lips to stifle a sob.

'Twas as though she were peering through a magic looking glass, tumbling back fifteen years to when she had been four years old and her life had been full of daisy chains and unicorns and the infinite love brimming from her own father's eyes.

Unbidden, her gaze drifted slowly to where Charleton Lansdowne slumped against the chamber's wall—his face unutterably old. He was an eternity away from that wondrous, young father who had indulged her every whim, who had built his life around her. Yet in his eyes she had committed the one unpardonable sin.

She had grown up.

"Cecily." Ransom's voice sent the fragments of her childhood spinning back into the rose mists of the past, and she started, a sudden sharp alarm stinging her at the grim set to his jaw. "I need you to take Lacey. Settle her in with Jessamyn at Rosetree."

"Rosetree?" Cecily regarded him warily as he gently but firmly disentangled himself from Lacey's grasp, putting the child in her arms.

"Don't want to go, Papa!" Lacey's whimpered protest made Cecily feel her own rising uneasiness. "Don't—"

"Hush, now, 'tis all right. Jessamyn will give you ginger cakes, and Jagger—tell Jagger I ordered him to carve you a new toy."

"But why can't she stay here? Why can't you—" Cecily hated the threading of dread in her voice, the dewing of sweat on her palms. It was as if Ransom no longer saw her, heard her, as though his mind had already flown from Tradewinds to set off on some knight-errant's quest.

"Aye, Cecily, and then take your father and hie back to Moorston," he continued as though she'd not spoken. Snatching up the pantaloons crumpled on the floor, he bent to jam his lean legs into them, with menace all the more terrifying because 'twas so savagely 'neath his control. "Stay there until . . ."

"Until what, blast it?" Cecily felt alarm tighten about her, grating across her frayed nerves. "Where are you going? Why . . . ?"

Ransom turned on her, yet the lines of rage in his face were not the clean, biting fury she had seen before, but rather cutting, cold like ice shards in the sea. And they were far more frightening than any raw fury could have been. "You can ask why after what Lacey just said? After what I told you last night?" His eyes pierced hers, chilling her to her marrow. "Do you know what this bastard Aaron White did to Nicky? What the boy suffered? If he hadn't gotten away . . ."

Cecily's stomach churned with fear, with horror, the image of Nicky's peaked, frightened face as he pleaded for his violin haunting her, shadowed only by the raw terror of yet another image . . . that of Ransom Tremayne dead at the hands of the vicious beast capable of so torturing the boy. "There must be a way to inform the authorities," Cecily flung out desperately, clutching Lacey closer against her. "Let them—"

"The authorities don't give a damn about one nameless beggar-lad whom a murderer's craft has kept from the lists of their parish poor." Ransom's eyes were granite hard as he rammed on his boots. "I'll handle this by *my* methods. I'll go to the factory—'reason' with its master. And when the sonofabitch tells me exactly who this Aaron White is . . ." A muscle in Ransom's jaw pulsed dangerously. "Then I am going to find that murdering bastard—and kill him."

Lacey gave a tiny squeak of protest as Cecily's fingers dug into the child's sturdy little waist. "Kill . . ." Cecily echoed. "But what of Lacey? Rosetree? What of *me*, blast you? If you kill a man—"

A laugh like iced silk rippled out from grim lips. "Don't fear, Gloriana. I've too many dependent upon me to face the Reaper now. When I've dealt with White, I'll come to Moorston. To you." Those eyes, so distant, so frighteningly calm, flashed from Cecily to her father.

"I battled my better judgment with Nicky," Ransom said between gritted teeth, his eyes again fixing upon Cecily's face. "I was patient, gave him time until it was too cursed late. But that's not going to happen again, not with you, angel." His jaw set, hard. "'Tis time we all stop running—*from the truth.*"

"I halted no better inspiration with scarce. Ransom told
colleen; pulling name. He tried could bring upon Cecily
done. It was do not save, and then until it was so misted
free, bay saary's and coming to broken there, not with you
and... I'm not sure." "Ransom as all stop courage—
now for your..."

Chapter Eighteen

Moorston's kitchen stretched in immaculate magnifi-
cence, testament to Cook's militant command. Cecily
sagged numbly onto a wooden stool, her fingers trembling
with a sick dread more chilling than the late spring breezes
whisking in off of the Thames. The lamp cast weird shadows
across the cooking implements placed about the room with
such care, the stooped figure fussing over a Wedgwood cup
in the far corner bringing back memories to Cecily that bore
a bittersweet sting. Memories of a hundred like raids in the
Briarton kitchen when she and her father had been in
happier, safer times.

"I've put a deal of sugar in it, just as you've always
favored your chocolate." The catch in Charleton
Lansdowne's voice made Cecily's heart feel heavy as a
mountain stone.

"I told you on the ride back, I'm not—not hungry. Or
thirsty." Cecily forced herself to her feet, pacing across the
room. "I'm angry and I'm terrified, and I wish to God
Ransom would come! A man desperate enough to murder a
child would think nothing of driving a knife in the back of
anyone daring to stalk him. And Ransom . . . when he said
farewell to Lacey . . ." Cecily clenched her fists, fighting
back the whisperings of panic that would give her no
peace—panic exacerbated by the memory of Lacey's tear-

streaked face, her soft sobbing when they had entrusted her to Jessamyn's care at the cozy rose-brick cottage. Lacey had clung to Cecily, as though she held some small part of the father the child adored. Yet despite the compelling need Cecily felt to keep Lacey with her, she knew that even Ransom's love gave her no right to disregard his wishes concerning his daughter. So she had tucked the little girl into Jessamyn's narrow bed.

Cecily let her lashes droop to her cheeks, remembering the feel of Jessamyn's work-rough hand upon her own as they watched Ransom's child drift into sleep. The open challenge in the housekeeper's blue eyes, which had once confronted Cecily, had been replaced by weariness, grief, yet also a gentle acceptance that braced Cecily's courage.

"He'll come back to you," Jessamyn had whispered. "God couldn't be so cruel as to give Ransom so much love only to snatch it away."

The words had wrapped a stirring of comfort around Cecily's heart, and she had hugged the older woman, sensing in Jessamyn the same desperate fear that was roiling within herself.

It had been a healing . . . some small healing between the two, bound now in their love of and fear for the man off daring London's streets.

Yet did all the love in the world hold the power to drive a pistol ball from its course? Could it deflect the deadly piercing of a stealthy dagger?

The soft sound of Charleton Lansdowne's tread as he crossed to where Cecily stood made her start, thoughts about Jessamyn and Lacey fading to a dull ache as Cecily turned to confront a more immediate, piercing pain.

"Drink this." Charleton Lansdowne's voice was sympathetic, pleading, full of the same loving tones that had formed the very fabric of her life. Yet now they seemed a travesty, a harsh reminder that she had been lovingly duped. Her nails dug deep into her palms as she battled not to scream.

"Papa, I'm not a child!"

His pale eyes filled with a patient kind of sorrow, and she

was certain he sensed the rage inside her. "After tonight," he said softly, "even I could not shut out the certainty that you are a woman grown." Cecily's cheeks fired with remembered embarrassment, but she met her father's gaze steadily. He sighed, the effort seeming to wrack his narrow shoulders. "Saints, but I wish you were yet a moppet in hair ribbons and short skirts. Wish 'twas as easy to patch up your hurts now as it was when you were scraping your knees climbing fences. At least then I was able to delude you into thinking I could aid you instead of bumbling about like a useless . . . useless weak fool."

"Papa . . ." Cecily ached at the condemnation in her father's tone, the beaten look in his lined face. In the weeks since they had come to London worry had cut dozens of new scribings into his skin, drawing away the serene, loving scholar who had drilled her in Greek and Latin with infinite patience, the father who had filled his life with her small childish joys and sorrows . . . mayhap because he could not bear to confront the realities that had battered in the misty dream world he had once dwelt in.

"Nay, child. You needn't seek to defend me. God knows I should hold myself fortunate you'll even deign speak to me after . . . after what I nigh did this night." He rubbed his palms on the fabric of his pantaloons as though he could yet feel the hilt of the pistol against his skin. His mouth twisted in revulsion. "When I was young, idealistic, Bayard Sutton hied me off to some entertainment . . . the hanging of a man who blasted the life out of his wife and three children because, in his delusions, the sick-minded wretch had believed they were plotting against him—aiming to send him off to Bedlam." Charleton Lansdowne set down the cup of chocolate, the saucer chinking softly against the polished wood table.

"I never knew you attended hangings."

"I don't . . . didn't." Her father sucked in a deep breath. Released it. "I spent the entire time doubled over in the gutter, spilling out the previous night's kidney pie. When the execution was over, Bayard looked so patently unaffected, it made me shudder inside, question how he could look upon such a brutal wretch as the one who had dangled from that gallows. Bayard, he smiled at me, and said, ''Tis but looking into the face of our own darker sides, my innocent friend. That side even men like you possess, buried beneath your notions of honor.' I thought 'twas just more of Bayard's cynical driveling. I refused to believe . . .''

Her father dragged his hand back through his graying hair. "I never knew, Cecily, when I was young and bursting with hope, that one day I would stare into the memory of that hanged murderer's face and see there my own."

"You are no murderer!" Cecily cried, unable to bear the sadness in her father's face. "You—"

"Had my hand been but a wisp steadier in that bedchamber, I well could have been. Not to mention the fact that I"—his mouth twisted, eyes bright with tears of self-loathing—"that I nearly shot an unarmed man in my blind ravings. When I saw you, so terrified of me, as though . . .''

He gave a sick laugh. "As though I were that monster of a man at Tyburn Tree, then I saw so clearly what Bayard had meant that day so long ago. 'Twas like staring into the devil's looking glass, seeing all pretense of nobility, honor, decency carved away, exposing cruelties I had not known myself capable of, emotions so dark and terrifying that to face them was to die inside."

Cecily felt the overwhelming need to leap to her father's defense, hating the despair that made him seem to shrink into himself. But the agony of those burned in the *Ninon* had seared away something inside her. "You thought you were trying to protect me," she managed, her voice stiff, edged with a coolness she fought to banish.

"Nay, Cecily, I was struggling to cover my own cowardice. To secret away my hideous mistakes by fastening some kind of righteous outrage upon a man whom I saw as shattering your faith in me. A man who I was terrified would tell you the truth about what I was . . . what I *am.*"

"What you are is a . . . a loving father and—"

"What I am is a failure, Cecily. A failure in everything

except in the love I bear you." His fingertip reached out, tracing her chin with halting tenderness. "And now, mayhap I have cast that to the devil as well."

"No. You're talking with me, really talking to me for the first time in weeks. From the beginning, it is all I wanted, Father." Cecily's eyes pleaded for forgiveness for the morass of hurt and misunderstanding that had risen between them, still separating them like a castle wall. "Whatever is wrong, let me help you, Papa. I know you didn't intend for—for anyone to die—"

"No. I had not even the strength to stand and commit myself to doing that which I knew was wrong. I closed my eyes and let myself be conveniently duped into casting hundreds of souls into a life worse than hell, in order to gain a purseful of gold. You were all I had after your mother died. You were my whole life. Because I had dared marry beneath my station, my father, the duke, had cast me out without a farthing. Only the dower estate, left me through my grandmother's will, kept Anastasia and I from genteel starvation. 'Twas wrong, Cecily, I know that now. But I wanted you to have every comfort, every privilege the world held to offer. When Bayard offered me interest in a shipping venture, I leapt at the chance to secure the money I was so desperate for."

"The shipping venture . . . it was the *Ninon?*"

Charleton gave a weak smile. " 'Twas called the *Lightskirt Annie* then. Bayard, he had it rechristened to placate me, and he brushed over the fact that the cargo the ship would be carrying was a human one. Even then, I think I knew. But I would have bartered with Lucifer and all his angels if in so doing I could secure a safe haven for you, my tiny daughter with Anastasia's eyes."

"You always made sure I felt safe." Cecily struggled to remember the coverlet of security and love that had warmed her during her childhood.

"And if I had died, who would have cared for you then? Your mother's people were all dead. Harry . . . I knew that he would not let you starve. Even my father would be forced to take an orphaned granddaughter into his household or risk the wrath of the rest of the ton. But I also knew what lot befell those who were cast under the title 'poor relations.' I knew that they were barely tolerated, with a callousness that chilled me to the core. There was little hope of marriage, more like bitterness and spinsterhood. And, knowing Harry's bride—well, even then Honoria was scarce capable of loving her own babe, let alone 'that foreign woman's bratling.'"

"So you turned the other way while Uncle Bayard entangled both of you in slaving?" Cecily prodded after a moment.

"It was not illegal then, only immoral. And I intended only to be involved in the one voyage—I planned to glean the quick profits from that first cargo and then invest it wisely, live frugally, gain enough to give you a comfortable life. That was how I rationalized plunging my hands into Sutton's blood money. I meant it then, meant never to let it taint me again. But when the new-christened *Ninon* sailed back into London, the profits were huge, and it became a temptation beyond my power to resist. If I were to leave my investment intact for but a little while longer, I could double, triple what I had, I could guarantee you not just a life filled with small comforts, but the life of a princess."

"So you continued with the slaving? Until the *Ninon* was set afire?"

"'Twas not my doing!" Her father spun, his face betraying his inner anguish as he pressed trembling fingers to his temples. "God, had I known, I would have stopped him!"

"Stopped who?"

"Bayard Sutton, of course. We had had a series of misfortunes, and our losses were increasing. I was furious with myself for having plunged on for three years, when, had I held to my original plan, the money I had earned would have been plenty to raise you. Still, I had tucked away enough that, combined with my grandmother's dower, there was a tidy sum in my name at my solicitors. But Bayard . . . everything he owned he had poured into Acanthus Diversified. If, in truth, the *Ninon* sailed back into port this time without bearing profits, Bayard would have lost his estates, everything. He was desperate, and took out insurance money to be paid in full should some disaster snuff out the lives of every slave upon the ship. But to gain the payment, *every* slave would have had to be lost—through some sort of disaster. *Every one.*"

Cecily felt a cold nausea creep through her stomach, the flesh at the nape of her neck crawling. "You mean that because the *Ninon* . . . *sank*—" The word caught in her throat. "You and Uncle Bayard . . ."

"Recouped every loss we sustained." Charleton Lansdowne kneaded the back of his neck with shaking fingers.

"But the ship did not 'catch' fire, Papa. Ransom said that the captain—"

"Put the *Ninon* to the torch and burned every man upon it alive." Charleton sank down onto the stool, as though the weight of the stars pressed upon him. "The one thing your Ransom Tremayne had no way of knowing was that the captain of the *Ninon* had been *ordered* to set the ship ablaze."

Charleton dragged a gaze laden with guilt to Cecily. She shook her head, disbelieving, her mind filling with the images Ransom had spun for her of the raging inferno the *Ninon* had become, of the slaves, chained, helpless in the ship's flaming belly, of the crew members trapped while the captain and a few of his cronies rowed away.

"Aye, you do well to look upon me with such horror," her father said wearily. "Whilst I was playing at patty pans with you at Briarton, hundreds of men and women were being burned to death at the orders of the man in whose hands I had placed not only my faith, but my honor as well."

Cecily wanted to comfort him, ease the misery etched in his beloved face, but the flooding of truths was too painful, too new.

"When I read in the London *Times* the horror that had befallen the ship, I was stunned. Sickened, because in my soul I knew what Sutton had done. I confronted him . . . railed at him until I got him to admit the truth. But even deeper than my horror ran my fear." Her father gave an anguished laugh. "The account of the fire fueled public outcry against slaving and any who profited by it, until London's streets seethed with outrage. Those who already abhorred the slave trade held the *Ninon* disaster up to the rest of England, demanding that justice be wreaked upon those responsible."

Cecily sank to the floor, curling her legs beneath her as she had when a child. She stared down at her hands, twining upon her lap. "Did they know—know the *Ninon* had been burned on purpose?"

"I think some suspected. But there was no way they could prove it. The man who had captained the *Ninon* was"— Charleton shivered—"was found dead in a back-street brothel in the Caribbean soon after, and he was the only man who could have linked the ship with Charleton, Lord Lansdowne or the glittering Baron of Wythe. Bayard had been meticulous about keeping our names from being linked with anything concerning the slave trade or Acanthus Diversified. I know not how he managed it, only that this secrecy was vital to him. Even then his eye was roving toward the prime ministry."

Cecily bit the inside of her lip, the soul sickness gnawing inside her intensifying as she dared not meet her father's eyes. "You were trying—trying to protect me."

"And what I've managed to do is plunge you into the midst of an abyss of shame, scandal, that will not only ruin me, but ruin your chances as well." Charleton Lansdowne's fingers curved gently over hers, the woman-softness of those palms a stark contrast to Ransom's hardened ones. "That was why I wanted to give you a London season—I was desperate to see you properly wed. That first card . . . it arrived on your birthday, and I knew . . . someone else knew the truth, would try to expose me."

His hand tightened about hers, his expression pleading, pathetic. "I feared it was but a matter of time before the whole of London would know my shame."

"So you forced me upon Aunt Honoria, were even willing to thrust me into the marriage mart in order to—"

"Only to gain you safety, child. I couldn't bear the

thought that I might have destroyed your chance at the happiness your mother and I shared. I was so distraught, shaken—" He gave a weak laugh. "Bayard has attempted to calm me since that first night at Drury Lane, but—"

"The theater? 'Twas Bayard Sutton who was in the box with you? Bayard Sutton who was the man in the cloak?" Cecily felt her hand grow suddenly damp in her father's grasp, remembering the sense of brooding evil that had clung to that sinister figure.

"Aye. I fear I was making a scene . . . Sutton, well, he refused to speak with me any longer, there amidst the crowds, said he would meet with me later, in the gardens here. Yet all his attempts to ease my conscience have been for naught." Charleton squared his narrow shoulders, his hands rising up, tentatively curving about Cecily's cheeks. She steeled herself not to flinch away from her father's touch, but as though he sensed the sick disgust yet within her, Charleton let his hands fall awkwardly to the table.

Lansdowne swallowed convulsively, chafing at his knuckle with an inkstained finger. "I had been coming to instruct you to make ready to travel to Briarton, when I discovered you missing earlier this evening."

"You were sending me away?"

"Aye. I wanted you off somewhere, insulated from the cruelties of the gossip mongers. I didn't want you to see—" His voice cracked. "See your father held up as a twisted monster before the whole of London when the truth about the *Ninon* was emblazoned across every rag-sheet or posted upon every fence in the city."

"But 'twas all so long ago. Surely no one remembers—"

"People remember touching hell, child," Charleton said. "Even an eternity after."

"You said Uncle Bayard destroyed any evidence there might have been. Even Ransom bears no way to prove that you had anything to do with the *Ninon,* and he was aboard the ship when it was burned."

Charleton winced, his waxen face whitening further. "So, that was how he knew about the torches, that the fire was no accident. Well then, I may be forced to ask him to testify to the truth in my behalf."

"Testify? Papa, I don't understand . . ."

"Child . . ." Charleton gripped her shoulders in desperate hands, his eyes burning deep into hers. "'Tis time to pay for the misery I wrought—time to confront the scorn I so richly deserve. And Bayard . . . 'tis time his dreams of rising to the top office in the nation were dashed as well. There is danger in him. The same sort of danger that lurked in that man on the gallows."

Cecily shivered, remembering the day Sutton had walked with her in Moorston's gardens, trying to cow her with subtle threats, dark promises. "But if it is only your word and Ransom's against Bayard Sutton's . . ."

"Whatever transpires will be far more than a bandying of words." Charleton withdrew his gold pocket watch, and Cecily saw his eyes skim the ornate clock's face. "Time . . ." she heard him mutter. "Not much time." He stood, drawing Cecily to her feet as well. "Come."

His fingers closed about the lamp base, and Cecily followed him as he made his way through the silent, dark house. The elegance of Moorston's new wing faded behind them, the lamp's glow entrapped in eerie blue shadows upon the armor lining the corridor to their own suite of rooms.

Cecily fought back the chill of foreboding, the shadow of her own mortality seeming to wisp over her as her father bent down to fumble with one of the iron helms. He reached his hand into the black interior of the armor, and when he again turned to face Cecily, he held a small, plain-wood chest.

"What is it?" Cecily eyed the casket as though it brimmed with evil, and flinched back instinctively as her father moved to place the chest in her hands.

"'Tis what I returned to Briarton for when I was almost killed in that carriage accident. 'Tis the evidence Bayard Sutton has no idea yet exists. The evidence that will blast the shroudings of mystery from the *Ninon* disaster forever. Take it, child."

"But . . ." Cecily swallowed hard, her gaze shifting to her father's. The inner agony that had tormented his thin features for weeks was gone, replaced by a kind of resigned serenity that clutched at Cecily's heart. She bit her lip, battling to remember where she had once seen that same expression—one so wrenchingly said yet so peaceful that it had branded itself in her consciousness years past.

The coldness about her chest tightened as the memory waxed clearer . . . her mind filling with remembrances of the high, arched ceilings and intricate stained glass. It had been in a tiny church in a Lancashire village. Above the altar she had seen that resigned, bittersweet expression in a rendition of Thomas à Becket about to be martyred.

Cecily's fingers knotted into fists, and she took a step back. "Papa, you keep it. I don't—don't want to be responsible for—"

"Nay, child. Don't you see? You are the only one I dare trust with it. The only one . . ." Clasping the casket in one hand, he reached up to smooth the tendrils of night-black hair from her forehead. "If anything should happen—"

"If what should happen? Curse it, Papa, you're driving me mad with these evasions." Cecily could not stay herself from sounding like a lost waif. "Papa, I'm frightened."

She had seen that gentle smile a thousand times before, soothing her in childhood nightmares, easing her fears, loving her, ever loving her. "Whist, now, sunshine," her father said softly, brushing her cheek with his knuckles. "Retire to your chambers, sleep. 'Twill all be over soon."

Cecily felt spikes of ice drive through her spine, the gentle-sad smile tipping her father's mouth haunting her.

Charleton Lansdowne folded her hands over the wooden chest, brushing her lips with a soft kiss.

"I don't want to sleep. I want to stay with you."

"This is one thing I must face alone, child. At least let me salvage my pride, my honor, to that small degree."

Cecily felt the rising of panic in her chest. "Papa—" she began, but something in the silent plea within Charleton Lansdowne's eyes stopped her. She battled to keep her voice from shaking as he drew away. "I love you, Papa," she whispered, her fingers clutching the box's smooth surface.

"And I love you, child." Her father's eyes filled with tears. "No matter what happens, Cecily, cling to that."

She wanted to reach out to him, embrace him as she had when she was a starry-eyed poppet chasing kittens in Briarton's stables. But a hundred frayed ribbons spun of vanished dreams held her as she watched him stride away.

She stood there, numb, aching, clutching the wooden chest in icy fingers as she heard the latch scrape back from where it barred the garden door. 'Twas a hollow sound—an empty one. Empty as her life would be without the love of her father. The father who had made a terrible mistake, that even yet sluiced waves of bitter horror through her.

But he was willing to pay for that mistake, confront it at last—alone.

"Nay, not alone!" Cecily whispered fiercely. "Blast it, not alone!"

Her chin rose in stubborn defiance that boded ill for any who dared challenge her, her eyes blazing violet fire.

With all haste, she jerked up the helm's visor, jamming the box she held back into the suit of armor, the clatter of wood against metal echoing through the vast hallway.

But she cared not if the noise woke the whole of London, felt nothing except the desperate need to find her father.

Scooping up her skirts, she ran through the corridor.

The door latch her father had loosed moments before was cold in her hand, the brisk dawn breeze chilling her face. And she felt as if she teetered upon the edge of some gaping void, whirling in flame, and screams, and a thousand long-dead terrors.

Her fingernails dug deep into her palms as she hesitated but a heartbeat. Then, choking back her fear, she plunged after the father she sensed even now was slipping away.

Chapter Nineteen

LIKE PHANTOMS, LOST, the mist trailed over the garden, its clumsily wrought sculptures and tangled rose vines still sinister specters untouched by the first whisperings of dawn. Cecily caught her lip between her teeth as she ran, fighting the shiver of dread born of her fanciful imagination.

"Papa?" She paused, shivered, trying to pierce the obscuring haze with her eyes to gauge which direction her father had gone. But the maze of shrubbery stretched in inky shadings before her, no sign of the stoop-shouldered figure to be seen.

She tried to stifle the flights of her imagination, to drive back the rising, almost supernatural evil she sensed within the walled enclosure. Knotting her hands in the folds of her skirt, she hastened down a path leading to the secluded alcove formed of bayberry and sweet juniper, where her father had been wont to sit with his journals in the first days after their arrival at Moorston. But even before she reached the copse of shrubbery, Cecily harbored only an empty hope that her father had merely strode out into the gardens to contemplate the tempest he was about to unleash.

She struggled to see through the mist, the curved marble bench wrenchingly empty. If he were yet in the garden, 'twould have been this quiet haven he would have sought.

She knew it with a certainty. Unless . . . unless he were no longer in the garden at all.

Battling the panic clamoring in her chest, she wheeled, trampling through her aunt's masses of roses, the thorns tearing at her skin, the vines seeming to snarl out sharp-spined lashes to bind about her ankles as she hurried in the direction of the gate. She could just make out the darker shadow of the portal's wood set against the lighter-shaded stone of the walls encircling the garden, when a sound drifted to her upon the eerie mist.

Voices.

Their words were as yet indistinguishable, but the menace in one speaker's tones raked clearly through the dawn air, while the other voice was icily calm, soul-wrenchingly familiar. Her father, aye, confronting his demons alone.

Cecily started to call out, but her slipper caught upon the snout of a marble dolphin, sending her sprawling into the roots of a tree. She was scraped upon her elbows and knees, the warmth of blood welling upon her skin, but she ripped her skirts free of the yet-clinging thorns, scrambling to her feet as though Hades himself were trying to drag her down into the dark earth.

The voices were louder now, angrier. Cecily's bruised fingers clenched, some sinister spell seeming to yet wrap poisoned tendrils around her, binding her slipper soles to the ground.

". . . may leave off scattering your little cards about." Her father's voice was clear, strong, with the first hintings of pride she had heard in the weeks at Moorston. And in the rich timbre of the tones, she could sense he was struggling to grasp at some elusive sense of honor. ". . . whole of London will know the truth about the *Ninon* from my own mouth before . . . sun sets this evening, and you . . . have to suffer without the coin . . . battled to extort."

"Extort?" Venomous silk, a woman's husky laughter drifted low from behind the partially opened garden gate, setting pulsings of fear, indecision bursting in Cecily's chest. "Thrice . . . kept the knife from your throat. Consider the coin I demand rightful payment for sparing you the cut of a far deeper blade."

"Rightful payment? For attempting to rob me ... endangering my daughter?"

Sweet God, Cecily thought wildly, he was defying whoever had precipitated this hellish storm of events—was threatening someone desperate enough to steal into a houseful of servants, to slip insidious terror like a dagger into a man's heart.

". . . precious daughter," the other voice sneered. "She is no better than I! Barters her wealth, position, to gain security, just as I barter . . . beauty of my face, skills of my body, to keep from starving in the gutter. But after today I'll ne'er again be under the power of some cursed man. At his mercy—"

"Nay, indeed you'll not." Cecily could hear a threading of reluctant sympathy through the steely tones of her father's voice. "For you'll never see anything except Newgate's cells after this night."

"Nay, Papa!" Cecily choked back the whisper, pressing her fear-whitened knuckles to her mouth as she struggled with her resolve to allow her father to regain a measure of his much-battered honor. But the pervasive sense of evil played upon the taut threads of her nerves like a harpie's fingers, shattering the importance of all except the safety of the father she cherished.

Cecily ran toward the voices, her consciousness filling with whisperings of the occult, mysteries spawned of the dark one . . . threats of death . . .

Obeah.

"Newgate?" A laugh hissed, ice on a steel-honed razor. "I think not, Lord Lansdowne. You'll but pay my forfeit another way. . . ."

Cecily shoved her palms hard against the wooden gate, scarce feeling the splinters being driven into her hands. The panel banged outward, slamming into the stone wall with a deafening crash, opening what seemed a gateway into blinding terror. The veilings of mist were all but swept away upon the narrow street beyond, as if Satan himself had commanded the hazings to vanish. Only thin wisps of white twined like serpents about the two figures that spun now to face her—her father, and the other, slender form, robed in scarlet.

In that frozen instant it was as if a woodsman's axe had split wide Cecily's chest as the newborn sun cast a feeble light across the face of Charleton Lansdowne's enemy.

A cloth of bloodred was bound about the woman's hair, highlighting features spicy brown, elegantly beautiful. Features Cecily had seen before, supposedly battered, bruised in the great room at Tradewinds.

"Khadija!" Cecily gasped out the name, a hundred fragments of confusion whirling like the pieces of some macabre puzzle, crashing into place with devastating force.

Khadija, who had staged a Cheltenham tragedy to gain sanctuary with Ransom; Khadija, who had buried the knife blade in Cecily's pillow—Khadija, who bore an employer desiring Charleton Lansdowne's death.

Cecily darted toward her yet-stunned father, saw him take a step in her direction, but in that instant, Cecily's gaze flashed to the woman standing but an arm's length away. Silent, swift, the African beauty's hand flashed up to the scarlet turban, her fingers sweeping away from the cloth something thin, long, gleaming blue.

Cecily started to scream warning, terror cutting, jagged-edged, through her body, but 'twas too late. Like a snake Khadija struck, her eyes cold with evil as the wicked needle that had pinned her turban drove deep into Charleton Lansdowne's skull.

Pale eyes widened in surprise for but a heartbeat, then rolled in a horrifying path upward. "Papa!" The anguished cry tore from Cecily's lips as she caught her arms about him, trying to brace him as he staggered, but her own legs buckled beneath his weight and she tumbled to the ground beside his slumped form.

Her eyes flicked but a heartbeat to her yet-unmoving father. Still. He was so still. A pin the like of which had

anchored a hundred different bonnets upon her own head—
nothing but a wire-thin length of steel. Surely it could not
deal . . . death?

"'Twas you!" Cecily accused the other woman, fingers
clutching at her father's limp form. "You who came into my
room . . . who . . . oh my God . . ." Cecily gasped the
curse, feeling as though an iron-toed boot had been driven
into the pit of her stomach as she remembered Lacey's
terrified babble, remembered the doctor's diagnosis when
he had seen Nicky Dolan.

Mind blurred with horror, Cecily released her crushing
grip upon her father and stumbled to her feet, confronting
the woman who had so terrorized the gentle child. "You . . .
you murdered Nicky . . . killed him . . . why . . . ?"

The laugh that rippled from the African woman's lips was
sultry, sinister as a heavily poisoned flower. "The little
wretch recognized me from my . . . former associations.
But the obeah know well how to deal with any who can cast
them into chains."

"He was only a little boy! So frightened!"

Cecily saw the woman's lips slither into a grim smile.
"Had I known what your precious Captain Tremayne would
cost me, I'd have murdered his bastard as well that night.
But then, there may yet be time to dispose of the spoiled
chit, and her father, *after* I dispatch *you* to the demons."
Khadija paused, and Cecily knew her own death lay reflected in those night-dark eyes. But all she could see was
Lacey's trusting eyes, Ransom's heart-wrenching smile—
both soon to be crushed into death by the evil woman before
her?

A primal rage possessed Cecily as she hurled herself at the
statuesque Khadija, instinct driving her to claw at those
smooth cheeks, that beautiful face. Cecily's hand caught in
the folds of red turban, the garment, loosed of its pin,
ripping away from Khadija's head.

Thick, black, a waterfall of tresses tumbled down the tall
woman's back, an arresting flood of hair Cecily knew in a
heart-stopping instant she had seen before—adorning the
mysterious beauty she had witnessed deep in conversation

with Bayard Sutton the day she had fled through the shopping district.

In that instant the image of Sutton's blandly handsome face swam before her eyes, his mouth twisted with the barest hinting of danger. But she shook herself free of the numbing horror, shock rushing through her, just as Khadija charged, glinting silver in her grasp.

Cecily bit out a denial, catching Khadija's wrist with both her hands, heart leaping wildly in her chest as the jungle-bred beauty bore down upon the lethal weapon. The tip of the wicked needle glowed red with blood, Khadija's impassive features more terrifying than any blood-lusting snarl could be.

Witch-woman . . . Cecily could hear Lacey's terrified cries, felt in her own breast the roiling, supernatural terror as Khadija chuckled softly, bearing downward, ever downward, upon the deadly bit of steel.

Cecily clung, fierce, to her love of the dark-curled child, clung to her love of the man who had taught her the meaning of honor. The man and child who would die at Khadija's hands if the blade-sharp needle drove home. With a snarl of pure rage, Cecily drove the toe of her slipper into the other woman's shin, one hand releasing Khadija's wrist to slash, lightning fast, in a scratching, tearing path at the woman's eyes.

Cecily heard Khadija's breath catch, a curse in some language Cecily did not understand bursting from her attacker's lips as the fragile skin under Khadija's eye tore.

Yet despite the cry attesting to the African beauty's pain, the needle flashed down. Cecily attempted to dive out of the way, knowing that she could not evade the other woman much longer, knowing too that the needle in the woman's finger bore death upon its glinting point. The garden wall's harsh stone grated against her back, cutting off her escape. Khadija's teeth gleamed, an asp's fangs, eyes narrowing with thirst for the kill. With a cry, Cecily darted low, slamming her shoulder into the woman's midsection, feeling a sharp tearing across her collarbone as the needle bit flesh. Cecily crashed to the ground, her mind reeling with agonizing pictures of Ransom's pirate-rogue face, Lacey's impish smile, Charleton Lansdowne's kiss across Cecily's own childish cheek. A wave of dizziness washed over her, Khadija's laugh of triumph piercing through the roiling colors in Cecily's head.

"Nay won't . . . let you . . ." Cecily gritted her teeth against the blinding pain, her fingers groping for something, anything, to use against the woman closing in to kill her. Her hand brushed something hard, rough, her hand clutching the object desperately as Khadija charged.

With all her might Cecily arched her hand up, cracking the jagged cobblestone into Khadija's cheekbone, hearing the sickening sound of bone cracking.

A sound of stunned fury came from Khadija's mouth, the woman's blood splashing warm upon Cecily's arm as Khadija drove the knifelike needle in a wild slash.

Yet at that moment the crashing of boots through the garden brush echoed through the street, both women freezing as a voice boomed loud.

"Who goes there! You! Who goes—" 'Twas the footman. Cecily nigh sobbed with relief.

"John! John, help!" she cried out, her eyes blinded by the light of a lantern slicing through the shadowy dawn.

"Milady? Milady, is that you?"

Cecily glimpsed the servant's livery straining over burly shoulders, heard Khadija's frustrated snarl as the woman spun away, the sound of pattering footsteps fading as the African beauty vanished into the mist.

"For the love of God, milady, what befell you? The master?" John's florid face was creased with concern as he knelt beside Cecily, encircling her with his arm to draw her upright.

"Papa . . ." Cecily choked out the plea, crawling over to where Charleton Lansdowne lay, his graying hair capturing the lantern light, his mouth slack. One hand reached toward her in silent supplication, as though he were yet pleading with her for forgiveness.

"Papa, you have to listen to me, you have to . . . sorry . . . I'm so . . . so sorry . . ." But as Cecily drew his head into her lap, she knew he would never hear the words he had so desperately longed to hear. Would never know how hard she was battling to understand what he had done so many years ago.

For her, he had said, in that broken, despairing voice. *For love of her.*

"Milady . . ." John's warm tones were gruffly sympathetic beside her, but Cecily scarce heard him, scarce felt the gentle hand he laid upon her arm.

"Papa, I love you," she sobbed, burying her face against her father's chest. "I need you." But the arms that had comforted her through a thousand childhood sorrows lay limp upon the cobbles, the beloved, ink-splotched fingers never again to brush a tender caress upon her tear-wet cheek.

Chapter Twenty

THE BARON OF WYTHE pored over the missive in his ring-bedecked hands, his lips splitting in a smile of stark triumph. *'Tis time for all of England to acknowledge Lord Bayard Sutton's most noble leadership,* the neatly penned lines scribed by the Duke of Montclieff proclaimed. *The honor of not only the Whig party, but of this whole noble isle of Britannia shall lay within your hands.*

Bayard Sutton's immaculately gloved fingers clenched tighter about the invitation bidding him to celebrate his ascendency at a grand political dinner to be held at the duke's house of Montclieff. Lud, but it seemed Sutton had been awaiting this moment for a lifetime, had plotted and planned, and tilted with a hundred subtle weapons to gain the power that would be placed into his grasp this night.

'Twould be heaven, aye, to take up the reins of the Whig party, to drive it again high into glory, battering down the rule of the hated Tories. No small feat for any man, the gleaning of such an exalted position. But for the son of a drunkard who had borne nothing but huge gambling debts and a nigh bankrupt baroncy to pass on to his only son, it was a miracle.

Sutton chuckled, stepping over to where a cheval glass glinted in the sunlight streaming through the mullioned window. Yes, but this "miracle" had had a deal of aid from a mind ruthless enough to destroy any enemies that dared threaten its dreamings, and yet cunning . . . aye, so cunning that any scurvy minion who had dealt death in the name of the Baron of Wythe kissed the Reaper's stiff lips themselves soon after. None of those insignificant wretches he played like a puppet master would live to shatter the facade Bayard Sutton had spent a lifetime weaving.

Sutton looked at his reflection, lost there in the mirror, one gloved fingertip tracing the tiny lines at the corners of his eyes as he affected his gravest smile, his eyes filling with the deep compassion of a Christ image in a Michelangelo painting. 'Twas most effective, this ability to call into play any emotion that suited him, even to willing a single crystal tear to appear at the corner of his eye and trickle down his soft cheek . . . or yes, even weeping solemn manful tears at some injustice that called for great show of emotion.

He swiped the tear away with infinite satisfaction, rubbing the dampness into his fingertips. His last performance had been worthy of the Bard himself—the noble, philanthropic Bayard Sutton, reaching out his hand to aid the wretched climbing boys so piteously ill-used in the city. The whinings of that cursed contingent of do-gooders who had brought the children's plight to Parliament's attention last session had almost made Sutton laugh, with their solemn faces and gravely sorrowful eyes.

Their masters force them up the tiny flues by searing their legs and buttocks with flaming sticks—children of six, five, even four years old—their bodies naked, half starved. Sometimes they needs must extinguish fires caught high within the chimneys . . . can fall to their deaths far below.

Sutton's mouth hardened as he straightened his cravat with impatient hands. Of course the little wretches had to extinguish fires in the chimney flues. For Chrissake, *somebody* had to do it! And if 'twere those cursed philanthropists who bore a smoking chimney, they would well drive the spikes into the climbing boys themselves to keep the soot from spoiling their Aubusson carpets.

Of course, no one bore the slightest idea that the great humanitarian of the age, the noble Baron of Wythe, bore any such thoughts. Nay, he had stood at the end of the speeches, striking his fist to his chest, addressing the assemblage in a voice that cracked with just the proper amount of emotion.

. . . 'tis a noble quest you embark upon, to aid these lambs of God, lost in the midst of such unspeakable horror. You may count Lord Bayard Sutton as a champion of these innocents, and take this small token to aid in easing the children's plight. He had drawn a pouch full of coin (it made a much more satisfying thud upon the table than the lighter, paper currency), and had cast it down to where the contingent stood.

A man with a weathered face and a mouth curved as though it had witnessed too many sorrows had taken up the purse, thanking the baron solemnly for all his good works.

Sutton felt a grin play about the corners of his mouth, saw it reflected back in the cheval glass ornamenting the wall of this, his most favored sanctum. Good works, he thought with a spicing of irony. The single good that had come of that cursed encounter had been that it reminded him that 'twas time to clean the chimney in the East Drawing Room. And, when the master sweep Farnham had come, dragging along his bevy of big-eyed waifs, there had been a new one amongst them, with dark gold hair and a face like the archangels, despite its layering of soot. He had long had a weakness for golden-haired boys.

Sutton shook away the memory, refusing to allow the slightest tarnish to dull the gloss of the evening stretching before him. A muffled grunt of irritation came from his lips as he rubbed the ring he wore beneath his glove, the crest cutting the slightest bit into his flesh. 'Twould be a relief to get the cursed circlet of gold off of him and onto the slender finger of his intended bride.

Lady Cecily Lansdowne—with the haughty beauty of generations of nobility etched in her features, and her bearing infinitely regal despite her scant nineteen years— she was the final shading Sutton needed to complete the image he had striven so long to portray. His teeth clenched in an unguarded moment of aggravation at the memory of how the chit had dismissed his suit in the garden of

Moorston that day, pining, no doubt, for the broad-shouldered, rough-hewn Ransom Tremayne, with his animal eyes and his gritty passion.

Well, the lady would perforce have to endure being disappointed. Bayard had labored too long, risked even being tied to the murder of a man he had once used in the guise of friend, and all to gain her as an ornament to pin to his waistcoat pocket.

Aye, and he would have her now, damn it, even if he dragged her kicking and screaming to the blasted altar. With an oath he stalked to where a cut-glass bottle of Madeira rested discreetly upon a dark-wood stand.

The sound of a disturbance in the hall made Sutton cast an annoyed glance toward the doorway, the voice of his most favored footman mingling with another muffled sound, the thudding of some sort of scuffle setting Bayard's teeth on edge.

". . . told you, my lord will not see you here . . . be furious you dared . . ."

Sutton heard the comely servant hiss out in alarm, but the baron's own temper was now rearing its ugly head. "What the devil is the meaning of this?" he blazed, slamming open the huge door to reveal the scene in the corridor beyond.

The footman's pleasingly lean body was pressed against the wall, his eyes fastened fearfully upon a wretched creature that seemed to have been dragged from the Thames—hair of a ridiculously long length tangled about bloodied features, the material of a once rich gown torn and soiled while she held the footman at bay with something that looked like a biddy's knitting needle.

"How dare you intrude—"

Sutton started to draw up the full force of his dignity, his eyes glacial as he took a step toward the woman. But he had scarce moved before she wheeled upon him, her lips drawn over perfect teeth in a feral snarl.

"You'll see me, my fine lord, and immediately." The hissed words, the wild eyes, made Sutton's heart still in his chest.

He cursed, lunging forward, grabbing the woman's wrist

in a crushing grip, his gaze darting about to ascertain whether or not any of his other servants were nigh. But the corridor was deserted, except for the faithful Aloysius.

"Witling bitch," Sutton spat low under his breath. "How many times have I warned you not to come here?"

Khadija sneered, and the sight of it sent a spike of dread through Sutton's frayed nerves. "When you hear why I have come, *my high lord baron,* you'll be more than grateful I burst into your palace."

Sutton glared down into that perfect, spice-brown face, hating what he saw within it—disaster, aye, something so terrible he wanted to crush that slender throat before the woman could speak.

"Very well," Sutton said between clenched teeth, releasing Khadija as though she were a particularly distasteful piece of refuse. "Aloysius." He gave the pretty-face youth a meaningful look. "See to it that the rest of the staff is, er . . . occupied elsewhere in the house."

"Y-Yes, my lord." The footman peeled himself away from the wall, skirting around Khadija as though she were a madwoman.

Silent, Sutton gestured for Khadija to enter the sanctum of his Red Salon. With hands that belied his fury, he shut the doors deliberately, locking them.

When he heard the nervous rustle from where Khadija stood, he looked up at her, arching one brow in haughty disdain. "Come now," he said. "Even a brainless whore the likes of you can surely see how . . . inconvenient should anyone barge in to see the noble Lord Sutton in conversation with someone of your ilk. The whole of London would be abuzz with the news by the morrow."

The woman gave a grating laugh that made Sutton want to slap her. "I vow to you, London will not give a damn on the morrow if you've entertained every harlot in the city upon the Regent's own lawns. Every silk-smothered member of your precious ton will be buried in gossip of a far different sort—*murder.*"

"Murder?" Wariness stole over Sutton, his eyes scanning his hireling's face. Had the wench discovered already that he had planned to have her eliminated? Had she come to confront him now? Kill *him?* He turned away from her with a laugh of feigned carelessness, his eyes fastening for an instant upon the heavy fireplace poker in its stand beside the hearth. He paced in that direction with practiced negligence.

"I'd advise you not to attempt anything foolish." The awareness in the woman's voice startled him, and he stopped, turned toward her. "After all, I've already taken one life this night." Sutton saw those dark, dangerous eyes narrow as Khadija continued. "My lord will be pleased to know that I have finally managed to dispose of one more of the . . . inconveniences you've hired me to rid you of."

"Is that so?"

"I regret to inform you of the death of your most cherished friend."

"Charleton?" Bayard could not keep the eager gleam from his eye.

"He lies dead even now, outside the garden at Moorston."

Sutton's brow wrinkled and he caught the corner of his lip between his teeth in puzzlement. "Of course, I wanted the weakling dead, but I do not recall instructing you to take the risk of approaching him at his brother's town house. . . ."

"You did not." Khadija gave a low laugh. "And 'twas an unfortunate miscalculation on my part. For I fear it has caused something of a difficulty."

The insolent tone of that sultry voice raked across Bayard's temper, his lips stiff with scarce-controlled anger as he faced her. *"Difficulty? Just what do you mean by difficulty?"*

"I fear you shall have to render me payment for Charleton Lansdowne's murder immediately, so that I may exit London as soon as possible."

"Damn it, tell me what the hell—"

"'Tis your precious Lady Cecily," Khadija said. "She had the misfortune of bearing witness to her father's demise."

"Cecily!" The leash Sutton had held upon his temper snapped, and he stormed toward Khadija, full intending to take her by her slender arms and shake her until her teeth rattled. But before he could reach her, the woman's lips parted in sly danger, the firelight running red down the length of the subtle silver weapon she yet held.

Bayard stopped, knowing full well the depth of menace in the deceptively small bit of steel.

"Aye, that is better, your lordship," Khadija taunted softly. "'Tis most unbecoming for a man of your station to so forget himself."

"You stupid doxy, do you not know what you have done? For God's sake, if she should ever discover that I—that you—"

"I judge that she has guessed already. And has also linked me, and you as well, to the death of that urchin Nicky Dolan."

A violent rage boiled inside Bayard Sutton, murderous, unbound, seething through him like poison. But it was the masterful violence of a cobra—hood spread, eyes mesmerizing its victim. "So," he said in silky accents. "You desire I should pay you, aid you in escaping London, when, because of your bungling, I might well be forced to flee the city myself within the week."

"Cecily Lansdowne is too distraught with grief to make any intelligent recounting of what happened this night. Even if she wanted to, she could get no one to believe her, upset as she is. And by the time she is recovered enough to do you ill . . ." Khadija let the words trail off.

"I can what? March into Moorston and put a pistol ball in her heart?"

"'Tis of no concern to me what you do. I want only the money you promised me. And I will have it, even if I must add another death to my tally."

"You are threatening me, Khadija?" Sutton smoothed the soft leather of his gloves over his slender hands. "Most unwise. However . . ." He forced his lips to split in a smile. "As you well know, I would hardly dare to attend to you as I would like to here, in a house filled with witnesses."

The woman's face went still, and Sutton took fearsome pleasure in the lurking darts of fear in that impassive beautiful visage. Graceful fingers waved the needle in an expert path before her. "You forget," Khadija hissed, "I know exactly how much you would dare."

Sutton snorted. "Despite the pleasure it would give me to kill you, I can hardly throw to the winds what little chance I bear of salvaging the havoc your carelessness has wrought. Very well. I'll give you your payment, and you, my fine harlot, will never show your face in London again, or I swear, by God, I will see you dead."

He turned, pacing to where his desk stood near the fireplace, and tugged open a drawer, ever aware of Khadija's eyes upon him as he reached for a pouch of money. Deftly, the nail of one finger slipped into the pouch's strings, stealthily loosening the cord as he swept the bag of coins into his hand.

Every muscle in his body tensed, ready. "Here." He extended the pouch toward her. "And may you burn in hell with it."

The look of victory in that beautiful face ripped at the webbing of control he yet held over himself as he tossed the pouch at her. Her eyes flicked away from him for an instant as she leaned forward, attempting to catch the object in her other hand, but the loosened strings snapped open, showering her with the coins that flew from the leather bag.

At that instant Sutton dove, his fingers gripping the poker's handle, ripping the instrument from its stand.

He caught a glimpse of Khadija's stunned face as she battled to regain her balance and saw the hooked point arching toward her. Her smooth skin burst as the iron cracked into her fragile-boned countenance, shattering her jaw, her scream of pain garbled as her mouth filled with blood. Sutton's face twisted in a grimace of ecstasy as the darkness took him, whirling him away into welcomed madness as he drove the weapon down onto her crumpled body again and again and again.

How long he had beaten the fallen woman he never knew, but only felt the scarlet rage ebbing. His arms and shoulders ached abominably with the effort he had expended. The snowy white of his shirt was spattered with blood. With the toe of one gleaming Hessian he nudged the fallen Khadija over onto her back, saw her face, now unrecognizable, staring lifelessly up at him.

Sutton sighed. He would have to dispatch Aloysius at once, to rid the room of the body. And then, of course, there were the carpets to clean. Bayard bit back the tang of distaste in his mouth, his gaze falling upon the once-pristine leather of his gloves, now stained bright scarlet.

She had deserved to die. And now, the other . . . Sutton closed his eyes, seeing Cecily Lansdowne's ivory beauty devastated in the same way as the dead woman before him. Now he bore no choice but to kill her as well, aye, and that bastard rogue Tremayne.

However, Bayard thought, he dared not trust these affairs to anyone save himself. The stakes were far too high. After the dinner at Montclieff . . .

With careful deliberation, he turned toward the hearth, replacing the poker into its holder. The entire morass was unfortunate, most unfortunate. He gave an aggrieved sigh, deftly peeling away his ruined gloves. Ah, well, mayhap that spineless chit of a cousin Cecily had, Lady Mirabelle, would suffice as his wife in Cecily's stead. She was, after all, a duke's daughter, and an heiress as well. A poor substitute, mind you, but he would have to sacrifice.

Sacrifice . . . such an apt expression.

A grim smile creased his lips as he cast his gloves into the flames.

Chapter Twenty-one

Ransom DROVE HIS HEELS INTO the exhausted gelding's barrel, spurring his mount through the streetlight's glow. It seemed that he had stalked for days instead of hours through flats stinking of cabbage, through rivers of gin and the cheap perfumes of the ladies of the evening. Yet nowhere, from the scrawny, terrified factory master to the most drunken sot in Covent Gardens, had Ransom been able to glean the slightest bit of information concerning one Aaron White or Nicky Dolan.

To the denizens of the streets, the child had been just one more skeletal bundle to trip over on the corners. Yet if anyone did conveniently remember aught that would aid Ransom in his search, he doubted not that that person would show themselves at the shipping office at Defiance Enterprises the next morn.

A grim smile played about Ransom's lips as he recalled the sum he had vowed to pay for any such information. Aye, he would make it well worth the while of any who would dare come forward. And no matter how much this White was feared, an empty belly would be sure to drive someone to betray him.

Ransom rolled his stiff shoulders beneath his cape, the wind's chill fingers penetrating the layers to the muscled flesh beneath.

Yet now there were other dragons to tilt with. His gaze strained up the street to where Moorston stood, a brooding shadow in the night. Dragons that might well cost him the greatest treasure life had ever granted him. He transferred both reins into one hand, wincing at the memory of Cecily's stricken face, the agony he had sensed in her at Tradewinds hours earlier. For weeks the two men she loved most in the world had been rending her apart, neither of them giving a damn about the torment in her dark-lashed eyes.

His mouth twisted in self-disgust. Well, by the saints, there would be no more plottings behind her back, no more secrets that held the power to destroy her, no more fits of accursed masculine temper, arrogance, stubbornness, to shatter the serenity within that regally beautiful face. Before this night was past, he would cut away a thousand lies and reach the bloody truth about the hell ship and the father she adored. And then . . .

Ransom grimaced. Then, maybe, there would be some small chance they could gain a life together.

The very thought twisted deep in Ransom's heart, bitter-sweet, so wondrous it seemed sin to even hold the hope in his own sullied hands. And yet he could not stay the wild longing that seemed to sink fiery talons into his very soul. Never, even in those Satan-spawned years in the slave port, had he ever wanted—needed—anything the way he needed Lady Cecily Lansdowne. Her delicate features, an angel's face spiced with a touch of the devil's own temper, her hair, night black, pouring like liquid silk through his fingers, and her eyes . . .

The memory of the outrage, the fierce love that had shone in their depths when he had told her the horrible truth about his boyhood, would be one remembrance he would cherish for the rest of his life. Instead of shrinking from him, eyeing him as though he were some sort of freak in a street-caller's fair, she had caught him in her arms and loved him.

He swallowed the knot that rose in his throat, the outline of Moorston blurring before his eyes. This one gift, then, he would give her tonight, if it cost him his own life. Peace.

He reined his horse to the right, cantering toward the

town house's grand entrance. But instead of the liveliness that usually announced the commencement of the haute-ton's evening festivities, the house lay silent, nigh as though a sorcerer's wand had set all within it into some enchanted sleep.

Something was wrong.

With a curse, Ransom flung himself from the saddle, rushing up two stairs at a time to reach the wide doors and pound upon them, but the footman whose duty it was to mind the entry was nowhere to be seen. Ransom paused but an instant, then biting out an oath, jammed his shoulder against the unbolted panel, flinging it wide. The entryway was darkened, the lowest of murmurings disturbing the smothering silence as Ransom stalked in. But he had scarce shut the door behind him when he noticed the dark drapings about the vaulted room.

Crepe. Midnight-hued crepe.

Ransom's heart plummeted to his boots, fear cold upon his skin. Moorston was in mourning.

The entryway swam before his eyes, its walls blotted out by the obeah death symbol and the image of a dagger thrust into the embroidered pillow upon which Cecily lay, helpless in sleep. God's wounds, what if the obeah had made good that threat?

"Damn it, where is everybody?" Ransom shouted, not caring if he shattered the delicate plaster carvings gracing the ceiling overhead. "Get the hell out here!"

His voice boomed, echoed, demolishing the silence that had lain so heavy over the household. There was an alarmed sound from one of the distant rooms, the scurrying of feet. Then a footman burst from one of the doorways, a black armband stark about the sleeve of his bright orange livery, his pale face stained with two bright spots of red.

"Who—Who goes there?" the footman demanded with a belated attempt to cling to the appropriate dignity. But his eyes were rounded with the fresh fear of someone who has too recently been witness to something that had shaken him to the core. "Sir, state your business."

"Where is Lady Cecily?" Ransom roared, catching the

servant by his starched neckcloth. "By Christ, you tell me, or—"

"Milady is not receiving anyone this eve." The footman eyed Ransom with barely concealed fear. The spiked bands of terror digging into Ransom's chest eased, relief driving the breath from his lungs as he clutched to himself the certainty that Cecily was alive, safe.

He glared at the footman. "Milady will damned well receive me. Tell her Captain Tremayne—"

The footman had regained enough dignity to deal Ransom an icy stare. "The lady is not to be disturbed under the direst of circumstances. She is grieving for his lordship's passing."

"His lordship? Damn it, man, what the devil are you babbling about?"

"Lord Lansdowne, sir, was—was murdered before dawn outside the garden gate." Ransom's mind reeled, struck through with gritty horror that magnified itself a hundred-fold as the footman continued in stony accents, "My Lady Cecily, she witnessed—"

Ransom choked back the bile that rose in his throat, his stomach churning with denial, rage. He shoved the footman away from him, anguish roiling inside him at the certainty that his angel, his Gloriana, had seen the father she worshiped die, seen his life snatched away by some ruthless cutthroat.

"Where is she?" The words were harsh, torn from lips taut with grief.

"Wh-What, sir?"

"I said, where is Lady Cecily?"

The rustle of silk upon the stairs made Ransom look up, his eyes fastening upon the pointy features of Lavinia Lansdowne. The girl bore the look of a sly cat that had been relishing some particularly delectable cream, and Ransom's fists knotted against the urge to drive his open palm against that smug face.

"Captain Tremayne," Lavinia sniffed, with most obvious relish. "You can hardly expect my cousin to disgrace this household further by trysting with you when her father is not even cold. I fear your sordid little affair will have to wait until after—"

Ransom charged up the curved stairway and took infinite pleasure in the squeak of fear the chit emitted as she scrunched against the railing. "Blast it, you take me to her now, before I knot those cursed hair ribbons about your neck."

Lavinia's fingers fluttered up to the pure white skin of her throat, and Ransom saw her lick her full lips in the very wicked excitement that had turned his stomach when he had seen it upon the faces of other ton beauties.

He caught a glimpse of the footman rushing up the stairs behind him, heard servants hastening from other parts of the house. Curse them all. If he had to fight his way through a score of the burly bastards to reach Cecily, he would. His shoulders stiffened as he tensed for battle, violence pulsing raw in his veins.

But before he could move, the tiniest swish of silk against silk made him freeze, a hush falling over all within the entryway as every eye angled up to the head of the magnificent staircase.

Every sinew in Ransom's body was wracked with agony as his gaze locked upon the slender figure standing so still above them. The ebony hair was drawn back from an ash-pale face, a gown of silver tissue over lilac silk molding the curves of Cecily's body in regal perfection, a delicate chain of amethysts around her neck. Her eyes were huge with grief, but every plane of her delicate face was rigid with a kind of courage that humbled Ransom, hurt him.

"Cecily . . ." Her name was a breath on his lips, choked with emotion as his eyes held hers a second that stretched into eternity.

"I will receive Captain Tremayne in the drawing room." The words were icy, so calm that Ransom wanted to clasp her in his arms, force her to cry, scream out her agony, but he feared that if he touched her, she would shatter. His fingers knotted into helpless fists as he turned, following her stiff back into where a bevy of gilded cupids cavorted about a winter-blue room.

Ransom caught a flash of crimson-shaded cheeks beneath moon-pale curls, Lavinia Lansdowne's face a study in indignation as she bustled after them. "'Tis not proper to close yourselves in a room unchaperoned . . . you'll not shame this house yet ag—" The door slammed inches from Lavinia's upturned nose.

He stared down at where his hand yet held the door handle, searching for the right words to say to the woman he sensed behind him. The woman he loved. Damn, why was he so blasted terrified to turn to her, hold her? Why did he feel that she had somehow already slipped beyond his reach?

He knew if he rushed to her as he wished, crushed her in his arms, forced her to rail, to weep, he could destroy some innate strength she needed to possess right now.

Drawing in a deep breath, he swiveled to face Cecily, willing his face not to betray the alarm racing through him.

"Angel," he said in a low, unsteady voice, his jaw knotting. "Sweet God, I'm so blasted sorry. . . ."

"Don't be." Her words were colorless as her face, and they sent shafts of fear through him. "Papa . . . he is at peace now. He doesn't—doesn't have to feel guilt any longer . . . endure . . . the scorn of people he called friend."

"Cecily, all of London respected—"

"Aye, they respected him a day past, a week past, years . . . years he was known as a grand scholar, a truly learned man. Mayhap 'tis a twisted mercy that he did not live long enough to hear the very people who had lauded him whisper out their horror that the noble Charleton Lansdowne had dealt in human flesh."

Ransom winced as the quiet words cut him deep, her gaze leveled at him, hurting . . . damn, she was hurting so cursed much. He would have welcomed blame, searched for it, there, in the rich violet beneath lashes undampened with tears. But there was only a detachment—a terrifying absence of the life that had driven him to the first real passion he had ever felt. He could not find any words to say, so he stood, silent.

"Papa . . ." How could one sweet voice hold so much

pain? "He didn't want me to be . . . ashamed of him anymore. Wanted to gain back some measure of my respect, even if he lost that of the rest of England. So he—he arranged to meet with the person who had been trying to extort money from him. Gathered enough evidence to condemn both himself and Bayard Sutton as well."

"Bayard Sutton?" Ransom struggled through the waves of guilt, that single, hated name gifting him with someone upon whom to unleash his fearsome anger. "What the hell did that bastard have to do with—"

"He murdered my father."

The words slammed like a morning-star mace into the pit of Ransom's stomach. "Sutton came here? Killed—"

Cecily gave a harsh little laugh, her fingers knotting in the fragile silver gauze until Ransom was certain the delicate fabric must tear. "He might as well have—would have been more honest if he had plunged the—" Her voice faltered, and Ransom would have cast himself back into the misery of Satan's Well just to hold her for a moment.

Her eyes flashed up to his, the violet depths huge pools of grief, anguish, indomitable courage. "I will not allow my father to be crushed beneath Sutton's heel, not let that animal get away with murdering. . . ."

With a muttered oath Ransom strode across the chamber, but he only dared to reach out, capturing her white, icy fingers in his own. His mouth set in a hard line. "I'll kill him for you." The words were a harsh, soul-deep vow.

"No."

He stopped, held by the daunting resolve in that single word, her face, turned up to his, beauteous as a warring queen's.

"Sutton has destroyed enough lives," she said. "Papa's, little Nicky's—"

"Nicky's?" Ransom reeled with confusion. "What the devil does Sutton have to do with—"

"He murdered Nicky through Khadija's hand."

"Khadija?" Ransom felt as though he were tumbling through a dark labyrinth.

"Sutton sent her to Tradewinds to spy upon your investigation into the *Ninon,* or more likely, to kill you while you slept. But when Khadija was shunted off to Rosetree, near as I can judge, she had to rethink her plan. 'Twas more difficult to reach you. Would take time. But . . ." Cecily picked up a feather fan abandoned upon a table and absently ripped the down from the elegant plumes. "Nicky recognized her from her dealings with the man who had . . . attempted to hurt him."

"Sweet God." Ransom felt talons tear his chest, slashing fury, hate, to his very core. "Jessie—I have to warn—"

"I sent a message to Jessamyn as soon as I knew. And one to the docks as well. The footman I dispatched said that Jagger and about eight men from your ships hied off to Rosetree at once. Khadija knew I had recognized her. I vow she'd be afraid to go near Rosetree now."

"Damn it, Nicky must have been scared. So cursed scared."

"Too terrified to tell anyone," Cecily whispered, "until that night before he died. He must have told Lacey, but she mixed up the sounds a bit. 'Twas not some Aaron White who abused him. 'Twas the Baron—"

"Of Wythe." Ransom spat out the title. "Damn him to hell, I *will* kill him now. Murder him with my own hands." He spun toward the doorway, wanting to feel Sutton's throat between his palms, wanting to crush the murdering bastard who had turned Nicky's last days into hell, who had done Christ knew what to the helpless lad before he had found haven in Rosetree.

Ransom reached for the door handle, full intending to rip it open, stalk into the night, but before he could, a ghost-pale figure with huge violet eyes swept between him and that exit.

"I'll not let you kill him, damn you." Cecily blazed, her whole body trembling. "I've already lost my father. I can't lose you. I won't!" There was the tiniest choke in her words, stark desperation that struck through Ransom. "Don't you see?" she pleaded, her fingertips catching hold of his shirt, her dainty hands icy against his skin. "If you died . . . were hung . . . I would have nothing."

"Cecily—" Ransom's voice grated deep in his throat.

"I said *no!*" Like a tigress she faced him, the mouth that had melted away years of abuse set now in an unyielding line. "If you love me at all, Ransom, you'll not allow Sutton to drown anyone else in his evil. You'll never let him taint anyone again. I spent the afternoon reading two of Papa's journals. The one we found missing the night we searched, and the journal he has been keeping of late. And I found . . ." She gave a sharp laugh, rife with grim satisfaction. "They say on the streets that nothing can prevent the Baron of Wythe from assuming leadership of his party this eve, and from thence, leadership of all England." She paused but an instant, her eyes the hue of chilled violets. "They are wrong."

Feral joy tore through Ransom's grief and fury, at the knowledge that at last there was hope of bringing down the dangerous baron. "You mean we bear the evidence we need to crush Bayard Sutton? Bear the power to destroy him?"

"Not *we. I.* I will make Sutton pay. Pay for my father's death. For all Sutton has done."

The fierce pleasure he had known for an instant vanished, melting into a stark, gut-wrenching fear born of the stubborn light in Cecily's eyes. "Gloriana, the man had a child murdered—killed your father. If you think for a moment I'll allow you near that monster when he's desperate, I—"

"Don't take this away from me, Ransom." The words were gritted between clenched teeth, a plea, for all their strength. "If you love me at all, you cannot take this away from me."

She drew her hands from his, and Ransom's jaw knotted as those cold, steady fingers curved over his cheeks, the sensation plunging to the core of his soul. "Of anyone, you should understand that I have to cut this hatred out of my heart myself—" Her voice gave a heart-wrenching crack. "Or else it will never heal . . ."

Ransom closed his eyes, seeing behind his lids a golden-haired youth of fifteen, feeling the bite of the razor-honed knife carving away the brand seared into one lean cheek.

Never in his life had he been able to leash his ferocious temper for his own good. Could he chain it even for Cecily?

Her words echoed in his mind. . . . *cut this hatred out . . . 'twill never . . . never heal . . .*

Sweet God, with the touch of her innocent lips, Cecily Lansdowne had healed so much in him, driven back the abyss of pain, self-hatred, that had tormented him his whole life. Could he, then, steal away from her the chance of exorcising her own fierce demons? No matter what the risk?

"Help me, Ransom." Her voice broke through the hazing of painful memory, the sound crushing his heart. "Please, God, I need you to help me."

Ransom opened his eyes, staring full into that shattered angel's face beneath its coronet of amethysts.

"Aye, Gloriana," he rasped, surrendering the last wisp of his soul. "I will."

Chapter Twenty-two

THE MOON SHONE HIGH in the mist-laden skies, a silvery galleon laying siege to the stronghold of a druid king. Cecily drew deeper into the shade of her wide-brimmed bonnet and peered out of Ransom's coach as it wound up Montclieff's long, arching carriage circle. There was so cursed much she should be feeling, she knew—dread, fear, or at least the dull throbbing from the scorings of bruises and scrapes gained in her battle with Khadija. But she felt only a blessed numbness. That, and a kind of frightening fascination with the house rising before her.

There, amidst the stark practicality of London, Gothic spires of the edifice were set against the backdrop of an eccentric labyrinth of gardens renowned throughout half of England. Heavy night clouds of velvet blue and ebony seemed to drive themselves against the sprawling structure like rival armies, limning the town house's walls with roiling shadows.

Cecily struggled to etch in her mind every line, every intricate carving revealed to her through the veiling of darkness, groping at anything that would keep her from acknowledging the taut-coiled danger in Ransom's hard-muscled frame. It had been madness, madness to bring him here, a voice buried deep inside her whispered, but she forced it away, wrapping it with the rest of her emotions in a counterpane of ice as she focused yet again upon the building before her.

'Twas already evident the fiend was holding court, she thought bitterly. Scores of windows melted the mist with the bright gold of candles, the bronze-hued livery of the Duke of Montclieff's servants flashing past the polished glass panes as they bustled about rooms that had no doubt been bursting with guests but a little while ago. With detached interest Cecily's eyes swept the windows of the chamber where she had attended a soiree some weeks past, but the vast room with its elaborate paintings of nymphs and satyrs appeared to be empty of the whirl of London's richest silks and satins, the polished elegance of stark black evening clothes and startlingly white cravats.

Most likely the entire company had retired to the mahogany table that stretched the length of Montclieff's huge dining room. Scores of servants were probably even now hastening about with silver platters heaped with enough culinary delights to feed half the starving in Covent Garden's slums. While in the midst of the glittering crystal and gleaming silver, the assemblage of the most powerful Whigs in London and their most beauteous ladies, the Baron of Wythe sat in state, gloating over this, his most stunning victory.

Cecily felt a sick stirring in her chest, felt talons honed of grief, fury, and soul-shattering pain threaten to tear away the blessed numbness that had settled over her emotions. But she forced all feeling away, clinging to the icy hate that lay like a stone within her chest.

Her fingers clenched about the box she held in her hands, the small, carved hinges cutting into palms that felt nothing. It would all be finished soon—Bayard Sutton's grasping glory, his bloody hands slipping forever from the dreams he had almost captured. Yes, it would soon be over.

"Cecily?" The rough-soft sound of Ransom's voice startled her, the brush of his hard shoulder warm against her own as the coachman reined the magnificent team of matched bays to a halt before Montclieff's broad steps. She looked up into that savagely handsome face and knew that if she were capable of feeling anything at that moment, the fierce light in those emerald eyes would have filled her with terror. "There is yet time for you to change your mind," he said. "Let me deal with Sutton, and—"

"He murdered my father." Cecily met that intense gaze levelly. She saw Ransom's jaw clench, saw him bite back the urge she knew was raging inside him, the urge to dissuade her, bind her hand and foot, if necessary, to prevent her from sweeping into Montclieff's elegant hallways and denouncing the conquering hero the Whigs had gathered to honor this night.

"You gave me your word, Ransom." Her chin lifted in a stubbornness to match his own. "Vowed on your love for me that you would let me lance the wounds Sutton has dealt me."

"You cursed well don't need to remind me what a fool I was."

"Nay, not a fool." Cecily couldn't stay her fingers from reaching up for an instant, touching the corner of his mouth. "A knight . . ." The words were breath soft. "A knight who has quested for so long, he understands about others needing to conquer their own dragons."

Cecily felt the stirring to life of her emotions, felt warmth seeping into her soul from the moist, firm line of Ransom's lips. But at that instant the coach door opened at the hand of the footman, agonizing reality driving back the faint pulsings of feeling. Yet even still, Cecily noted the glint in Ransom's eyes, an exasperated pride, and strength enough to lean on for a lifetime.

With an athletic grace that would be the envy of the most accomplished of regency bucks, he swung down from the coach, his broad shoulders accented gloriously by the folds of his cape, a glimpse of his exquisitely tailored evening clothes revealed for an instant by the flowing velvet garment. He had stopped at Tradewinds just long enough to garb himself in his finest and to order his most elegant equipage—a coach, yes, and an escort fit for a warring princess, he had said.

Cecily's gaze held his for an endless moment. Then he

extended one hand, the ruggedly beautiful planes of his face struck with moonlight and infinite love. "You win, Gloriana," he said softly. "I'll be your cursed knight."

"Forever," Cecily whispered, her heart memorizing the bittersweet smile he gave her so that she could take it out later, marvel at the beauty in it.

Gripping the box tight against her bosom with one arm, Cecily put her fingers into Ransom's and stepped down onto the ground. From the town house's daunting Gothic spires, to the ghostly moon above, it seemed an eve fashioned for hauntings. Pray God, Cecily thought grimly, it would be Bayard Sutton who was beset by specters this night— dragged down by the scores of souls dead at his command.

Cecily shook herself from her musings to see a sour-faced footman peering down his nose at her and Ransom, the servant managing to regale them with his opinion of late-comers without so much as opening his miserly lips. Ransom gave the servant an arrogant glare as he guided Cecily toward the doorway, and the combatant light in his eyes would have forced any pirate upon the Spanish Main to luff sails and flee.

"Sir? Milady? May I inquire as to whom—"

Ransom's voice cut, rapier soft, through the man's nasal tones. "Captain Ransom Tremayne and—"

"Lady Cecily Lansdowne." Cecily raised her face, the light streaming from the open doorway splashing over her features beneath their sheltering of rose-pink bonnet. The footman looked as though he had swallowed his tongue, and Cecily could well see that the roundings of gossip had already spread Moorston's tragedy on invisible wings throughout the city.

"L-Lady . . . my Lady C-Cecily—" the man stammered, his eyes widening in shock and disapproval.

Cecily fixed him her most patrician stare. "What is amiss? Has my name been stricken from the list of guests? My father and I received an invitation to dine here at Montclieff this night."

"Nay . . . I mean, aye," the footman stammered, and Ransom looked as if he'd relish throttling the man. "'Tis just that—" The servant's gaze skittered away. "I will . . . will announce you at once," he said, divesting them of cloaks, bonnets, gloves, and almost hurling them at a bauble-eyed underfootman.

Cecily watched the two usually efficient servants all but tumble over each other in their stunned haste, and her pulse lurched for an instant at the thought of the stir her entrance into the dining room would make in but a few seconds more. She turned her face up to Ransom's sun-darkened one, seeing the sharp-carved features, taut and grim. But as his gaze fell upon her, his fierce countenance softened but a whisper and he reached out a callus-roughened fingertip, smoothing back a tendril of dusky-black hair.

"You would do honor to any crown this night, love," he said in a voice gritty with emotion. And she knew how dearly his control was costing him. "You make me proud, Cecily. So damned proud."

She swallowed hard, willing her eyes to remain dry, struggling to crush the painful sensation of feeling his words loosed in her. Nay, she dared not—*dared not*—let anyone, anything, break through the brittle shell keeping her from flying apart. For if she allowed the first tear to fall, she would sob forever.

Her hand clutched the wooden box tighter, one corner cutting deep into her ribs. She welcomed the distraction of the slight pain.

"Captain?" the footman's voice broke in, and Cecily saw the eager light in his face, no doubt from anticipation of the scene to come. "Milady? If you will follow me?"

Cecily drew in a deep breath, felt Ransom's fingers grasp her chilled hand, tucking it in the warm crook of his elbow as he guided her after the servant's livery-clad back. Cecily tightened her grip upon Ransom's arm, that single contact the only thing that held the slightest shading of reality.

She shook herself inwardly, suddenly aware that they had left the corridor, spilling into a room so brightly lit it hurt her eyes. A maelstrom of color, silks, satins, scores of faces, seemed to spin before Cecily's eyes.

"Captain Ransom Tremayne . . . Lady Cecily Lansdowne . . ." The footman's words echoed through the dining room like cannon fire, every wisp of the conversations that had been buzzing about the room dying in that instant, as though someone had stolen in and severed the throats of all within the room.

Cecily could feel Ransom's body tense beside her, a jungle cat scenting danger, the deafening silence roaring in her ears as her gaze swept the length of the vast table.

She glimpsed a figure in gold satin hastening toward them, the Duchess of Montclieff's features beneath their layering of rouge a study in outraged disapproval. But Cecily bore scarce an instant to register the grande dame's wrath before her eyes locked upon the single person seemingly unconcerned with their arrival.

Bayard Sutton, Baron of Wythe, lounged back in a gilt-legged chair, spooning honey from a silver bowl onto a crusty roll, his eyes revealing naught.

Supreme confidence was etched into every plane of his face, the tiniest of sneers curling his upper lip as he regarded her. Cecily felt a sudden, sharp welling of hate jolt through her, the memory of her father's gentle, tormented face, and of Nicky Dolan's small hands, filling her with rage. Sutton bore no right—no right to sit there so calm, pampered, and adored by every person in this room. Bore no right to appear so unaffected by the horrors he had wrought. She wanted to take the box she held, batter it against that bland countenance, drive it against his flesh until he revealed the hideous mask of evil he had kept hidden beneath his urbane facade for so long.

"Lady Cecily!" The voice of the duchess made Cecily start, and she turned her gaze to the woman's features, puffed out with indignation. "Really! I vow I've never seen such a display of ill-breeding. Trouncing about to fetes, with your father dead only this morning—and wearing . . . wearing not so much as a stitch of black!"

"Your grace," Ransom's voice cut in, edged with the sharpest of warnings, "if you insist upon an example of ill-breeding, I shall be happy to—"

"I can assure you, your grace, that no one mourns my father's passing more deeply than I do," Cecily's regal tones interrupted with astonishing smoothness, filling the whole room. "Unless, of course, it is his most trusted friend." Her eyes swept away from the duchess's face to where Sutton sat, dabbing at the corner of his lips with an immaculate napkin. She felt Ransom stiffen, but she shot him a glance filled with warning more savage than that he had dealt the duchess. His mouth twisted in a furious grimace, then hardened again into a stark line. Cecily drew in her breath, turning back to the roomful of gaping faces.

The baron placed the square of white linen next to his crystal goblet of wine, his mouth curving into an expression of such solemn grief, Cecily wanted to blast a pistol ball into his black heart. "Cecily, my dear, 'tis too courageous of you to venture out so soon after your loss." His tones carried the warmest of concern across the dining room, and Cecily could see the faces of those about him turning to their most compassionate leader as he rose slowly to his feet. "Lord Charleton's death is a great tragedy, not only for you, but for all of England."

"Not for *all* of England, my lord." Cecily pulled her hand from beneath Ransom's fingers, her spine blade straight, her hands curving about the box as though she bore the queen's own scepter. Her gaze held Bayard Sutton's as she glided with slow deliberation down the length of the room.

A hundred whisperings stirred around her like the hissings of snakes, and it seemed an eternity before she stopped an arm's length from where Sutton stood. She was aware of Ransom, standing behind her as though he didn't trust himself within reach of Nicky's murderer, and she was aware of a latent danger in the depths of Sutton's eyes.

She lost herself in those chill brown orbs for an instant, seeing the real Bayard Sutton for the first time. "In fact," she continued, "I am certain my father's death serves a great relief to some."

"A relief?" Sutton said silkily. "Surely not. You must accept the most sincere condolences from—"

"From the man who murdered my father?" Cecily's voice carried throughout the room, raising stifled gasps, tiny cries, from those yet seated at the duke's table.

"Man . . . ?" Sutton raised one brow in feigned bewilderment, his lips curving into the condescending smile one reserved for a witling upon a street corner or a child concocting the wildest of tales. "But I understood 'twas a woman, some, er, wretched lady of ill-repute who had this unfortunate . . . *quarrel* with Lord Charleton."

Cecily heard Ransom hiss a curse, could feel the will with which he was chaining his fury. Her own chin jutted higher, her flesh crawling, fury bounding, as she saw what the wily baron was attempting to do—destroy the credibility of not only herself, but of her father as well, by hinting at some seedy liaison with a Fleet Street harlot. Cecily wanted to scream at him, strike him, but she dared not loose her hold on her emotions, dared not betray by any action that she was not in total command of herself.

"Now, my dear," Sutton all but crooned in his most patronizing tones, "if you would take your . . . gentleman, here, and be seated, I am most certain the duchess can have the servants lay out another setting. . . ."

"I fear I bear a distinct lack of appetite," Cecily said, allowing her lips to tip into a frigid little smile. "And I greatly fear that you will lose whatever relish you may have been taking in your own plate as soon as you are privy to the purpose for which I've come."

"The *purpose* for which you've *come?*" Sutton mulled the words over his tongue with the slightest hint of sarcasm. "Aside from doing your father dishonor by rollicking off with this"—his gaze flicked to Ransom—"this notorious rakehell, while no doubt the servants are yet laying out Lord Charleton? Aside from creating a scene amidst some of the most noble families in London? Come now, my lady, 'tis most evident you are overwrought with grieving. Whatever purpose you meant to serve here, the single thing you have achieved is to make a most pathetic showing of how low your grief has brought you."

"'Tis not myself, nor my father, who will be brought low this night, but rather, a man who has bathed his hands in the blood of his opponents, who has gleaned a fortune through trading in human flesh, aye, and who has abused and murdered defenseless children, all to gain some twisted ambition—"

Sutton's laugh rippled out, so blatantly unconcerned, Cecily feared Ransom would ram a fist down the baron's throat. "I am afraid that Lady Cecily's lover bade his coachman take the wrong turn," Sutton said, casting a sneering glance to his supporters. "I vow, he must have been escorting her to Newgate—"

"You bloody bastard!" Ransom's curse grated across the room, silencing the flutter of appreciative laughter that had risen after Sutton's silky insult. "You're not worth one of the poor wretches buried in those prison walls! But I vow you'll bear your chance to—"

"Captain Tremayne, Lady Cecily!" The duchess's silks gave a militant rustle as the lady stalked toward them in high dudgeon. "This is the outside of enough!" The duchess's bosom quivered as she confronted Cecily. "You barge in here, insulting—"

Cecily saw Ransom wheel toward the duchess, could sense that what little control Ransom yet held over his fury was about to snap.

"I bear proof," Cecily declared, determined to show him she could fight this battle alone as her gaze pierced Sutton's. "Proof that the Baron of Wythe gained a fortune from the slave trade. And with my own ears, I heard my father's murderess claim she was Bayard Sutton's minion."

The hush over the room exploded into a mass of indignant cries. The Duke of Montclieff bounded from his chair, his paunch nearly upsetting the wine goblet in his hand. "Of all the preposterous—"

"'Tis all right, Malcolm." With bored dismissal, Sutton's gaze flicked down to the simple lines of the box she held. "I confess guilt to the charge. 'Tis ever my way to send out hordes of lightskirts to murder men who would support my rise to high office." A round of strained laughter rose from those seated at the table.

Cecily felt hot color rise to her cheeks, caught a glimpse of Ransom lunging toward Sutton, eyes ablaze. "Damn you, you cursed—"

"Ransom, no!" Cecily held out her arm to stay him. "Let him laugh . . . while he is yet able." She fixed an icy stare upon the duke, allowing frosty violet eyes to meet those of the assemblage. "I was but a little girl when a ship called the *Ninon* was burned at sea, but I would judge that most of you were old enough to bear the clearest of images regarding what befell that vessel."

She could sense the rage in Bayard Sutton as she spoke, but by not so much as a tightening of his urbane smile did he betray his emotions. "I am certain we all read about it in the *Times.* Some sort of unfortunate accident, as I recall. Mayhap we should entertain this company with a recounting of every disaster known to man—the plague, mayhap, or, know you any tales regarding the Great Fire? 'Twould bear an equal amount of relevance to this gathering tonight."

"I beg to differ, my lord." Cecily laid the small wood chest on the table, unfastening its tiny latch with deft fingers. "I think that most of these honorable gentlemen would be quite distressed to discover that they are wasting their time, energies, and considerable money, in attempting to raise the Whigs to power through a man who has been involved in slaving. A man so desperate to gain a fortune that he ordered the captain of the ship he had invested in to burn the vessel and everyone on board if it appeared that too many of his . . . cargo were not going to make it to port in salable condition."

"You will remove yourself from this house at once!" Malcolm Montclieff blustered, his face red above his too-tight cravat. "If you were the niece of the Regent himself, I would not allow you to stand here, flinging such ridiculous, unfounded accusations!"

"Accusations so 'ridiculous' that my father died for

them?" Cecily slipped the leatherbound volume of one of her father's journals from the chest. Her gaze confronted Sutton's. "Surely, 'Uncle Bayard,' you recall these," she said, holding the book up for the baron's inspection.

Menacing edges showed about Sutton's lips as they widened in a scornful smile. He gave a long-suffering sigh. "What? You have come to Montclieff to regale us with all that tiresome Greek and Latin your father stuffed into your brain? God knows, 'tis obvious to anyone here that his educational zeal has robbed your woman's brain of what little sense it must once have possessed."

"You are right on one account. None of us—not myself, not anyone in this room—bore sense enough to see you for what you really are. But Papa . . . my—" Her voice gave the tiniest of catches. "My father . . . he knew. Not until it was too late to save himself from being entangled in your evil. But he knew. And from the time you first suggested to him that he might increase what little income he had by taking a gamble upon a shipping venture, until just last eve, when he decided to rid himself of the burden of guilt he felt for being ensnared in your wrongdoings, my father—Lord Charleton Lansdowne—recorded all the dealings of the partnership you named Acanthus Diversified."

Cecily saw a tiny muscle jerk tight in Sutton's jaw, the blood vessel at his temple standing out in relief against his smooth skin. "Enough, my Lady Cecily." She took the fiercest of pleasures in the sharpness of his voice. "We have all attempted to wax patient with you, what with your father's demise, but now even I find your babblings tiresome. Unless you leave at once, I will be forced to request that the footmen remove from this room both you and this . . . blackguard you have been, shall we say, gracing with your most maidenly virtues."

"If you dare lay a hand on her, it will be the last thing you ever do," Ransom grated from behind her.

Cecily saw the duchess bustling off, whispering to three stalwart footmen, saw the servants abandoning their heavy trays, their faces setting, grim.

"You needn't concern yourself, Lord Sutton," the haughty dowager said, flanked by the burly servants. "Lady Cecily and Captain Tremayne are both departing. At once."

Cecily saw Ransom's fists clench, felt a desperation that chilled her blood. Every servant in Montclieff would not be able to stop Ransom once his temper raged loose.

"Have you not heard a word I said?" Cecily cried, darting to the side of the table away from Lady Montclieff's guards. "Are you all so blind to the evil in this man? Lord Walcott," she pleaded, hastening over to a bone-thin man who had often discussed Plato with her father. "Surely you remember how meticulous Papa was in recording all that befell him. The time we spent a fortnight at your country home, you were forced to send for fresh ink when he ran out." The older man averted his gaze, and Cecily felt frustration and the first fluttering of fear course through her as the old lord refused to answer her.

She turned her gaze desperately to the others about the long table, catching a glimpse of Sir Farraday Holt. "You, sir." Cecily tried to keep the threading of anxiety out of her voice. "You once thought Papa's journals were such a grand jest that you sent him a trunk to carry them in. I remember—"

"Have a care, girl," the crotchety Sir Farraday grumbled out of the corner of his mouth. "For pity's sake, I can hardly question the word of a gentleman the like of Lord Sutton. 'Twould be inexcusable to—"

"Inexcusable to question his *word?"* Ransom roared, slamming his fist onto the table. The footmen started to make a grab for him, seemed to think better of it when they saw the killing light in his eyes. "The man had Charleton Lansdowne murdered, killed a child!" Ransom raged. "Sweet God, if one of you had borne the courage to question Bayard Sutton's word ten years ago, fifteen years ago, both would yet be alive!"

"Sir Farraday, you held deep affection for my father," Cecily burst out accusingly. "And you, Lord Walcott, you numbered him amongst your dearest friends. But you will allow this murdering beast to be raised to the prime ministry because it would be unseemly to glance through the pages of my father's journals, see the truth?"

The triumph carved across Bayard Sutton's face made bile rise in Cecily's throat, and she turned, catching a flash of Ransom's face, rigid with loathing as he glared at the crowd of London's most elite.

"Damn you! Damn all of you!" Ransom bellowed, his face that of an avenging god. "Open your eyes! Look!" Cecily started as he swept up the chest, flinging its contents across the table. Dozens of scraps of paper, yellowed with age, drifted within the reach of scores of the guests. Shipping receipts, notes penned in Charleton Lansdowne's precise script, letters in the sprawling, elegant hand of the Baron of Wythe.

The footmen lunged forward to restrain the furious Ransom, their faces pale, eyes wide as though they wrestled with his might. She saw them stumble back, cowering, as Ransom wrenched free of their hands, lunging between her and the tableful of indignant guests as though to shield her from the scorn of her peers.

But Cecily needed none of his sheltering. She drew her dignity about her like a velvet mantle.

"My father spoke most highly of your intelligence, both of you, Sir Farraday and Lord Walcott. I am certain that if he had been forced to weigh serving an 'insult' against bringing to justice a man guilty of effecting your murder, Lord Charleton Lansdowne would have borne you each enough loyalty to take whatever means necessary to prove or disprove the accusations. I regret that neither of you holds that same sense of honor."

"Leave questions of honor to your elders, milady," Sutton gloated, smoothing the ends of his cravat with beringed fingers. "I think 'tis obvious that no one here appreciates your interference. If you would be so good as to depart, we can carry on with—"

The dry, raspy sound of paper being handled made the triumphant smile upon Sutton's face go brittle. His eyes flashed up in the direction of the noise. The despair that had been gripping Cecily's heart cracked beneath the sudden surge of hope jolting through her, as Lord Walcott's mouse-quiet wife took up the wisp of paper nearest her.

"Geoffrey, please." Her soft voice split the rumblings all around her. "Lord Charleton rode clear from Briarton the day little Geoff fell from his horse, and he waited with us, minded all our affairs until . . . the end came. Do you not think we owe it to him to at least glance at what his daughter has risked so much to bring us?"

"Eliza, for the love of God, don't add to this farce by—" The nobleman cursed under his breath as he looked down at his wife's upturned face. Cecily caught her breath, knowing that all she had battled for, all she had striven to reveal, hung by the most fragile of threads within that single glance.

Bayard Sutton's hearty laugh burst out as he slipped easily from where he stood, approaching the Walcotts with negligent grace.

"My, my, I knew not that your lady bore such a taste for melodrama," Sutton said in insinuating tones. "Nor, Geoffrey, did I know she bore such a hold on your . . . decisions. Of course, if, in the interest of marital tranquility, you feel you must humiliate me by believing that I am a traitorous cutthroat, then by all means . . ."

Cecily fully expected Walcott to wither beneath Sutton's skilled regard, wilt beneath the scarce-veiled suggestion that the lord was ruled by his wife. But Walcott's thin cheeks washed dull red, his narrow shoulders stiffening as his hand closed over the supplicating one of his lady.

Slowly, so slowly, Walcott's veined hand reached out to take the faded letter his wife held. Cecily saw Bayard start to lean forward to snatch it away, saw Ransom's feral smile as he barred the path.

"Come now, Geoffrey." Sutton's voice dripped scorn. "Don't make a cake of yourself. 'Tis absurd to—"

The shifting of expression upon the nobleman's face drained the color from Sutton's skin. Lord Walcott's close-set eyes flashed up to the baron's, laden with loathing.

Sutton forced a strained laugh from his throat, and Cecily could feel the desperation in him as he heard the crinklings of other bits of paper, the sound of fingers leafing through the thick-bound journals. "This is madness!" Sutton snatched a shipping list from the hand of Sir Farraday and battled to scoop the remaining evidence into the wooden box. "A chit of a girl thrusting herself in here, bearing a boxful of lies. Malcolm, shall we all repair to the library for our brandies?" Bayard appealed to Montclieff. But the duke's brow was puckered as his gaze swept about those even now regarding snippets of paper, penned lists, letters.

"Damn all of you, don't be fools! We're close, so close to crushing the cursed Tories. If you would but pause, reflect—"

Cecily stepped back from the table, the light of the chandelier pouring over her in waves of warmth, some tiny part of herself breaking painfully from its casing of ice. She looked to where Ransom stood, his eyes fiery with savage pride and joy. With all the strength she could muster, she struggled to force her lips into a tiny smile, for the lump of emotion in her own throat would allow no words to pass.

"You've done it, Gloriana." His voice was rough with fierce triumph.

"Aye, she's done it, the stupid chit!" Sutton blazed, his eyes boring into Cecily's face with poisonous hate. "Made a mess of things with her blasted trivialities, just like her cursed father. Well, this I can vow to you, I'll not stand here any longer and be insulted by a bastard-born rogue and his third-rate Cyprian." Sutton started to spin away, to stalk from the room, but Ransom's strong hand shot out, clenching upon the baron's arm.

"I think you will remain here and be insulted a considerable time, my lord. At least until the constabulary arrives to make further inquiry into the murder of Lord Charleton Lansdowne and Master Nicholas Dolan."

"You will release me at once, sir, and meet me at dawn upon the field of honor." Sutton's hissed words broke through the murmurs about the room.

"Honor!" Ransom's laugh grated, his eyes raking the baron as though he were something that had crawled from beneath a rotting midden heap. "What the hell do you know about honor? A monster who vents his lust upon little boys,

and has them murdered when he fears being discovered."
Ransom's fingers dug deep into Sutton's arm, and he shoved
the baron against the edge of the table with a force that sent
delicate china clattering to the floor.

The savage joy of a tiger closing for the kill ripped through
Ransom as he saw the lurking darts of wariness in Sutton's
eyes. "Khadija did not murder Nicky Dolan before the boy
told the truth about the scars on his back, and about the
man who had put them there."

Sutton's face waxed gray, his eyes holding the danger of a
trapped animal. His hand swept back, his knuckles cracking
against Ransom's scarred cheek. Ransom felt the sting of
flesh tearing upon something hard, cold. A ring.

Lightning fast, his fingers clenched about Sutton's wrist,
holding it, frozen, there between them, the warm wetness of
blood trickling down to Ransom's jaw.

"Nothing would give me greater pleasure than to kill
you," Ransom said between gritted teeth, his eyes slashing
across Sutton's face to the fist smeared red with Ransom's
own blood. "'Twould almost be worth the hanging to—oh
my God—" The last words caught low in Ransom's chest,
trapped there by a tempest of disbelief and blind fury as his
gaze fused to the ring glinting upon Bayard Sutton's soft
hand.

Ransom battled to cling to reality, sanity, warring his way
through a thousand memories that ground like shattered
glass into the depths of his very soul. In that instant, some
evil demon had hurtled him back through oceans of flame,
into a room reeking of violet water and the stench of death.
Will's room. Will.

Ransom closed his eyes but an instant, seeing again the
bludgeoned body of the gentle child, seeing the bloodstained
fingers of the man who had murdered him curled even still
about the ornate candlestick that had dealt Will death.
Seeing, too, the ring winking upon that murderer's hand like
an evil eye.

A serpent piercing a quatrefoil.

The gold embossing seared into Ransom's heart as he
lunged for Sutton's throat.

Chapter Twenty-three

THE DINING ROOM ERUPTED in shrieks, curses, the Duchess of Montclieff's elegant Wedgwood china shattering as Sutton smashed backward onto the table. A dozen chairs crashed to the floor, the men springing to their feet, diving toward the two combatants locked in death grips. But as they grappled to tear Ransom away from the baron, it was Sutton upon whom they leveled a sickened scorn, Ransom whom they held as one would a righteous gladiator.

"Don't soil your hands upon him, Captain Tremayne," Sir Farraday growled. "He's not worth bruising your knuckles upon."

"Aye, and the ladies . . . I vow the honorable Miss Reardon looks like to swoon."

"He's crazed!" Sutton choked out as Ransom's fingers were ripped free of his windpipe. "You are crazed, Tremayne!"

"Nay," Ransom accused. "'Twas you who were crazed. Mad with lust, mad . . ."

"Ransom?" Cecily's alarmed voice seemed to reach him through a labyrinth of agony. "Ransom, what—"

"The ring," Ransom raged, battling like a pain-maddened wolf against the grasp of the four men holding him back. "Angel, 'tis the ring."

"Ransom, I don't—"

"He's the bastard who murdered Will!"

"My God." He felt Cecily's hands curve about his arm as she darted between him and the gasping Sutton, knew she feared that in his rage he would kill the evil baron. And he would, swear God, if he could but break the hold of these oafs that held him.

"Can you not see it?" Sutton shrilled. "The man is insane! Look at his face, those eyes. He is—"

"I saw you—saw the candlestick in your murdering hand, saw Will dead!" The words tore at Ransom, huge claws slashing at wounds that had festered what seemed an eternity. "Christ, he was only eight years old. I couldn't . . . couldn't even recognize his face after you killed him."

"You're babbling like a Bedlamite. I know nothing of—"

"Baytown? Satan's Well?" Ransom saw Sutton's skin pale, saw a furtive, deadly light in those narrowed eyes. "Well, I'll refresh your memory. A back-street hovel nigh the settlement's outer wall, run by a man as twisted, perverted, and cruel as you are."

"I am sure I have no idea what—"

"Oh, yes, Sutton. Lie, lie. It's what you are best at!"

Sutton straightened, straining at the men who held him. "Let me go." The emotionless calm in the man made his captors ease their grasp, their hands falling away, despite the fact that they yet blocked any chance of escape. The room was silent as a new-dug grave.

Sutton's eyes swept slowly to Cecily, his lips sliding over his bared teeth in a smile that made a shiver pierce through Ransom's rage. "So." Sutton's voice was silky soft, his gaze slowly raking the faces of those all around him. "You believe him. You look at me as though I am some kind of animal." His laugh was ugly, terrifyingly calm, as those eyes again found Ransom's own. "Well, what about your precious, noble Captain Tremayne? Or is Tremayne even his name?"

Cecily caught her breath sharply, a tiny cry breaking from her lips. "Ransom has done no wrong! It is you who—"

"Who what? Might reveal some dark secret the honorable war hero has locked within his soul? You have both seen fit to strip my own soul this night."

"Don't, for the love of God—" Cecily's voice broke, and Ransom was torn by the anguish in her plea.

"Don't what? Don't ask the captain to inform these ladies and gentlemen who have chosen to champion him *how,* exactly, he is privy to a murder in a back-street brothel?"

A chain seemed to cut deep into Ransom's throat, his eyes boring into the evil ones of Sutton, and he saw in those cunning, lethal depths the dark vengeance the baron would exact from him. A vengeance that would wrest Cecily from Ransom's grasp forever. And there was naught he could do to prevent it.

"Come, Tremayne, why suddenly so silent?" Sutton smoothed the rumpled front of his waistcoat. "You would have been, what, somewhere betwixt fourteen and sixteen at that time?"

Cecily wheeled on Bayard, the sob choking her voice wrenching Ransom's very soul. "Quiet, be quiet, damn you, or I—I vow I'll kill you myself!"

"You have already done worse than merely *killing* me, Lady Cecily. So now you may make amends by telling us all exactly what business a lad of that age could have in an establishment the like of which your lover describes?"

"Damn you!" Cecily's hand struck at Sutton's face, a smearing of blood appearing at the corner of that sneering mouth.

"Cecily, no." Ransom tried to jerk free of his captors, wanting only to catch her in his arms, shield her from the tempest Sutton was intent on loosing upon them, but the hands banding Ransom's arms and shoulders held firm. Still, as tightly as they bound him, Ransom could sense a subtle change, could sense them shrinking away, eyeing him with a kind of revolted fascination.

"Did your mother play the whore, Tremayne? Is that why . . ." A sudden, sinister light flickered in Sutton's eyes. "Nay, 'twas more than just that, was it not?" Sutton raised one finger to the corner of his mouth, wiping at the blood, then holding the red-smeared finger to lips curled with the devil's triumph. "Ah, I remember you now," he said, with a low, wicked chuckle, boring into Ransom with his gaze.

"You were a most comely lad, with all that golden hair, and savage eyes that challenged a man to tame you. 'Twas you I wanted, that night at Satan's Well, not that puling dark-skinned urchin Wolden attempted to foist upon me—but you ran . . . ran away."

With a feral snarl, Ransom ripped his arms free of the men who had struggled so hard to bind him, saw Sutton's former captors attempt to grab the baron. Screams and curses pierced the room as Ransom dove toward Sutton, murder in his fierce eyes.

It happened in but a heartbeat, yet whirled out like the most hideous of dreams, spinning on forever. Cecily cried out, plunging between him and Sutton, her angel's face wild with fear, torment. The smooth politician's hand that had been plying the folds of his waistcoat swept free of the garment, something small, metallic glinting in his hand.

Ransom tried to catch hold of Cecily's arm, fling her out of the way of the deadly pistol, but Sutton's other hand knotted in the ebony waves of her hair, jerking her back against his body with bone-jarring force, the pistol barrel flashing up to the vulnerable softness just below the curve of Cecily's jaw.

"Sutton, don't!" The cry tore from Ransom's throat as he slammed to a halt inches from where Bayard stood.

Thin lips on a gloating, suave face, pulled into a sneer, visible over the barrel of the gun. "'Tis a pity you didn't think of your harlot's safety *before* you charged in here like some thrice-cursed avenging devil, Tremayne. She could have been wife to the prime minister, had all of London scraping at her feet. But now . . ."

"Had you been the king himself, I would never have married you." The words were fierce, goading, Cecily's chin jutting with desperate stubbornness despite the kiss of death upon her throat.

"'Tis most unfortunate." Sutton's crooning, solicitous tone was tinged with madness. "But I can hardly allow you to humiliate me further, by becoming a whoreson's doxy."

Ransom's gaze flashed to Cecily's face, white, so white, her eyes dark, battling raw terror. "Sutton, killing her will gain you nothing. There are scores of witnesses here, and you—"

"It may well be that I have nothing to gain." The fingers that clutched the pistol's pearl handle did not so much as tremble, the eyes regarding Ransom's as chill as the gun's dark barrel. "But I bear nothing to *lose* either." He forced Cecily's head back farther.

"Damn it, Sutton, 'tis me you want to kill. Let her the hell go, and you can blast as many cursed holes in me as you want!"

Sutton's lips split into a strange smile, a smile like that of an insane child's mischief as he scanned the faces that a few hours past had regarded him with nigh worship. "'Tis ever the problem of low-born scum attempting to ape their betters. They bear no subtlety. None at all." Sutton took the pistol barrel, running it in a sadistic caress down Cecily's cheek. "I would hardly be so vulgar as to 'blast holes' in anyone. I prefer more elegant methods of dealing death."

Ransom saw Cecily flinch just the tiniest bit away from the weapon, could sense her steeling herself against her fears as if resolving to meet Sutton's final vengeance bravely. *Don't die, angel,* a voice screamed inside Ransom. *Please, God, don't die . . .*

With iron will Ransom chained his temper, struggling to think clearly, to match his wiles with the cunning enemy before him. "Sutton, for the love of God—" Ransom began, but his words were cut off by a harsh laugh from the baron.

"'Tis too late now, Tremayne. Do you not see? You cannot wipe away the accusations you made this night. Cannot place in my hand once again the power I've battled so long to gain."

"Damn it, Sutton—"

"You have left me no choice!" Sutton shouted, his face twisting in rage and accusation. "Now, the lady and I will take our leave." The deceptive mildness of the words, after the fury of seconds before, terrified Ransom to a depth he had never known. "Anyone foolish enough to attempt to detain us will bear the guilt of Cecily Lansdowne's death upon their head."

"Here, now, Bayard," Montclieff broke in, his face fish-belly white. "Do not hurl yourself into a morass deeper still. I—"

"Thank you for your concern," Sutton said, pulling Cecily with him back toward the doorway. "But I assure you, 'tis unnecessary. I plan to go to the devil as expediently as possible."

Ransom started forward, helplessness, rage, crushing his chest, but Lord Walcott's hand caught him. "No! He'll kill her, Tremayne."

Ransom's gaze flashed to the older man's earnest, worry-etched features, then back to Sutton, framed in that instant in the dining room's wide doorways. Ransom wanted to shake off Walcott's restraining grip, bolt after the angel he had let slip into Sutton's ruthless hands. But he could not—dared not—if Cecily were to have any chance at all.

"Ransom!" The sound of his name upon those pale, beloved lips drove a fiery stake in his heart, as Sutton dragged her toward the corridor beyond.

"Ransom, I love you." The words were defiant, imbued with the certainty that it might well be the last time she could say them. She held Ransom's gaze, memorizing the tormented planes of his face, the love in his forest-hued eyes.

Nay, she'd not let his last memory of her be one of a child-woman cowering in terror. She would be the Gloriana he had once named her, savagely proud, strong, as she faced her fate.

She battled back tears of loss, love stiffening her spine as Sutton urged her out into the misty night. But as she espied the direction the baron was dragging her, her blood turned to ice, the vast garden maze that was Montclieff's pride seeming to gape before her like the jaws of some horrifying dragon. Cecily felt a spirit-crushing dread curl like a corpse's hand upon her flesh as Sutton propelled her inexorably away from Montclieff's bright-lit windows, away from Ransom.

"You might as well kill me now," she challenged with feigned arrogance. "Even bearing me as hostage, you will never escape."

"Escape whom? Your bastard lover? Montclieff's doltish footmen? If I intended to escape, the whole of Napoleon's army could not bar the way. But what is there for me to escape *to* now? You and Tremayne have left me nothing. Nothing."

Cecily winced as his hand tightened in her hair, forcing her to stumble into the garden's entrance. "You bear your life," she bit out accusingly, trying desperately to retain her balance, to think of some way, any way, to escape the iron-strong hold Sutton bore upon her as he shoved her into the night. "'Tis more than you left my father. More than you left Nicky Dolan."

"Think you *life* matters when I shall be stripped of all power? When I would have to flee, loathed in the very city where I was to rise to the pinnacle of state? I only regret I did not wait until Khadija had disposed of you and your lover before I had her cast into the Thames."

A chill slipped like a dagger blade, cold between her ribs, the image of the African beauty's face rising before her, then dissolving into a mask of death. But Cecily bore no time to relish the sudden, fierce surge of satisfaction driving through her at the knowledge that the evil woman lay dead, bore no time to do anything but battle to leash her own mounting dread as Sutton rambled on.

". . . could have had everything, you and your dolt of a father," Sutton was saying. "Wealth, high position. I would have lavished you with jewels and gowns. Christ's blood, as long as you were discreet, I'd not even have denied you the pleasures of your lover's bed."

She felt Sutton's hand loosen in the tangle of her hair as he lost himself deeper in his railings, the slightest stirring of hope fluttering to life in her breast. If she could but tear free of his grasp, force her way through the snarlings of vegetation, she thought desperately, mayhap she could lose him in the dark labyrinth. She steeled herself to bolt, rip free of the baron's fingers.

But as though he had pierced her very soul with those chill, all-seeing eyes, Sutton chose that moment to shove her with stunning strength into a curved marble seat. Her thigh cracked into the hard stone just visible in the moon glow. Cecily cried out, clamping her teeth over her lower lip, stifling the moan as her flesh bruised, tore, the pain driving up into her hip robbing her of the fleetness that had held her only hope of escape.

She sank down onto the bench, her eyes spitting defiance. "Even if you kill me, I'll never be sorry," she grated, staring, she was certain, into the face of her own death. "Never be sorry that we destroyed you before you could gain the prime ministry, before you could abuse another little one the like of Nicky."

Sutton's laugh rumbled low, his voice cracking. "So you think you and Tremayne have rid London of some dread scourge in eliminating me, do you? 'Twill but leave others like me to stalk the streets, claim children whom no one else wants. And if he were God himself, Tremayne could not be at every flash house, in every alleyway and gutter to stop them."

The truth in his words gnawed deep into Cecily, filling her with hopeless rage. "You're despicable! A beast who—"

"Enough!" Sutton's screech of fury split the night, and Cecily feared he would snap her neck with his own hands. "Enough." He seemed to shake his eyes free of the madness, fixing a bland, terrifyingly emotionless gaze upon her.

"Now, my fine lady," he said in silky-soft tones, "you will do exactly as I bid you. You will turn. Walk—"

"If you're bound to kill me, you'll blasted well have to look into my eyes to do so."

"Defiant to the end. Well, I am neither your doting father nor your precious Captain Tremayne, and I'll not tolerate your fits of temper. Do as I say, or I will utilize upon you some of the more painful arts my vast experience has taught me."

"I won't—"

"Walk, goddamn you!" Sutton raged.

Cecily stared into that face, stark white in the moon's light, etched with insanity. If she seemed to obey, mayhap she would be able to dart into the darkness and get away, she reasoned quickly, her nails digging deep in her palms. And the more distance between her and the baron when he fired, the more hope she would have of being but wounded, of Ransom finding her. For she had no doubt that already Ransom was stalking the beast who threatened her, his senses honed in a hundred such preyings in the jungle, in the most savage parts of the city. She took a step forward, her eyes struggling desperately to pierce the darkness, find some opening in the unfamiliar, twisting maze. Yet there was nothing. She took another step.

"It was not my fault, you know, that the boy died." The absent, contemplative tone in Sutton's voice frayed like knife strokes against Cecily's sanity.

"Nicky?" Cecily choked out, forcing her feet onward. "You ordered Khadija to murder—"

"Nay, not *that* boy. The one at Satan's Well. I had ordered Tremayne specifically from Master Wolden. Payed handsomely to pluck the boy's virginity."

Bile rose in Cecily's throat, and it took all her will to keep herself from flying at the beast who had so attempted to victimize the proud man she loved.

"When Tremayne escaped me," Sutton plunged ruthlessly on, "the disappointment put me in the foulest of humors. Then, when that Will lad began to scream . . ."

Cecily jammed her knuckles against her mouth to keep from retching, the horror of Ransom's childhood striking her more deeply here, where she confronted death, than it had in the safe haven of Tradewinds. "Animal . . . you disgusting, depraved—"

"No one else wants the children I take. Their parents cast them to the devil, and people like those in Montclieff, they'd not cast them a coin if they were starving. But I . . . I love them, you see. . . ."

Cecily heard the hammer of the pistol click back. Her fingers scooped up her long skirts, her slippered toe digging deep into the path, propelling her forward as she started to run.

"I love them!" Sutton shrieked.

Cecily screamed as the pistol exploded.

Chapter Twenty-four

THE NIGHT WIND struck Ransom's face like a rapier, knifing through the blind panic that gripped his heart. *Don't let her die, God, please don't let her die,* he pleaded with the stone-hearted deity that had ignored a thousand of his childhood cries. Yet no plea, prayer, he had ever uttered had been torn from more deeply in his soul than the one he offered now. His eyes swept over Montclieff's grand landscape, the sinister darkness seeming to have swallowed the two figures that had plunged into its secreting depths. But despite the fact that he had hastened after Sutton and Cecily as soon as he had dared, he saw nothing except mist, hopelessness.

"Where are you, angel?" he hissed under his breath, straining every sinew in his body as though, if his will were strong enough, he would somehow be able to sense where she was, keep Sutton from harming her. "Damn it, where are you?"

He closed his eyes, listening, battling to hear some sound, any sound to guide him—the merest creak of a tree branch, the rustle of new spring leaflets being stirred by the folds of Cecily's shimmering gown.

He started, not even daring to breathe as a noise, muffled by distance, drifted upon the still night, then snapped into a harsh, crazed scream.

"Walk! Goddamn you!" The sound seemed spawned from the gates of some unseen hell, and Ransom stiffened at it, gauging the direction from which it had come.

The labyrinth . . .

Ransom cursed inwardly, bounding down the stairs, out across the wide lawns, silently as a jungle cat on a death stalk. Damn it, Cecily was lost somewhere in the eccentric Montclieff's maze. For hours the gentlemen and ladies of the town had attempted to find their way through the clever maze of hawthorn, to no avail. And now Cecily was trapped with a madman somewhere within its twisted paths.

Ransom paused for an instant at the maze's opening, struggling to judge which of three paths to take, fighting to hear again some sound stirring. Nay, there was no time to stand, deliberating. No time. Ransom plunged into the twisting corridors of the maze.

Anyone who follows us will bear the chit's death upon their heads. Sutton's jeering voice echoed in Ransom's mind, the cunning cruelty, cold rage, that had been in the baron's face seeming to tear at Ransom's sanity.

Thorns ripped at his shirt, raked his arms, leaving trails of warm blood welling in their wake as he ran, the mists that swirled within the labyrinth's paths seeming to taunt him with glimpses of silver gauze, violet eyes melting with love for him.

Don't let him hurt her! he railed silently. *Damn it—*

The sounds were nearer now, terrifyingly, tauntingly near, yet the night wind seemed to be gaming, delighting in whisking a thousand rustlings of leaves and stirring of branches, a dozen night creatures adding to the rippling of sound.

Ransom held his breath, the rushing of air in and out of his lungs seeming deafening as he instinctively veered to the right, then left again, praying as he ran, striking wild bargains with any angel, any devil who might hear him.

Cecily, I love you! his heart screamed. *Damn it, I—*"No!" The denial was torn from the depths of his soul, the night sounds shattered with the report of a pistol, a hideous scream.

With a tortured cry, Ransom plunged through the tearing wall of thorns, not feeling them rip his clothes, his skin, feeling naught except the starkest of terror. "Cecily!" he cried out, tears searing his cheeks. "Sweet Christ—"

His knee slammed into the curve of a marble bench as he broke through the mass of thorns, and he stumbled, crashed to the ground. His hand cracked into the earth as he jammed himself upright. But he had scarce gained his feet before he felt it, warm, wet, there, upon his palm.

Blood.

The sound that tore from his throat was that of a beast tortured beyond endurance. And a horrible, primal grief threatened to rend Ransom into a thousand tiny pieces as his eyes focused upon a shadow-veiled form lying twisted beneath the maze's wall.

He dropped to his knees, a hideous sob ripping from his chest as his hand reached toward the bloodied form.

"Ransom!"

He started, wheeled, almost crashing backward into the thorns as something hurtled toward him from the labyrinth's depths—a lithe figure glittering silver with moonlight, sobbing wildly, desperately.

Cecily.

His hands caught hold of satiny ebony hair, silken, rose-scented skin. "Angel . . ." He choked out the word, clutching her to him, burying his face in the delicate curve of her throat. "God's blood, what—"

"He—He told me to walk. Told me to . . . and then . . . oh, God, Ransom, I heard the pistol . . . thought . . . was going to kill . . ."

"Hush, angel, hush."

"But he—he didn't . . . he . . ."

The moon glided from its sea of mist, its light gliding up Sutton's immaculately tailored pantaloons, his elegant coat, to his face. . . .

Ransom felt bile rise in his throat, turned his gaze away. Face? Nay, 'twas naught but a gaping, wet hole.

He heard Cecily suck in her breath, felt her recoil deeper into his arms, her whole body quivering.

"Oh, my God," she choked out. "My God, he—"

Ransom's hard palm curved about her nape, straining her closer against him, as though the very force of his love for her could drive the ghastly, gruesome scene from her mind. But he knew that what had transpired in Montclieff's elegant dining room, and here, within the web of night-darkened hawthorn, would haunt them both forever.

Ransom cast one last glance down at the baron's body— seeing instead of the nobleman's lean, graceful form, Nicky Dolan's thin back, raked with scars, seeing also the delicate coffee-shaded skin of the innocent Will bleeding from a score of hideous wounds.

Ransom's stomach turned. Nay, death had been too quick, too kind a fate for Bayard Sutton. 'Twas too cursed easy . . .

And even still, from the brink of the grave, Sutton's evil had triumphed in a way that must have sent him to the devil with a sneering smile on his face.

He had won.

Won in a way that the woman trembling now in Ransom's arms did not yet understand . . . won so thoroughly that Ransom would never be able to cradle her thus against him again.

But she was alive, he thought fiercely. *Alive.* Even if he spent the rest of his life in a barren wasteland of misery without her, the knowledge that she was safe would be enough.

Gently, Ransom scooped her into his arms, the slight weight of her against his chest driving pain, bittersweet, into his heart.

"I love you, angel," he whispered, soothing her, comforting her as she sobbed out the grief that had been imprisoned within her since she had seen her father murdered, sobbed out the terror of the moments when she had kissed death's cold lips.

Slowly he wound his way through the maze of thorns, away from the stench of blood, death, but certain, also, that he was not walking toward any joyous future with the woman in his arms.

The buzz of alarmed voices, shouts of those who had poured from the dining room onto Montclieff's broad lawns, seemed to blend with the night sounds into a subtle, evil jeer as Ransom carried Cecily into the light blazing from candles and lamps held in a score of hands.

Yet instead of the wild clamoring of questions, joyous cries at the knowledge that the baron's hostage was safe, a strained silence fell over the crowd.

Ransom glared at them over Cecily's head, seeing in those faces, lit by the miscellany of tapers and lamps, revulsion, scorn. As if the Captain Tremayne they had all welcomed in their midst since Trafalgar had suddenly become the breeding ground of some dreaded, malignant plague.

"The baron . . ." Sir Farraday broke the heavy silence in his gruffest tones.

"Dead." Ransom's gaze met the old knight's levelly. "Bore the sense to put a bullet 'twixt his eyes before I did it for him."

Despite the fact that Farraday had seen his share of battles, the knight's mouth curled in distaste as he turned away.

The thin countenance of Lord Walcott separated itself from the milling group, the nobleman saying in an uncertain voice, "May I, er . . . aid you in dispatching your carriage for Lady Cecily? Or, uh . . ."

"Yes." Ransom's gaze slashed up to the lord's flustered face, and saw that no one, not Sir Farraday, not even the kindly Lord Walcott, could bring themselves to meet his eyes.

And the ladies—those few who had most likely defied the orders of their menfolk and trailed out into the night, unable to forgo witnessing the conclusion to the drama that had unfolded that evening—they gaped at him, the bolder amongst them not even attempting to shield the speculative gleam in their eyes as they ran their gazes down the planes of Ransom's hard-muscled frame.

'Twould be like that always now, Ransom knew with sick despair. Whisperings behind hands, skirts being whisked clear of so much as brushing against London's newest pariah, sick, cruel curiosity tearing away at the life he had built away from African shores.

And never could he shackle the proud Lady Cecily Lansdowne to a man who would draw nothing but scorn from all of London.

"R-Ransom . . ." Cecily's choked, broken crying seemed to crush his very soul. ". . . love you . . . need . . ."

"I know, angel. I know." He bent his head, laying his lips upon her cheek as he heard the rumble of coach wheels approaching, and he tasted of the same bottomless despair he had known in Satan's Well.

Chapter Twenty-five

T HE ROOM THAT HAD SERVED as Charleton Lansdowne's study was lit with a single taper, the wavering light dancing across faded ribbons, letters penned in a lopsided, child's hand. Cecily ran her fingers lovingly over pieces of her childhood, gathered there within the pages of her father's journals, each pressed flower, each tiny curl of baby-fine hair, a treasure from within Charleton Lansdowne's heart. 'Twas most impossible to believe that the man who had so cherished his only daughter could be the same man who offered Bayard Sutton coin to buy the *Ninon*.

And more impossible, still, to believe that her father was dead.

Dead.

Never to call her "sunshine" again, never to tease away her poutings, to challenge her mind and her heart with the learnings of great scholars. Never to bring her chocolate in the midst of a stormy night.

"'Tis naught but a cluster of rubbish, just as Lavinia says," Cecily murmured aloud, her throat raw with tears. But to her father—to Papa—it had been as if he were trying to save bits of the child she was, bits of the gangly girl who used to spoil her copybooks and use his volumes of Plato to build fortresses on the library floor. She only wished . . . wished she had saved something of him. . . .

Something besides the cool ebony of the mourning ring upon her finger, the onyx brooch pinned at the collar of her stark black gown. Something besides the empty ache that never seemed to leave her chest.

An ache left by the absence of the two people in her life whom she had loved most deeply. One beyond her reach forever, barred by death, the other . . .

Cecily huddled back farther into the leather chair, her eyes shifting toward the window, aglow with the mauves and roses of twilight. Was he lost to her as well?

Ransom had left with scarce a word the night he had brought her away from Montclieff. He had but bundled her into the arms of her uncle, then brushed her cheek with the softest of farewell kisses. No words spoken about the future, about the love that they bore each other. He had said only "Good-bye, angel," in a voice rough with sadness.

As the first day passed, and then the next, without so much as a word from Tradewinds, she had been confused, wounded, then angry at his seeming desertion.

Yet in the week that had followed, grim with the ceremonies of death, she had caught glimpses of him, cloaked all in black, his gold hair the single splash of color in a world gone gray. He had hung about the fringes of her life, like the rebellious waif he had been as a child. And every time she tried to approach him, he had melted into the shadows.

Yet even still, she knew he had watched her. Watched her make her way from that first painful visit to Charleton Lansdowne's grave, watched her as Mirabelle forced her out in the carriage to take the air in St. James Park. She even sensed him when the darkness came and grief bit fierce, could feel him somewhere beyond the cold, mullioned panes of glass, loving her.

And with every new bevy of the curious who flocked to Moorston in the guise of mourners, there had been the whisperings—righteous indignation and horrified fascination yet rippling through the London ton at the scandalous knowledge that one of their own had proved a common murderer, and another, a brothel's issue.

Only the condolences of Mirabelle and Aurora Lyton-

Snow had seemed genuine; aye, and the solemn apology of the gentle new Baron of Wythe, Arthur.

Cecily gave a weak smile. At least some small good had come of all the madness. With his baroncy, Arthur was no longer a suitor to be summarily dismissed. Once the scandal died, he and Mirabelle might yet find happiness. And with the man's sensitivity and his quiet ways, perhaps he could gild the tarnished name of his family in some trappings of decency.

But no one, not from the beauteous Countess Lyton-Snow to even Cecily's own bluff uncle, Duke Harry, could take the name of Ransom Tremayne and restore it to its former honor.

They'll take it all from him . . . Aurora's voice drifted across Cecily's memory, the countess's perfect face holding a subtle challenge as she stood in the grief-shrouded drawing room. *They'll take his pride, his sense of worth, justice. It will all mean nothing, unless* . . . Cecily would never forget the intensity in Aurora Lyton-Snow's eyes. *Unless you have the courage to give it back to him.* . . .

Cecily forced herself up onto numbed feet, making her way slowly to the window. Her eyes skimmed over the garden, her heart twisting with a still-fresh pain as she glimpsed the gate where her father had met his death. The city stretched out beyond the fortressed elegance of Mayfair, the winding, dark streets of Drury Lane, Covent Gardens, the stench-ridden flash houses, rookeries. Ransom's world. The world he had battled alone from the day his child-mother had abandoned him.

The world he would war with alone forever, unless she took her heart in her hands and offered it to him.

Ransom leaned his throbbing head back against the wood of the rocking chair, nestling the sleeping bundle that was Lacey closer within his arms. Not a night had passed that he did not cradle her thus, rocking her gently until the first rays of dawn trickled across the sky. 'Twas as if some part of him yet battled to recover the sense of peace he had once found here amongst his little daughter's hair ribbons and scraped knees. As if, in the child's unconditional love, he could touch some small, secret corner of his heart, untainted by Satan's Well, Tuxford Wolden, and men the like of Bayard Sutton.

Yet even that meager scrap of peace seemed lost to him now, lost with the elegant, stubborn set of Cecily's chin, lost with her smiles, her laughter.

Lacey shifted in her sleep, tucking Lord Nelson's china head more closely in the crook of one small elbow, the damage done to the doll's face repaired by the ever-resourceful Jagger in the days since Ransom had parted from Cecily.

Wish't I could fix ye up wi' a bit o' tar an' gluin', the grizzled sea dog had grumbled, fixing Ransom with a canny glare. *Aye, ye an' that spitfire o' a princess ye fancy.*

But 'twas not so simple to repair lives once they were shattered. And only rarely could the most loving of hands restore hope, once it had died.

Ransom sighed, his chest raw, aching. If the merest stirring of hope had been left somewhere in him after the nightmare in the labyrinth at Montclieff, the days since that catastrophe had driven away all thought of it now. All but the fewest of the friends he had secured within the ton dared so much as speak to him, and even those who scorned grand society's cruelties could still scarce meet his gaze. They were *kind* to him. *Kind* in the way one was kind to a beloved animal who has broken its leg. Christ, Ransom thought, if they could, the long-faced hypocrites would blast a bullet into his head, and think they were putting him out of his cursed misery.

But then, it might have been more merciful if that long-ago day in Baytown, Tuxford Wolden had slit Ransom's throat, rather than but sear the brand deep into his cheek. Or if he would have but loosed his hold upon the bits of wreckage that had kept him afloat whilst the *Ninon* went down. At least then he would never have known how desperately he wanted things he could never have—a name that bore with it shadings of honor, respect, a wife to adore him, defy him, love him.

His past. It hung there, betwixt him and the rest of the world, so hideous that he could never breach it. Could not touch the angel his heart railed for, burned for, because always his past would tear her away.

Ransom trailed his finger down his daughter's innocent, pink cheek, the strains of the lullaby he had been struggling to sing to her catching in his throat. Nicky's song . . . the song he had played that last day in the park . . . the song of the sailor who had lost his love . . .

"He went to sea, Lacey, to forget . . ." Ransom said in a broken whisper. "I wonder if he ever did . . . forget how it felt to kiss her, to hear her laugh, rage, to see her smile. . . . I wonder if he ever stood beneath her window, desperate for but a glimpse of her, the need to know she was safe, happy, gnawing in his belly like the fiercest of hungers." Ransom curled a silky black tendril about his rope-toughened finger, wishing it could soothe the jagged hole within his soul. "I wonder . . . if she cries yet at night, needs me. . . ."

The slightest stirring at the bedchamber doorway made Ransom drag tear-blurred eyes to the open portal. He blinked, struggling to focus upon the apparition seeming to taunt him there, with his angel's face, his angel's winsome smile.

"You should know that spoiled princesses—" the voice quavered, broke. "Princesses never waste their efforts weeping into their pillows. They take what they want, the devil count the cost."

"C-Cecily?" He breathed her name, his starved soul feasting upon the sight of her, so regal, beautiful despite the sorrow grief had blushed about her face, her eyes. Yet even still, he dared not go to her, take the love she was offering to him with that soft, tremulous smile. "I think this one time, angel, you had best count the cost yourself," he said, tearing his gaze away from her so that she would not see the desperate plea in his eyes. "You would be no princess at all here in this house, saddled with a man who can only gift you with shame."

"Shame? Shame for what? For bearing the courage and

the wits to rise from the hell of Satan's Well? To have nigh sacrificed your life defending a country that is so shallow it forgets the honor you bestowed upon it, clinging to dark things you bore no control over? Shame? Yes, I vow you should know shame—shame that for one instant you would let these worthless, pampered hypocrites steal away from you that which you have rightfully won." She crossed the space that separated them, so achingly graceful, beautiful, she seemed but a sea dream come real. "You are more a man than any of them, Ransom Tremayne," she said. "The most wondrous, brave-hearted, loving—"

His heart wrenched as a tiny sob broke through her words. "Angel, I—"

"But this is one cursed time you can cast your noble selflessness to the blasted winds. Because I damned well am not going to let you walk out of my life and leave me . . . alone, Ransom. So alone . . ."

Tears—tears for him welled upon those dark, lush lashes, her eyes glowing with such savage love, that Ransom could scarce breathe. She knelt down beside the rocking chair, her arms gently curving about the sleeping Lacey and him. And 'twas as though, in that magical circle, his angel had banished the world outside Tradewinds' windows, had conquered the demons that had tormented Ransom for so long.

"Angel, I . . . Christ, I need you . . . need you so badly." Ransom raised a shaking hand to her face, gathering her tears upon his fingertips. He leaned over the daughter he cherished and took the lips of the woman he loved in a long, gentle kiss.

Cecily pulled away from him, and the beauty in her passion-hazed eyes crushed his heart with soul-shattering joy. "Let Mama tuck Lacey in for the first time," Cecily said softly. "I want to get used to tucking your babes in bed. Because I plan to lay a great many of them in your arms, Ransom Tremayne. And into your heart." Her fingers traced over his lips, over the scar slashing down one high cheekbone, her touch infinitely healing, tender. "You have such a beautiful, loving heart, big enough to take in the whole of Rosetree, every child in London. Big enough to take in a pampered, willful girl and turn her into a woman."

Gently she took Lacey from his arms, and the sight of that dark, curly moppet cuddled close against Cecily's breast filled Ransom with raging, tender need. He stood, bending to brush a kiss across his daughter's brow as Cecily tucked the covers up beneath the stubborn little chin that seemed a miniature of her own.

Cecily snuggled the ragglety-tag Lord Nelson in beside the drowsing child, then leaned over, dropping a kiss upon one of Lacey's plump cheeks, then the other, and Ransom could see the bittersweet smile on Cecily's lips as she paused to nuzzle her nose but an instant against Lacey's upturned one.

"Papa . . . Papa always used to kiss me good night that way," Cecily said as she straightened. "It made me feel safe. Loved. That is the hardest thing of all for me . . . knowing you never had anyone to bring you chocolate, hold your hand when you were frightened. Never had anyone to make you feel that way . . . until now." She turned into Ransom's outstretched arms, curving her hands feather light against his face, rising up on tiptoe to brush each cheek with her lips, touch her nose softly to his.

"Cold . . . I've been cold for so long," Ransom choked out, threading his fingers through waves of silken ebony. "Angel," he breathed against her trembling lips. "Warm me."

With a tiny cry, she pressed herself against him, all softness and warmth and fierce loving. Ransom swept her up against his chest, his lips never leaving hers as he bore her out of the whimsical wonder of Lacey's bedroom and into the barrenness of his own.

But 'twas not barren now, even the stark lines of his sea chest and the big, plain bed seeming blushed with the beauty glowing in his angel's eyes, the hunger in her lips.

He laid her upon the downy counterpane, wanting desperately to draw upon every skill he possessed, wanting to give her such pleasure as no woman had ever known, but the fingers that could dance drugging passion with their merest brush upon a cheek were clumsy as a green lad's, the fastenings Ransom had worked upon a hundred women's gowns seeming to tangle about his hands, snarl hopelessly in his fingers.

Cecily whimpered, her hands tearing at his own clothes, her nails raking his skin in their haste. Her mouth was everywhere, her hands hungry, not to take, Ransom sensed, but to give. . . .

To give him a thousand dreams he had never dared touch before. With a guttural groan, his fingers knotted in the black fabric of her dress, his hands tearing free the fastenings that had so mystified him. Rosy, infinitely sweet, her breasts seemed to cry to him, plead with him to take them into his mouth, suckle them, tease them. He started to pull her down to his lips, but already Cecily was drawing away from him, her hands struggling to bare that part of him even now aching with the need of her.

"Nay, this time . . ." Her voice came through the haze of heavy, honeyed need throbbing in his loins. "This time 'tis my turn to gift you with loving."

Loving . . . Had he ever known what that was like, in the sordid crannies in Satan's Well? In the perfumed beds of countless shallow beauties? Had he ever thought to drink of such wonder that the last shades of horror, pain, that lurked in his heart washed away?

Amazement, disbelief, raged within him as Cecily's tumbled, midnight hair rippled over his taut belly like waves of silk, pooling upon his thighs, stealing away all reason. And when she bent to touch him, taste him, he arched his head back into the pillow, slow tears trickling from his lashes as the raw waves of exquisite pleasure jolted through every fiber of his body.

A ragged sob tore from his chest when he could bear the torturous wonder no longer. He rolled her beneath him, plunging deep into her welcoming softness, losing himself in sensations raw, primal, agonizingly new. He felt her tremble, the beauty of the love in her face hurling him out of a past that held no meaning and into a future that promised more than he'd e'er dreamed.

With a choked sound he buried his face in the lee of her neck and let the tears come, healing tears, cleansing tears, tears of such joy it seemed to spill from his heart in waves of molten rainbows.

"Hush, love, hush." Cecily kissed his wet cheek, her fingers stroking his hair with fierce love.

Clenching his teeth against the pain, the wonder, Ransom raised his head, catching her face between his hands. "I never . . . never knew before . . ." He struggled to steady his voice. "I never knew what it was like to make *love* . . . until now."

Violet eyes brimmed with tears, the lips that had given him such pleasure quivering. "I'll fill your life with love, Ransom Tremayne," she vowed as she raised her mouth to his. "Let me."

His mouth melted against the healing wonder of his angel's, the last wisps of the hungry-eyed child he had been, spinning away into dawn.